PRAISE FOR *WHAT THE DOG ATE*

Named one of the best dog books of 2012 by NBC Petside.com.

Bouchard "writes in a natural, accessible style and Maggie is a profoundly appealing character that the reader roots for. Yes, it's about a broken heart, but it's also quite funny." —Dorri Olds, NBC Petside.com

"Dog lovers take note! *What the Dog Ate* is a cheer-me-up read, the story of a smart woman putting her life back together. Maggie is the character women have been waiting for—she's clever, funny, and REAL. You'll root for her with your whole heart." —Elsa Watson, author of *Dog Days*

"Belongs on reading lists everywhere. It is good reading at its best!" —*Readers' Favorite*

RESCUE ME,
maybe

ALSO BY JACKIE BOUCHARD

What the Dog Ate

House Trained

RESCUE ME,
maybe

JACKIE BOUCHARD

Text copyright © 2013 Jackie Bouchard

Published by Lake Union Publishing, Seattle

www.apub.com

Amazon, the Amazon logo, and Lake Union Publishing are trademarks of Amazon.com, Inc., or its affiliates.

ISBN-13: 9781503946170
ISBN-10: 1503946177

Cover design by Laura Klynstra

To Bailey, my "Barnum," and Abby, my "Maybe"

CHAPTER 1
WIDOWHOOD 101

The funeral hasn't even started, but I already feel a blister forming. I should never have let Mom talk me into buying these pumps yesterday. My flats would have been fine. But Mom insisted that a widow doesn't wear her broken-in work shoes to her husband's funeral. If there's an Emily Post book for widows, or maybe *Widowhood for Dummies*, then I need a copy because I clearly don't know the rules.

My heel rubs against the hard leather, and all I want to do is go home and take off my shoes and get in a hot bath with a cupcake and a glass of Jack Daniels. But it's time. Time for the four of us to follow the altar boys and priest in their silent crepe-soled shoes.

We walk up the long aisle, in a cloud of cloying incense that makes my head feel like a helium balloon. Ryan's parents are ahead of Mom and me. I stare at their black wool-covered backs: Barbara so petite, Jeffrey so tall. Even in her grief, Barbara maintains her perfect posture, while Jeffrey's normally square shoulders slump. Barbara carries a rosary; Jeffrey holds the cherrywood box containing Ryan's ashes. I was supposed to carry them, but they felt too heavy. Before the service started, I asked Jeffrey to please carry "the box" for me. I worried it would make Jeffrey feel worse if I said "him." Or maybe it would make him feel worse if I didn't. I hadn't known what to say, but it wasn't "him" anymore.

Instead, I carry the framed photo of Ryan. It's not my favorite, but Barbara rejected the eight-by-ten I'd suggested—Ryan laughing, happy in a Hawaiian shirt, on our wedding day in Maui (his "happy place," as he always called the island, and one of my favorites as well). No, Barbara chose the professional photo of Ryan taken for Jeffrey's company website. Ryan, handsome with his dark hair and green eyes, wearing his blue suit and his "I'm an accountant, you can trust me" face.

My mom hangs on to my elbow. If I pass out, there is no one behind to catch me. Hopefully, Mom will keep my head from cracking on the marble floor. She squeezes my arm and tries to muster an encouraging smile, but her coral-painted lips tremble. I want to pat her hand, but my hands are clutching the picture of Ryan. I'm so afraid I'll drop it. I try to smile back.

Our heels echo, keeping time with the somber organ (something Ryan hadn't wanted) as we move up the aisle. Everyone stands and watches us pass. It's a big turnout, probably sixty people, maybe more. Barbara was right to put the funeral off for a month so more of their relatives could fly in, but I don't even recognize half of them. I want to study who's here, what they're wearing, but I take only a glance, look at Jeffrey's back, glance again. Everyone's wearing gray, black, midnight blue, even though I asked Barbara to tell people that Ryan's favorite color was purple. That was another of his requests—that the guests would wear purple or their own favorite colors. He wanted a party, wanted us to put the "*fun* in funeral." Barbara hadn't been amused when he'd said that. I'd thought it was admirable; he'd faced death like it was nothing more than a trip to the dentist. At least up until the very end.

Everyone is turned toward the aisle. Some look at the box of ashes, some at me. Most don't seem to know where to look. And a few, toward the outer edges of the nave, look down. It's a pious pose, but I wonder if they're texting.

In my lavender suit, I feel like a rogue thistle on a manicured lawn. Not to mention the fact that my legs feel naked since I haven't worn a skirt in ages. But Mom said no pants—another one of her rules. I'd needed to go out and get something purple anyway, but I don't know where my head was when I let Mom talk me into this suit.

So far, I've noticed very few splashes of color: Jeffrey wears a purple silk tie; Mom hides her neck, which she hates, under a gauzy plum-colored scarf; my best friend Mirabella's mauve wrap covers her black sheath dress. I saw Uncle Graham and Aunt Sugar before the service, so I know, true to form, they are dressed alike—bless them—with violet button-down shirts under navy blazers. So there are only six of us wearing purple—the five people I mentioned it to personally, and myself. Nice of Barbara to ignore Ryan's only other request. I should have been more involved with this.

Since my sweet beagle, Barnum, got sick two weeks after Ryan died, I've been running between the vet, the hospital, and, five days ago, the pet cemetery. I've been an incoherent mess this week and, consequently, haven't been up to helping Barbara with the final plans for today. I don't know if she's irritated with me about that or happy. Probably a bit of both. I'm sure she wanted me—and my pushing for things like people wearing purple—out of the way, but she still wants to complain that she's had to handle everything. At any rate, I'm glad she decided against a full Mass. ("We'll be celebrating a funeral Liturgy outside Mass," she'd reported to me on the phone one day, "since so many of the guests aren't Catholic . . . or don't practice." I figured that was a dig at me, but then Ryan didn't *practice* either. Although, I suppose she thinks that was due to my influence.) I'm surprised but relieved about her choice. The funeral's going to be difficult enough to get through; at least it'll be relatively short.

We reach the table that stands below the altar steps, and Jeffrey sets the box down. Its burnished lid glows under the soft lights. Barbara drapes her rosary over the box, and I set the framed photo beside it, turning it out toward Ryan's gathered friends and family.

We take our seats in the front pews: Mom and I on the left with my aunt and uncle, Jeffrey and Barbara on the right with her sister. Father Llewellyn, a jowly man under a white robe and purple stole (at least he's in purple), says an opening prayer. He sums up that we're here "to mourn the passing of Ryan Jeffrey Waynesfield." As if we could forget.

During the first reading, I hear Barbara sob when Uncle Graham gets to the line "A time to be born, a time to die." I look at the box with Ryan's ashes. A tear scalds my cheek.

My thoughts creep toward the night Ryan died: his nails, brittle from the chemo, on the back of my hand; how his jaw hung slack; the way the hideous pale pink lampshade on his nightstand painted a mockingly healthy glow on his face. I think of the things he said to me, and the things he tried to say, but couldn't. I've relived that night so many times. Did I give him too much morphine? Did I deny the man his final say? God, I don't want to think about that night. I force myself back to the present and look at the altar, which is empty, waiting for the next reader. Out of the corner of my eye, I see Jeffrey move. It's time for the eulogy.

Jeffrey walks at a measured pace, gripping a piece of paper. His grief, like a heavy-browed gargoyle, hangs over him, its breath rattling the page in his hand. He leans into the lectern. A lock of his salt-and-pepper hair falls across his forehead.

"I've had the privilege, these last six years, of working with my son every day . . ." He pauses and presses his lips together, then clears his throat and continues. "I was proud of him, as a businessman, a husband, a son."

I hear Barbara weeping, but it's Jeffrey's sharp-taloned grief that claws at my heart. Maybe it's because Barbara and I, forced together, cried so many times over Ryan's hospital bed. Her tears have fallen on me, inoculated me. But it's Jeffrey's raw anguish I can't bear to see.

He gave me a copy of the eulogy last night, but I didn't read it until I got home and crawled under the covers. It was more emotional than I'd ever known him to be, describing his happiness when Ryan accepted Jeffrey's offer to come work at the company he'd started, his pride in Ryan's many accomplishments, his "throat-closing fear" when he first heard the word *cancer*. He talked about the helplessness he felt, watching his son grow weaker, and the struggle with his own faith in the final days when we brought Ryan back to their home. He admitted that sometimes it's hard to understand God's will, but said he believed that someday, through the grace of God, he would see his son again.

When I woke this morning, the eulogy was still on the bed—our bed, which used to overflow with six-foot-four Ryan, five-foot-eleven me, and thirty-two pounds of beagle. Today it held only a curled lump of me and a tear-stained, blotchy piece of paper.

Although I already know the words, I can't stand to hear them in his faltering voice. More tears come. I hold my breath to keep them from turning into ugly gasps. My heart pounds so hard I can no longer hear Jeffrey, but I can see his grief, ready to devour him. I look away. I don't want to think about Ryan or Barnum. I don't want to break down, sobbing, in front of these people.

Instead, I focus on the crucifix. It keeps my mind from unwelcome topics, although it reminds me of the painful conversation I had with Ryan, speculating about what happens after death. It occurs to me that I don't know where Jesus went when he was dead for those three days. Limbo? There's a bible in the pew, right there within easy reach. The trained librarian in me wants to look up the answer, but I imagine reference work during a funeral is one of those things widows aren't supposed to do. I still can't fathom that the word applies to me. *Widow.* This is not how things were supposed to work out.

Why the hell did you have to die, Ryan?

I try to not be so crazy—so everything's all about me—as to think Ryan's death is somehow my fault, that I willed it upon him. But I can't help it. Voices in my head taunt: *You wanted out, and now you're free. You win.*

My heart still pounds, but slower now, a blacksmith's hammer on an anvil. To avoid looking at Jeffrey, I keep staring at the crucifix, especially the hands and the painted blood. Why does that image of suffering have to be the focal point in every Catholic church? The church loves to lead with the guilt. Always the guilt. Why not Christ rising from the dead? Wouldn't the miracle be a better draw? The church needs new PR people.

My diversionary tactics work, and the tears stop, so I continue to study the carving of Christ: his shoulder-length, matted hair, the slight curve of his fingers. I count his ribs. I notice his belly button. It's an innie.

Silence snaps me back to attention. Jeffrey gathers himself for the walk back to the pew. I cannot believe that I've been thinking about Christ's belly button. I am a terrible person. Just like I was a terrible wife. I look again at the box of ashes and think, *I'm sorry, Ryan.*

Father Llewellyn rises. He stands, relaxed, hands clasped. I pay attention now, but I don't believe it when he claims Ryan is in a better place. Well, better than Philly, I could buy; maybe that's what he means. I close my eyes until it's over. Until Mom nudges me that it's time to file back out. Follow the priest and the altar boys. Stare straight ahead.

At the back of the church, Father Llewellyn stops to speak to Barbara, but Mom and I keep going. We step out of the dark gloom of the church and into the barely brighter gloom of a gray-sky fall Philadelphia day. The smell of wet asphalt greets us. It must have just started raining, since I can see where fallen drops darken the street. The guests stream out, fumbling for their cell phones. *It wasn't even an hour, people.* Who are these self-important jackasses?

Mom asks if I'll be okay alone for a moment, then goes with the altar boy to unlock the rental so he can place Ryan's ashes in the backseat. When Mom flew in, she insisted on renting a sedan. She said we couldn't use my car because "a wife does not attend her husband's funeral in a bright red Subaru Outback."

Someone pops open an umbrella over my head. I turn and look. "Thanks, Jeffrey."

"Ryan always loved rainy days as a kid." His voice is stronger, more like his usual boom, but his eyes are pinched. He looks out at the rain pattering on the concrete bank of church steps where we've stopped, neither of us sure where to go, what to do.

"He loved them as an adult too," I say. "He'd get annoyed with Barnum, because . . . Barnum didn't want to go for walks in the rain." Barnum's name catches in my throat as if I'd swallowed a foxtail. I bring the handkerchief Mom pressed into my hand earlier to my mouth.

"Hey, a penny." Jeffrey bends to pick it up.

He turns the shiny coin over in his hand. I'm confused about why he seems so touched by it. Is he hoping the rest of the day will bring good luck? I suppose it can't get any worse.

"My mother used to say found pennies were messages from loved ones who'd passed," he scoffs—but pockets the coin. "Pennies from heaven; a little sign, sometimes a penny, sometimes something else—maybe something unexpected—that lets you know your loved one is . . . is okay." He stares out at the street. He's changed a lot since Ryan's illness, aging almost overnight, but he's also softened from his all-business all-the-time ways. It's heartbreaking to see this softer side of him, knowing the reason behind it.

"Jane." We turn and see Barbara coming toward us, under her own umbrella, steering a slightly younger, less angular version of herself. Barbara still teaches beginning ballet, and it shows in her ramrod spine. Her usual severe bun perches high on the back of her head. She always pulls her hair back so tightly that I imagine her whole face would droop if someone plucked out the bobby pins. Ryan used to make us all laugh, teasing her about her mini-face-lift-in-a-bun look. He used to say it was a twofer—a hairdo and a facial rejuvenation treatment. I've never seen anybody but Ryan tease laughter out of her like that. I wish my memory would only conjure up the happier times with Ryan. I wish I could control which scenes run on the movie screen in my head, but I'm not in charge of threading the reels up there.

As Barbara comes close, I notice that the necklace she's wearing with her black suit has an amethyst pendant dangling from it. Ryan's birthstone. Okay, she did wear a *little* purple. I smile. She pushes her sister at me and says, "Jane, you remember Bea."

"I'm so sorry for your loss," Bea says. She takes my hand.

Barbara passes dozens of other relatives before me: aunts, uncles, and cousins, once-, twice-, permanently removed. An older cousin calls me Mrs. Waynesfield, which is fine—how would he know I didn't take Ryan's name—but Barbara corrects him, "It's *Ms.* Bailey." They offer condolences, then move on. Some say how unfair it is: "He was too young." "Not even forty!" "Melanoma took my Bill as well." Thinking of both Ryan and Barnum, I want to shout, "Cancer sucks!" But I only nod, feeling awkward and too tall in my heels. Not knowing where to look, I mostly watch their hands. The older women clutch handkerchiefs, some embroidered, while crumpled tissues hide in the palms of the younger ladies. The men don't know what to do with their hands and shove them deep into their pockets. Some of the relatives hug me, their umbrellas battling Jeffrey's; he still stands tall and stoic by my side.

Jeffrey notices me shiver. "Where's your coat?"

"In the car." I look toward the parking lot and see Mom coming with it.

"Honey, you'll catch your . . . you'll catch cold." She wraps the black raincoat around me, covering my lavender suit and turning us all into a stormy sea of proper gloom—except for one little girl with a yellow umbrella. She twirls and taps her shiny black Mary Janes in a puddle. A kid can get away with any behavior at a funeral, but not a widow.

"Barbara, you can introduce everyone to Jane back at the house," Jeffrey says. "Let's get out of this weather."

On the highway, with Mom driving, I sit in silence. I watch the raindrops that hit the top corner of the windshield, out of reach of the wipers. They splatter, then jig and dance in the wind across the corner of the glass. They look wild and free.

"You doing okay?" Mom asks.

"Yeah." We ride in silence for a while until I ask, "Do we have to go to this thing?"

"Yes. I know it's going to be hard, but I'll be right beside you. We can leave early."

"I don't want to go. I want to go home. I'm tired. Besides, even on the best of days, you know I hate being the center of attention. Everyone's going to be staring at me." It's not just the staring I can't stand the thought of; it's the pity. Plus, this has already been more togetherness than I can handle. But then, even if we skip out, Mom would still be back at the condo with me. If only I could get her to go to the Waynesfields' without me.

"Believe me, I know. Your father and I wanted to give you that nice big wedding, but you two ran off to Hawaii instead, all because you didn't want to be the center of attention."

"Still with that? Isn't six years the statute of limitations or something? We tried to pay back the deposits you lost, but Dad wouldn't let us. And we didn't 'run off.' You and the Waynesfields came with us."

"All I'm saying is if there's anyone who knows how much you dislike interacting with people, it's me. You are your father all over again. Bless his antisocial heart. But this isn't only about you, honey. It's about everyone's grief."

"But I don't even know most of these people. I'll never see his Ohio relatives again. It seems pointless to meet them *now*."

"It's not pointless. Everyone wants to offer you their condolences. It's all they can do at a time like this, and it will make them feel a little better. And you'll draw strength from them too. That's how I felt at your father's funeral."

"It's not the same." I think, *You were madly in love with Daddy.*

"Of course it's not the same. Your father died way too young—only sixty-seven!—but it's still nothing like what you and poor Ryan went through. We won't stay long. I promise."

My head falls against the headrest, set too low in the nondescript navy-blue sedan, and I end up staring at the beige fabric-lined ceiling. Mom doesn't understand. It's not about being brave. It's about not wanting to be found out as a fraud, the not-so-distraught-after-all widow.

*

AT THE RECEPTION, I spot Mirabella—she's easy to pick out with her mauve pashmina and cascade of chestnut hair—and make a bee-line for her, like an exhausted swimmer heading for a buoy. She looks beautiful, like she's ready to step in front of the TV camera, as she does every morning in San Diego to deliver the weather forecast on the local CBS station.

She strokes my hair after we hug. "I like your hair that way."

"Mom came at me with her straight iron. You can't believe how much beauty-related crap she's traveling with for a three-day visit. She insisted on putting makeup on me too." She nagged all morning until I let her dab at me with some powder and blush. At thirty-seven, it seems I am old enough that new signs of sun damage from my beach volleyball years appear almost daily, but still young enough to experience stress zits. I'm hoping the powder and my bangs hide the Vesuvius on my forehead. I reach up, self-conscious, and pull at a strand of my super-straight hair. "Be honest, do I look like Tom Petty? I mean, without the facial hair."

"No. You look pretty. Tired, but pretty. How are you holding up?"

"I'm hanging in. It helps having you here. I'm really glad you could come."

"I wish Max could have come, too, but someone had to stay with the kids. He irritates me though. He tells everyone he's 'babysitting.' Babysitting! Like they're not his kids or something." She rolls her eyes, then looks down and pokes at her plate of chicken and Barbara's usual fat-free, taste-free pasta salad. I assume she feels guilty for bitching to me about her annoying-but-at-least-he's-alive husband. Mirabella straightens. "Anyway, I'm glad I could be here. And I know Karen wanted to come too." Karen, our third musketeer, from way back in our Catholic grade school days, had planned to be at the funeral, but then called to say she and her partner had to fly to Portland. The surrogate they were working with went into labor early. She'd texted this morning to say the baby—a girl—had come into the world at 3:00 a.m.

"She's got a good, healthy seven-pound reason for not being here. I know how much she's been wanting this baby."

"Yeah. It's an exciting time for them. It's just been so long since the three of us were together."

"Too long." I want to say more, much more, but Barbara taps my shoulder, says there are more people she'd like me to meet. I don't want to meet more people, but I let her steer me. She swings me past the buffet first, for a plate of food, telling me I looked "peaked" (this from a woman who couldn't look any more peaked if she were a vampire), but I say I'm not hungry.

She stations me next to the fireplace. People stream by. I shake hands with Ryan's coworkers, more relatives, some of his friends from Penn who still live in town. I let them hug me. Some of them smell like fruity perfumes or heavy hairspray, some like cigarettes, or breath mints, or combinations thereof. I thank them for coming. Eventually, I start to sway from low blood sugar coupled with lack of practice wearing heels. I reach for the mantle.

Jeffrey insists I sit and eat, but Mom swoops in. She ushers me to the guest room—where our coats lie on the bed like shed snakeskins—stage-whispering behind my back, "I better get her home. She's worn out." Mom leads me to the front door. I grab at Mirabella as we pass and ask if we're still on for breakfast; she says she's sorry she didn't mention it earlier, but she can't. She had to book an earlier flight—Max called this morning; the twins are sick. We hug, and she promises she'll call soon for a long talk. But I know she won't. She'll get busy; she works full-time and has two-year-old twins. It's fine though. I don't want to tell her everything over the phone and, if all goes well, I'll be back in San Diego soon anyway.

At the car, Uncle Graham gives me a hug, says he'll see me the next time I'm in Arizona.

"Thanks for coming. It can't have been easy to leave the B&B for a few days." It's been good to see my aunt and uncle, whom I haven't seen since my dad's funeral. Ever since my uncle's hair turned white, he reminds me of a clean-shaven Santa—although on this trip, his eyes lack their usual twinkle.

He hugs my mom, his younger sister. They look so alike, except for my uncle's belly and Mom's dyed cocoa powder–brown hair color. "Good-bye, Cordelia. We'll see you soon." My mom lives in Phoenix, about two hours south of Prescott where they live, so they see each other often.

"It was no problem to shut down the B&B." Aunt Sugar hugs me, my eight hundredth of the day. She's always been thin, but it feels like hugging a hanger. I didn't realize until now how tired she looks. Her hair is still ashy blond, which hides her few grays, but it seems thinner. She wears the same chin-length cut she always has, but the bounce and shine are gone. I ask if she's okay. She insists she's fine—it's the time difference, the too-hard hotel bed.

Finally, I collapse into the serene beigeness of the rental car. I have survived the funeral.

I even survive the rest of Mom's visit, which lasts less than twenty-four hours. I survive it by sleeping through most of it—or, sometimes, lying in bed, pretending to sleep.

The truth almost comes out once. Late that night, I get up, starving, and stumble out of the bedroom for a muffin. She's already up, like she's expecting me. She practically has the frying pan heated by the time my sock-covered feet cross the kitchen threshold. While I fill my stomach with pancakes, I almost tell her everything. Maybe because I finally feel like the cared for, instead of the caregiver. But when I look up and see her gazing at me, I can't ruin the picture I know she has of me in her head: the perfect wife turned perfect grieving widow.

Before I go back to bed, I already know what list I'll make. Making lists helps me fall asleep. Something about the orderliness keeps my thoughts from bouncing around like Tigger, keeping me up. Tonight's list seems pretty obvious to me; there's no sense avoiding it.

WAYS I WAS a terrible wife, or rather, for some of these, ways my mother-in-law would say I was a terrible wife:

1. Didn't even consider taking Ryan's last name. I mean, Jaaaane Waaaaynesfield? No, thank you. My last name is the only part of my name I like, so no way was I giving it up. Besides, as I'd told Ryan, Barnum Waynesfield was meh as a dog's name, whereas Barnum Bailey was a perfect name for my little circus clown in a beagle suit.

2. Insisted on keeping separate bank accounts. Ryan wanted to go joint with everything, but I'm too independent for that. Mix our bodily fluids? Okay. We even shared a toothbrush once on a poorly packed-for weekend. But mix our money? No way.

3. Never helped him pick out his clothes for work. Never ironed his shirts. Never made his lunches. He claimed to be incompetent at those things, and I let him be. It meant he often looked like a slob at work, but that wasn't my problem. And it meant he wasted time, money, and calories going out to get lunch every day, but I'm sure the man could have learned to make a damn sandwich.

4. Made too big of a deal of some things. Like, maybe the whole lunch thing wasn't a war game. Maybe it wasn't a classic gender struggle. Maybe he was simply lazy and spoiled, and not trying to bend me to his will. Maybe I made much ado about lunch meat.

5. Often nixed the idea of having his friends over. I always ended up doing all the cooking and cleaning, and they'd eventually turn to reminiscing, leaving me feeling like an outsider in my own home. (I thought he was a loner, like me, when we met. I didn't realize he just hadn't lived in San Diego long enough to build up a stash of friends like he had back in Philly.)

6. Didn't say I love you very often—even back when I was still in love with him. The thing is, we rarely said that in my family. Of course, he didn't say it very often either. It's not like he said it, and I sat there going, "Gee, that's nice." (I'm not sure why I had no qualms about saying it daily, or almost hourly, to the dog, which brings me to number seven.)

7. Was way more demonstrative with the dog. Cuddling with Barnum was one of my favorite things, probably because Barnum was stingy with the cuddling and didn't want to unless he was cold. Barnum playing hard-to-cuddle made me want to glom onto him even more. Plus he was furry. Furry goes a long way in making something irresistible, in my book. In contrast, Ryan liked to cuddle, but—maybe because of his super-fast metabolism or something—being wrapped in his embrace was like being inside a kiln. I could only stand it for about five minutes before I'd push him away. And then he'd always make the same joke: "Do I make you hot?" To which I would respond by rolling my eyes.

8. Stopped loving him. I didn't mean to. I didn't try to. But I did.

I search for a while for a number nine, but realize nothing could be worse than number eight, and I eventually fall asleep.

CHAPTER 2
RASH DECISIONS

"I signed up for a bereavement group." There's silence on the other end of the phone. "Aren't you going to say anything? You're the one who suggested it."

"Oh, Jane," Mom says. "I don't know what to say. I'm sorry you have to go through this." I hold the phone away from my ear as my mother sighs, long and loud, into the phone. Mom's always been a sigher, but it's gotten progressively worse since Ryan first got sick. The sigh barely finishes leaving her lungs, when she adds, "Wait a minute. You signed up for one, or you actually went?"

"I signed up. I found it online."

"Are you going to go?"

Now it's my turn to sigh, although I have to admit: she knows me well. There's a meeting tomorrow night, but I'm pretty certain I won't go. I'd go if I could sit, mute, in the back and observe, but after I signed up, I read the full description. It ended with "everyone will have time to share their feelings." I'm not big on sharing my feelings, even at the best of times. And grief—who wants to share that? Brownies. Brownies are for sharing. Grief is for burying at the bottom of the bed, under a pile of blankets and duvets and quilts so heavy that it'll be smothered and unable to come back out. No one wants a piece of that.

She accepts my sigh as my answer and says, "You should go. It would help, I think. I'm sure there'll be other widows there. Probably not as young as you, but still."

"Widows?"

"Don't you think there will be other widows?"

"It's a bereavement group for pet loss. I'm going because of Barnum."

"Oh, Jane." The words ride a tsunami of a sigh. Her lungs must look like shriveled balloons.

"Mom, don't start." I know she doesn't understand. We already had a fight the day after Barnum died, when she asked me if I was going to get another dog. The day after! I may be remembering wrong, but I'm pretty sure she used the word *replace*. As if I could ever replace Barnum. Barnum was a once-in-a-lifetime find. I'm never getting another dog. It wouldn't be the same. And besides, it hurts too much when you lose them. Mom's never had a pet—she would never let me get one as a kid; "too much hair and they're always licking their privates!"—so I know she can't fathom the huge hole that Barnum's death left in my heart.

"I thought you were talking about Ryan."

I thought about telling Mom everything way back when Ryan and I started fighting on a regular basis about moving back to San Diego, but I never did. Even if Mom hadn't verbalized some form of the phrase "I told you so," it would have hung there between us, like a blinking neon sign. I have to give it to her. She was right. When I told my parents that we were engaged, Mom said we shouldn't do anything "rash" and asked repeatedly if I was sure about "all this." I'd spent my childhood declaring I never wanted to be a "dumb bride in a dumb poofy dress"; the adults' chuckling irritated me and would cause me to restate my position all the more emphatically.

I managed to avoid the poofy dress, but get married I did, after knowing Ryan for only six months. And our marriage is the one instance where I wish I'd listened to Mom. What can I say? I was knocked senseless by love madness. It was my first time really being in love, and I didn't realize how addlebrained it would make me. He made me feel special. We loved all the same sports and hated the same football teams; we had the same sarcastic sense of humor; we were both athletic and took Barnum hiking almost every weekend at Mission Trails. When I went swimming, Ryan would come along and jog up and down the beach. I felt like he was looking out for me. I felt like the center of his universe. And I was, until we moved to Philly.

"I know you don't believe me, but I'm doing okay about Ryan. Really." I think about adding, "Barnum was in my life fourteen years—twice as long as Ryan." But there's no point.

"I believe you. I believe you think you're doing fine. But you're still in shock. Being by Ryan's side these last few months had to be very hard. I know you feel a . . . a sense of . . . well, relief that at least he's not suffering anymore. But it's only been a little over a month, and I'm afraid it's going to hit you hard when you finally accept that he's gone." She pauses for a moment. "And you're there all by yourself now. I wish I lived near you."

I'd just been thinking, *Thank God she doesn't live here; she'd be on my doorstep.*

"I'm not going to be alone here for long. I'm moving back to San Diego."

"You are? When? Isn't that sort of a big decision to make, so soon after . . . after everything? That grief book I bought when your father died said you shouldn't make any major life decisions for a year."

No way was I going to wait another year. I've had it with waiting. I had that argument, that just-another-six-months fight, a million times with Ryan. Now he's gone, and there's nothing keeping me here. I hate Philly. I want to go home, to my friends, to swimming at La Jolla Cove with Karen, to Wednesday-night volleyball, and to decent weather. "It's too late. I already told my boss I quit."

Mom sucks in so much air I swear she affects weather patterns in three states. "Quit? Is that a good idea? With the economy the way it is, uprooting yourself right away?"

"I thought you'd be happy. I'll be close enough to drive over and visit on long weekends."

"I'd love that, but I don't want you to do anything rash you'll regret later."

A pregnant pause hangs in the air. What she means is, I don't want you to do anything rash *again*. This could easily devolve into a fight, but I don't have the energy, so I let it go. "I've been planning this for a long time. It's not a rash move."

"I didn't know you and Ryan had decided to move back. You mean, before he got sick? You never tell me anything. I never know what's going on with you until the last minute."

I decide to let her believe that Ryan was in on the idea. After all, that was supposed to have been the original plan. We were only supposed to live in Philly for two years. He was going to help his dad get his new software business up and running, then they'd sell, and we'd move back to San Diego in style. Oh, the dreams we had. We were going to get a house by the bay or in Pacific Beach—nothing huge, just a cute, little beach cottage. We'd go back to our routine of me swimming while he ran. He promised to learn to play volleyball, and we were going to join one of the Wednesday-night coed intramurals teams. But slowly, I realized "our" dreams didn't seem to be part of the plan anymore. For one thing, it took longer to get Jeffrey's business running than they'd anticipated. And then Ryan and his dad loved working together; they no longer wanted to sell right away. Ryan claimed they were waiting for the right buyer, the right price, but he just didn't want to sell and have to make good on his promise to me to go back.

Six long years later, I'm finally free to leave. "I should go," I say. "It's getting late, and I've got an early meeting with my boss to go over my open projects." Total lie. Our meeting isn't until eleven.

"I'll call you tomorrow. I want to hear more about this move." Her voice perks up. "When do you think you'll head to San Diego? Maybe you could stop on your way?"

"I thought you didn't want me to move?"

"I want you to be happy. If moving will make you happy, you should do it. I'll talk to you tomorrow."

One unfortunate side effect of Ryan's death is that my mother now finds it necessary to call and check in every damn day.

I turn on the TV—for the noise. I channel surf, but everything's so . . . banal. Nothing is funny anymore. And the dramas are so melo-dramatic, not to mention that half of them are set in hospitals, which I've had enough of. That leaves sports. But sports remind me too much of the good times with Ryan: watching baseball with our long legs intertwined on the sofa, eating pizza while Barnum begged for a pep-peroni. Or if it wasn't baseball, it was football, a cycling race, a rugby tournament, heck, even table tennis. We watched it all. Now, coming across a game on TV just makes me sad, because the good times are long gone, and Ryan's gone with them. And maybe also because Mom's right. I do feel a sort of relief now, and that just seems wrong.

Maybe she's also right that I haven't processed everything yet. My brain is a jumbled mess of emotions, and I haven't been up for sorting them out. I miss Barnum so much it physically hurts. I'm depressed like I've never been depressed before. And I feel like a complete jerk for not being devastated like a good widow ought to be. I do miss the good times we once had together. Watching sports reminds me of that. And makes me feel shitty.

I give up and turn off the TV. In the kitchen, I stand under the too-bright overhead light. The cabernet that Ryan used to like calls to me, so I pour a glass. I head back to the living room with the intention of reading, but end up sitting cross-legged on the floor, staring at the sofa. It's been a little over a week since the vet came to the house and euthanized Barnum, right there, his soft, warm body going limp and heavy in my arms.

At least I didn't have to take him to the vet's office, a place Barnum hated. And at least I could make it peaceful. Wish I could have done the same for Ryan. He was in so much pain at the end. I felt so helpless. And useless. Completely not up to the task of trying to offer comfort to someone so sick. I missed out on that whole mothering gene, that innate impulse most women seemingly have to care for others. I wish I were normal. But frickin' Florence Nightingale, I am not.

Why couldn't I save a human family member from pain the way I could a furry loved one? I take a swig of wine and try to turn off my mind to the memories.

I head back to the kitchen for more of the cab, but decide instead to get one of Ryan's leftover sleeping pills and go to bed, even though it's only a quarter to nine.

In bed, panic awaits. I sink into it like quicksand. My thoughts race: headlines about the economy, apartment rental rates, whether I can get all my junk into my Outback. I've done the math and can last about five months without a job. I could last longer if I got a room-mate, but I hate the thought of living with a stranger. If only I could stay with Mirabella or Karen. It'd be like old times, when we roomed together in Pacific Beach after graduating from San Diego State. We used to have so much fun: going out drinking, playing pool, and making fun of the slutty girls. Not that I want to relive my youth, but I miss spending time with my friends. But there's no way I can horn in on them—Mirabella has the twins plus her parents most weekends, and Karen and Elaine just brought home the baby. Besides, I've never been convinced Elaine likes me. And let's face it: even if they had room, I can't get excited about living with a twin set of two-year-olds or a new-born. I've got to go it alone.

I'LL NEVER FALL asleep unless I can reassure myself this isn't a rash decision, so I get started on my list of things that bug me about Philadelphia:

1. The weather. It's too damn cold in the winter. Though it's not exactly Fargo here, I'm a weather wimp, the result of a lifetime spent at an average daily temperature of about seventy-one. And it's too damn sticky from April to September. The locals say the humidity's only bad in July and August, but they lie. (Okay, I admit autumn is nice.)

2. The booze-buying laws. I hate having to go to a special store for alcohol, and then when I do go out of my way to get it, I can't buy a six-pack of beer. I have to buy a case. So dumb.

3. The women at my train stop. They're some of the most miserable ladies ever. It looks like they're from the old USSR, standing in line for a loaf of bread. We've waited for the same train downtown every day for years, but never once has any of them cracked a smile or said hi.

4. The lack of decent Mexican food. Once, when I decried the lack of tasty street tacos, my neighbor suggested Taco Bell. I wanted to punch him.

5. The lack of access to the ocean and accompanying breezes. Yes, Fairmount Park is wonderful, but it's no Pacific Ocean. Where's an open-water swimmer like me supposed to go?

6. The lack of normal roads and decent freeways (emphasis on *free*). There's a toll road full of potholes, but it takes forever to get to since the streets run at weird forty-five-degree angles. It takes an hour to get anywhere. In San Diego, everything is within a twenty-minute drive.

7. The lack of friends. I've been here six years and have not made a single friend.

Drifting off, I realize it's really the things I miss about San Diego that make me not want to live here anymore.

Maybe you're not that bad, Philly. This is about me, not you. Still, I can't wait to see you in my rearview mirror.

CHAPTER 3

BEGGIN' AND EGGS

"We want Ryan's ashes back." Barbara's green eyes, so like Ryan's except for the missing twinkle, stare into mine, unblinking. I look down, concentrate on my pancakes, and think, *So this is why they invited me out.* When Barbara called early this morning, I'd thought they were worried about me, wanted to make sure I wasn't wallowing in bed, was eating a decent breakfast. I didn't want to come. I wanted to stay home and wallow in bed; I wanted to drink stale coffee and pick at four-day-old muffins. I tried telling Barbara I had a lot to do today, what with getting ready to move, but she insisted.

I should have seen this coming. After all, they hadn't honored any of Ryan's wishes for the funeral; why did I think they were going to go along with his final dying wish?

"So, you're going to take him to Maui yourselves?" I know this is not what she means. I look at her, then Jeffrey. Now it's his turn to look at his plate. I'm sure this is her idea.

"We're going to bury him," she says. "We already have the plot. It's next to ours in the Huntingdon Valley Peaceful Hills Cemetery."

Never mind that Ryan didn't want to be buried. Never mind that even if he did, why would he want to be buried next to his parents? Did they even consider that maybe he'd want to spend eternity next to his wife? Of course, they don't know about our fights, but still, they should assume that if the man wanted to be in the ground, he'd want to be next to his wife, not his mama. Barbara's got some long-ass apron strings—they extend right through to the afterworld. "You know that he made me promise to take him to Maui someday; you were there."

"I—we—can't let you simply toss him into the sea." Barbara widens her eyes, making it look as if someone's just tugged her bun even tighter.

The waitress, dressed like a clown (I'd forgotten today was Halloween until I walked into the café), tries to pour more coffee, but Barbara waves her away. I hold up my cup, but it's too late; the clown's gone. I hate clowns.

I set my half-empty cup back down. "You say that like I'd be tossing him out like . . . like the trash. I know you guys are grieving, and of course you want him near you, but Ryan didn't want to be buried. He wanted to be in his favorite place in the whole world." I'm under-caffeinated, and this conversation is starting to make me angry.

Am I trying to be difficult? I'm sure as hell sick of Barbara dictating how everything's going to be. She already nixed Ryan's "fun" funeral ideas, and I gave in because I felt terrible for her and Jeffrey—and because Barnum had just died, and I didn't have the energy to fight about it.

But now I feel terrible. I'm letting Ryan down. And it wasn't like those discussions with Ryan were easy to have in the first place. It was unbearably hard to talk to him about what I'd be doing after he was gone—even to acknowledge that I'd keep going. I felt sad, angry at the universe, guilty knowing that I'd still be around, a functioning person. I'd be able to get on a plane and fly to Maui after he was gone. (Well, technically, he'd be getting on the plane with me—but he wouldn't be able to enjoy the view or the macadamia nuts.)

After enduring those painful conversations and promising Ryan everything would happen exactly as he wanted, and then caving about the funeral because I was distracted dealing with Barnum's death . . . *No, this time I'm not backing down.*

"I know that's what he said he wanted, but, Jane, I'm begging you to reconsider. Those ashes are still Ryan. You wouldn't throw Ryan's body over the side of a boat, now would you?"

"Of course I wouldn't, but—" I look at Jeffrey, hoping he'll be the reasonable one and help me out, hoping he'll stick up for what his son wanted.

"The thing is," Jeffrey begins softly, "Barbara and I talked to Father Llewellyn, and he said we need to bury the ashes in one place, in consecrated ground."

"We want his body to be ready on Judgment Day." Barbara squeezes Jeffrey's hand, which still holds his fork suspended over the egg-white and spinach omelet Barbara ordered for him, although he'd said, "Belgian waffles sound good!" while perusing his menu. The poor man can't order his own breakfast; I should have known better than to think he would come to my aid on something as big as this.

I lean back against the red Naugahyde seat. "But Ryan didn't—" I stop. I'm angry that they'd suggest I go back on my promise—a promise made right in front of Barbara (why didn't she bring up her objections then?)—but even though I'm pissed, I can't bring myself to say that Ryan didn't believe in the things they hold dear, the things they cling to like little neon-colored life jackets in the face of their son's death. They already know anyway, but I'm not going to be the one to verbalize it. Ryan believed in being a good person, in treating others with respect, but he didn't share their faith.

I look at their anguished faces—Jeffery a weathered version of Ryan, Barbara with Ryan's sea-green eyes. I don't want to let Ryan down—but they look so miserable. They wait for me to finish what I started to say. I take a deep breath and hope Ryan won't mind. "What if we compromise? I'll take half of his ashes to Maui. You can bury the rest. Then you'll have your visitation spot, and he'll . . . mostly be in consecrated ground."

They look at each other, then back at me. "We can't do that," Barbara says. "Father Llewellyn was adamant that we shouldn't scatter the ashes—not even some of them. He says Ryan should be interred in whole."

For a second, I'm tempted to suggest they think outside the box, so to speak. I can't help it. Bad jokes pop into my head when things get serious. I chew my lip and say nothing.

"Someday, he'll be resurrected," Barbara says. "He's going to need his body."

I'm not sure at what age I stopped believing in a vision of heaven that involved angels and harps and fluffy clouds, but I did stop. I don't believe we're going to be resurrected, that we'll each float up to our own predesignated La-Z-Angel cloud recliner. (I'm willing to admit there's a small chance I could be wrong, but I doubt it.) I think if there is going to be some sort of resurrecting going on, God, or whoever's in charge, wouldn't be cruel enough to saddle us with these same old bodies. Won't we be . . . I dunno, some sort of asexual things? All beautiful and ethereal and floaty. Are people going to still need their funky feet and their double chins and their . . . scrotums? (Or is it *scroti*?) Wouldn't we be better off without that . . . baggage? I think any sort of loving God has got to have a better plan than that.

On the other hand, I must admit I have imagined Barnum being there to greet me when I die. And I always picture him as his usual fuzzy self. So, how will that work? He'll be his regular dog self, but I'll be some sort of shape-shifting mist? Will he recognize me? Will I smell the same?

The whole thing is very confusing and makes my brain tired. I want to go home and go back to sleep.

"I'll have to think about it." I want to end this conversation and buy myself some time. Jeffrey and I finish our breakfasts; Barbara taps her wedding ring against her coffee mug.

As I stab the last bite of pancake, I think there is no way I'm breaking my final promise to Ryan. The funeral stuff was minor. I can let that go. But this is a big deal. My last stand.

So . . . I'll just keep *some* of him. They'll never know! I'll keep a scoop, maybe two, and let them have the rest. It's a perfect solution.

I lick syrup off the back of my fork, satisfied with my plan.

Jeffrey asks the waitress for the bill, and we wait in silence. Why does this matter so much to me? I'd grown apart from Ryan, planned on leaving him while he was still alive and kicking, so how come I'm so determined, now that he's gone, to hang on to him—if only for a brief while until I can afford to get him to Maui? I guess I feel like I owe it to him, because I'm the one who got to go on living. Someone has to make this man's dying wish come true, and no one else is going to step up anytime soon. It's the least I can do for him now.

And maybe it feels good to defy Barbara. Any time there was ever a choice between what I wanted to do and what Barbara wanted to do, Barbara won. Like, every Sunday was family dinner night at the Waynesfields'. Even if I had a headache (or faked one), or the weather was bad, Ryan would go without me, saying it was tradition and his mom would be upset if we didn't go. And we always went to their house on Thanksgiving and Christmas. I tried to talk Ryan into visiting my parents for the holidays, but Barbara convinced him it was too much of a hassle to fly at that time of year, and—I can still hear her voice saying sweetly—"Wouldn't it be better to visit Jane's parents in the summer or fall, when the weather's good for traveling?"

This time Barbara will compromise, whether she knows it or not. I look down to hide my face because I'm afraid they'll read my thoughts.

In the parking lot, I say, "You know what? I don't need to think it over. You're right." Barbara clasps her hands beneath her pointy chin. "You should be able to have your son near you." *Or most of him anyway.*

"Oh, thank you so much." She holds her hands up in what is either a praise-the-Lord or raise-the-roof gesture, I'm not sure. "You've made me so happy!"

Jeffrey grips my shoulder. "Thank you, Jane."

I don't like lying to them, or to Jeffrey anyway, but I hate the thought of going back on my promise to Ryan even more. Technically, I'd never broken a promise to him during our seven years together. Of course, I'd planned to break the biggest one—the "Till death do us part" one—but then, before I got the chance to tell Ryan I wanted out, he came home from a checkup and said the doc had lopped a mole off his back. And then the biopsy: cancer. And that one word decimated the neat row of ducks I'd lined up. I was almost ready—had money saved for a lawyer and the move back home—but I couldn't leave him then, not when he'd just entered the hardest battle of his life. I figured I'd help him fight it. And then, once he was strong again, I'd ask for the divorce. I'd put my plans on hold until he beat this thing. Only, he didn't beat it. Cancer knocked him out; Ryan fell flat on his back on the mat, and the ten count was over before any of us knew what happened. So, I did end up hanging in until the end. But it was all a matter of timing and circumstances beyond my control.

We say good-bye, and I retreat to the quiet of my car. It's a good plan, so why do I still feel bad? I guess because all I want is to be a regular ol' divorcée instead of a much-pitied widow. Maybe keeping this one last promise will make up, in some small way, for the lie I lived our last months together, the lie I'm still stuck living.

I'm lost in thought when Barbara taps a pointy, painted fingernail on my window.

"So, about the ashes," she says after I crack the window. "I'll swing by one day this week and pick them up. I know you'll be busy getting ready for your big move. The Rite of Committal is next Saturday, a week from today. I assume you're free?"

"Rite of Committal?"

"The burial." She shimmies her shoulders as if to say, "Isn't that obvious?"

"The burial's already scheduled? For next Saturday? But—"

"We knew you'd see reason, so we went ahead and made plans with Father Llewellyn."

Heat creeps up my face. I clutch my keys. Of course Barbara would assume she'd get her way. Doesn't she always? I'm about to say I've changed my mind, I'm keeping the ashes, when Jeffrey appears behind her. Sweet, devastated Jeffrey. Barbara can be so passive-aggressive that I forget that, at the heart of it, she is a grieving parent. With him, I never forget.

"Thank you again." His voice is gruff. "This means so much to us. It's . . . it's all we have left of him." He looks down, and his face lights up. "Hey, another penny."

"Oh, Jeffrey, that's filthy." Barbara waves a hand at him as he bends to retrieve it.

He ignores her and passes it to me. "I'm pretty sure this one was meant for you. It was right under your car door. You've got to look out for these things, Jane." He smiles at me, and I can't help but smile back. It might be the first time I've smiled all week.

CHAPTER 4

DOG WAS MY COPILOT

On the drive back, I decide that as soon as I get home, I'll set some of Ryan's ashes aside. But in what? I guess a Ziploc, for starters. I'll find a nice receptacle later. Something meaningful. With a snug lid. Ryan always loved the peppermint bark Williams-Sonoma sells at Christmas. Maybe . . .

Wherever you are, Ry, I hope you're not mad. I hope you don't mind that only part of you is going to Maui. Sometimes, Ry, I swear, your mother . . .

Outside our—*my*—condo door, I jingle my keys. Damn. It's habit, letting Barnum know Mama's home. I open the door and silence greets me. There's no wagging tail, no wiggling butt. No tip-tap of happy feet dancing on the hardwood floor. No sweet beagle kisses. Coming home is the absolute worst part of any day since Barnum died. And also eating, because I'd always share a bit of my food with him. Yeah, eating sucks too. Sleeping is good though. Sleeping equals forgetting. *Maybe a nap,* I think, before noticing the blinking of the answering machine light.

"This is Serenity Pet Cemetery," a soft voice says. "Barnum is ready to be picked up."

Of course, the woman was too tactful to say, "what's left of Barnum." The thought causes a sharp pain, deep in my chest, like someone's driving a long needle into my heart. Tears creep up on me like silent ninjas. My hand goes to his dog tag—his thin metal bone-shaped tag—that I've worn on a long chain inside my clothes since he died. With my thumb, I trace its outline under the soft fabric of my T-shirt.

I wish I could think of someone to drive me, because I'll sob the whole way home.

I've always loved those "Dog Is My Copilot" bumper stickers. I'd planned to get one, but never got around to it. It would have been perfect, since Barnum always rode shotgun. Any other passenger, generally Ryan, would have to accept having a beagle on their lap—that was the rule.

But now, Barnum will be riding shotgun in a receptacle. A box of beagle. I can't help myself; I picture the bumper sticker: "Dead Dog Is My Copilot." The ninja tears flip themselves up and over the wall of my lower lid, landing hot and silent on my cheeks.

I try to think of someone I can call who'll take me. Although we've lived in Philly six years, I don't have any real friends here. There are other dog owners in the condo complex, but Barnum hated other dogs, so I never had to stop and talk to those people. As for coworkers, they were just that. I kept thinking we'd be moving back to San Diego soon, so what was the point of getting to know any of them? Sure, Ryan had his good buddies, and as a couple, we had going-out-to-dinner friends, occasional weekend-barbecue friends, but not the type of friends I could now call and ask to help me pick up my poor dead dog's ashes.

If you weren't such a loner, weren't so "I can do it myself" all the time, you might have a friend you could call when you need one.

But that's precisely the problem. Most of the time, I don't need one. And most friends don't want to operate under that sort of arrangement. Why do I have to be this way?

The phone rings and, caught off guard, deep in my thoughts, I answer rather than screen like I normally would.

"Hello, Jane."

Barbara. *What now? His ashes aren't enough? You need some DNA too?* We already spent a painful day last week going through Ryan's things, so what could she want now? (I kept his Padres baseball cap, a reminder of happier times, when we dated in San Diego. Jeffrey kept his briefcase and the Swiss Army knife he'd given Ryan when he joined the Boy Scouts. Barbara kept every last one of his work shirts, holding them to her face and saying they still smelled like him. Of course they did; he never did laundry.)

I'm not in the mood to deal with her again so soon, and my annoyance almost overrides my grief about Barnum's ashes. Almost. "Yeah?" is all I say, but Barbara hears the weepiness behind my attempt to sound normal.

"What's the matter?" The concern in her voice unhinges me. If it had been a fricking telemarketer, I could have held it together. I am not a weeper. I hate being like this, but when I hear all that horrible sympathy, I can't help it—I lose it.

I start the kind of sobbing where I can barely talk. I haven't cried like this since I was little. The words blurt out, sharp and staccato. "It's . . . Barnum. He's . . . ready to . . . pick up."

"You're in no shape for that. I'll drive you. It was bad enough you took him by yourself in the first place." She's right. I went alone that day to the cemetery, Barnum's lifeless body wrapped in a blanket, me crying the entire way. My face crumpled, and incoherent words fell out of my mouth when the woman in a droopy gray cardigan asked if she could help. She told me she'd "settle the deceased" in the back where I could spend as long as I wanted saying good-bye. The room was big and cold, with exposed construction block walls and a concrete floor. Barnum, laid out on the pull cart she'd used to bring him in, was still warm. I hated to see him so still, like a broken-down stuffed animal. I rested my hot forehead against his soft brown one, and then buried my nose in the ruff of fur at his neck. Barnum always had a lovely smell, like a mix of peanut butter and tortilla chips, which sounds odd but was wonderful. I sat there for a long time, breathing in his scent, stroking his fur, getting up the courage for the seemingly endless drive back to my empty condo.

Barbara's voice scatters the memory. "Do you want to go now?"

"Okay." I've been turning the penny Jeffrey gave me over and over in my jacket pocket. I pull it out. It was minted the year Barnum was born.

*

AT THE PET cemetery, it's the same woman in the same stretched-out sweater but with the added attempted cheer of a cherry-red lipstick. She says she'll bring Barnum out, and I notice a bright splotch of lipstick on her teeth. Even in my grief, I think, *Gross*. I hate lipstick—the smell of it, the greasy texture, the soapy taste. I look over at Barbara, who gives me a "buck up!" smile with her burgundy lips. I peruse the shelves displaying wooden boxes and ceramic urns, while Barbara reads a framed poem about rainbows and bridges. I read that damn poem the last time I was here. I'm not going near it again, or I'll be a puddle on the floor.

No, the urns are safer to look at. Some are ornate, carved with curlicues; others aim at the hunting set, engraved with trees, fields, and ducks. Most of them look too fussy for Barnum, who'd never liked being dressed up—no costumes on Halloween or sweaters in the winter. I find a plain cedar box at the far end of the top shelf. The deep, spicy scent of the cedar sells me on it. I figure he'd like being in something so aromatic, since I'd always called him a nose on four feet.

The woman reappears with a small white cardboard box with a label. It looks like a package ready for shipping.

I hand over the cedar box, and with her back to us, she transfers the ashes as though to shield us from the sight. As she turns back, she snaps a small lock shut on the lid. She hands me the box and two small keys. I look at Barbara, her lips stretched tight. She must be thinking the same thing I am: Ryan's box didn't come with a lock. Did we get ripped off at the funeral home? Where's *his* lock?

On the way home, I'm calmer than I thought I would be. Probably because exhaustion weighs me down like the lead apron they use for dental X-rays. I still cry, but slow, cool tears now, rather than the hot, nonstop streaming kind. With Barnum's box on my lap, I watch the browns and yellows—the remains of the mostly spent fall colors—stream past the window in a tear-blurred mosaic.

Back home, Barbara insists on seeing me in. She holds Barnum's box while I dig for my keys. Inside, she sets the box on the bookcase beside Ryan's. I see her eyeing the much larger box, and try to head her off from asking about Ryan's ashes, since I haven't set a scoop aside yet.

"So, do you need me to do anything for the burial?" I ask, pulling her attention to me.

"The Rite of Committal. And, no, everything's taken care of. It will be a small group: my niece and her husband, and the Denofreys. We'll have a luncheon at our place after."

"I'll bring the ashes that morning."

She looks at the box and back to me. "Fine. You should take a nap. You look tired."

"Thanks," I say sarcastically, but then realize I owe her a proper thank-you. "I mean . . . really. Thanks for taking me."

"It was no problem. Get some sleep. I'll let myself out." She watches me head for the stairs. I turn back halfway up, and she waggles her fingers. "Sweet dreams."

When I wake up, Ryan's ashes are gone.

THAT NIGHT, I'M still angry with Barbara for stealing Ryan. I can't sleep and end up listing slights and/or outright insults Barbara perpetrated against me, my home, and my dog:

1. I know she's done the white-glove test here, running her finger along the sideboard. (She wasn't actually wearing gloves, but still, the test is the same.) I caught her, sneering and showing her finger to Jeffrey, when I came into the dining room with dessert.

2. She used to get up and move to the armchair if Barnum jumped up on the sofa beside her.

3. One year for Christmas, she and Jeffrey gave me a vacuum. Ryan got new golf clubs. She got two digs in for the price of one: she let me know she didn't think my carpets were clean enough, and also sent a signal about how she thought we should each be spending our weekends (even though I know she'd heard me say many times that I wanted to learn to golf). Subtle, Babs.

4. She equates my being tall with being big, and buys me sweaters in size large. I've told her several times that I wear medium, but I guess she thinks I'm lying to myself. She clearly thinks I'm a moose, but then again, everyone looks like a moose next to her tiny dancer frame.

I could go on and on, but it all pales in comparison to stealing Ryan right out from under my roof. Okay, I told them they could have the ashes, but still. I said I'd bring them, so it really wasn't necessary for her to take them. She makes me insane, always managing to get her way. But not this time. Sleep comes while I make a new list: items I'll need for stealing some of Ryan back.

CHAPTER 5

ASHES TO STASHES

The next day, I'm on the Waynesfields' doorstep, holding a plate of carrot cupcakes slathered with cream cheese frosting for Jeffrey, who I'm hoping will answer. I arrive at 1:00 p.m. Sunday, knowing they'll have just finished lunch after attending late-morning Mass.

"A thank-you present," I say when Barbara opens the door. "For taking me out to breakfast yesterday." I try hard to sound sincere, hoping she doesn't realize that I know she won't eat a single cupcake.

"You shouldn't have," Barbara says with a look on her face as if I'm offering chocolate-dipped rats instead of my heavenly cupcakes. And I know these babies are heavenly. I broke out my old recipes when Ryan was sick. I'm not a bring-treats-for-people type, but Ryan seemed to get a little extra attention from the nurses once I started bringing home-made goodies to his treatments. I used to love to bake for Ryan—he was especially a fan of my pies and Sunday-morning scones. But then Barbara had to go and say that he looked like he'd gained a few pounds. She said if he wanted to keep up with his buddies on the basketball court, he better cut back, and then he started having the nerve to look annoyed if I'd bake for him. Give me a break. The basketball burned off the few extra calories.

On the other hand, Jeffrey has never stopped appreciating my baked goods. He drifts over, as if lured by the scent of sugar and butter. The expression on his face reminds me of one of those hyperspeed films of a flower blooming: he transforms from bored to delighted in a fraction of a second. "Cupcakes!"

"Really, Jane, you shouldn't have," Barbara repeats.

"Let her in!" Jeffrey elbows Barbara out of the way and puts an arm around my shoulder, steering me through the front door.

"I wanted to thank you guys. And I felt like baking. I haven't made cupcakes since that last batch for the hospice people. I miss it. And it seemed depressing to bake for myself." Barbara might be tempted to close the door on cupcakes, but she won't close it on grief.

"Oh, Jane, of course it did," Jeffrey says. Barbara's face softens—as much as her bun will allow—and she motions for me to have a seat on the pristine cream-colored sofa. She takes the plate and sets it on the coffee table, then heads for the kitchen. "Coffee, Jane?" she asks over her shoulder. Jeffrey bites into a cupcake, leaning forward in his seat and holding his other hand out as a crumb catcher.

"No, thank you." As I answer, I glance around, hoping to see the cherrywood box. There it is on the mantle. But there's something new. A gold padlock catches the light from the dining room chandelier; it glistens and winks at me.

Damn! I drop my purse. I won't need the Ziploc bag and Tide detergent scoop hidden inside.

Barbara returns, placing a cup of coffee before Jeffrey and a huge stack of napkins next to it. She must have seen me looking at the box. "I knew you wouldn't mind if I brought him home. No sense waiting until Saturday." She walks to the mantle and strokes the polished lid. "And I got the idea to add the lock after—well, it didn't seem right that

Ryan was unlocked. So I had the clasp added on my way home yesterday. They did a lovely job."

I take a cupcake, trying to eat carefully over a napkin. I contemplate that now my only chance to steal back some ashes will be Saturday morning before the burial. And I'll have to figure out what to do about that lock. I finish my cupcake, then hold the plate out to Jeffrey, knowing it will irk Barbara. "Have another."

*

MONDAY AT WORK (Hooray for my second-to-last Monday here! I'm counting the days until my two-week notice is up.) I again spend my lunch hour searching Craigslist for a decent-looking, affordable apartment in San Diego. The reality of moving without the benefit of gainful employment is hitting me, and I've already spent hours searching for jobs and apartments and working out budgets based on various scenarios. My excitement about moving back is being squeezed out by my worries about how I'll make this happen. I only have eleven days left before my big move, and panic is setting in.

But during my nightly phone call with Mom, I don't let on that I'm worried. "I'm sure I'll find something once I get there," I say, unsure if I'm convincing her. I'm not even convincing myself, especially since my line of work is rather specialized. I'm good at what I do—my undergrad degree in business combined with a master's in library and information sciences makes me an excellent market intelligence analyst. But, as I'd found out when I began my original job search postgraduation, not that many companies have MI departments. Usually it's just the big corporations. So in San Diego, where academia, the military, and small biotech firms make up most of the employment pool, it's especially tough to find an MI position. The place where I worked in San Diego before moving to Philly went bankrupt the year after I left. (Which, at the time, I took as a sign that we'd done the right thing in moving.

As a maker of rash decisions, I'll admit I sometimes spend a good deal of energy looking for signs afterward that confirm that the decision, although rash, was in fact the correct one.)

"You should come to Phoenix and live with me," Mom offers. "Just until you find work. San Diego's close enough that you could job hunt from here. I don't want to pry into your finances, honey, but I know you must have had a lot of hospital bills with Ryan—even with his insurance. Can you afford this move?"

It's true that the deductible and out-of-pocket expenses from Ryan's illness devoured his savings and took a massive bite out of mine as well. Ryan had said we could get money from his parents, that I shouldn't have to pitch in. I told him that was ridiculous; we were in it together. But then, on top of Ryan's bills, there were Barnum's, and I didn't have pet insurance.

"It'll be fine, Mom. Don't worry." *It'll be fine* is my new mantra. Besides, if there's an emergency, that's what credit cards are for.

*

AHHHH, SATURDAY. I luxuriate in my goose-down cocoon, happy for the weekend and the chance to sleep in. I roll over and see the clock.

Nine thirty! I never sleep this late. I shouldn't have taken another of Ryan's sleeping pills. I flail out from under the heavy duvet. I'll have to rush to make it to the Waynesfields' in time. If I'm late, there'll be no hope of keeping my promise to Ryan.

I veto showering and pull on black pants and my nubby gray wool sweater set. I glance in the mirror, and Barbara's words come back to me: *"Please wear something . . . appropriate. It's going to be a solemn day."* A dig at my lavender suit, no doubt. But in homage to Ryan, I find a pair of purple-and-black striped socks in the back of my drawer, left over from a witch costume. As I sit on the edge of the bed and pull up the socks, I notice a few Barnum hairs clinging to the hem of my pants.

I don't bother to brush them off; a bit of Barnum should come along and say good-bye to Ryan. I sigh, slip on my black loafers, and grab a blueberry muffin to eat while I drive. My heavy purse smacks against my hip as I run to my car.

Managing to break only a few traffic rules, I get to the Waynesfields' at 10:35 a.m. Barbara's niece, Lucy, and her husband are already there, along with the Denofreys, a couple that Barbara and Jeffrey have been friends with for forever. They mill about the living room, waiting to leave for the cemetery.

Barbara greets me with a stiff hug that morphs into an attempt to tame my hair. At least that's why I assume she's patting my head—a move she's never tried before. I squirm away, and we survey each other's outfits. Barbara wears a black skirt and jacket over a frilly white blouse with a waterfall of ruffles down her chest.

"You look very nice, Barbara."

"So do you, dear." She points at my cardigan and whispers, "There's something all over your sweater."

I look down. Bits of muffin nestle into the woolly nooks of my twinset. "Oh. Breakfast." I am tall, thin, and flat chested, but not so flat that my boobs can't act as a landing strip for crumbs. I pluck the biggest one from my sweater and think about popping it into my mouth, but I notice Barbara's hand extended, palm up—a move that reminds me of being busted for chewing gum in school and having to hand over the confiscated blob to withered Sister Mary Richard. I deposit the crumb in Barbara's palm and brush away the rest. "Sorry."

Barbara accepts the offending crumb and turns to address the room. "We'd better go," she announces.

"Uh, Barbara," I say loudly enough for everyone to hear. "Can I have a quick minute with Ryan—alone?" Barbara looks at her watch, then at Jeffrey. I press on. "I'll be quick. I . . . I want to say good-bye . . . one more time before we . . . You understand, don't you?"

Barbara glances at her watch again, but Jeffrey pats my back. "Of course," he says. "Use my office. But we must leave in a few minutes."

I heft Ryan's box off the mantle and head for the first room down the hall. "I'll just be a moment." I try to sound solemn, but a nervous, higher-than-normal edge creeps into my voice.

After closing the door, I set the heavy box down on Jeffrey's desk, plopping my purse next to it. It's dark in the wood-paneled office, so I turn on the desk light. My hands shake while I pull out my tools. I whisper a silent prayer to the universe: "Please don't let anyone come in!" With one hand, I hold the box, then stick the tip of my screwdriver into the U-shaped loop of the small, decorative lock. I push down hard and fast on the screwdriver handle, sending the tip up. A pop sounds as the lock comes apart, but I cough several times and hope no one noticed.

The good news is it works—the lock yields. The bad news is two-fold: the tip of the screwdriver scratched the box, and the U-shaped piece popped off with such force that it flew past me. Frick! The scratch isn't bad. I think the replacement lock, found at a luggage store last night, will hide it. The missing piece is the bigger problem. I scan the floor. It must have fallen on the carpet, since I didn't hear it hit anything, but I don't see it; it'll have to wait.

When I open the box, I see a dark purple velvet bag with black cording pulled tight and piled on top. The bag's a nice, unexpected touch. And the purple is fitting for Ryan, but I can't help but think of the bags Crown Royal whisky comes in. I loosen the cording, revealing a plastic bag full of pale ashes. It really does look like ash or dust. I don't know what I was expecting. I guess I was afraid there'd be . . . bits. But it's simply gray powder.

"Oh, Ry," I sigh as I undo the gold twist tie holding the plastic bag shut. I take a deep breath, afraid if I exhale, I'll scatter Ryan, like powdered sugar from a doughnut, across the desktop. I hold my Ziploc bag with one hand, while measuring out ashes with my green plastic

Tide scoop with the other. I pick up the Ziploc and judge the weight: not much. Even as a symbolic gesture, it doesn't seem like enough for Maui.

Maybe one more scoop.

I'm almost done pouring in the second scoop when a knock sounds at the door, a quiet one-knuckle tap, tap, tap. It startles me, and I drop the scoop—it hits the desk, sending a fine spray of dust into the air.

"Are you ready? We need to head out."

Jeffrey. Damn. "I'll just be a sec." My heart races. Hopefully, he'll think the shaky sound of my voice is from crying.

A thin layer of ash dulls the previously shiny desktop. It's too fine to try to brush it into the Ziploc. Besides, there's no time. I blow.

Forgive me, Ry! But think how happy your mom would be if she knew a bit of you will always be here at home with her.

I quickly twist tie the plastic bag shut again, pull tight the velvet bag's cord, and close the lid. I drop the scoop, now covered in a fine film of ash, into my Ziploc, zip it shut, and stuff it, the gold twist tie, the bottom piece of the old padlock, and the screwdriver into my purse. I snap the new lock on and position it so it covers the scratch.

Everything's perfect, except for the broken piece from the old lock. On hands and knees, I search the carpet. My head is fully under the desk when I hear the creak of the door hinge.

"Jane?" Barbara. "Are you—what are you doing on the floor?"

I spot the missing piece. As I crawl back out from under the desk, I yank out one of my amethyst stud earrings. I palm the bit of lock in one hand and, with the other, display my earring.

"My earring came out and bounced under the desk."

"Oh." Barbara's eyes narrow. She looks at me, at my hair (which I'm sure now looks worse from sweating while I worked and from crawling under the desk), then at the box. I look at it too, assessing the scene with fresh eyes. Everything looks good.

"I guess I was a bit distracted this morning. Must've forgotten to put the back on my earring. It fell out when I bent over the box to . . . to say good-bye." I pick up the box and hold it against my chest so Barbara can't inspect it.

Barbara looks like she wants to pry it away from me, but instead clasps her hands together. "I guess you can hold him on the way there. But please, set him back down for one second. There's one more thing I want to do before we go." Her hand emerges from the pocket of her suit jacket, holding a small gold key.

New and improved beads of sweat—bigger and hotter than the ones I felt earlier while stealing the ashes—form on my back and at the edges of my hairline.

"Wh—what are you doing?" My arms seize up, rigor mortis from knuckles to shoulders. Barbara will never get the box away from me now. "You're not going to, to open him up, are you?"

Barbara reaches for a photo that I hadn't noticed, lying on some loose papers on the desk. It's of the four of us at our wedding on Po'olenalena Beach in Maui. Ryan, in his Hawaiian shirt, grins at me in my simple white dress. A band of pink-and-white plumeria flowers circles my head; my long toffee-colored hair floats on the breeze. Jeffrey and Barbara stand on either side of us, smiling. The ocean behind us sparkles under the sun. I remember my dad snapped the picture. The happiness we felt on that trip seems a lifetime ago. Seeing the picture makes me know I'm doing the right thing. I've got to get Ryan's ashes back to that idyllic paradise where he golfed to his heart's content, and I swam every day in the warm, clear waters.

"I know you think I'm terrible, not honoring Ryan's wish about Maui." Tears well in Barbara's eyes. "And I do feel bad about that." She holds the photo out to me. "Look how handsome he was, my poor, beautiful boy. I . . . I thought we could put this in the box with him; it's the next best thing to being in Maui."

"That's very sweet. And I don't think you're terrible. I understand." My sense of triumphant indignation turns to pity.

"Thank you. Now set him down." She reaches out for the box, but I hold on. "Jane, give me the box." Barbara tugs at it.

I let go. What else can I do? I hope, by some miracle, the key will work. These locks are all the same, right?

Barbara inserts the key while my heart uses my ribs like a ladder and starts climbing right out of my chest. I put my hand over my mouth, afraid I might gasp, scream, curse—I'm not sure what might come out, maybe my heart.

Barbara turns the key. Nothing. She jiggles it. Still nothing. "That's odd."

"I'm not surprised. Everything's so poorly made these days." Nervous words tumble out. "There's no quality control anymore. Everybody just wants the cheapest price nowadays, and stuff's just slapped together . . ." Barbara fusses with the lock while I ramble.

Jeffrey walks in, and I clam up. "We need to leave now, or we'll be late."

"I can't get this lock open." Barbara stands back. "Will you try?"

"Why?" Jeffrey, as I know from years of Ryan dashing out the door to make it to work on time, hates tardiness. He raises his arm and makes a show of yanking his shirtsleeve back to reveal his watch, then taps the face. "Father Llewellyn is waiting."

"I told you I wanted to put this picture in with Ryan. And now the lock won't open."

"It's your own darn fault for installing that thing. I told you it was unnecessary—especially since we're burying him. But, no, you insisted. You never listen to me." He grabs Ryan's box and the photo and strides off toward the living room. "We'll put the photo in the plot alongside him." I breathe for what seems like the first time in minutes.

Barbara and I follow along as Jeffrey herds everyone out. I fall back and finally drop the broken bit of the old lock into my purse.

CHAPTER 6

PENNIES FROM HEAVEN

After a bland postburial—sorry—*Rite of Committal* lunch, during which Mrs. Denofrey worked hard to keep the conversation flowing, I offer to help with the dishes. We take our places in the straight-from-the-seventies kitchen, at the same stations we've manned after countless Sunday dinners. Jeffrey washes. I dry. Barbara wraps leftovers and puts away clean dishes. It's funny, yet also terribly pathetic, that we don't miss Ryan in the kitchen; there's no spot for him in the lineup because Barbara always insisted that he sit and watch TV while the rest of us cleaned.

"I'm not sure when we'll see you again," Jeffrey says. Sadness tinges his voice as he hunches over the sink. "You're leaving for San Diego next weekend?"

"Yeah. I have to finish out my last week at work, then Saturday, I hit the road."

"Maybe we'll come and visit sometime." He turns to Barbara. "It's been a long time since we were there. Remember that trip we took to visit Ryan, before he met Jane?"

"I remember how disgusting his apartment was," Barbara says. *That's because you never taught him to clean up after himself.* "I was so glad when he met you, Jane. I thought, Now he'll have a nice girl to take care of him." Her eyes drift. I imagine she's seeing the perfect daughter-in-law she'd hoped I'd be: combination maid, chef, personal shopper, and nutrition expert who'd care for her son in the manner to which he'd become accustomed. I can't believe I never noticed how useless he was at, oh, just about everything domestic, until after we got married. We should have lived together first. Me and my rash decisions.

Returning from my memories, I see that Barbara and Jeffrey still seem lost in theirs. Even if Barbara does consider me a disappointment in the daughter-in-law department, she's probably at least a little sad to see me go. If nothing else, I'm a reminder of Ryan's life.

"I should get going." I place the last pot on the gold Formica counter.

"You must still have a lot to do." Jeffrey rolls his shirtsleeves back down. "We don't want to keep you."

"I do have a lot of packing to finish. And I need to drop off Barnum's crate and some of his other stuff at the Humane Society." It amazes me that I don't choke up.

"I'm surprised to hear you say that. I know how much you loved Barnum. I assumed you'd get another dog."

"No . . ." Ah, okay, here comes the choking. "I better go." I head toward the living room. "Need to grab my purse."

"I put it in the guest bedroom." Barbara follows me. "Jeffrey, be a dear and fetch it."

"No, I'll get it!" I didn't realize Barbara had moved my purse. I'd brought my biggest one to fit the scoop, screwdriver, and bag of ashes, but it doesn't have a zipper closure, only a silver snap. I don't want to chance Jeffrey seeing, or feeling, anything suspicious in there. Obviously Barbara hadn't, or we'd still be scraping her off the ceiling.

"Don't be silly." Jeffrey's already down the hall, and I figure it will look odd if I dash past him. In a moment, he's back, holding the bag out like a rabbit from a magician's hat. He shakes it. "Heavy! What do you have in here? Power tools?" He laughs, and I force one too; it sounds like a donkey's bray.

I snatch the bag. "Ha! No, just regular tools." Jeffrey laughs again.

"Oh, dear, we're going to miss your sense of humor." He puts an arm around Barbara and pulls her close. "Eh, Barbara?"

I can't remember Barbara ever laughing at one of my jokes—maybe a smirk now and then, but never a hearty laugh. She manages a smile now. At the door, she clutches my shoulders in her usual grab-and-pull move that I've never gotten comfortable with.

"Take care." Barbara eyes me with almost-motherly concern.

"We worry about you driving cross-country alone." Jeffrey pulls me into a bear hug. "I wish Barnum could be with you. I'd feel better knowing you had your guard dog along."

I look down. "Me too" is all I can manage.

Barbara hands me a tissue, pulled from her apron pocket. "Don't worry; he'll be watching over you." She looks heavenward and points.

"He always was a good guard dog." I blow my nose.

Barbara's chin droops. "I meant Ryan."

"Of course."

"They'll both be watching," Jeffrey says.

We say good-bye, promise to keep in touch, and I'm free. I turn as I walk down the flagstone path to the street and wave.

"Look for the pennies!" Jeffrey yells. Barbara turns to him with a what-the-hell-are-you-talking-about look on her face. I wonder if this is the last time I'll see that face.

As I drive home, I try to decide if I'll miss Barbara or Philadelphia more, once I'm gone. I decide on Philly, because at least it has cheesesteak going for it.

*

"I HAVE THE answer!" Mom sings into the phone.

She never says, "Hi, how are you?" Like a normal person. She's always got to open with flair. "What was the question?" I ask.

I'm leaving town in three days and still have tons to do, so I keep packing while I wait for my mother to enlighten me, my shoulder shoving my cell phone against my ear. My mom calls so often and talks for so long that I know I have to keep busy. During calls over the past few days, I've reorganized and culled my huge collection of recipes and cookbooks (I probably kept way too many, now that I'll be cooking for one, but I couldn't part with most of them); cleaned my stove with a toothbrush (I need every cent of the security deposit back); and, one by one, picked dog hairs out of the sofa. They'd embedded themselves so snugly into the weave of the fabric that the vacuum couldn't suck them out (again, I need that deposit).

"The question of where you're going to live while you find a job!"

"I already told you, I'm moving to a short-term furnished apartment."

"I have a better idea. But first, I have some news." Her voice goes from the about-to-lay-her-brilliant-idea-on-me lilt to downright melancholy. Knowing her penchant for the dramatic, I brace myself for something ridiculous and unrelated to my housing needs. "Sugar was diagnosed with rheumatoid arthritis this summer."

"Seriously?"

"Of course, seriously. I wouldn't make something like that up."

Now I feel bad—for suspecting Mom would dump her usual silliness on me in the guise of a real problem, and especially for not questioning something was wrong with my aunt at the funeral. I knew she didn't look like her usual vibrant self, but I believed her lie that it was jetlag.

"I can't believe you waited until now to tell me this." I stop packing and sit on the edge of the bed, piles of clothes tumbling toward me.

"Your aunt didn't want to burden you. She found out right after Ryan was first diagnosed. She made Gray and me promise we wouldn't tell you until the time was right."

"It's been months since then!"

"And now is the right time. Even if you'd known before, there was nothing you could do."

"It still would have been nice to know." I drop a stack of T-shirts into the suitcase at my feet.

"If you want to help them, now's your chance." Mom explains that Aunt Sugar needs operations on both her hands, which will hopefully help her regain some mobility. I can't imagine how she's been doing her usual cooking and baking duties at the B&B, with that pain in her hands. Mom explains that they only have catastrophic health coverage, so their plan is to visit Sugar's niece, an orthopedic surgeon in Rhode Island. She offered to do the surgery for free, so my aunt and uncle only have to cover the outpatient hospital and rehab costs. "They're going to take the RV—" My groan interrupts her. "What?"

"If they hadn't spent the money on the airfare for Ryan's funeral, they could fly for the surgery."

"Nonsense. You know how much your uncle loves that RV. He's excited about the chance to drive it across country. Between the long drive there and back, and the rehab," Mom continues, "Graham thinks they'll be gone about three months. Other than the holiday weekends, it's a slow time of year for the inn, so it's a good time to go away. And he said Sugar hardly ever gets to see her sister and her niece, so it'll be nice for them to have a long visit."

She goes on to explain their plan to leave their lone longtime employee, Selene, in charge of the B&B. "This, my dear, is where you come in!" Her voice trumpets back to that of the bearer of great news. "It's the perfect answer for everyone! You move there and work with

Selene as the official breakfast chef-slash-baker. You get free room and board while they're gone, and you only have to work mornings, so you have the rest of the day to job hunt. Your uncle said he immediately thought of you for the job. You know how he loves your pies!"

My initial reaction is that, baking skills aside, they must be pretty desperate if they want me to work at their B&B. There must be better options—options where the person involved actually *likes* interacting with others. This makes me think of full-of-bull Harrison, my "cousin."

"Why can't Harrison do it?" Harrison isn't really my cousin, since we're not blood relations. He's Aunt Sugar's son from a brief, foolish marriage in her youth. He's about my age and not super reliable, but he loves to "shoot the shit," as he always says. I can't blame him for his reliability issues, since his dad took off when Harrison was a baby, and never came back. Uncle Graham tried his damnedest to be the best stepdad ever, but Harrison never accepted him in that role. He dropped out of high school and spent a long time roaming the country on his motorcycle. The last I heard, he was working at a tattoo parlor in Flagstaff, about ninety minutes north of Prescott. "He's her son. He should be the one to step up and help out." Not that Harrison's ever been great about stepping up, but he'd probably be better at the job than me.

"I can't believe you're not excited about this idea." After an exasperated sigh, she says, "Harrison has a job. *You* are about to be unemployed. And I just can't picture Harrison in an apron."

It's so annoying that she's right. "I'd have to think about it." On the one hand, I'd like to help them, and it'd be great to have free rent while still having plenty of time to job hunt. On the other hand, I've got a yearning to get back to San Diego—I need to be back near the ocean, not to mention that it'd probably be best to have a local address on my resume. And, finally, the thought of working at a B&B—even if it is the slow time of year—sounds like torture. The cooking part? Fine. But the people? No, thank you.

"What's there to think about?"

"What if I find a job right away? I don't want to have to abandon them."

"I know you don't want to hear this, Jane, but with this tough economy, the odds are slim that you'll find something right away. Plus, it'll be Thanksgiving soon, and I doubt many companies will be hiring over the holidays. I think it's best if you spend that time at the B&B, helping your family and not wasting your savings. And 2010 is bound to be better, so I'm sure you'll find something in the new year."

I search for a decent excuse, but nothing comes to me, so I go with the truth. "I don't want to live in Arizona. I'm going to San Diego." I'd e-mailed Mirabella and Karen my plans; they'd both replied right away. Karen said her weekly four-on-four beach volleyball team has room for me when they start up again in the spring, which gives me time to get back in shape. I can't wait. (A volleyball court is one place I don't mind meeting people; your arms and legs do the talking.)

"You'll get there, but in three months instead of three days. Sugar and Gray will be there with you the first few weeks, while you learn the ropes—get you over the Thanksgiving hump when they're fully booked—and then you'll help Selene until they come home. By then, you'll probably have a job lined up. It'll work out perfectly!" There's silence, Mom no doubt waiting for another argument. But I've got nothing. She's right. It makes sense. And I'll still be in San Diego in time to join Karen's team in the spring. Since I don't object, she says, "It's settled! Graham and Sugar will be so pleased."

When we hang up, I grab the vacuum. On the face of it, the plan makes sense, but it's already freaking me out. I take my frustrations out on the carpet, yanking the vacuum backward, shoving it forward.

It's not like I have a choice. What would they do if I didn't help? But, ugh, a B&B. I ram the vacuum into the foot of the bed. Never in a million years would I choose to work at a B&B. I don't even like to *stay* at B&Bs. Everybody eating breakfast together, and the cozy, country-crap decor. Give me a big, impersonal hotel any day.

Okay, deep breaths. Selene will be there. I've met her a few times, when I visited with my parents. She's worked there for years; she'll be the one running the place. I'll hide in the kitchen, making breakfast. In the afternoons, I might have to help with some cleaning or laundry, but Selene'll be the one doing the interacting. Maybe it'll be okay. And like Mom said, the holidays are a bad time to look for a job. And this way, I won't blow through my savings.

I lie on my stomach to vacuum under the bed and attack the dog-hair dust bunnies huddled against the baseboard. Barnum will never be completely gone: there will always be some bit of him embedded in my clothes, in my rugs, in my heart. Under the bed, I see one of his favorite toys—his squeaky squirrel.

Using the crevice tool, I retrieve the squirrel. It's too tattered to donate to the Humane Society, so I decide to keep it. When I get up to go put it with his box of ashes, it squeaks.

I almost drop it. It hasn't squeaked since it was new. He killed the squeaker within a few days of my giving it to him last Christmas. Barnum and I played tug-the-squirrel almost every night after that, and it never made a sound. I try to make it squeak again but can't.

Jeffrey's words about pennies or other signs come to mind. What was it he said? It's a message that "lets you know your loved one's okay." Something like that.

I kiss the stinky, silent squirrel and feel my eyes start to burn. "I hope you really are okay, Barnum." I set it on top of his box. "I hope I'm going to be okay too."

MY LAST NIGHT in the condo, I'm too excited to sleep. I'm finally leaving. I guess Philly wasn't all bad. I need sleep because I'll be driving all day tomorrow, so I try making a list of things I'll actually miss about Philly:

1. The rusty oranges and reds of the trees every fall, and the dogwoods and azaleas that show off their bright pinks in the spring.

2. Pennypack and Fairmount Parks, where Ryan and I would take long, meandering walks with Barnum.

3. The cobbled streets downtown.

4. The chewy soft pretzels that you can find on every other downtown street corner.

5. Of course, the classic Philly cheesesteak, but not at Geno's or Pat's, where everybody goes, but Jim's. And I like it with the provolone, and not "wit' the Whiz" like most locals order it.

6. The water ices, especially the lemon flavor. And the margarita. And the watermelon.

7. The juicy chocolate cordial strawberries from Lore's Chocolates, red as garnets in their dark chocolate shells. Ryan used to bring them home every Wednesday in early summer, the only time they were available. God, I'll miss those.

8. Tastykakes, especially the Peanut Butter Kandy Kakes. (Why can't you get those on the West Coast? Seriously, someone should get distribution rights.)

Wait. Why are these almost all about food? My stomach growls, and I end up heading to the kitchen for a banana. This was a bad bedtime list.

CHAPTER 7

THE TIN MAN

It's 9:00 p.m., and Philly is three days behind me when I finally pull into Mom's driveway, yawning. I've yawned roughly two hundred times over the last one hundred miles and stayed awake on a steady stream of Diet Coke and M&M's. In an effort to keep myself from devouring the bag in two minutes and having nothing to do, I made up a game for the monotonous miles. I'd dig two M&M's out of the bag each time a new song started. If they were the same color, I got a bonus M&M. It was pathetic how excited I got each time the colors matched. Like, holler-out-loud excited.

I stay in the car for a moment to assess myself. I know I'm not looking my best. I've worn the same sweatpants every day, and a pattern of fast-food stains charts my westward progress. I flip down the visor to look in the mirror, but it blocks the security floodlight that came on when I pulled in, so I only see the bottom half of my face. But it's the upper half I'm worried about. After three twelve-hour days of driving and two nights in strange beds, I know that dark semicircles sit under my eyes. My hair is in no better shape. I washed it this morning at the motel, but didn't bother to blow dry it, so I've got not so much a hairdo as a hair*don't*. I run my fingers through it, but the static in the dry Phoenix air makes the ends of my hair grab at my sleeves. I'm certain I've made things worse.

My plain gold wedding band catches my eye as I finish messing with my hair. I left it on for the trip. It made me feel safer, like it flashed a "don't mess with me because someone out there cares about me" sign. No one needed to know that that "someone" was my mother. I push at the ring with my thumb. I wanted to take it off the day after Ryan passed away. Had started to, but then thought Barbara and Jeffrey might react to my bare finger as another sad reminder that their son was gone. For their sake, I left it on. But now seems like the right time to take it off—before Mom notices. If she sees I'm wearing it, and then suddenly I'm not (and, on top of that, if she notices I'm still wearing Barnum's dog tag), she'll turn both into a huge deal. I drop Barnum's tag back inside my favorite "Life's a Beach" T-shirt, then scrape my ring over my knuckle and stash it in the pocket of my sweater.

Breathe in; sit up straight; try to psych myself up. My mom can be like a puppy that piddles when it sees you. I'm never as excited to see her as she is to see me; I can't even pretend to match her level of enthusiasm. I slowly breathe out. I better go in. She must know I'm here since this floodlight lit up the entire neighborhood. I remind myself to try and be patient with her, even if she nags me about my sweats and my hair and my posture.

I grab my overnight bag, and tuck Barnum's box into it. I'd had him riding shotgun, as usual. I consider leaving Ryan's ashes—in their Williams-Sonoma peppermint bark tin—in the car. But Ryan sometimes seemed a bit jealous of the attention I gave the dog, and I don't want him to think that, even now, I'm playing favorites. I tuck his tin into my canvas shopping bag, on top of the remains of my Triscuits, string cheese, and green grapes dinner.

Before I'm halfway up the path, the front door opens.

"You're here! I've been so worried." My arms overflow with my bags and my purse, but my mom scurries out and grabs me before I can get inside and set anything down. She reaches around me and clutches my shoulder blades, presses her powdered cheek against mine. She pulls me into her bright living room with its over-the-top Southwestern decor. "Let me look at you!" she says as I drop my things to the floor. You'd think she hadn't seen me in years.

I assess her outfit while she examines mine. Although only sixty-four, she's decked out in the sort of matchy-matchy sportswear type of outfit I imagine would be favored by eighty-year-old ladies on Mexican Riviera cruises—loose fitting peach-colored rayon pants, with a coordinating top that has some sort of funky fabric-painted pearlescent blob enveloping her left shoulder. If I were her, I'd be in my pj's and slippers; but, no, she's even donned matching peach flats. Her makeup, though excessive and entirely too peachy, is perfectly applied, and her dyed deep-cocoa hair has been hot-rolled and Aqua Netted to heights not naturally found in this dry desert.

She looks at me, from my static-y hair to my Converse-covered toes, shakes her head (on which not a hair moves), and clucks her tongue. "You look like something the cat . . . something that the cat didn't even want to bring in."

"I didn't know we were dressing for the occasion." So much for being patient.

I head to the kitchen and hip-check my grocery bag onto the counter, planning to unpack everything after I move my car into the garage and regain my composure.

"Can you open the door so I can pull into the garage?" I don't want to leave everything I own sitting in the driveway. It's a nice neighborhood, but still, I hate to chance it and be left with nada. It's little enough as it is.

She's left plenty of room next to her Lincoln for me. I pull my car in, then go hit the button on the wall to lower the door. Coming back into the house, I hear the sort of gasping breaths that can only mean one thing: big-time tears.

Geez Louise. Already? I haven't been here five minutes, and I've already somehow made her cry. I come up behind her, where she stands crying at the kitchen counter. "Ma?"

She turns around; the peppermint bark tin sits in her hands, the lid pulled back to reveal the Ziploc bag where I've written "Ryan: Maui or Bust" in Sharpie permanent ink.

"Oh no." I put my hand over my mouth. "You opened his tin."

"I . . ." She fights back a sob. "I thought you brought me a treat."

I take the tin from her unresisting hands and snap the lid back on. Plucking a tissue for her out of a nearby box, I apologize. "I'm really sorry, Ma. That must have been a terrible shock."

She blows her nose as she walks over and collapses into—and clashes with—her favorite mauve easy chair. She dabs her eyes. "Why's he in a candy tin? With the groceries!"

I sit on the sofa. "He was riding shotgun with Barnum. To keep me company. And I didn't want to leave them in the car. I put him in the grocery bag to bring him in. I was going to unpack the bag and take him to my room after I pulled the car in."

"Oh, Jane. Poor Ryan." She starts to cry again. "Poor you!"

I'm too exhausted to deal with her pity right now. "Ma, it's okay. Really."

"But why is he in a Ziploc bag?"

"It's a long story. I'll tell you in the morning. Right now, I want to take a bath and go to bed."

"It's early yet. I thought we'd stay up and talk."

I look at my wrist. "It's . . . what's twenty-one fifteen? It's . . ."—I do the math in my head—"quarter after nine, so that's eleven fifteen in Philly. Plus, I'm pooped from driving." I unfasten the watch and stab at the buttons. "I've never been able to figure out the settings on this thing. Ryan gave it to me." It was nice of him to get me a sports watch, but he should have known that a super-fancy, complicated one was not my style. "He used to set it for me. I changed it to Arizona time this morning and managed to get it on military time."

"You must miss him so."

I keep looking at the watch. I don't miss him. I miss that he's not out there, somewhere. I'm sad about that. But I don't miss him being with me. I don't miss the fights. I don't miss being his nurse. It doesn't mean I'm glad he died. I hate that he died. I hate this whole thing. I say nothing, and I assume she's reading the emotions on my face as grief, but it's only a handful of grief, mixed in with a boatload of guilt.

"If you two had had kids, you'd have part of him with you always."

Oh no. I'm not going down that road. "You know we talked about it, and neither of us wanted kids."

"I know. But I hoped you'd change your mind. I'll probably never have grandkids now."

She hangs her head, apparently out of self-pity, but she should hang it out of shame. Even my widowhood has to be about her. Of course.

What she doesn't know is that I've been so certain, for so long, about not wanting kids that I had my tubes tied before I even met Ryan. In fact, not simply tied, I had them macraméed into little plant hangers, just to be sure. Why does she say things like that when she knows I have zero maternal qualities? I'd like to say this to her because she's pissing me off, but instead I silently fume before saying, "I've been driving all day; I'm beat. We'll talk in the morning."

When I head for my room, she calls after me. "There's bubble bath under the sink. And I put a towel on the edge of the tub—the ones hanging up are for looks. And I turned down the bed already and put the bedspread on the chair. If you get chilly, that one's for show. There's a quilt in the closet. And I know you like an extra pillow, so there's one on the bed. And—"

I poke my head back around the door. "I know where everything is. I'll be fine. G'night."

She smiles at me. Tears still fill her eyes. "Sleep tight; see you in the morning."

"Thanks, Mom." I see the tears spill over, and duck back into my room.

*

THE NEXT MORNING, after waking to the smell of waffles, I find my mother bursting to tell me the "brilliant" idea she had in the night. Great. Not another one.

"When you're done helping out your uncle, you should come back to Phoenix. It's so much cheaper than San Diego!" She drops a steaming waffle on my plate. "And there are some big companies here. You might find one that has a department for . . . what you do."

"Market intelligence." I reach for the syrup. No one understands what I do for a living. I'm used to that.

"I know. I was going to say that." She sits and cuts prim bites off her waffle.

"I don't want to live here. I know you love it, and the dryness helps your sinuses, but look at me. I can't handle the lack of humidity." I point with my fork at my flat, lifeless hair. Mom raises a drawn-on eyebrow in a way that I know means it would take more than humidity to fix my hair troubles. She pats her own curled and coiffed mane and, for once, doesn't say any more. I ignore her subtle signal that it *is* possible for hair to be tamed in a desert climate. "I've been here less than twenty-four hours, and I already feel like my lips are falling off."

"Maybe if you wore some lip gloss." She dabs the corner of her mouth with her napkin.

That's my mother. Always trying to convince me to wear makeup. I get up for more coffee and grab another waffle on the way.

When I sit back down, she reaches over, circling her thumb and index finger around my wrist. "You're all bones. I bet you haven't been eating properly. Probably not since Ryan got sick."

"I am not all bones." I'd expected Mom to chide me about my wardrobe, but hadn't figured on an argument over my weight. I've always had what marketers of women's clothing label an "athletic build," which sounds a lot nicer than "a preteen boy's body." I've got thin legs, bird ankles, and no curves. Unlike my pear-shaped mom, any pounds I gain go straight to my belly. I can't believe she hasn't noticed my pouchy tummy, although it's hidden under my sweats. "I barely fit into my nice pants. And I need to be able to, in case I get an interview."

"Oh, Jane, pants for an interview. That's not right. You should wear a skirt. You never wear a skirt, and you have such lovely long legs. Let's go shopping today!"

"I have to head up to Prescott. Uncle Graham and Aunt Sugar are expecting me." Clothes shopping is the last thing I want to do with my mom.

I offer to clean the kitchen, since Mom cooked, but she insists on at least drying. I know that she sees domestic chore time as the perfect opportunity for mother-daughter chats, so I try to veer the discussion toward the weather and Mom's many social groups. Not surprisingly, she uses a brief lull in the conversation to bring up Ryan's ashes. The only surprise is that she didn't jump on the subject as soon as I cracked my bedroom door this morning.

"So, are you going to tell me why you have a sandwich bag full of Ryan's ashes in a candy tin? What happened to that beautiful wooden box? Where's the rest of him?"

"Like I said, it's a long story," I say as I wipe down the waffle iron. "Remember I told you he wanted his ashes scattered in Maui where we got married? His parents had other plans."

"Oh dear. It sounds like the funeral all over again." I'd vented to Mom when Barbara ignored Ryan's wishes for the funeral. Now, as I explain about the burial, I know she'll understand my being angry with Barbara for again pushing aside what Ryan wanted, but I'm not so sure she'll understand about stealing the ashes, so I gloss over that part. And by gloss over, I mean outright lie.

"Unlike the funeral, we compromised. I let them bury most of the ashes, and they agreed I could take some to Maui." I don't feel bad about the lie—after all, it's much smaller than others I've told her in the past, and it isn't hurting anyone.

"That's nice that you worked it out. As a mother, of course, I see Barbara's side of it. But, then, I see your side, too, wanting to honor Ryan's wish." She pauses in her dish drying. "I have another great idea! We could go to Maui together! Maybe this spring."

This idea needs an immediate dousing with cold water. I can't let her start dreaming about this, or she'll be calling the airline as soon as we finish the dishes. "I'll hopefully have just started a new job this spring, so I doubt I'll be able to get time off." Knowing my mother as I do, a greater quantity of icy water is needed here. "Besides, I need to save up some money for the trip. And . . . it's something I'd prefer to do alone."

"You always want to do everything alone." Mom doesn't try to hide her disappointment. "It'd be nice if we made an event out of it. I mean, what are you planning—you're going to walk to the water's edge and turn the bag inside out?"

"No. I mean . . . I dunno." That is exactly what I'd planned. I figured I'd go back to Po'olenalena Beach (that same southern end of the beach where we got married, obviously not the northern end where people sunbathe nude in the coves), and I'd step a few feet out into the waves to, well, scatter him. "I haven't thought about it that much yet."

"I think there should be a ceremony of some sort."

"Like, what, a Mass or something? You know Ryan and I weren't religious."

"It doesn't have to be religious. But something . . . with some meaning. A memorial-type thing. And you should invite Ryan's parents."

"No, no, no." I shake my head back and forth with each word. "That's not gonna happen. Honestly, I don't think I'll ever see the Waynesfields again. Jeffrey's a sweetheart, but I was never that close to Barbara. I don't think she likes me much."

"You always think nobody likes you. They love you."

"They understand that this is something I need to do by myself. It's a long ways off anyway. Ryan knew I couldn't afford to go anytime soon; he asked me to go whenever I could. It might be years. We'll worry about it when the time comes."

I know Mom doesn't like to wait to worry about things. She'd rather get a jump on the worrying.

So I exchange one worry for another to effectively change the subject. "You know, you were right about this whole working-at-the-B&B idea." With the addition of telling Mom she's right, I can now be secure in the fact that she won't go back to the subject of Maui. "Ever since I gave notice, I've been looking online for an MI job in San Diego. I'm a little worried I won't find anything by the time Uncle Graham and Aunt Sugar get home."

"By the time she gets through the surgery and rehab, and then their long drive back in the RV, I'm sure you'll have found something."

I'd expected her to be more doom and gloom. "I don't know. I saw a bunch of articles that say you need to give yourself at least six months to find something right now. Some say as much as a year." I don't believe it will take me a whole year to find a job, but it's force of habit to take the opposite view from Mom's.

"Maybe you should look at the bright side of all this," she says.

"What bright side?" I wait for her to get out of the way so I can wipe the counters.

"First of all, think of your time at the B&B as a minivacation. Like a—what do they call it?—a *sabbatical* from your career. And, as for work, you're brilliant. You'll find something. Besides, you're free now to do whatever you want. Live wherever you want, work wherever you want. Remember what Daddy used to always tell you: the world is your oyster!"

"Then why does it feel like *I'm* the one getting shucked?" I pull the plug in the sink and watch the dirty water swirl down the drain. I'd taken this stance to be contrary, and here I end up completely depressing myself. I'm jobless, homeless, dogless. Practically fricking friendless.

"*Jane.*"

"Seriously, Mom. And I can't 'work wherever I want.' I have to talk someone into hiring me, which isn't going to be easy, since I'm not great at selling myself. And as for living wherever I want, that's San Diego. So I need a job *there.*"

"You'll find one, honey. You will."

I might feel a little better if the conviction in Mom's voice matched the look in her eyes.

CHAPTER 8

HOW HAPPY ARE CLAMS?

About thirty minutes away from the B&B, I turn off Highway 69 at a rest area. As a general rule, I try to avoid rest stops, but Mom kept pushing glass after glass of iced tea at me during lunch. I knew she was trying to stretch our time together, so I let her keep refilling my glass. Besides, I wasn't that anxious to head north, toward my new life at the B&B.

But now that I can't hold out until I get to the B&B or to a gas station, I'm cursing that third glass. The high gray clouds give the day a gloomy feel, but when I park in the empty lot and open the car door, the cool breeze after the heat of Phoenix revives me. I racewalk to the bathrooms, hoping no mass murderer waits in one of the stalls. Desperate as I am, I still check behind each door before slipping into the last stall.

I trot back to the car. The rest stop's too quiet and gives me the creeps, even though there's still plenty of late afternoon daylight. The slight exertion makes my heart pump hard; whether it's due to the five-thousand-foot elevation or the adrenalin from looking for bathroom boogeymen, I'm not sure. I slow to a walk a few feet short of the car to catch my breath. With my Converse now making less noise due to my slowed pace, I hear other feet on the gravel.

I freeze. Silence. I'd love to think I imagined the noise, but I know I heard something. My car sits ten feet away, like an oasis. Oh, how I'd like to be in there with the doors locked. I'm afraid to turn around, wondering how far the madman/cannibal/rapist/escaped convict is behind me. The noise seemed far enough back that I could probably lunge for the car, get in, and lock the doors before he grabs me. But just in case, I work my car key—the sole survivor on my key chain now that I have no job and no home (*If I wasn't a nomadic, jobless loser I'd have more keys!*)—around in my hand so that it protrudes between my middle and ring fingers. The mere seconds I stand there last forever. I take a single step forward, straining to hear. My ears catch the slightest rustle of stones on the gravel. The madman/cannibal/rapist/escaped convict has taken a single step too. But he sounds far off, over by the other side of the women's restroom. As I gather myself for the lunge to the car, I can't stand it anymore and glance back.

Oh, geez Louise. It's a coyote. It flinches, hunkering close to the ground. No, wait . . . it's a dog. Relieved, I almost burst out laughing. I hold my fist that still clenches my key chain up to my pounding-harder-than-ever heart.

The dog, which looks to be some sort of tall, thin shepherd mix, cowers even more when we make eye contact. As my wits start their slow return, I notice how scared and skinny the poor thing looks, its tail tucked between its legs, hip bones sticking out.

Apparently, it crept out from behind the ladies' room to spy on me, but now that I'm moving toward it, it takes stilted steps backward. I stop so the dog won't literally turn tail and run. "It's okay. I won't hurt you." What the hell is this dog doing out here by itself? I look around again, although I know its owner is nowhere in sight. Taking a slow, silent step forward, I hold out my hand in greeting and crouch to make myself appear smaller, but it's no good. For each of my steps forward, the dog takes three back. It's almost at the corner of the building, and I'm afraid it will dash into the woods.

Cheese! I have string cheese in the car. Even though I'd had lunch with Mom, and although Prescott is less than two hours from Phoenix, she insisted on packing road snacks.

"Wait right there." I try to make my voice calm and gentle. "Wait." I tiptoe to the car, grab the cheese, and tear off the plastic. Barnum knew that crinkling sounds usually meant food, and I'm hoping this dog does too. The dog must have some experience with plastic-wrapped goodies, or maybe it smells the cheese, because it creeps a few steps forward.

Seated on the curb by the car, I face away. I know the dog might come to me if I don't confront it head on. Tearing the cheese into small chunks, I toss the first bit toward the dog. It lands close enough to tempt but still far enough away not to threaten. Perfect. I silently thank my dad for all the softball tossing we did in our backyard.

The dog's nostrils flare. It keeps its feet planted but stretches as far forward as it can. The cheese lies just out of reach. The smell gets the better of the dog—I'm assuming it's starving since I can see its ribs from here—and it lunges at the cheese, then retreats to eat it.

I smile; I've got it now. Thank you, cheeses!

Another hunk. If I can get the dog close enough, maybe I can see if it has a tag. It's wearing a pink collar, so I'm assuming it's a girl, or a sexually secure male, but she's got such a full ruff of neck fur that I can't see if there's a tag. We play the toss-sniff-lunge-at-the-cheese game until I'm down to the last two hunks. The dog is almost within reach. I set one hunk in my palm and hold it out, then turn my head away. I wait what seems like ages, until a warm tongue darts at my hand. I turn to find her eyes focused on the last morsel.

Now up close, I can see beyond the dust and burrs that she's one helluva gorgeous dog—or, she would be if she had some meat on her bones. She's got a thick, mostly strawberry-blonde coat and a long fluffy tail with a white tip. Her slender legs are white with reddish-blond speckles. A white ruff surrounds her face, with its adorable half-black, half-white spotted muzzle. Her red head blends into dark brown ears, edged with black, that stick out like the floppy wings on a homemade angel costume. Deep brown eyes, rimmed in black and stretched back in an extreme cat-eye effect, watch me, unblinking. She has a regal air that is very Elizabeth Taylor's Cleopatra.

"You're a pretty baby." I offer the final bit of cheese, then hold on as she nibbles it. Reaching out with my other hand, I feel for her collar. Although her ears go up and back in alarm, the power of cheese keeps the dog from pulling away. "It's okay. I'm going to help you find your people. Good girl." Groping along her collar, I find a tag. Eureka! It reads "Penny." That's it. No phone number, no address.

Penny. Seriously? I clench the dog's collar and look up to the heavens. *Ryan or Barnum, if either of you is behind this, it's not funny. This is not the sort of sign I need. This dog is going to the Humane Society, and they're going to deal with it.*

I look back down. "Hey, Penny." The dog flinches—she seems to know her name, but not like it. I can relate. But then, I don't like my name because it's the most boring name on the planet. If she doesn't like hers, maybe it's because someone yelled it at her a lot. Poor sweetie. I can't help but wonder how she ended up here alone.

"Wanna go for a ride?" I try to make it sound like an exciting prospect. I envision having to drag her to the car, but she follows along. Maybe I smell like cheese. Or maybe she has fond memories of car rides. Whatever the reason, when I open the door, Penny placidly rests her front paws on the floorboards and waits for me to boost her into the passenger seat. I pull back on the highway, wondering if she can smell my former copilot.

*

THE "CHICKEN & DUMPLINGS Bed and Breakfast": green cursive lettering on a white sign proudly marks the driveway. I can't believe I am going to be working here. Even the name kills me. Ever since Uncle Graham and Aunt Sugar bought the place and changed the name, twenty-plus years ago, I've thought it was ridiculous. They, of course, love it. Uncle Graham says it gives the place "country charm," and Aunt Sugar had fun naming the rooms after different chicken breeds and decorating each accordingly. She says it's educational, since few people can name a breed beyond Rhode Island Red. That explains the "chicken," but the "dumplings" part of the name is plain *out there*. Aunt Sugar says that, since she always includes biscuits and gravy—rechristened "dumplings and gravy"—with Sunday breakfast, it makes perfect sense.

I have a master's degree, I think as I crunch my way down the gravel drive. *Six years* of higher education. I used to provide valuable research and analysis to the executives at my job—a Fortune 500 company, no less. And now, I work for room and board—basically chicken feed—at the Chicken & Dumplings B&B. Yay, me.

On the plus side, at least it's tranquil. I'd forgotten what a pretty spot this is. The eight-guest-room house lies about five miles north of the heart of Prescott, out near Granite Dells and Watson Lake, an area known for hiking, rock climbing, and canoeing.

The three-acre property, edged by pine trees, is strewn with huge lichen-covered boulders and punctuated by tall cottonwoods that shimmer and whisper in the breeze. It slopes gently toward a stream at the back. A rooster weather vane stands sentry over the house, which is set back from the road, behind a border of horrid plastic tulips my aunt has stabbed into the parched earth. The porch, wrapped around the two-story Victorian house, features a row of rocking chairs, which would be quaint if it weren't for the window boxes overflowing with yet more plastic flowers, petunias this time, in garish pinks and purples that stand out against the white house and dusty-blue shutters.

A plastic doe and fawn tentatively approach the house from the side yard. How did I manage to forget about my aunt's love of plastic flora and fauna?

"Janie!" Uncle Graham throws the kitchen door wide and holds his arms open for a hug as I force myself not to trudge up the stairs. I try to put on an I'm-excited-to-be-here face. Aunt Sugar grins over Graham's shoulder. "We're so happy you're here! Happy as clams!" (Now, see, her face is what mine's supposed to look like. Pretty sure I'm not achieving that look.) She bounces while waiting her turn to hug me. I can't avoid the hugs, so I surrender to them, but I keep them short.

They ask how my trip was, and I say fine and tell them that Mom says hi. I'm relieved to see that Aunt Sugar looks a bit better than she did in Philly. More well rested at least.

"You guys both look great," I say. Uncle Graham tries to usher me inside, but I stop him. "You're not going to believe this—I found a stray dog. She's in the car."

"A stray?" they say in unison, which makes me smile because they're adorable in their matching khakis and red polo shirts with the B&B's chicken logo where the crocodile usually is.

I tell them the story. "I should try to get her over to the Humane Society or a shelter. I bet someone's looking for her. Do you know where I can take her?"

Selene comes through the swinging door from the dining room. "Welcome! Long time no see." It's been years since I've seen Selene, but she's as pretty as ever. She's petite, which makes me feel like the Amazon that I am, and her dark chocolate eyes and hair offset her perfect olive complexion. She puts a hand on her hip, and her arm is the lean, muscular sort of arm that brides pray they'll achieve when they buy strapless gowns. "I heard you ask about the shelter. I know where it is, but we better call. I think they close at five."

"Ugh. What am I going to do with this dog?" Damn that third glass of tea. If I hadn't taken so long over lunch, I'd have gotten to

Prescott earlier. Then again, if I hadn't had that last glass, I wouldn't have stopped, and that poor pup would still be out there, alone and scared.

"It's no problem to keep her overnight," Uncle Graham says. "The last guests checked out, so there's no one here but us chickens." He chuckles. I'm glad to hear this. I hoped the place would be empty for at least my first day or two. Or twenty. "She can be our first canine guest!"

"Not true," Aunt Sugar says. "Remember the couple that smuggled in their Chihuahuas? We caught them when the dogs started barking."

People suck. Smuggling in dogs? "Did you bust them?"

"No." Sugar smiles. "The little munchkins were so cute. And the couple was very contrite!"

"See? As my lovely bride reminds me," Graham says, "we have a precedent of having doggy visitors, so it's no problem for her to stay. You can take her to the shelter in the morning."

"Let's meet her!" Aunt Sugar looks out over the top of the calico café-style curtain.

With a bit of coaxing, Penny follows me up the stairs and inside. "She's got a tag, but it's just her name." Penny resumes her hunched, tail-tucked stance as they ooh and aah over her.

Aunt Sugar suggests we give Penny some space and let her get used to the house. With the swinging door closed, she's confined to the family's quarters: the kitchen, a den, my aunt and uncle's master suite, and the guest bedroom and bath, which will be mine. On silent feet, Penny inspects the floorboards while Uncle Graham helps me bring my bags to my room. When I walk back out to the kitchen, the dog wags her tail for the first time. Up until now, it had been drooping, almost touching the floor, but now she waves it like a parade flag, then curls it into a fluffy circle over her back.

"Look, she already knows you, Jane," Aunt Sugar says. "She likes you."

"Of course she likes me; I gave her cheese. She wants more." I scratch her behind. Penny leans into my legs, then lets her hind end sink to the floor. She sighs and flops down with her head on my shoe. I wipe my dusty hand on my jeans. "She needs a bath, big time."

"It's too cold!" Aunt Sugar says. "We'll wipe her down." She runs some water in the sink until it gets warm, then wets some towels.

While we clean the dog, who surrenders to our attentions by going limp on the linoleum, Aunt Sugar coos, "What a pretty girl! Look how gorgeous her coat is. What a beautiful spotted tummy! Why, this is the prettiest dog ever."

"She *is* gorgeous," I say. "I'm sure her family misses her."

I notice Sugar's stiff, swollen fingers. Her index finger looks misshapen, with a crook in the first knuckle that I wouldn't have thought possible. How could I have been so self-absorbed and not notice when I saw her at the funeral? I guess it is a good thing I'm here.

"Does it hurt?" I point at her hands.

"Not all the time." Aunt Sugar stands, with noticeable effort, and tosses the dirty towels on the porch. She takes the teapot off the stove and heads to the sink.

"She's being stoic," Uncle Graham says, getting up from the computer nook. "Don't believe her. Never complains." He takes the teapot and fills it. "Keeps working like it's nothing."

"Don't make a fuss, Gray." Aunt Sugar tries to wave him off and take back the kettle. "I can make a pot of tea. I'm not going to be *persona au gratin* in my own kitchen." I bite my lip so I won't laugh. My dear Aunt Sug has a tendency to butcher phrases so often that our family has coined the term "Sugarisms."

Uncle Graham, refusing her attempts and setting the pot on the stove, corrects her gently. "Oh, my dearest, you'll never be *persona non grata* with us! You sit and let me serve you a cup of tea." God, they're adorable.

She sits next to me at the kitchen table. "I admit, it's a bit harder to keep up around here. But that's life, isn't it? The work stays the same, but we get older." She laughs, but I can't imagine how she's managing to do her usual cooking and baking with those hands. She pats my arm. "I'm glad you're here, honey. You have no idea what a godsend you are!"

"I'm no godsend." I reach down again for the dog, embarrassed, and scratch behind her ear. "You guys are the ones doing me a favor." I stand up. "Hey, do you have some heavy twine or something? I'd like to take her for a walk. Geez, I hope she's housebroken."

*

THAT NIGHT AFTER dinner, Aunt Sugar gathers some old comforters to make a bed for Penny in a corner of the den. Penny seems exhausted and settles in right away. Poor thing. Who knows how many nights she was at the rest stop? I stroke her head as she falls asleep, happy that she seems to at least feel safe and secure here.

When I come back out to the kitchen, Uncle Graham asks me to join them in a game of cribbage. I say I need to unpack, which is true, but I'm also just ready for some alone time.

My room contains a double bed, a dinged-up dresser with a small TV on it, and a round table and overstuffed chair, perfect for curling up with a book. The room isn't part of the guests' quarters, or even seen by them, but Aunt Sugar has decorated it in the same country-cozy style. The wallpaper almost shouts, with its big cabbage roses. The forest-green carpet picks up the color of the leaves in the wallpaper. The bedspread echoes a similar floral print in magentas and greens, and the same fabric forms a partial canopy over the head of the bed. Crocheted doilies rest on every surface—a long narrow one runs the length of the dresser, the nightstands beside the bed display heart-shaped ones, a large circle covers the top of the table, and the arms and back of the chair are likewise bedecked. An oil painting hangs over the dresser, featuring chickens scratching in the dirt in front of a weathered red barn. Not exactly my style.

While I unpack, I wonder how long this room will be home. It doesn't feel like home—but then, I hated where Ryan and I lived the past six years, so what the hell does home even feel like? I flop on the bed and curl into a ball. I wish Barnum were here, cuddled next to me. Home is where your dog is; *that's* what home feels like—home is soft ears and warm breath and contented sighs. I swallow hard, and then get up and dig his cedar box out of my luggage. I place it on the dresser.

Uncle Graham taps on my open door. "You got everything you need, Janie?"

"Yeah." I blink, wondering where the tears go when you manage to keep them from spilling over.

"If you need a computer, we have one set up for the guests to use in the foyer." He seems oblivious to the tears filling my eyes. Thank you, dim lighting.

"I've got my laptop. And since you guys have Wi-Fi, I'll make this table job-search central." I sit in the big chair, pulling my feet up under me.

"Well, you can at least use the printer here if you need to. It's wireless too!"

"Deal. Wow, wireless printing. That's impressive. Mom can barely do e-mail."

"I can't take the credit. It's Selene. She's our IT department. She did our website, and she takes care of the online registration. She's got us on Facebook too. Have you seen the Chick's page?" He puffs up like a proud rooster. This place hasn't aged gracefully since the last time I was here, and I wonder, with a stab of guilt, if maybe he shouldn't change the nickname to the Coop instead.

"I haven't; I'm not on Facebook."

He deflates. "You should join. It's great for staying in touch with all your friends."

All my friends. Yes, right. Maybe I'll start an *anti*social networking site. That'd be more my style. A place where everyone could post complaints about the annoyances they deal with over the course of their days. "I'll think about it."

"Okay, I'll leave you to your unpacking. Sleep well. That reminds me—never tell the guests to sleep tight. We don't want them thinking of bed bugs!" I laugh and wish him good-night. He stops in the doorway. "We're sure glad you're here. And . . . we're real proud of you, Janie. You're a very strong woman. I think about losing . . . If anything happens to your aunt . . ." He purses his lips together. I fiddle with the frayed hem of my jeans. I hate that he's comparing my so-called strength in the face of Ryan's death to what he'd go through if he lost Sugar—his soul mate for over three decades.

I want to reassure him he won't lose her, but after the last few months I've had, I feel like I'm not in a position to hand out those sorts of promises. "She'll have her surgery and be good as new before you know it."

"You're right. Of course." He pulls a handkerchief out of his back pocket and wipes his eyes. "Don't tell your aunt that I'm worried, okay? It'll upset her."

I promise I won't, and we say good-night again. I sit, curled up in the chair, and stare blindly at the tabletop until I start to feel pins and needles in my feet.

As I crawl between the cold sheets, I glance at Barnum's box. I feel his bone-shaped dog tag under my T-shirt and press it into my skin. It was always so cozy having him in the bed. Okay, and Ryan too. But Ryan snored sometimes. Well, Barnum snored sometimes, too, but sometimes Ryan would steal the blankets, and Barnum never did that. And sometimes Ryan talked in his sleep, which was creepy; he sounded possessed. But, for the most part, I guess it was nice to wake up and find him there. Yeah, it was nice, having a beagle and a man to share the bed with.

Being alone is nice too. Maybe nice isn't the right word, but it's comfy. I can sleep diagonally if I want—which apparently I'm going to need to do since I bang into the footboard when I stretch out. I resituate and try to get comfortable. Then flop over on my stomach. I can flip around like a fresh-caught trout, and no one will complain. It's good to sleep alone.

After a few minutes, I get up and grab an extra blanket out of the closet.

Back in bed, I try sleeping on my back. My side. My back again. I stare up at the canopy.

I know you're not excited about being here, I lecture myself, *but you're helping your family—and who knows, maybe being here will be a nice break.*

Besides, what other option do I have at the moment?

At least I have this comfy bed to myself. And it's dead quiet, unlike the condo complex in Philly, where we could hear traffic, and people pulling in at all hours, and neighbors slamming doors. It's peaceful here.

In fact, it'd be a pretty nice setup, if only they didn't have a bunch of strangers roaming around the place.

I TRY TO lull myself to sleep and shut off the "what am I doing here?" soundtrack by trying to list the chicken names for the rooms:

1. Rhode Island Red. Okay, that one's easy, especially because that ugly room comes right to mind. I assume Aunt Sugar still has it done up in shades of red and maroon. It's like a chicken-themed bordello. It makes me imagine chickens in corsets, attempting to pole dance.

2. Iowa Blue. And a blue-and-white-decorated room to go with the name.

3. California White is easy, because that's my favorite room in the place, decorated the most simply. Although, same as my room, too many doilies.

4. Sicilian Buttercup. I know that room is Aunt Sugar's favorite, decked out in bright yellows.

5. There's one that sounds like coffee . . . It's a brown-and-cream room. Java! That's it.

6. And there's a black-and-white room, to go with the black-and-white stripy chickens . . . that are called . . . oh hell, I don't know. Who names rooms after chickens anyway?

I manage to fall asleep without ever remembering that those black-and-white stripy chickens are called Barred Rock, or the names of the other two rooms. I imagine they'll all be burned into my brain by the time I leave here.

CHAPTER 9
TAKE A PENNY, LEAVE A PENNY

The next morning, I struggle awake when the alarm buzzes at five thirty. I'd woken in the night, dreaming of Barnum, to find Penny sound asleep in the crook of my legs. I'd pushed her a bit, so I could straighten my legs, but she pushed back. That was the nice thing about sleeping with Barnum—he was an unobtrusive bed partner and always stayed curled in a warm ball by my feet.

"How'd you get in here?" I'd asked, but she'd ignored me. I distinctly remembered pushing my door shut tight before going to bed; the door seemed swollen and hadn't latched until I leaned into it with my shoulder. Someone—Aunt Sugar stands out as the most obvious suspect—must have opened the door and let the dog creep in.

Even with the calming rhythm of the dog's breathing, I'd had a hard time falling asleep again. I spent most of the night trying to convince myself I hadn't made a huge mistake in coming here. I drifted off sometime after three, by repeating over and over, in time with Penny's breathing, "It'll be fine. It'll be fine."

After the rough night, it ain't easy to wake with the chickens, but I know that working at the B&B means early mornings, so I need to get in the habit, even if there are no guests today.

"We're rising and we're shining!" Aunt Sugar greets me as I stumble out in my pj's in search of coffee. Penny ambles along behind, stopping to stretch in the middle of the kitchen, in a perfect downward-facing-dog yoga pose. "Why you little dickens." Sugar feigns shock. "Did you sleep with Jane?"

"Yes. And she took up more than her share of the bed."

"She's really settled in. She was so skittish yesterday, but today there's some pep in her step. I think she likes it here."

"It beats the rest stop, that's for sure," I say. Aunt Sugar's right; Penny seems happier. She nudges me while I stir up leftover rice and chicken for an impromptu doggy breakfast.

After coffee, cereal, a spin with Penny down to the stream for a quick game of fetch-the-stick, and more coffee, I start to feel awake.

"Here's my repertoire." Aunt Sugar hands over a binder full of recipes—some clipped from magazines, some handwritten or typed, all with notes and lots of exclamation marks in the margins ("Don't try to double!!" "Great with ham!" "Good for finicky folk!!!"), and each tucked into its own plastic sleeve. "For now, why don't you look through these, and over the next few days, we'll try out some of them together."

I flip through the binder. Everything looks tasty, and I actually look forward to trying some of them, especially the baked French toast stuffed with cream cheese and blackberry jam.

"With Jane's pie-baking skills, she won't have a problem with any of those delicacies," Uncle Graham says, coming in through the side door. He's always been a huge fan of my crust, saying it rivals his mother's. I never got to meet Grandma, so I have to take his word for it—although I take it with a full teaspoon of salt, not just a grain, since he tends to exaggerate the positive. "I cleared out some space for you in the laundry room, Janie." On a tour of the property yesterday afternoon, he showed me the combination storage shed and laundry facility in the yard, and promised to make room for the rest of my boxes. "I'll help you unload your car later."

"Okay, but as soon as Selene gets here, she's helping me take Penny to the shelter. That's the first item on today's agenda." My aunt pouts; I pretend not to see.

*

SELENE SIGNALS—HER old Ford truck making loud, slow clicks— and turns into the parking lot of a concrete building with "Prescott Animal Rescue and Eatery" painted on its side.

"Animal Rescue and *Eatery*?" I say, incredulous. "Are they aware it sounds like they're serving up the dogs that don't get adopted?"

"It's a small café—coffee, muffins, vegetarian wraps. That sorta thing. It's not like they serve shish kebabs in there. It used to just be PAR—Prescott Animal Rescue—but they added the 'eatery' a couple of years ago to help make extra money to sustain the place."

"But PARE's a terrible acronym. Pare down. Pare away. Not exactly a warm and fuzzy connotation."

"I know, but it's a good place. This is where my sister's family got their dog. Penny'll be fine. I mean, unless you want to turn around and take her back to the Chick."

"Nope. Let's go in." I don't want to get into it with her how I just lost Barnum, and that I can't handle the thought of having—and losing—another dog. Not now. Not ever.

We leave Penny in the truck until we know for sure they'll take her. Pushing open the heavy glass door, we step into a linoleum-floored waiting room with worn posters advocating adoption and spay and neuter programs. Behind a high counter, a poufy-haired woman, wearing a pink T-shirt with the shelter's logo, sits at a scuffed brown desk. She says into the phone, "Yes, I understand. You can bring the dog anytime today until five." She hangs up, shaking her hair-helmeted head. She sees us, and her lips and cheeks form a smile, but her eyes don't play along. "Worst part of this job: taking in surrendered dogs."

"That must be awful," Selene says. She glances sidelong at me—I'm too horrified at the thought of someone handing over their family pet to speak. We're not off to a great start.

"Yeah, and it's happening a lot. People are having a hard time affording pet food or the vet bills. Anyway . . ." She stands and moves to the counter. Her white plastic name tag reads "Roxie." Drawn in purple marker, beside her name, is a stick-figure dog with a wagging tail. "How can I help you ladies?"

I explain about finding Penny and tell her the dog's in the car. "I'm sure her owners are desperate to find her. I wanted to bring her last night but—"

"Hmmm." Roxie holds a green fingernail to her cheek. "I don't think we've had any calls about a lost pet. But I could be wrong."

"So . . . what'll happen if no one claims her?"

"After one week, and an evaluation of her personality—"

"She's sweet as can be," I interrupt. "She has an awesome personality."

"She should have no problem getting adopted then." Roxie smiles and hands me a clipboard. "I know she's not your dog, but it'd be peachy if you'd fill in as much as you can."

I start filling in squares. The first one, "Name," is the only one for which I definitively know the answer. I write "Penny," adding, "But she doesn't seem to like it" in parentheses. I guess at most of the rest, including "Breed" ("Shepherd mix?"), "Age" ("About a year??") and "Color" (I write "Reddish/Tri-color"). Selene looks through a rack of pamphlets while I finish.

"What happens if she doesn't get adopted?" I ask, sliding the clipboard across the counter. It hits me that something horrid could happen if no one claims her, and I start to panic. What sort of place is this? As I look at the walls of the dingy waiting room and the desks behind the counter, heat claws at my neck. I don't know what I'm expecting to see—a scythe? A man in an executioner's hood? A doggy door leading to a tiny gas chamber? They aren't going to . . . ? I put my hands flat on the counter.

"This is a no-kill shelter, if that's what you're asking." Roxie looks me straight in the eye. "She'll stay here until she finds a happy home."

"I'm sure that won't be long," I say, recovering. "I bet her family's here before the end of the day." A long howl emanates from the kennel area beyond. "End of the week at most."

On the way home, I try not to think about the look on Penny's face as Roxie led her into the back. I stare out the window while Selene drives. Penny had looked over her shoulder, watching me with doleful eyes and a low-slung tail. "It's gonna be okay!" I'd called out, hoping like hell her parents show up soon. How could they not have called already? Roxie was probably wrong about that. Maybe someone else took the call. Yeah, that's it. It'll all be fine.

"She'll be fine," Selene says, reading my silence. "We can call and check on her in a day or two. I'm sure she'll be gone by then." I nod. Selene pulls a shiny folded paper out of the pocket of her flannel shirt and hands it to me. "I picked up a pamphlet about volunteering. We don't have a lot of weekday bookings right now at the B&B, so I thought maybe . . ."

"You're thinking of volunteering there?" I take the pamphlet and glance at it.

She looks over at me, then focuses on the road again. "Uh, no. It's for you. Sorry, I just thought you might want something to, I dunno, *do*. The B&B's usually empty on Mondays and Tuesdays . . . Just an idea."

"I'm not going to be here that long, so . . ."

"Right. Of course not. Hey, you could come hiking with me. Sometimes, when things are quiet, I drive over to Thumb Butte on the other side of town. It makes for a good break."

"Maybe." I don't want to go hiking with Selene. She's nice and all, but she's even moving in. At first, I objected when Uncle Graham called to talk to me about working at the B&B and mentioned Selene would be taking their room. I told him it wasn't necessary; after all, I didn't want to live with a virtual stranger. But then I remembered the house would be full of strangers. What if one of them needs help in the night? Uncle Graham claimed that's a rarity, but said, just in case, it would be good to have Selene there. Since we'll be together day and night, I don't think it's necessary to spend our free time together too. "I'm going to be really busy job hunting—searching online and sending out resumes and whatnot."

"If you ever want to get some fresh air, let me know. I'm always up for a hike."

"I'll do that." I stuff the pamphlet in the back pocket of my jeans and resume staring out the window at my new temporary hometown.

*

LATER THAT AFTERNOON, in my room, staring at my laptop and considering whom in my meager list of LinkedIn connections I can hit up for a job lead, something crinkles when I shift in my chair—the pamphlet, still in my pocket. I'm about to toss it when the glossy pictures of smiling volunteers in their PARE T-shirts, posed with various cats and dogs, catch my attention. I study the picture of a woman holding an adorable beagle, then turn the pamphlet over, looking for more. The phone number runs along the bottom of the page. Four seconds later, I recognize Roxie's candy-apple-sweet voice when she answers.

"Hi, uh, I brought the stray dog, Penny, in earlier today."

"Aren't you a doll to check on her? She's fine; fine as my grandma's moustache."

"So, no one called about her?"

"I hate to say so, but I think the poor thing was abandoned. I don't expect we'll hear from anyone looking for our shiny little Penny-girl."

"Oh."

"Don't you worry! I could be wrong, but if I'm not, we'll find her a home. You call again anytime. Of course, if you adopt her yourself, we'll waive the fee since you brought her in."

"No, I can't. I don't live here. I mean, I'm only . . . I'll call again later in the week." I hang up, wondering how someone can abandon their dog. I mean, it's one thing to have to choose between feeding your kids or the dog, and surrendering it to a shelter, but to dump it at a rest stop to fend for itself? Sometimes people suck.

CHAPTER 10
JACKASS BEAR-MAN

"It's me." Selene knocks at my closed bedroom door. "Starting some laundry; thought I'd add your sheets."

I'm *in* my sheets, having retreated to my bed after the last guests checked out. It's 11:30 a.m. on Sunday, and I've survived my first working weekend. With the B&B only half-full, and even with Aunt Sugar there, the last three mornings rated surprisingly high on the stress-o-meter. Feeding four couples a fancy breakfast each morning reminded me of preparing Thanksgiving dinner: no single item is hard to make, but the trick is having it all hot and ready at the same time. Speaking of which, Thanksgiving is this week, and we're booked solid, starting Wednesday. I'm a bit concerned, but my aunt says not to worry: "It's breakfast, not brain science."

I hop out of bed, not wanting to be caught napping. It seems so pathetic. Like I can't handle the work, or the early hours, or the fact that I have no real life, that there's not much to do around here when there are no guests, and that there's also no job hunting to do since that's a weekday endeavor.

"Hang on," I yell, yanking the sheets off the bed.

"Sorry to interrupt," she says when I open the door.

"I was reading. And you're not doing my sheets. I can do them. In fact, I need to do a load of clothes. Uncle Graham hasn't shown me how to use that monster washer yet."

"Grab your stuff. Once the sheets are done, the laundry room's yours."

On our way through the kitchen, Sugar looks up from her cup of tea and *Woman's Day* magazine. "Where are you two headed?" She grins as if we are off on some girly adventure.

"Selene's showing me how to use the washer. I'm running out of clean underwear."

"Can't have you going Brando around here. Have fun!" she calls after us.

As we walk across the yard to the laundry room, I turn to Selene. "Going 'Brando'?"

"Graham and I have tried to tell her it's 'going commando,' but she doesn't believe us. She says that doesn't make sense, because she's sure"—and here, Selene pitches her voice higher, in a decent imitation of my aunt—"those military boys wear underpants, otherwise there'd be a lot of chafing." She switches back to her own voice. "She says it's got to be Brando, as in Marlon, because he's too macho for underpants." We laugh, but she stops first. "Sorry. I'm not making fun. Your aunt's super sweet." She flips on the light in the shed.

"It's okay. I understand. She is sweet. She's just not . . . um, yeah."

Selene smiles, then shows me the washer settings. "So, how was your first working weekend at the Chick?" Together, we stuff sheets into the machine.

"It was, ya know, okay, I guess." I know Selene loves this place—in fact, it might be the only place she's ever worked—so I don't want to let on I'm not thrilled about being here.

"Wow, that good?" So much for hiding my feelings.

"Honestly, it was better than I thought it'd be. I'm not great about meeting new people, so I was a little worried about the whole working-with-the-public thing." In fact, I managed to have almost zero contact with the guests over the weekend, which was good. Of course, the fact that I stayed squirreled away in the kitchen or my room the whole time had something to do with it.

"The guests can be annoying sometimes—especially the ones that treat me like I'm their personal maid—but they're mostly nice. They're on vacation, so they're more laid-back than the average person." She pulls the knob, and the washer begins to whir. "Hey, by the way, did your uncle tell you that once I move in, I won't be around on Monday and Wednesday evenings?"

"He mentioned a class or something."

"I'll be back around ten, so you'll be on your own for a few hours those nights." She opens the dryer, and the smell of hot cotton towels envelops us. We grab armloads and drop them on the table.

"I'll help fold." There's a chill in the air, and I want to bury my face in the warm towels.

"Nah. Your aunt likes to fold, says the warmth feels good on her hands. I think she feels bad that she can't help with all the things she used to." She leans into the sturdy old table.

"How's she really doing?" Selene's worked here so long I know she'll have witnessed the decline in Aunt Sugar's health.

"She's hanging in there. Your uncle and I try to make sure she doesn't overdo it."

"Thanks for looking out for her."

"I'm happy to. Your aunt and uncle are two of my favorite people in the world." She opens the door at the base of the dryer and swipes at the gray-and-white lint. "Don't forget the lint trap. If this baby dies again, your uncle might take an ax to it."

"What if it dies while they're gone?"

"We call Ky, the handyman who lives next door. You'll like him. He's great."

I want to say, Hello. Remember me? I just told you—I don't like meeting new people.

*

"IF YOU WERE a baked good, what would you be?" Aunt Sugar supervises while I make Baby Jesus cookies—dried apricots swaddled in flakey dough. We survived the madness of the Thanksgiving week- end and have resumed my recipe training. Apparently, it wouldn't be a Chick Christmas without these babies. We're almost to the back of the binder (the stuffed French toast was, indeed, amazing); and next week, they hit the road in their RV. I can't imagine how Selene and I will handle Christmas without them, since Thanksgiving weekend— in a word—sucked. We were booked solid, and on top of that, Aunt Sugar had a bad RA flare-up and barely got out of bed. Thank heaven my mom didn't come up, like she'd originally wanted to. She ended up accepting an invite to have dinner with friends. I'd have barely been able to spend any time with her if she'd come. Selene and I were running around like chickens, helping Uncle Graham keep everyone happy and supplied with extra towels and fatter pillows or thinner pil- lows and ear plugs and bubble bath and any shampoo that didn't smell like apples and liquid soap because bar soap is too drying and 2 percent milk because nonfat tastes like water and cream's too fattening and, oh, about eight hundred other requests.

On Thanksgiving afternoon, I made the mistake of answering the phone in the kitchen. It was Harrison offering to hop on his chopper and join us for dinner. He had "a craving for Mom's gravy." I told him she'd spent the day in bed, and he was welcome to come (I knew my aunt would love to see him), but we weren't having a real Thanksgiving meal since we were so busy. I offered to put his mom on the phone, but he hung up before I could finish. Poor Aunt Sugar looked so disappointed when I told her he had called but wasn't coming. She made excuses for him, and said she was sure he'd visit soon.

On the other hand, it was nice to be too busy to contemplate the holiday and the fact that I don't have a lot to feel thankful for this year. I should have called Ryan's parents, but at least I e-mailed.

Christmas, which I hate to think about, will be worse—in more ways than one. I don't see how Selene and I will survive it, and the last thing I'm concerned about right now is perfecting the doughy fold that's swaddling a dried-fruit version of Baby Jesus, but Aunt Sugar's excited to make them.

"Boy, I dunno what baked good I would be," I say, distracted, wishing she'd stop leaning over my shoulder while I diaper apricots. "You?"

"I'd be a cupcake. They're sweet and just the right size." She pauses and points to my first cookie lying on the tray, awaiting the trip to the oven. "See how the apricot looks like a peachy baby face sticking up out of a blankie? So cute! Tuck that dough in tighter. There you go." She beams. "Anyway, I wouldn't be a fancy cupcake, like on the cover of *Family Circle* at Easter. You know, with the candy corn for bunny ears or licorice-whip whiskers. I'd be a regular vanilla cupcake with chocolate frosting. And maybe some coconut flakes."

"That's a perfect choice for you." I finish another row. "I don't know what I'd be. Maybe a loaf of bread. Yeah, rye bread."

"Oh no, that's not right." She studies me. "You'd be a baguette. A bit crusty on the outside, but very tender—and sweet—on the inside."

I can't decide if it's nice or completely misguided that she sees me that way. Anyway, leave it to her to sum up our personalities as baked goods.

When the tray is full, she attempts to grab it to put it in the oven, but I move in. "Let me."

"Jane, I need to confess something," she says. "I've been calling the shelter every day."

She waits. I start wrapping the next batch of apricots and don't say anything—like, "Oh, that's interesting, because I've been calling every day too."

"Penny's still there." *Um, yeah, I know.* "Nobody claimed her. They put her up for adoption this past Saturday, and she's still there."

"It's Tuesday." I shrug. "That's only three days ago. She'll find a good home." I try to sound certain.

"That's my point—I know a good home."

She means me . . . *this* home, but I play dumb. "You know someone who wants a dog?"

"I know you say you don't want one, but I think she was put in your path for a reason."

"I don't want another dog." I've run out of dough, and there's nothing to do but wait for the first tray to bake, so I start washing dirty dishes. Now it's her turn to push me out of the way.

"Let me. The warm water feels good."

"Besides," I continue as I hunt for a clean towel for drying, "even if I wanted a dog, I don't have my own place. I don't have a job. Dogs like a routine. My life's up in the air."

"That's hooey. Dogs like to be with their people. And I think you are Penny's people."

"I'm not." I don't want to be short with her, but I'm tired of this. I love my aunt, but, being a very happy person, she wants everyone else to be very happy too.

She drops the subject, and we finish the dishes in silence. When the timer dings, the Baby Jesuses bring joy and reunification back to what, mere seconds before, had been a rather icy kitchen. They also bring a sugar rush, because I eat five of them.

*

"AHEM," A SOFT voice says.

I turn from the counter where I'm mixing up ginger cookies. (The guests get cookies in their rooms each afternoon, and I've decided it's best to make them while the kitchen's still a mess from breakfast so I only have to clean once.) A slim fortysomething blonde, probably only a few years older than I, but way better preserved, pokes her head around the swinging door. Guests aren't allowed in this part of the house, but after barely two weeks, I've already found that, at least every few days, some clueless person ignores the sign designating this section of downstairs as private.

"Can I help you?" I ask, my hands sticky with dough.

"This pumpkin bread has pecans." Her manicured and heavily diamonded hand holds out a napkin with a golden-orangey slice of my delicious bread on it. "And when we made our reservation, I told the man that I'm allergic. I guess he forgot." My aunt and uncle are leaving in a mere three days on their cross-country quest for RA relief. God help me.

"That's why there's a sign by the bread basket that says 'Contains Nuts.' And that's also why there's a basket of cranberry scones *next* to the bread, with a 'No Nuts' sign." I sound snippy, but seriously, can't she read? I force a smile as I remember what Selene said: *"No matter how absurd the guest, smile; because the customer's always right."*

I go back to plopping balls of dough on the cookie sheet. Uncle Graham says the problem is that I only deal with the demanding guests—the ones who ignore the "Private" sign and march on in. He assured me that if I'd sit and chat with folks, I'd see that, by far, the majority of the guests are very nice. Talking to strangers I'll never see again holds zero appeal, so I told him it's best if I stick to the cooking, and he and Selene stick to the hospitality. Speaking of . . . Where the hell are they? Uncle Graham probably snuck off to pack some final items, but who knows where Selene is. She's supposed to be out in the dining area, chatting and answering questions—like, what here doesn't have nuts in it?—and keeping these nuts out of my hair.

"I saw the scones." I look back up, tempted to say, "You're still here?" But she moves closer, bread still held aloft. "The thing is, I love pumpkin. And I hate scones." She actually shudders. "Terrible, dry old things." (You haven't tried *my* scones, I want to interject.) She pauses and looks my outfit up and down—my usual black sweats and "Life's a Beach" T-shirt plus my black-and-pink polka dot Converse high-tops. "My twelve-year-old has those shoes." She smirks. "Anyway, do you have some pumpkin bread *sans* pecans? Or any low-fat pastries? Would you have that, in this . . ." She looks around, and I see the country-kitsch decor—the rooster clock, the farmhouse wallpaper border, the hens stenciled on the chipped yellow cabinets—through her snooty eyes. ". . . kitchen?" The last word rolls off her tongue with disdain.

I'm about to say something when my uncle's silver head appears around the kitchen door. He steers her back to the dining room, listening to her troubles. He glances back, and I'm pretty sure he can tell that I'm picturing her tied to a spinning board at the carnival, while I throw damp kitchen sponges at her.

He winks, and I mouth, "Thank you." As they go, I hear him say, "Just try one of our scones, and I think you'll change your mind. The Chick's scones are world famous. And tomorrow, I promise we'll have some nut-free pumpkin bread on the table!"

Fine. I'll make some nut-free pumpkin bread, but it'll be extra fattening. Or maybe, I'll make pumpkin scones.

Wow. I used to have a real job, but now, I'm reduced to passive-aggressive use of baked goods. I blob a hunk of dough onto the pan so hard it rattles against the countertop.

When I'm done, and the kitchen's clean, I eat a sandwich in my room while obsessing over the fact that there's nothing new in my e-mail. I have alerts set up with Monster and Career Builder for market intelligence jobs in San Diego, and I check for hits, oh, about two hundred times a day. I check, finish my lunch, check again. I go to the bathroom and check one more time. Finally, I give up and decide a long, fast walk is in order. After I check once more.

It's windy, and the scent of the pine trees swirls around me. I breathe in, hoping it will clear my head.

Geez, this place! Sure, I like helping my family, and playing chef isn't horrid, but the guests leave me muttering and picturing ways to torture them with pastries.

As I walk, I think again that if it weren't for the guests, this would be a great gig. The baking and cooking part is actually pretty fun. Of course, a B&B without guests isn't the usual business model. Maybe I could do this sort of thing in San Diego—be a specialty baker for B&Bs and inns in the area. But then, I probably couldn't afford to live in San Diego on a baker's salary, not without turning it into a big commercial operation, and then you're stuck dealing with a lot of different people again. Anyway, I've just started looking for a job. It's too soon to start hatching desperate alternatives.

Back from my walk, I'm sweaty and windblown. I head to my room, intending to jump in the shower, but detour by my laptop to check e-mail first.

There's one from Monster. The job listing sounds similar to what I did in Philly. I perch on the edge of my chair, the idea of showering gone. The afternoon slips away while I tweak my resume to match the requirements. The final item in the bulleted list reads "Knowledge of market sizings a plus." We did a market sizing last year while considering an acquisition, but it's not on my resume. The details of the project now escape me, but I've got a box of work files in the shed. If I can find my notes, I can add something about that to my resume and look like the perfect candidate. Which I totally am!

The wind's picked up even more, so I grab my SDSU Volleyball sweatshirt off the floor. Flour dusts the front, but I'll only be a sec. My hair sticks out in seventy different directions, so I pull my baseball cap low. I'll dash out to the shed and find the file, then adjust my resume and fire it off with a cover letter. And *then* I'll shower.

Outside it's chillier than before, so I hunker down in my sweatshirt as I futz with the shed door, which refuses to yield. I jiggle the knob again and throw my shoulder against the door. It gives, and as I stumble across the threshold, I hear a deep male voice yell, "Hey!"

Looking around, I see the outline of a large man, backlit by the low afternoon sun. His shoulders look huge, and his tool belt jangles as he jogs over. "Betty! Get out of there! What're you doing this far out of town? This is private property."

What the hell? I stand in the doorway, stunned, watching this ranting bear come at me.

It isn't until he's about ten feet away that he says, "You're not Betty." His expression goes from concern to confusion. He looks my ratty outfit up and down. "Still, you're no guest here. What are you doing, busting into Mr. Roberts's storage?"

"I'm not busting into anything. I'm getting *my* things. Not that it's any of your business."

By now, Uncle Graham has come out to see what's going on. He must guess the situation when he sees me with my hackles raised and . . . well, whoever this big jackass is with the suspicious look on his face, moving in like he's going to put me in a headlock.

"Ky, I see you've met my niece. How about a little light on the subject here?" He reaches past me and flips on the storage-room light.

Ky, or Jackass Bear-Man as I've suddenly come to think of him, blinks and takes a step back. Now I can see that he's not so much bear-size as tallish (a bit taller than me) and is wearing a weathered suede letterman-style jacket with big rounded shoulders. He's got a ridiculously square jaw; I could use his jawbone to beat back an attacker. He hooks his left thumb into his tool belt and runs his other hand over his hair—although it's obviously just a habit since his dark hair is buzzed so short there's nothing to rearrange.

"Your niece?" He looks out from under his eyebrows at my uncle. "Sorry, Graham. I thought she was Betty, breaking into your shed. I know you keep spare cases of beer out here."

Uncle Graham roars with laughter.

"Who's Betty?" The way my uncle is laughing annoys the hell out of me.

"She's . . . uh . . . this . . ." Ky begins to answer, since Uncle Graham is still chuckling too hard, and searches for a word. "Uh . . . character who hangs out down on Whiskey Row." Whiskey Row, part of Prescott's downtown square, is named for the saloons it's been home to over the years. It's not hard to figure out that "character" equals "wino." Great. I look like an old rummy trying to break into the B&B's stash.

My uncle composes himself and points. "You owe *her* the apology."

I stand up straight. I know I look like more of a slob than usual, but, geez Louise, not like a wino. I put my fist on my hip and try to give off an I-belong-here air, but I just want to shut the door on these men and grab my box of paperwork. With an effort, I lift my chin.

"Oh right," Ky says. "Sorry about that . . . um . . ."

"Jane," Uncle Graham says. "She's our temporary resident chef. She's filling in, along with Selene, while we head back East. Janie, this is Ky. He does electrical work for us now and then. It's the one thing I can't do myself. Better safe than sorry, right, Ky? He lives over yonder." Uncle Graham points south. Across the grounds, I see a white van at the edge of the gravel parking area. "Kyle & Son: For All Your Handyman & Electrical Needs" the side reads.

"That's what I was thinking: better safe than sorry. I, uh, in the dim light, I thought . . . Never mind." He looks from my uncle to me. "I see the resemblance, now that you mention it."

Great. I've gone from thieving wino to looking like—bless him—a fat old man.

Ky must see my eyes flash, because he looks at Uncle Graham's paunch and then at me. "I mean, you have the same eyes."

I'm sure my nostrils flare as I exhale. I'm not about to stand here and chitchat, so I take a step backward into the shed. "If you two will excuse me, I just came in here to grab one of my boxes." I turn, hoping they'll both just go away, and spot the box I need stacked with the rest of my things beside the laundry-folding table. I bend down to retrieve the box.

I hear footsteps coming into the shed. "Do you need help with that?" I can practically hear the "little lady" he probably wanted to add to the end of his question.

Ugh. I do not need the "big man" to help little ol' me. To demonstrate that, I stand with the box—it weighs all of about five pounds since it's just some paperwork—and toss it into the air a few inches. Catching it again, I say, "No. I think I can manage." And I walk out, leaving Ky and Uncle Graham behind.

THAT NIGHT IN bed, I'm riled up—excited about the resume I sent out, but annoyed about the wino look-alike thing. The guy's an idiot. A myopic idiot. I try to focus on more pleasant thoughts. Remembering how Selene and I laughed last week over Aunt Sugar's "going Brando" comment, I list classic Sugarisms:

1. Once, she heard Mom and me talking about going to see *Don Quixote,* and said she didn't understand why someone would write a musical about a burro. Yup. Named Donkey Hoatey.
2. She once said she "ran Pall Mall," instead of pell-mell. Maybe she wasn't wrong on this one though; after all, she was a smoker way back when.
3. She makes my uncle drive when they visit any city that involves freeway driving because "big-city people drive on the freeways like it's Lamaze or something." I've heard Uncle Graham several times patiently say, "Le Mans, dear."
4. She's been known to "throw abandon to the wind."
5. She told my mom that "Gray loves to talk to people. You'd think he's running for mayor, the way he's always kissing hands and shaking babies."
6. She thinks it's "womanly wilds" instead of wiles. Which does kind of make sense.
7. This one's not a classic, but when I moved into the B&B, she took me on a tour to refamiliarize me with the place. At the first room, she pointed at the TV and said, "We upgraded our cable. We get that Hobo network now. Personally, I don't watch it—it's all a lot of cursing and naked people and naked people cursing, but the guests seem to like it." I had to chew my lip to keep from laughing. Uncle Graham, passing by, called out, "HBO, my love!"

So sweet, how he calls her "my bride" or "my love." They're about the most sickeningly cute couple ever. Pretty sure Ryan never called me "my love." But then, I never called him that either.

CHAPTER 11
PENNY SAVER

"Do you know where my aunt and uncle went?" I ask Selene as we meet on the stairs, me heading up with fresh towels for the rooms, her lugging the vacuum down.

"Sugar said they had one last errand before their trip."

"Yeah, but do you know what time they'll be back? I'm making a pecan pie—Uncle Graham's favorite. I'm hoping to get it cooled and hidden before they're back."

She squeezes past, saying more to the vacuum than to me, "Sorry, I don't know anything."

"You are staying for dinner, right?" I say to her back.

She turns at the bottom of the stairs. "Of course. Shoot, we should have invited Ky too."

"I met that jerk the other day. Why would we invite him?"

"He's their neighbor. And he's not a jerk; he's nice. Why do you think he's a jerk?"

I tell her about our encounter at the laundry shed, and she covers her mouth with her hand. I can tell that she's trying hard to not laugh. Annoying.

"Well, I need to call him anyway," she says. "I don't want to bug Graham, since they're so busy getting ready to leave, but the flushy thingy in the toilet tank in Java isn't working right." She makes an opening and closing motion with her hands to simulate the "flushy thingy."

"Sounds like the flapper assembly. It's no big deal. You don't need to call him for that. I can replace it."

"Seriously?"

"Yeah. My dad was really handy; I was always his assistant. That's easy to fix." I turn and continue up the stairs with my towel delivery, adding, "And it's too late to invite him for dinner, so don't be calling him."

*

AUNT SUGAR CRACKS the back door wide enough to slip her head in. "Close your eyes."

"I can't," I say over my shoulder. "I'm trying to get this chicken in the oven."

She squeezes through the door, then shuts it. "That can wait." She plucks the lemon I'm about to stuff into the chicken's nether regions out of my hand, then tugs at my sweatshirt sleeve. "Come on. I want you to meet someone."

"Who?" I resist, leaning back against the counter. "You know I don't like meeting new people. And look at me; I'm all grungy." I indicate my liberally floured jeans and sweatshirt. "I'm a mess."

"No, you're perfect. Wait!" She scampers back to the door, moving faster than I've seen her move in the three weeks I've been here. "Bring her in, Gray." She flings open the door.

There stands my uncle holding a red leash. Penny wiggles at its other end. She sees me and bounds forward. Graham lets go of her leash, and it zings along the floor as she charges me. She stands on her back legs, crashing into my chest with her paws. Roxie, from the shelter, had told me, one of the times I had called, that Penny had started to come out of her shell. Looks like she burst forth from it. I bury my hands in her thick ruff. I'm happy to see her too. So happy, but still . . .

I narrow my eyes at my aunt. "What have you done?" Penny bats her paws at me, demanding attention. I bend forward and let her slather my chin and cheeks with kisses. I shut my eyes, and she licks my eyelids; she moves on to my forehead. I want to laugh, she's kissing me so frantically, but at the same time, I want to know what the hell's going on. "Aaaaggh," I half shriek, half laugh, drawing more ardent licks.

"See, I told you you're perfect." Aunt Sugar sounds like she's purring when she says the word *perfect*. As in the perfect owner? I'm about to say, "No way," when Uncle Graham says, "Janie, meet your new cousin!"

"What?" I push Penny down. "What are you guys thinking? You're leaving town—tomorrow." I put my hands on my hips. "You didn't get her for me, did you?"

"No, she's not for you. She's for your aunt; she'll take her mind off the pain. Give her something else to focus on. Remember that article you found online?" It's true. I'd filled a quiet afternoon, doing some research for my aunt on diet and alternative RA therapies. But this?

"I think they meant, like, meditation or something. I'm pretty sure they didn't mean a puppy! Do you have any idea how much work an active young dog is? She's going to need a lot of exercise, and a lot of time and training. Do you have room for her in the RV?"

"Oh, um, she won't be in the RV." Penny tours the baseboards, reacquainting herself with the kitchen. She notices the raw chicken on the counter and stands up on her hind legs to investigate. Wow, she's tall.

"Off." I gently push her down and turn back to my uncle. "Why not? Where'll she be?"

"We thought maybe you could dog-sit for us." My uncle studies the tops of his worn walking shoes (which match my aunt's).

Aunt Sugar grabs my arm. "We know it's a lot to ask, what with you already B&B-sitting for us. But she's so beautiful, we had to have her. A cross-country trip in an RV's no place for her, and what could be better for a puppy than our acreage here? Tammy'll be so happy here."

"Tammy?"

"She still doesn't seem to like the name Penny, so we thought we'd change it."

"We were thinking about Tammy Faye Bakker," my uncle chimes in. "Remember her? On account of how it looks like the dog's wearing a lot of eye makeup."

I'm looking at the dog while they talk, and shaking my head. I look up, and they grin at me. I shake my head harder. What am I supposed to do? Tell them to return her? I have no choice but to go along with this madness. But I don't have to let them saddle this poor dog with an equally batty name.

"I'd vote no on Tammy. I mean, if I have a say."

They exchange a satisfied look. They know they've got me now.

"Of course you have a say! What name do you like, Janie? Since she'll practically be your dog. I mean, while we're gone."

I look sideways at my uncle. I'm pretty damn sure they've got it cooked up in their heads that I'll fall in love with the dog while they're away. By the time they get back, I'll be begging them to let me keep her. Well, the surprise is going to be on them.

"I think she needs a classier name. Maybe Sophia, like Sophia Loren."

"Your uncle dated a Sophia in high school, so I don't think we'll be using *that* name." Aunt Sugar assesses the dog. "How about something chicken related . . . like . . . Nugget? Oh no. That's no good. Or how about Topi? Like those antelopes, on account of her antelopey legs."

I have a vague memory of seeing something possibly called a topi at the San Diego Zoo, but given my aunt's history, I'd be shocked if she remembered the name right. "Maybe you shouldn't change her name. Maybe she'll get used to Penny." The poor dog must be so confused—abandoned at a rest stop, locked in a kennel for three weeks, now living with me until my aunt and uncle get home. And now, they want to confuse her more with a new name. "Maybe this is all too much for her."

"Maybe! That's it," Aunt Sugar says. "We'll call her Maybelline—Maybe for short."

*

THAT NIGHT IN bed, drifting at the edge of sleep, I hear a soft whine. Groggy, I roll over. In the dim moonlight, Maybe's nose sneaks past the edge of the bed. She kisses me. My door is open just wide enough for her skinny frame to fit through. I know I closed it, like I did the other time she ended up in my bed. Like I always do. She slaps at the bed with a paw. "You want in?" I pull back the covers. "Shouldn't you be in with your parents?" She jumps up and spins in circles, finding the right spot. She flops down and closes her eyes, as if to say, "Nope, I'm sleeping with you."

Her soft fur warms the bed, and me.

The next morning, I ask my aunt point-blank if she opened my door. Her wide-eyed innocence would play to the back row of an opera house, but I don't press the issue, since it's time to say good-bye.

As soon as Selene gets there, we do the hugging thing, and they fire up the RV. Aunt Sugar rolls down her window and flashes the iPhone they bought for the trip, with my help, so they can keep in touch. "You call if you have any questions!"

"We will," I say. "And you call us every few days and let us know you're okay. Or send an e-mail." Several times, I'd showed them the features of the phone, showed them how to look up directions or find RV campsites. I even typed up a list of steps to follow.

Aunt Sugar looks at the phone, then back at us, confusion written across her brow. If we get a single call or e-mail, I'll be amazed.

Selene and I stand in the yard, watching the RV slowly crunch along the gravel driveway. I see Aunt Sugar waving out the passenger window and realize she's yelling a good-bye to Ky, who's standing in his driveway. "Have a safe trip," he calls out, then spotting Selene and me, he starts walking our way.

"I think I might have left the oven on," I say to Selene, and head back to the house. She can talk to him, but I'm certainly not going to.

*

THEY'VE BEEN GONE one whole week and so far so good: Selene's done the heavy lifting with the customers; I've got the breakfast routine more or less down; and, okay, I'll admit it's even been kind of fun having a dog around the house. Maybe is no Barnum, but with her still very puppyesque inquisitiveness, she makes Selene and me laugh at least a few times a day. Like this morning, she insisted on being in the bathroom with me while I showered, then peeked around the curtain and got her head wet. She just stood there, with a big goofy grin on her face, while the water plinked off her head. Nut. When I got out, she tried to lick the water off my legs.

Then again, for each thing she does that's funny, she does something that's a pain in the butt. Like on the days I got up early this week, she was underfoot, wanting to go out and play. The property's fenced, but only with a rough split railing that delineates the property and adds to its country charm—it's not designed to keep anything in or out—so I can't put her outside. Unless I tie her up. And the one time I tried that, she managed to get tangled up. I'd looked out the window and she was standing there, hobbled, staring at the house like a roped calf. And on the three days this week when we didn't have any guests, and I could've slept in, she was breathing her kibble breath in my face at five thirty.

She's so much more energetic than Barnum was for, oh, the last six years or so. I have to take her down by the stream for at least a thirty-minute walk or play session every morning after breakfast and again for a longer walk before dinner, or she gets hyper and tries my patience: steals my socks, nips at my heels and herds me while I walk, barks at me for attention. I lost it this past weekend and yelled at her, then locked her in my bathroom. She immediately ate a good portion of the pink shag toilet-lid cover, and later threw up pink, slimy blobs in front of a guest who was checking out. Charming.

Selene's been helping as much as possible, reminding me that "a tired puppy is a good puppy!" Turns out, a comatose puppy is the best puppy of all, so we try to take turns wearing Maybe out. But since Selene's got more to do around the B&B, I usually end up being in charge of Operation Comatose Puppy.

I guess it's best that I'm in charge of OCP, since I'm the one who suffers most if she's not exhausted by day's end. Selene and I will be watching TV in the den, or I'll be hiding out in my room, and Maybe'll come looking for attention or trouble, whichever she finds first. She pokes me with her nose, and if I ignore her, she starts what I call "corn-cobbing" me: running her tiny front teeth along my arm or thigh, as if she's eating an ear of corn. Every once in a while, she gets a bit of flesh between her teeth. Thank heaven we're past the razor-sharp puppy-teeth stage, but still, I'm covered in little bruises. I look like a human Dalmatian.

Of course, this all makes me remember when Barnum was a puppy. Photographic evidence exists in a box in the shed, documenting some of the trouble he got into. (Like the time he grabbed the end of the toilet paper and ran around TPing my apartment, or the time he squirmed into the cupboard where his food bag was. I came home to a bowling-ball beagle.) But, I don't remember being terrorized. We've had to instigate a threat-level code. At yellow, we can buy some time with a bone. Orange means grab a ball or rope toy. Red equals walking shoes!

Like now. The determined set of her ears and the malicious intent in her eyes reads threat-level red. I drop the towels I'm folding and grab her leash and my sunglasses.

As we hit the rise in the yard where I have a clear view of the stream, I see Ky there with his husky mix. Selene told me the dog's name is Milo, and he's another rescue from PARE. Maybe noticed Milo right after she moved in. She seems to have fallen in love with him from afar, whining and wiggling whenever she sees him. I, however, am Lady Capulet to her Juliet, since I don't want to have anything to do with Romeo's dad. Selene suggested I set up a playdate for the dogs, but I nixed the idea. Now, as I see Ky notice us, I smack my forehead and exaggerate an I- forgot-something pantomime. I start to turn, but Maybe spots Milo and drags me behind her like a water-skier. Barnum would have been only too happy to turn tail and head the other direction (after some trash-talking to put Milo in his place). But, no, Maybe has to go and be friendly.

Ky and I have talked twice since the "Betty" incident. Well, not actually talked. It was more like he called out a hello from his yard, and I muttered a reply and darted off, wondering if he'd managed to get in for an eye exam yet. Even if I thought he was a nice guy, I'm not going to be here long enough to make friends, so I didn't feel the need to be chatty. But now, here by the stream, there's no avoiding him.

It's the middle of the day on a Monday. Shouldn't he be at work? He isn't wearing the standard blue chambray work shirt and big jacket I've seen him in the few times I've spotted him (and hid). Instead he's got on a forest-green chamois shirt. It deepens the color of his eyes, which I normally find to be a rather icy shade of blue.

"Is Milo friendly?" I call out as we approach.

"For sure," Ky says waving us over.

I unhook Maybe's leash. "That's Maybe," I say as she darts past Ky and lunges at Milo. They're off, tussling and chasing, like old friends.

I'm stuck. What the hell am I going to talk to this guy about? Plus, he's in *my* chair. (Technically, Uncle Graham put a couple of Adirondack chairs here for the guests to amble down and relax by the stream, but I've almost never seen any of them stay down here for more than two minutes, so I've come to think of the one particular chair, which has a drink holder for my travel coffee mug, as mine.)

"Hey." I acknowledge him with a lift of my chin. He snaps shut what looks like a jackknife and slips it and something else into his jeans pocket. Are there creatures hiding among these trees that I should worry about? Coyotes? I've heard the javelina can have a nasty disposition.

"Hello, Jane." At least he remembered my name and didn't call me Betty. He asks how things are going since my aunt and uncle left. I say fine, busy. Add that I'm on a short break to tire Maybe out—setting up my exit for when I'll say we have to go, five minutes from now.

"I'm taking a break too. You should sit. Relax for a minute." I sit, setting my coffee mug in the dirt and calling out to Maybe not to play too rough.

Ky says Milo can take it, then points at my mug. "I should have put a cup holder on both of these. Didn't get the idea until I made the second one."

I look at him. "You made these?" Now it's my turn to point, and I indicate his van, parked at the back of his house. "So, you really are a handyman."

"I try. But, with the economy how it is, everyone's attempting to DIY it these days. I'm not super busy at the moment." No wonder he's loitering in the middle of the day.

"My dad was a great handyman," I say. "He taught me a thing or two." I don't want to boast, so I don't mention how I've fixed a toilet already.

"That's good. Everybody should know how to take care of minor things around the house." What makes him think the stuff I know how to fix is "minor"? I helped my dad install a garbage disposal once, I know how to put in a dimmer switch, and I can unclog a drain with a snake. Kinda patronizing, Mr. Big Man. "But if anything major goes wrong while your uncle's away, you can always call me."

I just grunt.

We watch the dogs.

The only thing I hate worse than talking to someone I don't know is sitting in silence with someone I don't know. I try to think of something to say, but nothing comes to mind other than what a crush Maybe seems to have on Milo. I go back to the work thing.

"So . . . how long have you had your business?"

"'Bout five years. Took it over when my dad passed away."

"Sorry to hear that. So, if your dad was Kyle, does that make you Ky Junior?" It amuses me to think of this big jackass-bear as "Junior."

"Not exactly."

He doesn't elaborate, and I assume it's a sore subject. Probably hates being called Junior. After all, the word brings to mind a kid in short pants, skipping along with a lollipop. I picture Jackass Bear-Man skipping in short pants, and try not to smile.

He leans forward, resting his elbows on the worn knees of his jeans. "Thanks to my mom, there's constant confusion about my name." He snorts. "My dad wanted to call me Kyle Junior, but Mom insisted 'a boy needs his own identity.' She convinced him to compromise and name me Kai—K-A-I. It's Hawaiian; means ocean." He snorts again.

Guess he's not feeling the whole island vibe surrounding his name. "Everyone who sees the truck thinks I'm Ky, K-Y. And everyone who sees my real name in print pronounces it wrong, 'key' or 'kay.'" Yet another snort. He's turning into jackass pig-man. "I generally let people think it's short for Kyle."

"Kai's a pretty cool name though."

"Kind of a joke, if you ask me."

I'm not sure I should ask, but I do. "Why's that?"

"I've never even seen the ocean."

"You've never seen the ocean? Never? How can that be?" The ocean is the best thing this planet's ever offered up. I can't think of a place I'd rather be than on a beach or in the water. When I'm playing beach volleyball or swimming, I don't feel too tall or awkward. Now that I think about it, the ocean is the only place where I feel graceful. Every movement of swimming is a beautiful thing: the arm lifting up and out of the water, the hand cutting back in, the pointed toes and strong kicking legs. The water glides over my skin and makes it gleam. My hair fans out behind me. When my hair was long, I felt like a mermaid. Even my fingernails look nice when I swim, not grubby like my usual tomboy nubs. The tips gleam white in contrast to the nail beds, flushed pink from the activity. Geez, I miss open-water swimming. "I can't get over that you've never seen the ocean."

He's silent. I sense he's uncomfortable with me making such a big deal out of the fact that he's lived a landlocked life. I could poke the bear some more, but decide, instead, to steer the discussion elsewhere. "So, how about your mom? She still alive?"

"Don't know. Haven't seen her since I was ten."

"Oh." Great. I've landed on more rocky conversational ground. I should've talked about Maybe's crush. Just as I'm about to say that my break's probably over, he starts talking again.

"My mom was originally from the islands." That explains the ocean name. "One day, she up and moved back to Maui. She'd been telling my dad for long as I could remember that if she didn't get out of Idaho, she'd lose her mind. Can't say she didn't give us fair warning."

"Your dad wouldn't go? What's not to like about Hawaii?"

"He had his business there in Coeur d'Alene, where I was born. Wouldn't give that up. Besides, he was the old-fashioned type, didn't think a husband should follow his wife around. I think he thought his wife needed to stay where his work was."

"Huh." So, by old-fashioned I guess he means too macho for his own good. I wonder if the apple landed right next to the tree. I can certainly see his mom's side in this, but abandoning your own kid . . . As nonmaternal as I am, I can't imagine doing that. I can't even understand abandoning a fur-kid. "Maui's pretty great. But obviously, you never went to visit her there if you've never seen the ocean." What a waste. The water is especially spectacular in Maui. Doesn't seem like the same dark, cold Pacific Ocean we have in San Diego.

"She wrote, wanted me to visit. But neither of my folks could afford it. And then we moved, and moved again, and eventually, her letters stopped finding me. And I wasn't exactly a regular correspondent. I could've written, but . . ."

I can understand that. Poor kid's mom ditches him; it's not his responsibility to keep up the contact. But his dad, I don't get. "So, your dad refused to move to Hawaii, but then you guys moved anyway?"

"Yeah." He shrugs. "I think he couldn't stand living in our house without Mom, so we moved. Every few years it was the same—move, start over, get the business going again." Snort. Maybe *snort* isn't the best description; maybe it's more of a scoff. "Seemed like as soon as we settled someplace, and things started to get routine, he'd start missing her. I guess I can understand that—keep moving, keep busy so he didn't have time to—" He looks over at me, then down at this hands. "Hell. I'm sorry." He runs a hand through his buzzed hair. "Look who I'm trying to tell about what it's like . . . being lonely."

My eyes narrow. What right does this jackass have to assume I'm lonely? Maybe I am, but what the hell makes him think so? Besides, maybe I'm okay with it.

He sees my face and adds, "Uh, Selene told me about you being a widow and all."

Why would Selene talk to this jerk about me? "What else did she tell you?"

"Just that you're moving to San Diego soon. Well, once Graham and Sugar get back."

Not soon enough.

"I bet you fall in love with Prescott, though, and end up staying."

Now it's my turn to scoff. "Doubtful. San Diego's pretty hard to beat."

"I'm not much for big cities."

I could explain to him that San Diego actually has a nice beach-town feel, rather than seeming like a booming metropolis, but whatever. I won't waste my breath.

"Hmmm" is all I say by way of acknowledgment. "I better get back." I stand as Maybe bops Milo with a right jab. He responds by wagging his tail and kissing her repeatedly.

Kai looks at his watch and jumps up as well. "Shoot. I didn't realize it was eleven forty-five already. I gotta go."

He calls Milo to his side. I grab Maybe's collar so she won't tag along. She's covered in Milo's slobber. Kai turns back before he reaches the path through the bushes up to his house, and sees me using my sweatshirt sleeve to wipe a Zorro-like mark of drool off Maybe's fore-head. "Sorry about that," he calls. "He's a drooler. His full name's Slobberdog Milosovitch."

I can't help but laugh at that. He may be a jerk, but his dog's a sweetheart.

"We should meet up again, with the dogs I mean," he continues. "They'd like that."

"Yeah." Doubtful. "Maybe," I add. Maybe looks at me, expectant.

I look down at Maybe, wondering if Selene would bring her down here for me.

Oh, it'll be so nice to move back to the big city where no one talks to their neighbors.

UNCLE GRAHAM AND Aunt Sugar have been gone only one week. I can't believe I've been here almost a month already. One month down means I've got another two to three months left. Ugh. Although, I admit there are some nice things about working here:

1. I pull on my sweats or rattiest jeans and my favorite Converse tennies, brush my hair, and voilà, I'm ready for work.
2. Commute time equals twenty seconds. Man, how I hated that commute on the train in Philly.
3. I bustle around a warm kitchen with a view of the stream, instead of being confined to a fabric-padded cube under fluorescent lighting.
4. I'm much more active, compared with sitting on my butt in front of a computer all day, which is a nice change of pace.
5. Taking a break involves a peaceful walk with Maybe under the pines and cottonwoods, rather than a hurried visit to the vending machine.
6. I really enjoy the baking: the squish of cookie dough between my fingers (reminds me of my mud-pie tomboy days); the smells of lemon zest, vanilla, and cinnamon, even the earthiness of flour; the golden-crusted delicacies that come out of the oven. There's something calming about it—maybe it's the precision of it all. I like that you have to measure everything exactly, right down to the leveled half teaspoons. There's such order to it. And if you do it just so, you're rewarded with perfection at the end. What else in life is that . . . fair?
7. I even sort of like some of the cleaning. There's something Zen-like about the tightly pulled corners of fresh linens, or the tracks of the vacuum in the long hallway. And, other than snuggling with Maybe, nothing beats the coziness of an armful of warm towels straight from the dryer on a cold winter's day.

But for all the good things, there are still the guests. And, although I avoid them, they still manage to make me crazy. Like the woman I overheard the other day at breakfast, saying, "Of course, after that we had to get our nine-year-old the unlimited messaging plan." Yes. Of course you did. Because a nine-year-old should be texting without limits. Who are these people I'm sharing a roof with?

CHAPTER 12
WHAT'S IN A NAME?

Selene has asked me to go hiking at least five times. My excuses are always at the ready, mainly job hunting. (And one time, when I could have gone hiking, I even found a couple of jobs to apply for.) But today, both Selene and Maybe had approached my room—where I was obsessively checking e-mails—at the same time.

Selene said, "Sorry about the interruption. I know you're busy, but I thought I'd see if you wanted to come along for a hike."

Maybe said, "If you don't get up and take me out *now*, I will chew everything you own. Including, and beginning with, you." She mostly said it with her eyes.

"You've got to take her out anyway." Selene had laughed while Maybe pulled at my sleeve and snarled an invitation to play. "Come on; we can wear her out."

I couldn't argue, so now, here we are in Selene's truck, heading through Prescott toward its western edge and Thumb Butte trail. Maybe trembles with excitement in the backseat. She leans over my shoulder, hanging her head out the window like Barnum used to love to do.

"I still can't get over those maple-bacon scones," Selene says. The sky looks huge and deep blue; it's a gorgeous day, chilly but sunny. "Everybody raved about them. You have to make those again."

"They were an experiment; I wanted to use up the last of the bacon."

"They were a successful experiment. You've got a knack for that stuff."

I shrug. It's nice to hear everyone liked the scones, but all I did was crumble some crispy bacon into my usual recipe and add a maple glaze. No biggie. I change the subject. "Did a guy walk through the dining room this morning without his shirt on? I heard his wife give him hell."

"Yeah, he'd been out for a run and strutted on through."

"What a clown. Besides, it was frickin' freezing this morning."

"I guess he wanted to show off his pecs. They were nice pecs. Anyway . . ." So, now it's her turn to change the subject. Whenever I say anything remotely negative about a guest, she finds something good in them. "I'm glad you came along. It's good for you to get out of your room." After a beat she adds, "You spend too much time in there."

"I spend time in my room, searching for a job." And sleeping and reading and lying on the bed staring at the ceiling. I like Selene and all, but it's not really her business how I spend my time. "And I do get out. To walk Maybe." At her name, Maybe licks my ear, which sends a tickling shiver down the backs of my arms.

"Sorry. I didn't mean to sound bossy." She glances over and smiles apologetically. "Anyway, this should definitely wear her out."

"How long is this trail?" Are we going to wear me out instead? I'm still not used to the elevation, and my heart pounds simply walking Maybe by our favorite spot, Watson Lake, which is pancake flat. And if Thumb Butte is, in fact, a butte that means my butt will be going up.

"Only three miles," Selene says, pulling into a dirt-packed parking lot with a big wooden trail marker. She grabs a fanny pack with two water bottles out of the back of the truck. At the trailhead, the dirt path forks. She points to the right, and we start walking. "It's a loop; we'll go this way today. Next time we'll go left. It's a lot steeper that way."

Both trails curve off, in opposite directions, and upward around what, to my eyes, looks not so much like a butte but a small mountain. Instead of asking about the length of the hike, I should have inquired about elevation gain.

"Next time won't happen if I have a heart attack this time." I better get her talking, since I'll soon be out of breath. "Your parents live around here?"

"Yeah, my whole family does. My parents are in Cottonwood—about an hour northeast. My brother's in Prescott Valley. And you know my sister and her family are here in Prescott." Selene lived with her sister before temporarily moving into the Chick.

"You miss living with them?" I ask. The uphill trail is already making my lungs protest. It'll have to be short sentences from here on out.

"I miss my nieces. My sister, Mary, is a nurse, and her husband, Alain, is a manager at the Prescott Resort. They both work nights, so it worked out well with me being home with the girls. Luckily, Alain rearranged his schedule for the next few months. The older one, Danielle, is seven and the younger one, Veronique, is five. They're adorable. You'll have to meet them."

Yeah, we don't have to do that. "Pretty . . ."—huff—". . . names." Puff.

"Alain's French Canadian. He and my sis met when they were both at U of A. He said he picked it because he wanted to go to college in the hottest place he could think of, after surviving eighteen Quebec winters. He's a kick. Anyway, he insisted the girls needed French names."

How can she rattle off so many words at this pace? She's not even breathing heavily.

"Cool." I gasp. My lungs scream while we work our way up the hill. My saving graces are (a) my long legs that, at least for now, are managing to keep up with Selene's quick but short strides, and (b) Maybe. The dog darts from tree to tree like a butterfly. She stops to sniff, then lunges forward. With each lunge, I get an extra pull. "I like . . . your name too."

"My mom got it out of a book. Beats my sister's name, Mary. She's bummed because she's stuck with the traditional Catholic name. But our last name's Levine. Selene Levine. Cruel, huh?" She laughs. "Being raised by a Mexican American Catholic mother and a Jewish father from New Jersey made for an interesting childhood. My siblings and I like to say we're Cathlish. My parents are more spiritual than religious, so we were raised on a mix of the two. Anyway, it took me a long time to like my name, but I love it now. It means 'goddess of the moon.'" She strikes a pose, fanning her fingers out below her face and gazing up to the sky. She drops the pose and laughs again. I just smile, because laughing requires breath.

She grabs the water bottles from her pack and hands me one. I stop, grateful for the rest. She stops, too, and takes a long drink, then squirts some water for Maybe to lap at. "Ready?" I'm not, but I nod. "What about you? You like your name?"

"Jane?" I shake my head with as much vigor as I can muster. "No."

"But think of all the cool Janes. Everyone thinks of Celine Dion when they hear my name. But you've got Jane Fonda, Jane Russell, Jane Goodall, and, um, what's her name—Lady Jane Grey or whatever. Wasn't she a queen or something?"

"Yeah. Beheaded. And. Clamity Jane." Yes, I say "clamity." There's not enough oxygen to waste on the extra syllable.

"Hell yeah! Calamity Jane." She kicks a rock with the toe of her hiking boot for emphasis. "Now you're talking! That's a cool namesake."

"Nah. Plain Jane. 'S'me." As a kid, I used to ask my mom why she picked Jane out of the universe of available names. Sometimes, she'd say she wanted me to be my own person, not saddled with "an old family name" like she was with Cordelia. She said Jane was a blank slate, and I could be anybody. Other times, she'd say she just thought I looked like a Jane the first time she saw me. That's not a good thing in my book, because there's no way a girl can get through the American school system with my name and not constantly be labeled *plain*. I guess she not only wanted my name to be a blank slate, but she thought I looked like one too.

I decide to change the subject back to the nieces. "'S'nice . . . of you . . . to babysit."

"It works for all of us. They need someone to be with the girls overnight, and I need to save up my money. Sort of like you with your aunt and uncle."

"How'dja mean?" Maybe sees a squirrel, giving me a boost as she tries to nab it before it dashes up an alligator pine.

"You're helping them out. But it's mutually beneficial, right? I mean, it must be incredibly hard . . . losing your husband and your dog, plus looking for work."

"Yeah." My eyes stay on the trail. I don't want to step on a rock and twist my ankle. Strong as Selene looks, at only five foot four, I know she won't be able to drag my five-foot-eleven butt back down, even with Maybe helping to pull. Besides, I know I'm still not managing the correct widow face. I don't want to pretend to feel something I don't, so I watch the ground.

"Sorry, I mean, it must be . . . tough." Her voice is soft with sympathy. It feels like she's trying to get me to open up, like she wants me to know I don't have to be brave with her. Even if I wanted to, I'm not physically capable of telling that long story right now.

I glance over, shrug, and attempt a sad smile, which doesn't last long since I have to return to open-mouth breathing.

We come around a sweeping bend in the trail, stepping out of the shade of the trees into full sunshine. It starts to get hot, but at least I can see a sort of plateau a short way ahead. "Summit?" I point hopefully up the trail.

"Yep, almost there, and we'll take a break." A few more moments and we're at the top. Hands on hips, I gulp in air, taking in the beautiful (if somewhat blurry because my eyeballs throb along with the pounding of my heart) view of Prescott and the rolling green hills that encircle it. In the other direction, a jagged purple mountain range dominates the far horizon.

"That's San Francisco Peaks." Selene points at the highest one, draped under a full white shawl of snow. We sit on a stone bench and drink our water. Maybe flops in the dirt at my feet, her tongue draped over the side of her mouth. I've never seen her look happier. "So, San Francisco—isn't that where Graham said you're headed?"

"No, San Diego."

"Oh, right. Sorry."

"You apologize a lot."

"I know. Sorry. I mean, I can't help it. It's the Cathlish in me. I've got guilt on both sides." I laugh. "Anyway, California sounds cool. I've never been. And coming all the way from the East Coast too. I don't think that sounds plain. Take it from someone who's lived in the same small town her whole life: to me, your life sounds exciting."

I look at her, and she smiles her gorgeous smile, then looks back out at the view. Her smile fades.

"Of course, that's why Devon left me. Because I said I'd never leave Prescott."

"Oh, are you coming off a breakup?"

"Yeah." She stands. "Come on, let's start back down." I reluctantly heave myself up off the bench. Maybe springs up like a jack-in-the-box, raring to go. Selene leads the way back to the trail. "Devon said we were never going to 'live big dreams' in Prescott. But my dream's *in* Prescott. I don't know. Maybe Devon was right. Maybe I do dream small."

"I dream small too. I don't see anything wrong with that." It's much easier going down. Hikes should always be downhill. "All I ask is to have an interesting job, and to be back by my friends and the ocean again. Besides, we can't all change the world. That'd be annoying."

"I guess you're right. I never thought of it that way before. That would be annoying."

"So, how long were you guys together?"

"A long time. Years."

"Sorry. Breakups suck." Now it's my turn to apologize. "Nothing like dating someone new, though, to get over the ex."

"Nah, I've got zero prospects. Besides, I've got no time right now either. Between work and school and hanging out with my nieces, I don't have time for dating. Maybe once my classes are done."

"I bet you've got lots of prospects."

"Sorry, but would you mind if we talk about something else?"

"Okay. But stop apologizing."

"Sorry," she says, but I knew she would, so we say it in unison. We both laugh this time.

"We should get a pizza or something tonight," I suggest. My aunt and uncle have been gone two weeks, but so far, Selene and I haven't eaten dinner together. She's got classes two nights a week, and most other nights, she goes home to eat with her family. If she is at the Chick, we usually fend for ourselves, and I eat in my room.

"Sor—I mean, I can't. That'd be fun, but it's Monday. I've got class. Last one before Christmas break. Woo-hoo!" Her comment reminds me that this will probably be our last bit of free time before Christmas: today is the twenty-first, and starting on the twenty-third, we're booked solid until after New Year's. And my mother insists on coming for Christmas. I told her I'll be busy working, but she says she can help, and this way we'll get to spend Christmas together. I hope she's not going to add to the stress. As I saw over Thanksgiving, guests can be more demanding on the big holidays, and my mom is not known for being a stress reliever.

"I forgot about your class. What're you taking anyway?"

"Basic business accounting."

"Ooooo, fun. I can see why you wouldn't want to miss that." Maybe's pulling is not so helpful on the way down. She galumphs down the trail, and I try to keep up without falling. I tug at the leash. "Slow down, Maybe!" She ignores me, darting forward again. I plant my feet and hold on tight. When she's semi-under control, I say, "That's not the usual hobby sort of class. I thought you were taking oil painting or something."

"I know. Believe me, it's not for fun. It's part of this pipe dream of mine. Which will probably never happen unless the timing works out, or if I borrow a bunch of money from my parents, but that's not—never mind." She groans and shakes her head from side to side, as if to knock the image of her dream loose. "Let's talk about something else."

We're almost back to the parking lot. The paved sections of the downhill trail provided good traction, but now we hit a last steep, slippery dirt stretch. I almost lose my footing because Maybe's back to pulling hard.

Selene notices and says, "You can let her off leash; no one's around."

I do, and Maybe bounds the rest of the way. She stops every few yards to turn and check on us. "Wait up," I call, as if she knows what that means. She races back to me, jumps up, and plants her dusty paws on my sweatshirt, then runs back down the trail again.

"I guess you're 'it,'" Selene says while I dust the dirt off.

"If she thinks I'm chasing after her, she better think again. Hey, is she limping?"

Maybe continues on down, still loping along quickly, but she seems to favor her right front leg.

"Stay, Maybe," I call. She has no concept of "stay," since I haven't spent time training her to do anything but sit. I've tried to teach her "off," and she's doing okay where the kitchen counters are concerned, but she still loves to jump at people and try to lick their faces. Amazingly, she stays, and I hook her up for the short walk to the truck.

Selene stops and watches us. "I dunno. She might've hit a rock or a hole on the way down. It's probably nothing."

"Gosh, I hope so. I didn't think to ask my aunt and uncle about potential vet visits." The thought of a vet bill leads me to worrying about the bigger issue of my aunt and uncle's general financial health. Once the holidays are past, future bookings look pretty sparse, and they'd mentioned more than once what a bite the bad economy has taken out of the business the past year or so. I broach the subject with Selene as we drive back.

"Do you think my aunt and uncle are doing okay? Financially, I mean." I'm not sure it's appropriate to ask this of their employee, but I'm worried, and I know Selene is more than a staff member. She loves them.

"For the most part, I think they're doing great and are the happiest people I know. But," she hesitates. "Oh, I hate to sound gossipy, but I did hear them fighting one day. It wasn't long after they found out about Sugar's RA. I remember because I never hear them fight." We stop for a red light and she looks over at me. "I don't want you to think I was eavesdropping."

"The light's green," I say.

"Anyway, I got to work early, and I heard them . . . not exactly yelling—it wasn't like that—but their voices were raised. I heard Graham say, 'We can't afford to,' only I didn't hear what. Then she said something, and she sounded upset. And he told her she wasn't 'being practical,' and she stormed off."

"Wow, I've never heard them fight either. They're always so sweet with each other."

"I know. It worried me a little, especially since the bookings haven't been great this year. But they've been doing this a long time, and there were a lot of years when business was good." She shrugs. "Anyways, I always get paid on time." She looks over at me. "It was just the one time. I shouldn't have said anything. They were back to acting like their old selves later that day. Graham was whistling, and Sugar asked me what mammal I wanted to be. She's so funny."

I smile at that. I hope she's right that they have some savings. I've started to notice more and more how run down things are around the inn. "I hate to think they might be hurting for money when they're so close to retirement."

Selene sits up straighter. "Do you think they'll retire soon?"

"I don't know. I mean, they're about that age, right? I just assumed."

"I thought maybe they'd wait a few more years. I mean, Graham does talk a lot about taking the RV and traveling. But he's been talking like that for years. Sugar always smiles and nods."

"I should talk to them when they get back. If there's one thing I learned from Ryan's cancer, it's that life's too short. If Uncle Graham's dream is to go exploring in their RV, they should sell the Chick and go." Maybe nose-pokes me from the backseat, and I roll my window down for her, letting in a blast of cool air. She squeezes her head through the opening, and the wind flutters her lips.

Selene doesn't say anything for a while. We're almost back to the B&B when she says, "Maybe they'll get really hooked on RVing while they're gone. They might want to go back on the road right away." There's something about the way she says it—like it would be a bad thing—that makes me look over at her. Her eyes are intent on the road ahead.

I suppose if they sold the place, she'd be out of a job. A job she loves. And she's got this big secret dream she's saving up for. I should probably shut up.

To change the subject I ask, "So what mammal were you?"

"Oh." She laughs. "A bat. I figured a bat might have a connection with the moon. Not very glamorous though, huh? What would you be?"

I don't have to think about it. "A dolphin."

When we reach the Chick, I can't be sure, but it looks like Maybe favors her right leg when she jumps out of the cab.

CHAPTER 13
IT'S A WONDERFUL LIFE?

Mom drives up to "help" a few days before Christmas. She says it's because she wants to spend Christmas with me for the first time in seven years, but the first night, I find out she has an ulterior motive.

"I had such fun today, playing innkeeper," she says while we watch TV in the den. Selene has gone to help her nieces with their parents' Christmas presents, so Mom and I are alone. Or as alone as you can be in a house full of strangers. I'm tired and want Mom to go to bed. I'm letting her have my room, and for the moment we both lounge on the sofa, which is where I'll be sleeping. I'm wondering whether Maybe will abandon me and the cramped sofa for the comfort of the bed with my mom. I would if I were her.

"We're not 'playing.' It's hard work, running this place." I yawn. "Tiring," I add, hoping she'll get the hint.

"But if you love what you do, it doesn't seem like work."

"Since when do you love being an innkeeper? You loved being a teacher for thirty years."

She tells me yes, she loved her career, but she's always been a little jealous of her brother and Sugar getting to share their work. And she thinks it would be "such fun" to meet new people all the time. Then she draws in a breath, turns to me, and says, "I have a wonderful idea! We should open an inn together!"

Are you insane? perches on my lips, but I swallow the words and cough out a "What?" instead.

"It'd be perfect!" She launches into several minutes of how great it would be: I could do the cooking and the cleaning and the computer "stuff" (i.e., all the work), and she could deal with the guests. She says Uncle Graham could help us find a place and show us the ropes. "How about Tucson? We don't want to compete with your uncle, and the weather's so nice."

"Before you start looking for available properties, let me remind you that (a) I don't want to be an innkeeper, and (b) I'm on my way back to San Diego." I leave unsaid, and (c) it'll be a cold, dark day in the synapses of my brain when the two of us partnering in business seems like a good idea.

The nice part about this conversation is that at least I realize my mom has no idea that she can drive me batty.

*

THE SHED DOOR is closed, and I'm expecting it to stick as usual, so I shift my laundry basket out of the way and shove with my shoulder. The clatter and plink of metal against concrete fills the room, alerting me too late to the fact that the shed is occupied. I've sent tools and an open cardboard box full of screws flying. Kai extracts himself from the lower half of the monster dryer and, sitting back on his heels, surveys the mess scattered under the big oak table. "Oops," he says. "Thought I'd moved that out of the way."

I plop my basket on the table and kneel down, resigned to helping clean up. Technically, this is his fault. He shouldn't have set his toolbox right in front of the door. Dummy.

"I can get this." He crawls over toward the mess, collecting screwdrivers and an oversize silver tape measure along the way. He rights a battered, old red toolbox and drops his collection in it.

"It's okay. I'm the one that burst in." I scrape together a handful of screws, and Kai shoves the cardboard box my way. "I didn't realize you were in here." *Or I never would have come in.* "The dryer died?"

"Yep. Selene called. I came right over. Can't have you ladies facing the busy Christmas weekend without a working dryer."

"Thanks. That'd be a nightmare."

I crawl under the table after more screws. I'm hoping Kai will head to the other corner of the room, but no such luck. At least he's at the opposite end of the table.

"Padres, huh?" He points at my sweatshirt. "I would've thought you were a Phillies fan. Thought that's where Selene said you're from."

"Nope. I was living in Philadelphia, but I'm not from there. Sadly, I'm a Padres girl."

"That's unfortunate." I can't argue with him slagging off my team; the Padres do suck. "Especially since Philly won the series last year and all," he continues. I grunt, remembering Jeffrey trying to get us tickets to a playoff game. That was before Ryan got sick, but we were fighting a lot back then. The two of them ended up going without me. "Anyway, could be worse. You could be a Cubbies fan like me." Ah, he also backs a losing team.

I move closer to the center of the table, continuing to collect scattered screws and dropping them into the cardboard box. "At least the Cubs have won the World Series before."

"Yeah, a hundred-plus years ago!" he says. "But at least we don't have a goofy mascot like that Padre you guys have. I'd rather have no mascot than a paunchy guy with a tonsure."

"Hey! That's *Mister* Swinging Friar to you." He's right. Our mascot *is* goofy, but he's our goofy mascot, and nobody else is going to make fun of him.

"Oh, I didn't realize he was a swinger." Kai laughs at his own joke, but I don't join in. "How'd you end up a Padres fan?"

"I grew up in San Diego; my dad was a fan. We used to watch the games together." I picture my dad and me on the sofa, sharing a bowl of popcorn. I can practically feel the scratchy fabric of that lumpy old sofa on the backs of my legs and the melted butter on my fingertips. He'd explain the plays to me; he could recite a million stats and remember past games like he'd played them himself.

"Here," Kai says. He leans toward me, and takes my hand with his left, dumping the collection of screws from his right hand into my open palm. His skin is warm and rough. The sleeves of his blue chambray shirt are rolled up, and I can't help but notice how muscular his forearms are. God help me, but I blush. *Why?* Yes, he's a hunk, but he's also a jerk. Stupid hormones. I guess it's been a long time since a handsome man touched me.

"Sounds familiar," he says, looking around the floor for strays. Thank heaven he didn't seem to notice my burning cheeks. "Dad was a Cubbies fan." Not seeing anything else to pick up, he slaps his hands on his jeans to get the dust off. "Since you grew up with a lovable loser team like mine, you probably heard the 'it's not whether ya win or lose' speech a lot."

"Oh yeah. But I'd take it a step further and say it's not even 'how ya play the game.' It's who you watch it with." My brain is really not cooperating here. It brings up an image of Kai and me, snuggled on a sofa together, watching TV.

He stands and offers a hand to help me up. "You're very wise."

I pretend not to notice the offer—I can feel that my cheeks have gone back to normal, and I don't want them flaring up all red again. I scramble up on my own. *He's a jerk, and you're only here for a few months*, I lecture myself. *Stick to sports talk, girl. Stick to sports talk.* "Best to be philosophical when you're backing a losing team."

He chuckles and thanks me for helping. "Did you ever play softball? You look like an athlete." He looks me up and down, and I almost blush again. But then, he also thought I looked like a drunk, and my annoyance at the recollection pushes any thought of his sex appeal out of my head. I want to say, "Which is it, Kai? Do I look like an athlete or a drunk?" But instead I answer, "Yeah, in high school. But then I switched to volleyball. You?"

He definitely looks like an athlete, too, probably a ball player, with his broad shoulders and strong arms. His body type, big and brawny, is so different from tall and lanky Ryan. I swallow. *Sports talk!* "Let me guess . . . right field?" With those arms, he's got to be a power hitter and have a strong throwing arm too.

He smiles. "Close. Center." I should have known. With those legs, he could cover some ground. "Sports is the best way to make friends when you move as much as we did. I still play on a team here."

"Cool," I say, inching toward the door.

He points at my laundry. "You can go ahead and start that. I'll move it to the dryer for you when I'm done."

"No. That's okay." I grab my basket before he can see it's mostly full of my undies. "I'll come back later." I dash out before he can see that my cheeks have gone red again.

*

ON CHRISTMAS MORNING, I'm actually glad Mom is here. I might even go so far as to use the word *thankful*. I felt bad about Selene working and insisted she take the day off. She fought the idea, but Mom and I convinced her we'd be fine. I'm not sure we will be fine (it's still early; lots could go wrong), but Mom swears we can handle it, and

Selene promised she could be here in ten minutes if we need her. She's already called twice to check in.

Mom's manning the dining room, socializing with the guests and pouring fresh-squeezed orange juice and mimosas, while I prepare an extra-special breakfast of eggs Florentine, bacon, cranberry bread with orange butter, roasted potatoes, and warm fruit compote. (Minus the potatoes, it's the same menu I used to make for Ryan and me on New Year's Day—one of the few holidays Barbara didn't insist we spend with them.) Mom comments, during one of her breezes through the kitchen, that "we're a well-oiled machine." Still bucking for us to work together someday. My lips remain tightly pressed together.

It feels odd to work on Christmas, but everything turns out pretty amazing, and I hear the guests oohing and aahing and *mmming*, so at least I feel appreciated.

When we finish stuffing the guests, Mom and I sit down to our own brunch of the leftovers.

Mom's been tiptoeing around me all morning, being solicitous of my every move, anticipating my every need. "More coffee?" "Can I get you some cream?" Etc., etc. I assume it's because she thinks I'm a soon-to-blow Molotov cocktail of depression since it's my first Christmas as a widow. (Pretty sure I won't find a "widow's first" Christmas ornament in my stocking; that doesn't make nearly as nice a keepsake as "baby's first" does.)

Now that the breakfast hubbub has died down though, what I'm really thinking about is the fact that this is my first Christmas in fourteen years (geez, it was the last century) without the Christmas beagle. Barnum had this red-and-green collar with jingle bells that I'd force him into every year. He'd squirm while I put it on him, but then he ate up all the attention he'd get when he'd come jingling into the room. (Of course, it also acted as a handy early warning sign if he leapt at the roast turkey or whatnot on the kitchen counter.) He was so cute, cruising around the house with his quick-stepping prance. Nothing like a

Christmas beagle to add massive amounts of cheer to your holiday. (In fact, those ghosts could have saved a lot of time by simply getting Scrooge a Christmas beagle. Would have changed his whole outlook on the holiday in a heartbeat, and everyone could have gotten a good night's sleep.)

I still have the collar somewhere, in a box in the shed. It's one of the few mementos of Barnum's I kept. I could go and find it. Put it on Maybe. Turn her into the Christmas . . . collie-shepherd mix, or whatever the heck she is. But it wouldn't be the same. She doesn't have that same adorable prance that Barnum had. She's more of a wiggler and a bounder. I look around for her, wondering where she is. She doesn't even beg like Barnum did. Whoever heard of a dog that doesn't beg? And we're eating eggs and bacon. Bacon! But she's nowhere around. Probably snuck off to go sleep in the bed (now that Mom's up and at 'em for the day), since we've been tossing and turning, crammed together on the sofa the last three nights.

"You okay?" Mom asks me, and I snap out of it, realizing I'm doing the Indy 500 of coffee-cup stirring. I don't say anything, but I put down my spoon, and she takes advantage of my stilled hand, reaching over to pat it. "Are you thinking about last Christmas? With Ryan?" A sad smile lifts the corners of her cranberry-red lips.

Ah yes. Last Christmas. When Ryan and I had a fight because he bought me the same Liz Taylor White Diamonds perfume he bought for Barbara. She was thrilled. I was pissed. I mean, seriously: What was he thinking? And when, in all our time together, had he ever known me to wear perfume? If I had to pinpoint the precise moment when I knew our marriage was over, it was then. I mean, okay, on the surface it was just a thoughtless present. But looking back on it, I think that was the moment when I realized that what *I* wanted wasn't a top priority for him anymore.

Later that afternoon, Jeffrey had too much scotch, and Barbara turned on Ryan and me for not being able to control our "beast."

Although she'd said we could bring Barnum, I guess she hadn't antici-pated him being underfoot in the kitchen. But where else would any self-respecting beagle be when there's meat cooking? I remember him snitching a hunk of leftover roast and dashing off to the hall to enjoy his ill-gotten gains. (Nobody'd heard the Christmas beagle jingling over the too-loud Yanni Christmas CD Barbara insisted on playing.) It's an irritating memory, but I can't help but smile, remembering how Barnum looked so pleased with himself.

"There you go, honey," my mom says, looking similarly pleased, but misinterpreting my smile. "Focus on happy memories."

"Speaking of Ryan, I better go call the Waynesfields and wish them a merry Christmas."

"I'm sure they'd like that. And we'll call your aunt and uncle when you're done."

I go to my room for some privacy, but dread comes along with me. I don't want to call. I've e-mailed them a few times, but haven't spoken to them since I left a month and a half ago. I know they'll be having a hard time getting through the holidays. I sit on the edge of my bed, where Maybe snoozes. She wakes and stretches, then rolls on her back, legs wide open. I rub her belly while taking a deep breath, and dial their number.

Barbara answers. "It's good to hear your voice, Jane. We miss hav-ing you here with us this year."

I know she means she misses having me there with Ryan. I don't know what to say. I take advantage of the fact that it's easy to fib over the phone and say I miss them too. "I hope you're having a nice holi-day," I add, and then regret it, because of course they're not. They're having the worst holiday ever. Before the silence can grow longer and more awkward, I change the subject. "Are you making your usual yummy roast?"

"Yes, I am. The Denofreys are coming for dinner. In fact, I was about to put it in the oven, so I'll pass you over to Jeffrey to say hello. Take care, dear."

"Jane!" The genuine pleasure in his voice makes me feel bad about not calling sooner. I should have called on Thanksgiving. This whole time of year must be killing them—holiday after holiday, and then Ryan's birthday in February. "Thank you so much for the homemade cookies. It was kind of you, and smart to send them to the office so Barbara couldn't keep me out of them!" He laughs, and the sound's as beautiful as sleigh bells. "They were delicious."

"I'm glad you enjoyed them." Okay, what the hell else do I say? "Barbara said the Denofreys are coming over?"

"Yes . . . it helps, having others around." The laughter in his voice fades. Serious subject change needed. I ask how his company's doing. "We still haven't found a new CFO." Another bad topic choice. Of course, work makes him think of Ryan. Everything does. I try to come up with something else, but he saves me by asking how I like the B&B. I try to make it sound like it's wonderful, but not *too* wonderful. I don't want them to know I'm not missing Ryan the way I ought to be. Now I feel terrible about remembering the fight Ryan and I had last Christmas over the stupid perfume. What's the point in remembering how we could make each other crazy?

"I hope you're doing well. We only want the best for you. That's what Ryan wanted too."

"I know, Jeffrey. Thanks. And I hope you have a good New Year." We promise to stay in touch, and I actually mean it. I hang up, intent on trying to honor Ryan by banishing the bad memories of our fights. I can focus on the good stuff, right? I think back to our first Christmas together, before we moved to Philly. We took Barnum down to Dog Beach and went for a long walk before going out to dinner that night at our favorite spot in Del Mar. Ryan made me laugh when he insisted on making an angel in the sand, and then we both cracked up when

Barnum joined him to roll on a clump of seaweed. Walking in shorts on a sunny beach, with Barnum trotting alongside, didn't call to mind the Norman Rockwell version of Christmas, but we loved it.

*

"LET'S LEAVE the dishes; it's present time!" Mom says. Busy all day, we'd put off opening presents until after dinner. We move into the den, where the meager pile sits next to a poinsettia with a shiny gold ribbon tied around its plastic pot. It looks a bit Grinchy compared with the tree and lights and over-the-top sparkly decorations Selene and I pulled out of storage and that cover every free inch of space in the common areas.

Four gifts await: two clumsily wrapped ones (a rawhide I bought for Maybe, and a stuffed duck for her from Selene), a gift bag with my present for Mom (I made Mom promise only one gift each), and a box in shiny foil paper with wired ribbon and bit of plastic holly from Mom to me. I fear it is clothing.

Yesterday, after Christmas Eve dinner, which Selene shared with Mom and me, Selene gave me a silver frame. She said since I didn't have any pictures in my room, she thought I might like to make it more personal. It was sweet, but now, at some point, I'll need to find my photo albums out in the shed so that I won't have an empty frame sitting on my dresser the rest of my time here. Anyway, I felt bad because I didn't think to get her anything. Ah, the true spirit of Christmas: feeling like shit over the often-awkward gift exchange. At least when Kai dropped by later in the evening, with cards and a bottle of wine for Selene and me, I was able to quickly put together a plate of cookies so he didn't leave empty-handed. It was nice of him to think of us, so maybe he's not a complete jerk after all. Luckily, he only stayed a minute, so my cheeks didn't have a chance to betray me in front of

Mom and Selene. Besides, I'd given myself a good talking-to after the laundry room incident.

First of all, Ryan hasn't been gone that long. Even if, to me, our marriage ended a long time ago, it's an affront to his memory to think of being with someone else already. Plus, I'm leaving town in a couple of months, so there's no point. And, I don't even like the guy. He's too old-fashioned and macho for me. He's probably one of those peaked-in-high-school guys. Mr. Big Man on Campus. Totally not my type. It's pathetic to be hot for someone I don't even like, so there'll be no more ridiculous blushing when he's around. And I'm not going to waste any more time thinking about him.

I look over at Mom smiling and nodding at me. She can't wait for me to open my present. She thrusts it at me before I even get comfortable. I pull my feet up under me, and she frowns. (I'm wearing my usual jeans and a SDSU sweatshirt, which she's sighed at off and on throughout the day. But hey, at least it's a red sweatshirt. Mom, in great contrast, wears a red, gray, and green plaid skirt, red angora sweater with a silver angel pin, black hose, and pumps. The bells on her earrings jingle every time she turns. It's not as cute as with Barnum.) I tear off the wrapping, and she makes an ooh sound, as if she can't believe I'm not saving the paper. Yanking the lid away reveals a bulky blue cardigan with a beagle appliquéd on one side and a giant bone on the other. I don't look up for fear she'll read my face.

"Try it on!" she says.

I look up. Her eyes are wide, hands clasped under her chin. She thinks this is the perfect gift. I can't help but smile, because if she's delusional enough to think that, she's not going to see through my fake gratitude. I contemplate leaving my sweatshirt on so I can say the sweater is too tight, but she probably won't fall for that. *Please let the sleeves be too short,* I pray. After all, at my height, it's a common problem. But no. It fits. Geez Louise.

"What do you think?" she asks.

"It fits great." No lie there. "It's very warm." Again, no lie.

"I'm so glad you like it!" I never said that, but whatever. Delusional. "I saw it at Sears, and it had your name all over it. Okay, now me!" She claps her hands. "Oooo, a silk scarf! Pretty, pretty, pretty." She glides the fabric across her cheek. "Oh, there's more! Perfume!" It was a gift with purchase, but she doesn't need to know that.

We watch Maybe tear open her packages. She stands on them and rips the paper off with her teeth. I've been keeping an eye on her. She's not limping anymore, but then we haven't done much the last few days—just quick jaunts around the yard or a game of tug—since we've been busy getting ready for the Christmas rush. It occurs to me now she hasn't corncobbed me in days, even with the minimal exercise. Weird. Could she be maturing?

Mom makes cocoa, and we settle in to watch *It's a Wonderful Life*. Mom wears her new scarf, Maybe gnaws her rawhide, and I sweat in my way-too-cozy beagle sweater.

"You seem happy here, hon." Mom mutes the TV during a commercial.

I grunt. *Do I?* Her delusions again, or do I actually *seem* happy? Well, whether I am or not is irrelevant, since I'm not staying. Where can a person open-water swim in this town? And there's no beach for volleyball.

"Hellooo?" I hop up, feeling ridiculous in my sweater. I go out to the kitchen, and one of the guests holds open the swinging door. "Sorry to interrupt." An actual apology for ignoring the "Private" sign. That's a first. "But I wondered if you had any more of this lotion." She waggles the travel-size bottle we put in each bathroom. "We're from Seattle, and I'm finding it so dry here!"

"Oh, Mrs. Wilson, hello." Mom emerges behind me. "You're right; it is very dry here." She pokes me. "Get her some more lotion, Jane."

"One sec." I go out into the hall. It takes me a few minutes because I knock over a box of little shampoo bottles and have to retrieve them.

Back in the kitchen, I find Mom dishing up two pieces of the delicious pecan pie I made for our dessert. "You take that up to Mr. Wilson, and I'm sure he'll find it an improvement over what you had at the restaurant."

"What are you doing?" I try to sound light and cheery and not oh-so-very peeved.

"Mrs. Wilson was telling me how they had a lovely dinner downtown, but the dessert was such a disappointment they didn't eat it."

"This looks delicious," Mrs. Wilson says, happily accepting the plates. She juts her right hip at me, and I realize I'm meant to drop the lotion into the pocket of her cardigan. I thought I was being so generous, bringing her three extra bottles, but now I see Mom is the generous one. "The thing is we're here with the Baumgartners. We're playing cards in our room, so I need two more pieces." She might have mentioned this before accepting the first two.

I'm about to get a knife to cut the pieces she's got in half. There. Solved. But Mom leaps in, the Wonder Woman of Pie, and scoots another piece onto each plate. She slips four forks into the pocket on Mrs. Wilson's proffered left hip.

"Fabulous. Merry, merry!" And she's off, along with the last of my pie. She turns back. "You really ought to consider putting bigger bottles of lotion in the rooms. It's so dry. And people can't fly with more than three ounces." She smiles and says, "Thanks again."

"You gave away my pie," I say when we're alone.

"We already had our pieces."

"I was hoping to have leftovers tomorrow. And I was saving some for Selene."

"But look how happy Mrs. Wilson was!"

"Yeah, look how happy you made the person who interrupted our Christmas night to come in and complain."

"She didn't complain; she made a suggestion. And now she'll think this is a wonderful place and want to come back again."

"You're too nice."

"One of us ought to be."

"I'm not mean, if that's what you're implying." I point upstairs. "I gave her *three* bottles of lotion."

"I didn't say you were mean. But you're not exactly nice either. You're . . . closed off." She holds her left hand in her right, and studies her wedding band, which she's never stopped wearing. "Like your father." Mom fluffs her silk scarf. "All I'm saying is that it's not that hard to be nice. You should try it sometime. And Christmas is the perfect time to be a little merry." She sashays back to the den.

"I've been merry. Didn't I make barn- and chicken-shaped gingerbread cookies for the rooms? I frosted feathers onto their chicken tails!" I follow along after her.

"Those were pretty adorable," she admits with a half smile.

We resume our places on the sofa and finish watching the movie. I've always felt an affinity with this movie—probably because George Bailey shares our surname. Plus, I can relate to that "the world would be better off without me" sulking. I've been there a time or two. The only bummer is that no angel would come and show me what a difference I made to the world. I didn't save my nonexistent younger brother, who went on to save a ship full of troops. I didn't save a town from a greedy old bastard. All I did was save one skinny dog from the side of the road. It's not exactly the stuff of movies.

ALTHOUGH I'M BEAT from sleeping like crap for three days, I lie awake, listening to Maybe breathe at the other end of the sofa, and contemplate reasons I dislike people so much:

1. Only-child syndrome. That's the root cause. If I had some siblings—even one—then I'd have learned about sharing and tolerance and not calling people names under my breath. (Actually, maybe I'd have done more name-calling, but at least I'd have learned sharing and tolerance.)

2. Teasing, part (a): tall at twenty is great; tall at twelve sucks. I was the Kareem Abdul-Jabbar of fifth grade, and, unfortunately, nuns are übermilitant about lining up kids by height. Nothing like having my most freakish feature highlighted daily when we'd line up after recess to trudge to class. To this day, if I hear, "Line up!" my head sinks between my shoulders.

3. Teasing, part (b): Mom made it worse by not accepting my tomboy ways. Although Bermuda shorts were an option with our uniform, she bought the skirt. Trees still begged to be climbed, so she switched to pants. It's not like I'd have frozen in shorts. It was San Diego! But, no, she insisted on the pants; and twelve hours later, I'd grow half an inch, and then be even more of a dork in my floods. Kenny Willis, head asshat at school, started a chant: "Jane" with the obvious "plain"; "freak" paired with "geek." In sixth grade, he and his moronic friends pinned me to the chain-link fence and made me smoke a cigarette—to help stunt my growth. At least I didn't cry. And I didn't throw up until after Karen chased them off with a softball bat.

Basically, most people just annoy me. It's that simple. If they weren't generally such idiots, they wouldn't annoy me so much. But they are, and they do.

CHAPTER 14
LIMPING ALONG

I hate this exam room. Maybe's never been here before (as far as I know), so she explores the corners and waves her tail; but to me, it's a bad reminder of Barnum's cancer. Veterinarian offices always have that smell—that mix of pet dander, disinfectant, and . . . I'm not sure what the other thing is . . . probably the scent of abject fear when the owner hears a diagnosis. And the estimate of what it will cost to treat it. Don't they ever have windows in these places? I'm looking at the usual mélange of pet art (a photo of a cat asleep on a keyboard, a drawing of a pug sniffing a daisy) alongside posters about gingivitis in dogs and Lyme disease, when the vet comes in.

"What brings the beautiful Maybe in to see us today?" Dr. Leo wears a slick ponytail and no makeup; she has a no-nonsense manner and doesn't bother with chitchat. Behind her horn-rimmed glasses, her eyes focus on the dog. I like her.

I explain how Maybe started limping on our hike, then stopped for a while, but started again on Friday. It was late morning after break-fast service when we'd headed down to the stream. I'd been trying to avoid Kai, but we ran into him and Milo there. Of course, Maybe had wanted to play, but when she yelped and started limping after attempting to leap over Milo, it was a good excuse to get the heck out of there. Friday was New Year's Day, so there was no chance to bring her in; plus, I thought it was a simple strain and would improve with some downtime. "I kept her quiet all weekend, which wasn't super easy, but even with the forced rest, she was still limping this morning."

Dr. Leo crouches next to Maybe, who leans against the beige wall, favoring her right front paw. The doctor speaks soothingly while she palpates the leg. Maybe tries to pull away.

"It's too soon to rush to do an X-ray," she says, filling me with relief, since I know doggy X-rays aren't cheap. "I'll give you something to make her sleepy. That will help keep her quiet, and give the leg time to heal. If she's still limping by next week, bring her back in."

I collect the pills and pay for the exam. Seventy bucks. I'm going to have to call and broach the subject of vet bills with Uncle Graham. I hate to bug them about this, since I'm sure they're nervous about Aunt Sugar's surgery, scheduled for this Friday, but Maybe's their dog, so I need to talk to them. In fact, I should have called them before I scheduled the appointment, but I'm hoping it'll turn out to be nothing.

Back at home, Maybe laps up a pill hidden in a spoonful of peanut butter, and crashes. Either this is an instant miracle pill, or the excitement and stress of the vet visit tired her out. I'm guessing it's the latter, but hoping the pills will help.

I go to my room to check e-mail when my cell rings. It's Aunt Sugar, which is surprising since this is the first time they've called me, instead of the other way around. Anyway, it's fortuitous timing.

"Hi, Aunt Sugar." Nothing. "Aunt Sugar?" I strain to hear faint voices. Tinny music plays, maybe "Beyond the Sea"? "Aunt Sugar," I yell into the phone.

I hear rustling; she must be fumbling with the phone. The music stops.

"Jane?"

"Yeah. What's going on?"

"Oh! I must have booty called you. We're just pulling into a Denny's." She laughs, and I hear her say to my uncle, "The phone was in my back pocket; I booty called Jane!" Speaking to me again she says, "I know you showed me how to lock these buttons, but I forgot."

"You did *not* booty call me. I think you mean butt dialed." Another Sugarism is born.

"*Butt dialed* sounds so coarse. *Booty called* sounds much nicer."

I am not about to define the phrase for her, so I change the subject. "I'm glad you called, even if it was accidental." I tell her about Maybe.

She sounds worried, but assures me they'll repay me. She tells me to do whatever I think is best. "I know you'll treat her like she's your own. Give that pretty girl a big hug from us. No, wait, make it two separate hugs!"

I say I'll call in a few days to check in before her surgery. She says how nice it's been spending time with her sister and niece. She asks about my job hunting, and I tell her there's nothing new. I haven't heard back yet from any of the three positions I applied for. Nowadays, companies get so many resumes, you don't know if they haven't responded because they're still wading through them, or they just don't have the time to formally reject each one. Rejection sucks, but it's better than limbo. I change the subject to the Chick, saying it'll be good to have some downtime now that the holidays are over. New Year's Eve was a bear. The guests were all up or coming in late, and then we still had to get up at o'dark thirty to make an extra-special New Year's Day breakfast. Happy New Year to me.

"Again, honey, we want to say how much we appreciate what you're doing," she says, making me feel guilty for my negative thoughts about the Chick. "I know you had some doubts, but the hard part's over! The rest should be smooth sailing until we're back." She's right. I should stop my internal whining. "And you know, we'll head home right after my rehab if you get a job and need us to hurry back. Promise you'll let us know if you need us to scoot our fannies on back there."

I promise, and we hang up. Oh, that is a promise I'd love to hold them to, but, at this rate, I feel perched at the edge of the Grand Canyon, with my new life out of reach on the far rim. It's close enough to see, but still damn far away.

Perhaps a cookie will make everything seem better.

In the kitchen, I find Maybe still crashed in a sunny spot, and Selene working at the laptop in the corner nook.

She waves me over. "Look at this. Are these your in-laws?"

"What?" I don't have in-laws anymore. I have *former* in-laws. She points at a notice in the online reservation system. "The Waynesfields; that's them."

"They reserved for the second weekend in February. In the dietary restrictions comment box, they wrote 'Surprise! See you soon, Jane.' I thought it might be them."

"Oh geez. Does it say anything else?" Ryan's birthday falls on that Saturday. Do they think I need help to get through it? Or do they need my support?

"No, nothing else. They're not allergic to anything, are they?"

"Barbara's allergic to sugar and butter and, well, fat in pretty much all its forms; Jeffrey will eat anything. I better go call them."

In my room, I dial and hope Jeffrey will pick up. He answers on the second ring. "Jane! Are you calling about our surprise?"

"I am. You definitely surprised me."

"We've been talking about coming to visit for a while. We wanted to know how you're doing." *I could tell you that in an e-mail. I'm fine. There, done.* "I told Barbara it'd be fun to surprise you. She wanted to call and make sure you were okay with us coming, but it's not the same as dropping in uninvited—after all, you live in a B&B now!"

The surprise will be on them if I'm lucky enough to get a job and be outta here. "You know there's a chance I might be back in San Diego by then."

"If you are, we'll change our flights. We talked about coming sooner, but Ryan's birthday seems like the perfect time." He pauses and adds, "His fortieth."

It just plain sucks that Ryan died so damn young, but that seems like an inappropriate thing to say to his dad. "It's awfully far to come for a long weekend."

"It's already arranged!" I'm glad to hear his usual robust voice again. "We're flying into Phoenix on that Friday and renting a car. You should invite your mother too."

"That's nice of you to think of her. She'd like that." It'll be easier to deal with Barbara with Mom around.

I call Mom and tell her the news.

"Oh, I'm tickled pink they wanted to invite me as well. It'll be nice to see them again." She pauses for a moment. "Funny, though, Barbara didn't mention anything about it in her letter last week."

"Whaddya mean?" Geez Louise, my mother corresponds with Barbara? I start to panic, wondering if she's mentioned anything about Ryan's ashes.

"We've been writing to one another off and on for some time now. In fact, I'd been thinking of suggesting that we all go to Maui for Ryan's birthday. So funny that you called, because I was planning to call you about that very thing this week."

My pulse throbs in my knuckles as I clutch the phone tighter. "But you didn't suggest that, right? You didn't say anything about Ryan's ashes, did you?"

"No-o!" She adds an extra syllable to the word for emphasis. "I wouldn't suggest such a thing without asking you first. Oh well, if they've already booked their flight to Arizona . . ."

"Mom, please, please, please remember that I don't have the time or the money to go to Maui anytime soon, so don't bring up Ryan's ashes while they're here. Please."

"All right. I won't say a peep." We say our good-byes and hang up. Although the visit is almost six weeks away, I'm pretty sure she goes and starts packing.

*

I OPEN THE side door and step out into the freezing, but sunny, January morning. The cold here feels different from the lung-burning winters in Philly. Here, it's got a crispness to it that I'm beginning to enjoy, like biting into a green apple that's been in the fridge. On my way to the shed with my basket of laundry, I hear Kai call out a hello. Under his usual big suede jacket, he's got that green chamois shirt on again. The one that makes his eyes look so nice.

He walks up the rise to where I stand on the path and points at my basket. "Want me to help you with that?"

I shake my head. "It's just some sheets. I've got it."

"Haven't seen you and Maybe by the stream lately. Milo misses her." It's eleven thirty on a Wednesday. Why isn't he at work?

"She's still limping. I have to dope her up and keep her quiet." I rest the basket on my hip. "Hopefully, she'll heal up soon. I gotta get this load started, so—"

"Wait, I, uh, was thinking maybe we could get a beer one night." He runs his hand over his barely there hair. "I mean you, me, and Selene."

"I dunno, we—" *Think of an excuse. Any excuse.*

"I mentioned it to Selene, and she said tomorrow's good. She said things are pretty quiet until the long weekend." He shrugs his shoulders, then rubs the top of his head again. Selene and her blabbermouth.

It's true; we're empty until ten days from now, at the start of the Martin Luther King Jr. holiday weekend.

"You guys should go. Have fun." If I could get Selene to go without me, I could have a nice quiet night at home, alone. Much more appealing than making conversation all night. "I should stay home, you know, in case . . ." I've got nothing. In case *what*? It's not like we have any guests. Even if we did, we don't have to constantly be in the house with them. And it's not as though I have anything else going on in my life in this town. "In case Maybe needs me."

"She'll be fine. She'll sleep. She's doped up, right? The quiet'll be good for her. And Selene said you guys could use a night out."

Thanks, Selene.

*

SELENE AND I pull into a parking space on Gurley Street, almost right in front of the Burl Wood Bar. I don't see Kai's truck anywhere. With any luck, he won't show, and after Selene and I down a quick beer, I can go back to the Chick and Maybe and my waiting bed.

It's cold tonight, so it's pleasant to enter the warmth of the bar. Not pleasant enough to make me glad that I came, but still, there's a quiet coziness to the place, plus the comforting yeasty smell of beer. There are only a few other patrons, which is how bars ought to be. I look around, sort of anticipating we'll get to see Betty, the town drunk, my twin. If she's in here, hopefully there won't be any confusion, since I brushed my hair and traded my usual grubby sweatshirt for a wool sweater. I'm disappointed not to see any female winos—only a few young guys sitting at the bar, in their dress slacks and shirts. Seeing them, I realize what a dork I am. I expected that small-town bars in Arizona would be filled with leathery cowboys in faded Levi's, flashy belt buckles, and ten-gallon hats, instead of just regular folks.

Selene points to a table in the back. We pull out our chairs, and they scrape on the wood floor that's littered with peanut shells. On the jukebox, a country singer I don't recognize (since I don't listen to country music other than the classic stuff like Waylon Jennings and Johnny Cash) whines about her troubles.

The waitress saunters over and tosses cardboard Michelob coasters on the table. She takes our order with one word: "Waddillyahave?" We order Stella Artois since that's Selene's favorite. She's always got a few bottles stashed in the fridge at the Chick, and she's gotten me hooked too. While we wait, I tell her I think Maybe seems to be getting better. "I just took her for a short spin around the yard to pee, and she seemed not to be limping as much."

"Good," she says. "We'll drink to that if the waitress ever brings our beers."

There's a rush of cold air as the door opens. We turn to look, but it's not Kai—just some hunched old man, walking slower than our waitress. And then I see Kai, looming behind the man. At first I think Kai's jostling for position, trying to work his way around, but then I realize he's steering the old guy our way.

Selene inches her chair closer to mine, leans in, and whispers, "He's cute, don't you think?"

I know what she means, and Kai does look especially handsome in a navy-blue wool sweater with a gray stripe across the chest and around his biceps. But, really, what the hell is Selene thinking? As far as she knows, I'm a grieving widow. And I'm not here to meet men; I'm passing through. I say, out of the side of my mouth, "The old guy? He's adorable."

She pokes me, and then leans back, smiling broadly. "You brought your gramps," Selene calls out to them.

Kai waves an awkward hello as they continue their slow progress. The old man's feet skim the ground with each step, and I'm afraid the peanut shells are going to be his downfall. Kai reaches for the old man's elbow, but he yanks his arm away and sets his jaw. I can see where Kai gets his square jaw from. The old man reaches for the closest seat, next to me. I think we're all relieved when he's settled. He wears a purple-and-white polyester trucker's hat that says "Magnusson Grain," and his face tells of the many furrows he's plowed in his day. I'm guessing he witnessed most of the last century; he's at least eighty-five if he's a day.

Kai takes the seat next to Selene. "Gramps, this is Jane and Selene. Ladies, this is my grandfather, Mr. Magnusson."

"Call me Weaver," he barks.

"Hello, Mr. Magnusson. Sorry, I mean, Weaver." Selene holds out a hand. "It's nice to meet you." I'm confused, since I didn't know Kai had any family in town, but Selene fills me in. "Weaver lives with Kai."

Weaver either ignores or doesn't see Selene's hand. "Where's the waitress?" He looks at the empty table and twists in his chair. With his back to me, the glow from the giant TV hanging at the end of the bar shines through his impressive ears.

The waitress returns with our Stellas. A smile lights her face at the sight of Kai. "What can I get for you, darlin'?" she asks in a voice that's all satin and honey.

"I'll have a boilermaker," Weaver says to her backside. She's clearly only interested in Kai.

"Gramps, maybe you should just have a beer. That's what everyone else is having."

"I'm having a boilermaker." He pokes at the waitress with his knuckle, which sticks out from the sleeve of the frayed canvas jacket he's lost in, and says, "Bring my nursemaid here one of those sissy light beers—the kind they put fruit in."

Kai leans toward him. "You said you'd be nice if I brought you." To the waitress, he says, "I'll have a Guinness." Damn. I forgot how much I like Guinness. I should've ordered that. I haven't been out for a beer in forever. I can't even remember how to do it right.

The fact that Kai's grandfather is here changes the dynamic I'd been expecting. I'd figured we'd talk about the Chick. Now I'm not sure what we'll talk about. I can't remember ever making conversation with an eighty-year-old before, my grandparents all having passed away long ago. I assume one talks to them about the same sort of things you'd talk to anyone about, but since I'm useless at small talk, I sit back and let someone else drive.

"It was freezing today, wasn't it?" Selene asks.

"It's February; whaddya expect?" Weaver says. "This ain't Miami Beach."

"True." She's undaunted, bless her. "But the winters here must be better than when you lived in Idaho."

"You're likely to freeze your left nut in Idaho this time of year."

"Gramps," Kai says as the waitress appears with the rest of the drinks.

Weaver downs his shot of whiskey in a surprisingly nimble move. He smacks his lips and lets out a satisfied, "Ah." He reaches for his beer and slurps. "That's more like it," he says. "Ain't one drop of whiskey in the house." He jabs a finger in Kai's direction. "All he keeps in the house is beer and wine. Wine." His disdain for the beverage is clear.

"Some people like a nice glass of wine with a meal," Kai says. I wouldn't have taken Kai for a wine-with-dinner kind of guy. The two of them squabble while Selene and I sip our beers and look around the room. Silence falls. We look at the TV, tuned to ESPN, hoping some sporting event will save us. But a hockey game has just ended, and it's followed by one of those interminable ads for erectile dysfunction medication.

"So, how long have you two lived together?" I ask, trying to divert attention from the embarrassing commercial.

They answer together: "Eleven months" from Kai, and "Too long" from Weaver. "He's waiting for me to die," Weaver adds.

"I am not." Kai's closes his eyes for a moment as he answers. Maybe I'm reading too much into it, but he looks like he could have used a night off from his grandfather.

"Why don't you two play some darts," I suggest, nodding at Kai and Selene. The poor guy deserves a break, but I don't want to play with him.

Kai looks at me and glances at his grandfather while the old man leans in for another slurp of beer. "Yeah?" he says, although his raised eyebrows say, "Are you sure?"

"Yeah, go ahead. We'll be fine." I wouldn't normally go out of my way to hang out alone with someone I just met, but Weaver strikes me as the kind of no-bs conversationalist—a fellow curmudgeon—who's happy to sit mute rather than suffer the inanity of small talk, and if that works for him, it works for me.

Weaver and I drink in silence, except for the slurping sounds he makes, while Kai and Selene play. Selene's squeal when she hits the bull's-eye on her third throw draws our attention. Kai laughs and says, "Boy, I didn't know I was playing a ringer."

Weaver and I watch for a while, and all of us but Kai laugh when he misses the board, his dart driving into the wall. "Waitress, cut this man off!" Selene jokes.

Weaver turns to me and says, "In my day, a woman didn't show up a man at sports."

"Oh, come on," I tease. "In your day the only 'sport' was hunting wooly mammoths."

Weaver looks at me, assesses my face, then bursts out with a loud guffaw. I can see his bottom denture shift when he laughs.

"I like you. You call 'em like you see 'em."

"Thanks."

"We should do this more often." He lands a glancing blow on the table with the side of his hand. "Get out, have a drink."

"You two don't go out much?"

"No, we sit at home and eat well-balanced, low-sodium meals. He comes home like clockwork every day to ensure I'm eating a proper lunch. Like Slim Jims dipped in Cheez Whiz ain't a proper lunch." Ah, that explains why Kai's always around when I take Maybe for her walk after the breakfast service. That's kind of sweet that he takes such good care of his grandfather. "And we watch educational bunk on PBS." PBS? Huh. "And the History Channel. Like I want to relive all that. Then we turn in early. We rise." He pauses, then adds with a growl, "We shine. You'd think he was trying to keep me around. He outta take me out at night, knock back a few! Be rid of me sooner."

"Maybe he likes having you around."

"Ha!" He contemplates his near-empty beer glass. "He don't need me. What he needs is a woman. Why, I ain't worth a hoot without my Viola, God rest her soul." He swipes at the corner of his eye with the cuff of his jacket. "Anyway, that's why I wanted to come along. Check out this gal he mentioned."

I lean in and whisper, "Selene?"

"He never said her name, but he talked about this gal that works next door. I teased him about being sweet on her. He said it ain't nothing; they're friends. I said I'd see for myself." I knew Selene liked him, but I figured they were just friends too. We watch them finish their game. Kai's face is shadowed, his head hung in mock shame over his loss; but Selene's face, laughing as she performs her victory dance, gleams in the rosy light of a faux Tiffany lamp. She dances over and links her arm through Kai's, leading him back to the table. They grin at each other. She's so petite and adorable next to his big bear frame. It does make sense for them to get together. They're both attractive, single Prescottonians. They'd make a great couple—she's the moon goddess; he's the ocean. It couldn't be a more perfect match if their names were Raspberry and Chocolate.

If Kai wanted to go out with Selene, though, why'd he invite me along? Guess he's shy. Which is kind of cute, in a way. And that's why she asked me if I thought he was cute—not to pique my interest, but because *she's* interested in him. *Of course he's cute, Selene. He's kind of a stud, as a matter of fact. You don't need my approval.* She's a bit shy too, I guess.

Well, this is good news, I think. I mean, I have no business being interested in him. And clearly he's not interested in me. So, yeah. Selene should go for it.

Weaver looks like he's about to nod off in the cocoon of his coat, so Kai says they better go. He helps Weaver up, and we say our good-byes. As they reach the door, Weaver turns back. "Jane," he calls, "you on Facebook? Friend me!" as Kai steers him out into the night.

When Selene and I get up to leave a few minutes later, Selene says, "Oh, sorry I didn't notice and mention this earlier, but your sweater is covered in dog hair."

THAT NIGHT IN bed, I keep thinking about what Weaver said and about what a beautiful couple Kai and Selene make. I don't know why I can't stop thinking about it. Could I be a little jealous? I mean, not so much that Kai likes her, but just jealous of the fact that they get to go through that whole infatuation thing. Thinking of Ryan, I remember how great it is when you first fall in love. Anyway, I'm glad he likes her. Now, to turn my mind to another subject, I think of uses for Maybe's hair. (Barnum was a shedder, but he was a total amateur compared to this girl.):

1. Build another dog, or a whole pack of dogs—plenty for a peck of Pomeranians.
2. Knit a stocking cap or scarf or sweater or king-size picnic blanket.
3. Scatter outdoors for the birds to pick up for nesting materials. They'd be the coziest baby birds in town.
4. Fashion Halloween costumes: make a wig and moustache à la Einstein, or dye it dark and form a Frida Kahlo unibrow.
5. Stuff pillows as an alternative to down, for people afflicted with goose allergies.
6. Staunch oil well leaks.
7. Repel any potential suitors by going out in public with it all over oneself so as to resemble a human lint brush.

CHAPTER 15
COME ON, INFECTION!

Dr. Leo's mouth moves. Words come out, and I hear sounds, like the underwater warbling of an adult in a Charlie Brown cartoon. All I can think is, *No, this is not happening again.*

"But let's wait and see." Dr. Leo's words reach me as she takes Maybe's leash.

I can't breathe. My ribs feel like I'm in an old-fashioned corset; an unseen hand tightens the stays. *Stop freaking out.* I never should have asked for the worst-case scenario. Dr. Leo is still speaking, but I can't look at her, or at Maybe. I stare at the gingivitis poster. Why can't she have gingivitis? *That* we could deal with. We'd buy a fricking toothbrush.

"Ms. Bailey? Are you okay?" I blink and look at the vet in her clinical white coat. "It's unlikely to be cancer, since she's so young. I only mentioned it because you pressed me for all possibilities. Let's see what the X-ray shows. As I said, the most likely case is an infection in the bone. Since she's a stray, and we don't know her history, there could have been some sort of trauma to that area, a small wound perhaps. Also, valley fever is common in this area."

"Right." I nod. "Infection."

"We'll just be a few minutes," she says, and leads Maybe out.

I'm glad to be alone, but still, I don't want to cry. Not here. Why am I going to cry anyway? I haven't known this dog that long. She's not even mine. But I scrunch up my face as tears pinprick the backs of my eyeballs. *Not again, not again, not again. Don't cry, don't cry, don't cry.* I dig my nails into my palms. Geez Louise, this is just like with Barnum. It's too soon to have to deal with this again. This is exactly why I'm never getting another dog. They all die. Sooner or later, they die.

She was getting better. Or maybe, I convinced myself of that. But, no, it wasn't just me; Selene said the limp seemed better too. But then this morning when we got up, a visible lump stood out on her skinny leg. I made an appointment right away, worried it might be something bad—but not *this* bad. Not *cancer* bad.

Okay, don't assume the worst. Rooting for infection!

But how can I not assume the worst, after what I've been through this year? For Pete's sake, Maybe's just a puppy.

Dr. Leo is going to think I'm a basket case. Get it together. Think of something funny.

Drawing a blank.

Or maddening, like the stupid guests at the Chick. Oh, like what the hell was that guy in the Sicilian Buttercup room doing this morning? I heard the shower when I walked past the room, and I also heard god-awful honking, hacking, and spitting sounds. Good thing the rooms on either side were empty. Repulsive.

While I focus on Mr. Repulsive, I lean against the wall and pick Maybe hairs off my sweatshirt, one by one. I collect them in the palm of my hand.

Dr. Leo opens the door, and Maybe limps over, wiggling and happy, to kiss me.

*

THAT AFTERNOON ON the phone with Uncle Graham, I don't mention the C-word. It's only been a few days since Aunt Sugar's surgery, and she's loopier than usual from the pain meds, so I just talk to Uncle Graham.

"The vet took an X-ray. She said she didn't want to give me her opinion until she sends the films to a radiologist." Which of course makes me think she suspects it is, in fact, bone cancer. But Uncle Graham doesn't need to know that. I haven't told Selene either. If I don't say it out loud, it won't be true. I did some research online when we got home, and it's not unheard of for young dogs to develop osteosarcoma—a genetic anomaly. Although it can strike any breed, it's most common in large dogs. Maybe's tall, with her long legs, but at under fifty pounds, she's certainly not large. She's a sprite. And I would have thought we'd be in the clear, what with her being a mixed bag of dog-knows-what. "She said it might be a day or two before we hear." I stopped searching for more information when I saw the word *aggressive*. I had to stop freaking myself out; it might not be cancer. Why scare the hell out of myself?

"It's not a simple sprain then?"

"Uh-uh." I explain what Dr. Leo said about a possible prior injury resulting in an infection or maybe valley fever.

"Alrighty then," he says, as if there's nothing to worry about. Of course he thinks there *is* nothing to worry about.

My eyes start to burn. "Okay then." I want to add that I'll call as soon as I know more, but I'm afraid my voice will give away the fact that I'm hiding potentially bad news.

"Call as soon as you hear from Dr. Leo. That poor pup. Who knows what happened to her, what sort of life she had before you rescued her. You're her angel, Janie."

*

IT'S A QUIET, empty morning at the Chick, and Selene takes advantage and sleeps in. I'm drinking coffee and reading the paper, a drugged Maybe at my feet. The phone rings. "Hello," a heavy British accent says, "my wife and I hoped you might have a room available?"

"Yes, we have some rooms." We have *all* the rooms. I pull up the reservation system.

"We looked at your website; we'd like the Rhode Island Red." I'm surprised someone would ask for the chicken bordello, but to each his own.

He books it for tonight and asks what time they can check in.

"Three o'clock."

When Selene gets up, I tell her about the call. After breakfast, she goes to prep the room. At lunchtime, we meet up for ham sandwiches, until a tooting horn interrupts our meal.

Selene goes to the window. "It's an older guy; he's motioning for me to come out." She washes her hands and heads out the kitchen door.

"Hello!" I hear. I look out and see a squat couple, in woolen hats, getting out of a sedan. "We're the Martins. We called earlier. We're checking in, and wondered if you might have someone who could help with our bag. Bit of a bad back, I'm afraid."

"Sure." Selene goes to help.

"I was thinking there'd be a gent. There's a man in the pictures on your website." On the About Us page, a photo shows Uncle Graham, about twenty years and thirty pounds ago, waving from the porch; another depicts Aunt Sugar dishing up a platter of her Sunday biscuits and gravy.

"Sorry, no gents today. Don't worry; I'm strong." Selene flexes as she meets him at the trunk. "Check-in's not until three, but you're welcome to leave your suitcase till then."

"Oh." He looks across the top of the car at his wife. "I'm certain the girl on the phone said noon." *First of all, I'm a woman, you asshat, not a girl. And I know I said three o'clock.* "We'd love to get into our room. My wife has a bit of a migraine." He pronounces it *meegraine*, which I find annoying. I'm about to march out and argue, but Selene caves. Of course. Worse yet, she apologizes. She's sorry for the confusion; their room's ready.

She leads them on the path around the side of the house, to the front door, while I go back to the kitchen and my half-eaten sandwich.

A few minutes later, she stands in front of me, hands on hips. "They hate the Rhode Island Red. Said the room was supposed to have a Jacuzzi tub and a fireplace for that price. I realized they wanted Iowa Blue—it's described right above Rhode Island. They said the website's confusing." She throws up her hands. "I offered to move them to Iowa and still charge the Rhode Island rate, but they said they'd just stay put. As long as I knock twenty percent off!"

"You said they could have twenty percent off? That room's a bargain as it is."

"I agreed to *ten* percent off. I felt guilty. I could have made the site less confusing."

"You always feel guilty. It's the Cathlish in you."

"I know. I'm sorry." She winces. "But they threatened to leave. I figured ninety percent of a room rate's better than none."

I shrug and start cleaning up the remains of lunch. "I suppose Uncle Graham would have done the same. Still, I think they were working you."

"I don't think so. Anyway, I'm heading out for a Costco run. Can you hold down the fort?" She doesn't wait for me to answer. "I hope the vet calls while I'm gone," she adds. Dr. Leo still hasn't gotten back to me about Maybe's X-rays. She said it might be a day or two, and we are now at day two. I hate waiting.

"I hope so too," I say.

After Selene leaves, I go to my room, followed by a groggy, still-limping Maybe. I help her up on the bed (I've been trying to keep her from jumping), then start logging on to e-mail before my butt even hits the chair. Nothing new jobwise (bummer), but there's something from Mirabella. I don't get excited, because it's her usual once-a-week-or-so "Hope you're doing well! Miss you!" along with a forwarded message. I know it's meant as a sign she's thinking of me, and I get that she's insanely busy, but still, can't she write a few lines of news? It's one of those chain e-mails about the power of female friends, which is nice in a sappy way, but then at the bottom, it threatens me with bad luck if I don't send it to my ten best girlfriends. Even if I were the type to forward these things, I couldn't come up with a list of ten, "best" or otherwise, friends—men included. I prefer quality in friendships, not quantity. I'll take my chances with whatever wrath the universe sends my way.

You e-mail chain letters don't scare me. Bring it, Universe.

I hit the delete button.

CHAPTER 16

WOW, UNIVERSE.
YOU'RE QUICK.

As I delete Mirabella's blackmail note, another e-mail pops into my inbox. It's from the company I sent my resume to before Christmas, the one that wanted a market intelligence person who could do market sizings. My heart pounds as I click on it. It's short; my eyes fly over it, scanning for the word *interview*, which I don't see. I go back and read it: they thank me for my application, but they've found someone more suited to their needs. How is that possible? I had a bullet point on my resume for every single qualification listed. It ends with the standard verbiage about how they'll keep my resume on file, but I know that means the circular file.

"Fuck," I say aloud. I try to not swear at the Chick. For one thing, Aunt Sugar literally frowns upon it, and also, I wouldn't want a guest to overhear, but there's no one around except the Martins in their room upstairs. I smack my head against the doily-covered table, one, two, three times. The third time, I leave my head on the table. The heavy thread of the crocheted scallop edging digs into my flesh.

I was perfect for that job. I hadn't allowed myself to fantasize about how much I wanted it, but now that it's not going to happen, I want to scream. I read the e-mail again, slowly, while I rub the grooves in my forehead. They wish me every success. Sure they do.

I try to console myself. The two other places I applied to have made zero contact; at least this place sent a letter. It's probably a terrible place to work anyway. I bet I dodged a bullet. I didn't want to do market sizings anyway. Market sizings suck.

I slam my laptop shut and drag myself to the kitchen. The stupid afternoon cookies aren't going to make themselves. I should have asked Aunt Sugar about this type of situation. Does she still make cookies when only one room is occupied? Knowing my aunt, she does. Do these annoying people deserve cookies? No, they do not. But it says on the website that we put fresh cookies in the rooms every afternoon, and we know they've been on the site.

I take a deep breath. Maybe some tea first, something herbal. Although it's going to take a claw-foot tub full of herbal tea—enough to drown myself in—to make me feel better. Thank heaven everyone's gone. I don't want to talk to anyone.

I put the kettle on the stove and stand there and stare at it. I don't blink or move.

When am I going to get out of here? When am I going to find a job? Okay, calm down. It hasn't been that long. And the holidays are over, so things should start to pick up.

The water rat-a-tats the stainless steel sides of the kettle as I'm picturing the HR person who rejected my resume, a withered crone wielding a "Reject" stamp. The word feels stamped on my forehead. This sucks. I met every one of their criteria. How could they not have at least called?

It's got to be the Arizona address on my resume. I mentioned in my cover letter I'm moving back, but they probably wouldn't consider someone from out of state over a local. Mirabella will let me use her address for the time being. I hate to lie, but I'll be living in San Diego soon.

The kettle screams, scattering my thoughts. I reach for the knob to turn the stove off as Mr. Martin bursts through the swinging kitchen door.

At the top of a long list of "things I really can't deal with right now" is having a guest—especially one that already annoys me—in my kitchen.

"I knew I heard a kettle." He eyes me and my mug. The hair mounted atop his head displays a much-too-even-toned caramel color, compared with the rest of his gray fringe. He wears a mustard-yellow cardigan over a beige dress shirt and rumpled tan slacks. A kelly green bowtie tops off his outfit, which seems a bit much for vacation wear. "Precisely what I was looking for!"

"The kitchen's not open to guests."

"But this is a B&B," he says, as if that explains everything.

"Exactly. Bed and breakfast." I point at the ridiculous rooster clock with its chicken feet hands. "It's past noon." What part of *breakfast* does the guy not understand? "Tomorrow—at breakfast—there will be tea." I know I'm being rude. I don't care. This guy's a jerk.

"But I have my own tea." He produces a sachet. "If I could trouble you for a bit of hot water, I'll be out of your hair in a jiff."

"Fine." I'm not in a sharing mood, but I want this guy out of my kitchen.

"And, of course, I'll need a mug."

Oh, of course. I'd planned on pouring the boiling water right into your cupped hands. I grunt and yank a mug out of the cupboard. I fill it with steaming water.

"Excellent." He smiles at me as he takes the cup and drops in his tea bag. I don't smile back. He stands there.

He looks down at the mug held in both hands, then at me from under his wild, overgrown eyebrows. My hands itch to take a Weedwacker to them. I so don't want to talk to this man that I develop annoyance-induced lockjaw. My voice comes out all Clint Eastwoody when I manage to say, "Is there a problem?"

"If you could spare a spot of milk and some sugar . . ." He points at my mug on the counter. "I thought you might be putting some in *your* tea."

I like honey in my tea, but I'd intended to wait until he left to doctor mine up because I knew he'd pester me for some. I don't say anything, but I'm pretty sure my perturbed message comes through loud and clear. The sugar bowl clatters when I pull it from the cupboard and plunk it on the counter. Yanking open the silverware drawer, I grab a spoon and drop it beside the sugar. I slam the fridge door with my hip after extracting the milk. I don't want to deal with these people anymore. I want to do what I used to do: sit in front of a computer for eight hours a day doing research and writing reports and being left alone and not having to wait on annoying people hand and foot. I've had it with people not reading the "Private" sign on the kitchen door. It's in caps, for Pete's sake. Don't people read anymore?

"Well, I have work to do." I lie, since after this encounter, I've decided, screw it—these people are not getting fresh cookies.

"If I could bother you for one more thing . . . My wife gets these meegraines, and nothing seems to help except a nap and wee nosh." He smiles in what I can only assume he thinks is a charming way.

I follow his eyes, which go to a rack of minimuffins behind me. They're from a failed attempt this morning at a new sweet potato and pecan recipe. I'd been meaning to dump them down the garbage disposal but hadn't gotten to it.

"Perhaps a muffin or two?"

"One of these muffins?" I reach behind me and hold one up in my right hand.

"Yes, and what about a slice of cheese. A spot of protein, don't you know."

"Oh, of course, cheese. Sure." This guy is too much. I pass the muffin to my left hand and reach for another with my right. My hands seem to move of their own accord.

"Would you have any soft cheeses? Perhaps some Camembert?"

I lose it at soft cheeses. I lob a muffin at him, and yell, "Here. Of course. Have a muffin." He catches it. It feels so good that I throw a second one, which bounces off his chest. I reach back for more ammo. Ohmigod, I know I shouldn't be doing it, but I unleash a minimuffin barrage. It's a rush, like great illicit sex. Not that I've had illicit sex, or great sex, or any sex in ages, but as far as I can recall, this is what it was like—the "I know it's wrong, but I can't stop myself!" release of pent-up frustrations.

"Miss, I . . . You're—" He tries to protect his face, but it's impossible, since his arms overflow with the tea and the spoon and the muffin he caught. He leans back and shrugs his right shoulder up, attempting to use his scapula as a shield. "I only wanted—" But it's too late; I can't stop. He drops everything on the counter, sloshing hot tea on his hand. "Blast!" He flees through the swinging door.

"Ha," I pant. "That'll teach you to come into my kitchen." *Jackass.*

I swipe at a hunk of hair that has fallen loose from my stubby ponytail and hangs in my face. Yanking the band out of my hair, I shake my head, hard. My hair's too thin to do that slo-mo swish-back-into-place thing like in shampoo commercials, plus the static electricity of this ridiculously dry air makes it stick out in eight hundred different directions. I look at the floor and see my shadow—a silhouette of thin clown hair, lit up by the afternoon sun streaming through the window. My eyes go fuzzy, then refocus on the spent ammo that litters the floor.

And now, as with illicit sex, the regret sets in on the heels of the release. I can feel the regret; it's on my back, scaling my shoulders, clutching at my throat.

I slide down the front of the cupboard, with its cheery yellow paint and faded red-stenciled hens pecking along in a chicken conga line. I collapse, cross-legged, on the rag rug. One muffin is mashed into the fringe of the rug where the enemy stomped on it as he retreated.

Crap. What did I just do? How am I going to explain this to Selene?

The sound of Selene's truck tires crunching the gravel of the drive had vaguely registered in the back of my brain as my freak-out had neared its crescendo. She's probably getting an earful from him right now. I should clean up the evidence before she comes in. But what's the point?

A few minutes later, the kitchen door swings open. Selene gasps. She takes in the mess with a blank, hard-to-read expression. I've never seen her angry, but a baked-good assault on a customer might push her to the edge of her eternally calm demeanor. She's got every right to scream. Fire me even. I may be the owners' niece, but Selene's the boss while they're gone.

I slump further and try to look pathetic. I certainly feel pathetic. As much as I hate working here right now, I can't get fired. I need the roof over my head.

"Wow. And here I thought Mr. Martin was exaggerating." She sighs and holds out a hand. "Come on, let's clean up. I'm dying to hear your version."

I wave off her hand and hug my knees to my chest. "I'm happy down here."

She sits on the opposite end of the rug and pulls her feet into lotus position like she's ready to meditate. I should've known she wouldn't be mad, but that look of understanding edged with pity—her eyes go soft but with a hint of a smile—makes me kind of nuts. I know she doesn't understand what I'm feeling. I like Selene, I really do, but I'd like her more if she'd stop feeling sorry for me.

"You know how it bugs me when they ignore the 'Private' sign."

"Other guests have come into the kitchen without facing all-out war."

"Plus, he was already on my bad side."

"I know."

"And then, after you left, I got this frickin' rejection e-mail for a position I really wanted. And . . . I guess I kinda took it out on Mr. Eyebrows."

She laughs. "Those things are something else, huh?"

"Yeah. Andy Rooney called. He wants his eyebrows back." She laughs again, and I start picking crumbs off the floor. "So, what did he say?"

"He said you're unhinged and that you frightened him."

"What? Oh, come on! Muffins, especially of the mini variety, are not frightening." I find an intact muffin under the cupboard and hold it aloft. "This is a wee baked good, not a weapon. It doesn't even have sharp edges." I saw at my wrist with it. "See?"

"He said you pelted him with muffins. He said that's battery."

"No." I hold the muffin up again and take a bite. "That's *buttery*." I make an *mmm* sound, then cough as I try to swallow. "Bleh. Man, these came out awful. Bitter." I remember now that Maybe came looking for me while I was in the middle of mixing up the batch. Her limp had me so worried, I must have added the baking powder twice.

Selene laughs again. "I know you didn't hurt him, but you get that it's not reasonable to throw food at a guest, right?"

I hang my head. "Yes, I know," I mutter. "I'm sorry." I get up and dump the mess of crumbs I've collected into the sink. "Were you able to smooth it over with him?"

"Yeah. But you might not like it." She gets up and crosses her arms.

"What did you do?" I turn my back to her, rinsing the sink.

"First of all, I told him I'd comp their room."

"What?" I spin around. "A free room? Because I zinged a few muffins off his head? He shouldn't have been in the kitchen. In fact, they shouldn't have been here at all until three! A free room is ridiculous."

"He writes a travel blog."

"So what? Everybody and their brother blogs. I doubt anybody reads the thing."

"He told me the name. I looked it up on my phone before I came in here. He has a lot of followers. Besides, he could leave a bad review on TripAdvisor. People read that stuff. I had to calm him down."

"Wait a minute. You said 'first of all.' What else did you do?"

"Don't be mad." She shifts from one foot to the other. "I, uh, told him you were recently widowed."

Hmmm. I turn to the sink and take my time washing my hands while I mull this over. She played the widow card. It occurs to me that I haven't thought about Ryan in . . . what, maybe a few days? I'd forgotten to feel the guilt of being the survivor. Without realizing it, I'd gone back to feeling like my old self. I wasn't good at being a wife, and I'm even worse at being a widow. When Selene mentions my widowed state, I feel it—that weight, the guilt—rush back.

"I'm sorry," she adds. "I know you don't like to talk about it. But I told him you're dealing with a lot of stress." She waits a moment, then asks, "Are we cool?"

I have to admit, I've played that card myself before, which is terrible. I don't deserve to have people cutting me slack on account of my husband's death—not like a real widow.

Still, this was for the good of the Chick, not me, so I guess it's okay. "We're cool," I say.

*

THAT EVENING, WE sit at the kitchen table in near darkness, with only the stove light on, and sip Stella Artois. We talk about my uncle and aunt. I wonder again what this dream is that Selene's been saving for. The way she talks, I get the sense she's holding back, that she doesn't want to quit and leave them hanging, since they depend on her for so much. I try to tell her that she's got to live her own life. It's the sort of conversation that would be better in front of a fire, or under the stars. But it's too cold to sit outside, and we're too tired to get up and go make a fire in the sitting room. With no night sky to contemplate, and no dancing flames to mesmerize us, we pick at the labels of our beer bottles.

"You know, you shouldn't let anything stand in the way of what you really want to do," I say. "If you have a dream, you should go for it."

"I know. I want to. Sometimes it isn't that easy, though, ya know?"

I think of my own dream, my longing to get back to San Diego, back to my old life. She's right. It's not always easy. Sometimes you know what your dream is, but it's beyond your grasp.

IN BED, I obsess about the rejection e-mail, and about how Dr. Leo hasn't called. Worries swirl in my head like cackling crows. Then I think about my fight with Eyebrow Man, which leads me to thinking about ways I've used being a widow:

1. Talked my way out of a ticket for rolling through a stop sign; widows get a pass for being distracted.
2. Before I left Philly, a telemarketer called and asked for Ryan. I said, "He passed away," and I actually enjoyed listening to the guy grovel and apologize profusely as I hung up. It was the most satisfying encounter I've ever had with a telemarketer.
3. I used it to get out of a particularly ugly project at work before I quit. I told my boss I'd do it, but that I wasn't feeling like I was at top form, so he said he'd do it himself. That was just wrong.
4. Today, I got a pass for rudeness. Rudeness tinged with over-the-top crazy.

I wonder if it's possible to work the whole widow-pity thing into guilt-sucking an interview out of some company. Maybe a carefully worded cover letter would do the trick. Would that make me a worse person than I already am? Probably.

CHAPTER 17
SOMETIMES YOU SUCK, UNIVERSE

"It's—" Dr. Leo takes the slightest hair's breadth of a pause. I clutch the phone, dreading what's coming next. "Cancer. Osteosarcoma." A longer pause. "I'm really sorry."

"She's just a puppy." My voice has taken on a weird pitch, like the vibrato tones a damp finger circling the lip of a half-filled wineglass makes. I could use a full wineglass right about now, even though it's only ten in the morning.

"I know; it's not fair. It's a fluke of her genetics. When it's in a young dog like this, it's nothing that happened to her, or chemicals she was exposed to, or anything like that. It's just one of those things."

"You're absolutely sure? Don't we need to do a biopsy or something?"

She explains that the radiologist is 99 percent certain it's bone cancer, due to the "classic sunburst pattern" of the tumor in the leg. She adds that a biopsy would only cost more money and, more importantly, cause Maybe more pain. "We can biopsy the tumor, to be certain, after the amputation."

"Amputation . . . ?" This can't be happening. I don't know what to say. She's less than two years old. It was a *limp*. I thought she just overdid it playing with Milo, and now she has fricking cancer, and the doctor wants to take her leg.

"I know it sounds extreme, but most dogs do very well on three legs. It's the best course of action, since bone cancer is extremely painful. Amputation isn't an option for every dog, but since Maybe's young and thin, she'll do great. I know this is a lot to take in, but right now, the obvious next step is a lung X-ray to see if the cancer has visibly metastasized yet. If the lungs look good, the amputation would take away her pain. She'd be back walking and playing as soon as she recovered; typically, that's about two weeks." She ends by saying that if we don't amputate, Maybe will most likely "not make it," as if Maybe's a contestant trying out for *American Idol*.

"Chemo will be another thing to consider." Chemo. I remember sitting with Ryan while he was hooked up to the IV. I hated those sessions; it felt like we were napalming his innards. And what good did it do? I know that pretty much any drug or medical procedure available for humans also has its canine equivalent, but can't imagine putting Maybe through that. I tell Dr. Leo as much, and she explains that chemo is different with dogs. "For one thing, with humans we hit them very hard, in an attempt to cure the disease; but for animals, it's a lower dose, meant to extend life. Most dogs experience very few side effects."

Dr. Leo's call interrupted my postbreakfast cleaning. I stare out the kitchen window while she talks. I want to put my hands over my ears and shout, "La, la, la, la, la! I can't hear you!" like a little kid.

"I don't want to overwhelm you with too much information." She gives me the name of an oncologist in Phoenix who does phone consultations. Zombie-like, I copy the number down on the back of Aunt

Sugar's baked French toast recipe. "Again, I'm really sorry. I can tell how much you love your dog."

"She's not my dog. She's my aunt and uncle's. I can't do anything until I talk to them."

"Of course. Speak to them, and then you and I will talk again, after you have a chance to talk to the oncologist."

Our only guests this morning are the annoying Martins, who, thank heaven, are checking out after breakfast. Earlier this morning, Selene had come into the kitchen to say that Mr. Martin requested a poached egg, instead of fried, which was what I'd planned to serve with the French toast. "I'll poach his eggs," I'd said through gritted teeth.

Now Selene comes into the kitchen again, saying, "You're not going to—" She sees my face and stops. "What is it? Oh no." She sees my cell phone still in my hand. I'm so shocked I haven't moved since I hung up. "Was that the vet?"

"May—Maybe has . . . cancer." I drop my phone and raise my hands to my face.

She wraps me in a hug and starts to cry. I don't want to cry. I'll cry later, when I'm by myself. Maybe, who's been sleeping under the kitchen table, curled in a beautiful ball with her long tail wrapped around herself for warmth, wakes at the sounds from Selene. She limps over, looking sleepy eyed and semistoned, but still manages to jump up on us. We pull her into our hug, and she gives us at least five kisses for every one we give her.

*

THE FIRST PERSON I call is Roxie at the animal rescue. She popped into my head, which I thought was odd at first, but then, the more I thought about it, the more it made sense. Besides Aunt Sugar, Roxie is the most cheerful person I know, and since she's not emotionally involved in the situation, I feel like she'll calm me down before I go into full info-gathering, cancer-battle prep mode. A mode I feel I know too well, but am also pretty ineffectual at.

Her perky voice answers with "PARE, we care! Roxie speaking!"

"Hi, uh, Roxie, you might remember me. I brought in a dog named Penny, in November, and my aunt and uncle ended up adopting her at the beginning of December."

"Of course I remember that gorgeous girly. How's she doing?"

"Not great. She's, um, we found out she's got," I stop and swallow, "bone cancer and—"

"And you want to return her?" she interrupts. She says it so matter-of-factly that I know it must happen on a regular basis. Not the bone cancer part, but the "this dog's defective, and we don't want it anymore" part.

"No! God, no." The thought makes my face feel hot. Perhaps this was a bad idea after all. "I thought you might have experience with three-legged dogs there at the shelter."

"Oh sure." Again, she's all matter-of-fact perkiness. Three legs. No big deal; it's not like they even need that extra one. Okay, yes. *This* is why I called. "We've had three-legged dogs and cats here before. They do great. Especially if they're young, like Penny. She'll be peachy!"

Peachy, I think, *except for that whole pesky cancer thing.*

"Let me give you a teensy piece of advice," she says. "Take your cues from her. Folks get much more upset about an amputation than animals do. We can't imagine losing a limb, but dogs just get on with it. They're not self-conscious like we are. She's not going to feel like a freak, and the other dogs aren't going to look at her funny. She might have to learn to adapt here and there, but I think you'll see she'll be her old self quick as you can say, 'peanut butter and sweet potatoes.'"

Peanut butter and sweet potatoes?

My instincts to call her were right. And so is Roxie: I need to take my cues from Maybe. Maybe's not afraid of tomorrow. She's not afraid of the C-word. She lives in the moment; it's all she knows. And, unfortunately, right now she's in pain, so I need to help her.

*

THE REST OF that day and the next pass in a blur—literally, because I'm more or less constantly on the verge of tears. The boost I got from talking to Roxie faded fast. Kai came up to the house that afternoon. I figured he was looking for Selene, but he said he wanted to check on Maybe; he was concerned since he hadn't seen us down at the stream in so long. When I told him the news, my voice started to shake. I almost burst into tears at the concern in his eyes. He said he and Milo and Weaver would all be sending good thoughts for Maybe. He might have wanted to say more, but I just barely got out a thank-you, and then I closed the door and ran to my room.

Now, I feel like I'm on one of those endless automated airport people movers. Here I go again, with a similar chain of events as with Ryan and Barnum: hours of Googling and asking questions in cancer chat rooms, talking on the phone until my ear hurts (with the oncologist in Phoenix, Uncle Graham and Aunt Sugar, my mom, and again with Dr. Leo), lying awake and staring at the ceiling. And today, taking Maybe for a lung X-ray.

Of course today, after we get home from the X-ray appointment, is when the market intelligence job search I've set up sends me an automated alert about an open position. Some biotech company called Golden Triangle Technologies. I don't research them first, like I usually do; I just fire off a rote cover e-mail and my resume in record speed, barely even checking for typos. I've got other things to think, worry, and obsess about.

If charted, my emotions over these past thirty-six hours would look like a seismographic printout following a 7.0 earthquake: deep dips of confusion, depression, and fear, spiked with hope at the clear X-ray, feigned strength for my aunt and uncle's sake, even giddy joy when the surgeon (usually booked three weeks out according to Dr. Leo) had a cancellation and said we can get in Friday. At least the timing is good. We don't have any guests checking in for the long MLK weekend until later that day. The surgeon wants to keep Maybe overnight, and then I'll pick her up Saturday, after the Chick's breakfast rush.

After scheduling the surgery, I feel almost confident. It's scary to contemplate the procedure itself, but I know it's the best thing. The oncologist I spoke with confirmed what Dr. Leo said: after Maybe recovers, she'll be 100 percent pain-free. He thinks the tumor's location helped us catch the cancer early. He explained that in most cases, when osteosarcoma presents itself in the front leg, it's in the radius, the larger weight-bearing bone. Maybe's, however, is in the ulna, the smaller bone that runs alongside. With it being a thinner bone, the tumor grew and showed an obvious lump more quickly than might have happened in the radius. The clear lung X-ray makes me think he's right; although Dr. Leo warned that there could be *micrometastasis*—tiny, evil bombs already planted by the cancer, too small to be seen on the X-ray.

I try hard to not think about micromets and median survival times. I hope that the oncologist is right; we've caught this early, and now the next thing is to remove the leg and the nasty tumor, to keep the cancer from spreading. The surgeon's cancellation is a sign—the universe is on our side. That's what I told my aunt and uncle too. They seemed a bit concerned about the cost, but they agreed we have to give this girl a fighting chance. And they agreed to let me pay for half of the surgery. Sugar gasped when I told her the estimate, and I didn't want money, or the lack thereof, to rob Maybe of her chance at beating this. I'm willing to chip in some of my money, because this time cancer's not going to win. I'm not going to let it.

*

THURSDAY NIGHT, BEFORE her surgery, Maybe and I lie on my bed together in the dark. I curl up facing her and stroke her side, feeling her ribs under my hand. Dr. Leo said it's good that Maybe's so thin, as a skinny three-legged dog gets around better than a heavy one. I feel each rib, each vertebra, thankful that she's not a chowhound like Barnum was. The clock shines a bright green 8:30. Usually at this time of night, she'd be harassing me if I hadn't given her enough exercise. I miss it. It's funny, missing the things that once seemed so annoying. Like before, all I wanted to do was avoid taking her down to the stream where we might see Kai; but now, I can't wait until she can get back to playing with her best friend, Milo. I want her to be the happy, healthy terrorist girl she was before.

I kiss the top of her head and whisper, "I know you're in pain, little girl, but we're going to get you well. You can trust me, sweet pea. It's going to be okay." She opens her eyes and, though she looks a bit out of it at first, she stares back into my eyes for almost a full minute before slipping back into sleep.

CHAPTER 18
RECOVERY MODE

I'm waiting for the tech to bring her out and I'm nervous as hell. My knee bounces. I stop it. It starts again. When the surgeon called to say the surgery went well (a call that reduced my tensed muscles to overcooked-spaghetti consistency), he warned me that her incision is quite large. "I don't want you to be shocked when you pick her up. The site looks great, but it covers her whole shoulder area." I think back to that now, while I wait and wonder what's going to come through that swinging door. Franken-pup?

I hear her tags. Jingle, jingle, jingle. She's obviously moving of her own accord. I didn't even know if she'd be walking already. I guess I expected someone would at least be carrying her, but no! Here she is! The door swings open and Maybe comes through, an inflatable collar like a swim float around her neck. A nurse in pink scrubs quick steps behind at the other end of the lead.

"There's my girl!"

Maybe hops over to me. Her eyelids droop from the sedatives and painkillers, but her back end wiggles, and her tail does its usual figure eight, extra-happy wag. I kneel down, and she kisses my face while I rub her ears. Aside from some dopiness, she looks amazing. I peek around the blue plastic collar at her incision. Geez Louise, it's huge. I know the surgeon said "quite large" but this is a giant Y-shaped incision with a bit of rubber tubing sticking out of the bottom end of the *Y*. It's raw and red along the line of staples, and so much of her beautiful coat is gone. I knew they'd have to shave her, but a quarter of her body is bare, pinkish skin. It looks so painful I want to cry into what's left of her fur, but she blinks at me, and I can see that she's already closer to her old self again. She seems so happy—happy to see me, happy to be busting out of here, happy to be rid of that painful leg. I kiss her nose, then close my eyes while she bathes my face in kisses. It's a good thing I've never been much of a makeup wearer.

When she's done, I stand and take the leash. "Doesn't she need a bandage?"

"Some surgeons recommend a bandage, but we think it's best to get some air to the area. To help keep it clean and keep the drain from dripping on your floors, you can put an old T-shirt on her." She hands me a bag of pills and explains the dosing, handing me a card for the pet hospital with a number to call if I have questions. "Bye, sweetie!" she says to Maybe, and to me, "That's one awesome dog you've got there." I just grin.

When I open the door, Maybe bolts so quickly I'm not prepared. I had no idea a dog that had a leg removed twenty-four hours ago could move that fast. Her lead flies out of my hand. She scoots across the parking lot—thank heaven it's empty—and plops on a patch of grass. She looks exhausted from her twenty-five-yard dash, but I'm so excited that she's already moving around, all I can do is praise her. "You're such a brave girl. Look at you!"

I ease her into the backseat, covered with old towels, and we're off.

Back at the Chick, I use a sling made from an old towel (a trick I learned in a chat room) to help her up the back steps. On the top step, we find a brown paper bag with Maybe's name on it. She sniffs at it as I pick it up. A note in what I know must be Kai's careful printing reads "Homemade salmon treats. Get well soon, Maybe. From Milo." That's so sweet. I look down toward the stream, but there's no sign of the boys. I give Maybe one of the small round treats, and she devours it before I can even get my hand on the doorknob.

Inside, Maybe goes through another round of tail flag waving when she sees Selene. I think about teasing Selene about "her boy-friend" bringing by treats, but now's not the time since Selene's busy gushing over Maybe. Instead I just hold up the bag and say, "Maybe got a care package from Milo." Selene tilts her head and simply says, "Awww," and then we get Maybe settled under the kitchen table on the orthopedic bed Selene picked up for her. Hopefully, she'll feel cozy and secure under there, but still be able to feel part of the action. We've closed off half the kitchen with plastic lattice we found behind the stor-age shed, so she's confined to the area around the kitchen table, and the den. The oncologist said she'd probably have trouble finding the best way to lie down and get back up, but she seems to have no problem with it. She sits, then eases herself down; as for getting back up, you can see the muscles working in her remaining front leg; but even with the narcotics, she manages to balance and power herself up.

Selene and I sit and watch her until she falls asleep. Then Selene dashes off to check on the guests before I have a chance to ask her any-thing about Kai. Why aren't they dating yet? Could Selene not realize he likes her? Hopefully, he'll get over his shyness soon and say some-thing to her. I get up and go finish cleaning the kitchen.

Maybe sleeps until dinnertime, waking when I present her with a special hamburger patty for her homecoming dinner. Considering what she's been through, I think her first day home has gone pretty well.

The first night, though, is a different story. Normally, Maybe springs up onto my bed, circles a few times, and curls up in a ball next to me. Springing is out of the question for now, so I drag my mattress onto the floor. I get under the covers; Maybe stands there watching me. She sways like a three a.m. drunk.

"Come on, Maybe." I try to coax her into the bed. "Come on." Kissy noises, which usually bring her running, draw no reaction beyond confused blinking. "It's okay." Nothing. I lie down and finally, with an apparent effort, Maybe gets up on the mattress with me. She circles, trying to get comfortable, then lowers herself down onto her good side and shuts her eyes.

It takes me forever to fall asleep; I'm afraid I'll roll over and hurt her, which is silly because I've never done that before. Once I do fall asleep, every time she makes the slightest adjustment, I wake up, wondering if she needs me. At two thirty, Maybe gets up and goes to the farthest corner under the window. She's lies flat out on her side, not curled into her usual ball. I go over to her. Cold air seeps down from the window and creeps up the back of my T-shirt. "Sweet pea, don't you want to come back in the nice warm bed?" Nope. No amount of coaxing works. I decide to let her lie there awhile. I go back to bed, but can't sleep while she's over there looking so miserable. After forty-five minutes, I get up again and go to her. I place a hand on her hip and feel her shivering.

"Oh, sweetheart. You're freezing. Come back to bed." More coaxing; again, I'm ignored. I get my comforter, wrap it around myself, and lie down on the floor next to her, draping the blanket over her. She promptly gets up and goes to lie on the far side of the bed.

Ah, okay. I can take a hint. She wants some alone time. I go back to my mattress and stay as curled on my half as I can so she has plenty of space. We manage to get two whole uninterrupted hours of sleep before it's time for me to get up and make breakfast. I rise, but shining is not gonna happen today. But then, does it ever?

*

TUESDAY AFTERNOON: FOUR days post-op and no poop yet. Apparently, the heavy-duty pain meds can mess with a dog's system, so I know it might take awhile—maybe up to five or six days—before we see any action. Still, I watch her like a hawk. She's mastered peeing, centering her front left leg and squatting. A look reminiscent of a football player's three-point stance. Her first time out in the yard, she made it look easy. Selene and I were so proud we high-fived.

But the pooping is another issue. Today, we stride out into the yard, confident. I murmur words of encouragement. She sniffs around one of her favorite spots, near some manzanita bushes at the side of the yard. She sniffs some more. Glances at me with a look that implies, "Can a girl have some privacy?" Out of my peripheral vision, I see the telltale hunched back. She wobbles a bit but steadies herself. And . . . success. She's done it. "Hooray!" I praise her, and she wags her tail. But then, as she backs up to turn around, she pogo sticks her remaining front leg right down into the soft center of the steaming pile.

"Oh, sweet pea." I'm dismayed, but by the time she hops across the grass, she'll have the worst of it cleaned off. I'll yell to Selene to toss me some damp paper towels before we hit the stairs.

We turn to go back to the house and see Kai trotting toward us. He hasn't seen Maybe since her surgery, and she wiggles and whines with excitement at the sight of him. "Maybe!" he calls out. She rears up onto her back legs and lunges forward. I holler, "Off!" but it's too late. Her poop-covered paw stamps squarely onto the front of his suede jacket.

He doesn't notice. "You look fabulous, beautiful girl," he tells her as he ruffles her ears and bends forward for kisses.

"Maybe, off," I say, more gently this time, trying to ease her down. I don't want her to get too excited, and I certainly don't want her to land too hard on that remaining front paw. "I'm so sorry." I point at his jacket. I hope he won't be mad.

"What? Oh. *Oh.*" He holds his hands out to his sides.

"I'm really sorry about that. I'll pay to have it dry-cleaned. It's her first, uh, success since the surgery. We were doing the happy hoppy poop dance and some missteps were made."

He looks down at his jacket again. "It's okay. Shit happens." Thank heaven he smirks, and I can't help but smile.

"Come up to the house." We begin to walk back, Kai with his hands swinging wide. "Selene can toss us some damp towels."

"She looks like she's doing great." She *does* look great, especially since we are still keeping her incision hidden under an old T-shirt. Assessing her now, I think this is the best she's looked yet. Mostly, she sleeps, but when she's awake she mopes, resting her chin on the edge of her orthopedic bed. If I come over to try to collect some kisses, she looks away. The first few times Selene walked into the room, she'd garner a tail thump and a kiss or two, but now, Selene can't get a reaction out of her either. I was so worried I called Roxie again, and she assured me this is normal. The new energy from Kai seems to lift her spirits.

"She seems to be adapting okay so far. But she's still really doped up. And seems sad. This is the happiest she's looked since we brought her home."

"I could come by anytime, uh, I mean, if you think it'd help." He looks at me, then looks away. I wouldn't have taken him for the shy type, but he's obviously angling for a way to get some more time with Selene. He should just come by if he wants to see her. I wonder if I should say something to him. Really, he's not such a jerk after all.

I call to Selene, but no answer. Shoot, there goes that plan. "Hang on." I run in and wet some paper towels. While I'm in the kitchen, my cell rings. It's Dr. Leo's office.

During the surgery on Friday, the surgeon took one of Maybe's lymph nodes, and they sent it, along with her leg, to the lab for a biopsy. "The biopsy confirmed the osteosarcoma." As hard as this is to hear, it still registers as good news: at least the radiologist was right.

"What ifs" had plagued me ever since I'd scheduled the surgery. "And," Dr. Leo continues, "there's no sign of cancer in her lymph nodes."

"Oh, what a relief." First the clear lungs, now the clear lymph nodes. *You are not taking this little girl down, Cancer. You may have taken her leg, but that is all I'm letting you have, you greedy bastard. You aren't going to win this time.*

Dr. Leo agrees it's a good sign and says she'll see me Friday for Maybe's appointment to have her drain removed.

I grab the towels and take the steps two at a time. "The vet called. Maybe's lymph nodes are clear!"

"Wonderful!" Kai starts to lift his arms as if to hug me, then looks down at the splotch on his jacket and runs his hand over his head. "Really, really great news," he says. I think this is the biggest smile I've had on my face since I moved here. I slap a wad of towels into his hand with the force of a game-winning high five. He grins back at me and squeezes my hand for a second before releasing it.

I blink and turn my focus to Maybe. We both rub her ears and sweet-talk her, but then remember the business at hand.

Kai swipes at his jacket while I tackle Maybe's foot. Since the poor kid's already minus a leg, she's not loving the idea of me picking up her foot and leaving her with only two to stand on, even though I'm supporting her. I pick her foot up; she stamps it back down. Kai notices our struggles and offers to clean her foot while I support Maybe with both hands.

He works diligently, getting everything out from between her pads. It's really nice of him to help, especially since he takes the nasty end of the job.

"Good as new," he says, releasing her paw and wadding up the dirty paper towels.

Maybe rewards him with one last kiss for a job well done. I say, "That would be awesome if you could come by again soon. I'm sure Maybe would like that."

I'm sure Selene would like that too. After all, I know she thinks he's cute and nice (and, I admit, she's right), so they'll probably be dating soon. If only he'd get over his shyness and ask her out already. I can just be friends with him then. I would never entertain thoughts about a friend's boyfriend. No matter how cute he is. So, yeah. Start dating already.

THAT NIGHT IN our room, Maybe performs her "I vant to be alone" Greta Garbo impersonation again, standing at the door until I let her out. I follow her to the kitchen where she lies down, on her bad side, on the linoleum. Ow. If I'd recently had my arm cut off, I wouldn't lay on that side, but perhaps it cools her incision. I go back to bed (leaving the door open in case she changes her mind) and, to keep from worrying about her, make a list of good news since Maybe's surgery:

1. She gets around amazingly well, except for going down the back stairs. But she can even manage those if I help with the homemade sling.

2. She can sit up and lie down fine. I guess being so young helps; it's easier for her to adapt.

3. Her appetite has been good. For her, that is—it's never been what Barnum's was, even back when she was healthy. Of course, it helps that Selene and I are babying her and hand-feeding her delicacies like cottage cheese, salmon patties, and mushy, organic canned dog food, instead of her usual same-stuff different-day dry kibble. She's going to be completely spoiled by the time she's fully recovered.

4. Her incision is almost healed.

5. Yesterday, she picked up one of my dirty socks from the floor and gnawed at it for a bit. The first sign that our terrorist might soon be back.

6. First poop!

7. Best of all, her lymph nodes are clear. I've never been entirely sure what a lymph node is—always thought it sounded like some sort of magical fairy or rare reptile—but, anyway, the node news is the best thing I've heard in weeks.

Or should I say months? God, years maybe? Seriously, when was the last time I was this happy about anything?

CHAPTER 19
NO EXPIRATION DATE

"I don't think we can afford that." Aunt Sugar's voice cracks, and I know she's trying to hide the fact that she's crying. We're discussing the treatment options, including chemo, that Dr. Leo went over this morning when I took Maybe to have her drain removed.

Sweet Maybe. She was so funny. It's only been a week since her surgery, and she's got to be in a lot of pain still—not to mention probably seeing pink flying squirrels from the meds. I worried about how I'd get her up and motivated to get into my car, but as soon as I jingled my keys, she was raring to go. I guess she needed a break from the Chick. I don't blame her. Then, I thought I'd have to drag her into the vet's office—I sure wouldn't want to go back to the house of horrors where I woke up without a limb—but she wiggled and whined in the backseat as soon as we pulled into the parking lot. She couldn't wait to get in there. She hopped in the door, wearing a huge grin, and greeted everyone from the receptionist to the vet tech to Dr. Leo, with kisses and tail wags. They treated her like a rock star, which is no less than she deserves.

After removing the drain, Dr. Leo inspected the incision site and said Maybe is healing nicely. She said the staples would be ready to come out in a few more days.

Then she went over with me, again, the stats and figures for median survival times with and without chemo. This confirmed why I like Dr. Leo so much. Her practice, which would work in consultation with the oncologist in Phoenix to administer the chemo treatments, would stand to make a good chunk of money if we opt for the chemo. And yet, she doesn't push me toward that option at all. She lays out everything she knows and leaves the decision to me. Or, to me and my aunt and uncle.

With all this, I've once again turned to the only thing that helped me feel like I had a useful role when I was going through this with Ryan and Barnum—online research. I know from my research and from talking to Dr. Leo that chemo's not a guaranteed cure, not even close. Conversely, I know Maybe doesn't have an expiration date stamped on her butt if we *don't* do the chemo. I know the various chemo drugs used and the usual protocols. I have pages of printouts about holistic options. I've researched a local vet that takes an East-meets-West approach, combining traditional drugs with various herbs. Only about 10 percent of dogs beat bone cancer completely, but there's no clear answer. It seems like luck, the dog's genes, butterfly wings flapping in the Amazon might all play a part in curing any given dog. I want to fight this disease with everything I have in me—but I also want to do what will be best for Maybe in terms of her quality of life during the battle.

"The chemo—it's too expensive," Aunt Sugar continues, bringing me back to our conversation. "And . . . I couldn't ask you to help her through that. Not after what you went through with Ryan. Oh, Jane, I feel so bad that this is happening while we're not there to do our part."

"Don't consider me in this. It wouldn't be like what Ryan went through. Dr. Leo said that chemo for dogs isn't like with people. They don't hit them as hard." But that's the part of the chemo option for Maybe that bothers me. If we're not going to try to hit her with it hard enough to save her, then why do it? I want to save her. And some of the holistic options can't be given at the same time as chemo, so we'd have to delay starting certain supplements.

I have to keep reminding myself that Maybe is their dog. It's up to them what path we'll pursue. Still, it doesn't hurt to offer my opinion. "We could try going a holistic route. It'll be easier on her system, and easier on the wallet." I don't tell her that the monthly bill for the supplements will be pretty pricey too. She doesn't need to know, and I'm willing to foot that bill myself. I know they'll insist on paying me back, but I'll show them a hand-picked subset of the bills. If I'm prepared to fight with everything in me, then I ought to also be prepared to fight with, well, not *everything* in my savings account, but a portion of it. Besides, I'll have a paying job again soon. It'll be fine.

"Okay. Get her whatever she needs. Thank you so much, honey. I don't know what we'd do without you. It's a relief to know you're there taking such good care of that lovable girl."

I'm glad I'm here too. If this had happened after they got home and I'd already moved out, who knows what decisions they might have made about Maybe's care, without my guiding them in certain directions. I look at Maybe, sleeping curled in a sleek golden-red circle at my feet, and my heart breaks, wondering if they might have . . . No, I can't let my mind go there.

*

MAYBE SLEEPS AWAY the afternoon, which doesn't alarm me—after all, she's still getting over major surgery, and we had our exciting outing to the vet today. When Selene and I meet up in the kitchen at dinnertime, after a fruitless afternoon of job searching for me, Maybe rouses out of her bed. Selene offers to take her for a short spin in the backyard while I make spaghetti. Selene and I have gotten into the habit of eating together on the nights she doesn't have class, or if she's not having dinner with her family. It seemed silly to be cooking our own separate meals, and I have to admit, it's less lonely than eating at the table in my room. We eat in front of the TV, so there's the bonus of not having to make a lot of conversation.

Selene and Maybe let in a gust of winter air. "They said we might get some snow tonight," Selene says, her cheeks flushed.

"I hate snow." I tell Selene about my worst snow experience in Philly, right after we first moved. A freak storm hit in October, and Ryan was away on a long Vegas weekend with some friends. "I dug the car out with a cookie sheet."

"The snow here's never that bad. A cookie sheet would be overkill. A spatula would be plenty." She laughs. "It's nice actually. We get enough for it to be pretty, and then it melts." She opens a can of salmon for Maybe while she talks. Since her surgery, Maybe has come to expect something extra stirred into her kibble. If she wasn't spoiled before, she is now.

When we settle in with our pasta in front of *Jeopardy*, Selene asks, during a commercial, about my conversation with Aunt Sugar. Maybe leans against the sofa and rests her head on my thigh, in prime position for sharing.

"Are you sure you can afford this? I think you should show your aunt and uncle *all* the bills. They'll be irritated if they find out you hid some of the costs from them."

"We'll have to make sure they don't find out then." I look at her pointedly. It's nice of her to worry about my finances, but it's Uncle Graham and Aunt Sugar that I'm concerned about. After all, they ought to be sitting on a decent-size retirement nest egg by now, but it seems obvious that they're not. Otherwise, why would they drive across the country in order to get Sugar's operation for free?

"Sorry, I don't mean to pry. But they're going to find out sooner or later. Once you're gone, they'll have to buy more pills when they run out."

"So I'll stock up. Don't worry about it. I have some money in my savings. I'd planned to use it for living expenses in San Diego while I looked for a job." I shrug and dangle a piece of spaghetti for Maybe. "But now, I'm living here free while I job search, so it's fine. Really." I repeat my mantra from months ago: "It'll all be fine."

*

SELENE COMES THROUGH the swinging kitchen door with the basket of scones, still half-full. A pair of couples who were supposed to self-check-in late last night didn't show, but I didn't know that when I started baking this morning. "The Millers ate two each, but we've still got all these. Hey, why not take them over to Kai and Weaver?"

"Good idea. No sense letting them go to waste."

"I'll wrap them up, and you can run them over there while they're still warm." She digs the foil out of the bottom drawer.

"Me? It was your idea." Here's a chance to get them to spend a few minutes together.

"I know, but you made them, so you should be the one to deliver them."

I'm about to add, "But you're the one he wants to see," when a long, somewhat panicked "Hellooo" rings out, sounding like it's coming from the stairwell. "Our toilet is overflowing. Help!"

Selene points at the scones, then in the direction of Mrs. Miller's voice, and holds her hands up in a "Which one's it going to be?" gesture.

"Scone delivery," I answer, but I'm not enthusiastic about it.

"Coming!" Selene rushes off.

I set down the cooled eggy frying pan for Maybe to lick. She can't come along since she still hasn't been cleared for doggy play yet. I duck out while she has her head in the pan.

As I hop down the back steps, I hope Kai will be by the stream. I don't want to go knock on their door. Nobody likes a surprise visitor, even if she's bearing baked goods. I just want to do a quick handoff and get out of there.

Sweet. I see him by the stream. I wave when he turns at the sound of my shoes thudding down the dirt path. Milo runs to greet me, and I stop to pat his thick, furry sides. "No Maybe?" Kai calls out, as I see him slip what looks like a wood-handled jackknife into his pocket— just as he did the first time I saw him down by the stream.

"She got her staples out on Wednesday, and Dr. Leo said to give her a few more days before she's back playing with other dogs. Probably Monday we'll be down here." I hold out the foil package. Milo stands on his back legs to sniff at it. "Selene thought you and Weaver might like some scones."

He stands and accepts the offering with a big smile. "Fantastic. That was nice of her. And you. I mean, you're the chef, right?"

"Yeah. But it was Selene's idea. We had a bunch leftover. Some guests didn't show up."

He opens the seam of the foil and inhales. "Man, these smell great. I'll take them up, while they're still warm." He starts to walk away, Milo close on his heels, then turns. "Why don't you come up to the house with me? Just for a minute. I know Weaver will want to thank you. Especially since he's always complaining to me about the 'gruel' I make him for breakfast. Steel-cut oatmeal with granola that I make myself, and he calls it gruel." He snorts.

I look at my watch and try to think if there's some excuse I can make to get out of it. "They're not really from me. It was Selene's idea," I say again, wanting to make sure he knows Selene was thinking of him. I should have made her write a note or something. Or made her wait and bring them after the toilet fiasco. That was dumb of me.

"It'd mean a lot to him. He never gets any visitors."

Oh, sure, guilt-suck me. "Okay. Just for a minute."

Milo troops along behind us up the path to Kai's house, an unremarkable house—nothing like the grand B&B next door. It's one story, covered in beige stucco, with little to distinguish it from the beige gravel that surrounds it.

Kai opens the back door, and I hear what sounds like one of those bass fishermen shows (the zing of a fishing line and "Oh, you got him!" "Hang on!" exclamations) blaring from a TV. Kai calls out, "Gramps! Jane's here. She brought us a little present."

"Eh?" Weaver yells from the other room.

"Jane's here!" We move through the kitchen, spotless except for Weaver's Magnussun Grain hat sitting on the counter, and on into the living room. The inside of the house is a surprise after the bland exterior—amazing butcher-block countertops in the kitchen, with a cool industrial-looking stainless steel backsplash, and there's a lovely pale shade of moss-green paint on the living room walls. Weaver looks right at home in his dark-chocolate leather recliner with a nearby table with slots underneath filled with crossword puzzle books and the TV guide. The burgundy chenille overstuffed couch begs to be napped on during a gloomy afternoon, especially with the cream-colored throw draped over the arm. The carved wood mantel above the brick fireplace holds black-and-white photos in wood frames. This is a home, cozy and warm, and definitely not the bachelor pad I was expecting.

Weaver looks even older without his hat on: smaller, all ears. He's backlit again, as in the bar, this time by the morning sun streaming through the front window. A halo of wispy gray hairs frames his nearly bald head.

He sees us and lowers the TV volume. "Jane!" he exclaims. "What a surprise." He grins and attempts to hoist himself out of the chair to welcome me, but I motion for him to stay put. He plunks back down and points at Kai. "This big lug never gets any visitors."

Kai sets the scones on the coffee table and explains the gift. Milo sniffs the package.

"They're from Selene," I add.

Weaver's eyes widen. "Heaven!" He turns to me. "You should see the swill he puts in front of me every morning. Makes a person want to go back to bed. The wife and I used to have doughnuts every Sunday after church. Now, if I tell him I'd like a doughnut, he looks at me as if I said I'd like to share a joint!"

I laugh. "I hope you like the scones. They're carrot-cake flavor. The whole-wheat flour and the carrots make them a bit healthier than a doughnut, so maybe I could sneak you our leftovers every once in a while. It's no doughnut, but still." In the future, I'll have Selene deliver them though.

"Oh, Jane, a leftover scone now and then would make an old man very happy. You'd think living like the bachelors we are that I could get away with eating whatever I want, but no." He points an accusing, crooked finger at Kai. "Granny, here, runs a pretty tight ship."

I glance around at their ship. It's tidy, but not in a don't-know-where-to-set-your-drink-down way. The room's comfy vibe is welcoming. I turn and look into the dining room and am surprised to see a miniature replica of Prescott's downtown square taking up the entire table.

"Oh my gosh, what's that?" I take a step toward it.

"That's his pride and joy," Weaver says.

"It's just a little hobby." Kai waves a hand as if trying to bring my attention back to the living room.

"A little hobby, ha! That's the reason why I can't get him to play gin rummy with me at night. He's always working on that thing."

"Can I look at it?" I don't wait for an answer. Kai follows. I bend to examine the tiny courthouse, and marvel at the intricately carved and painted storefronts. A smattering of people—simple, whittled shapes in painted shirts and hats—also dot the grounds. I guess this explains the jackknife I've spotted him with.

"Kind of silly, I guess. But once I got started, I couldn't stop."

"It's not silly; it's cool. What made you start?"

"I got bored with my work projects. The handyman biz is mostly odd jobs, fixing this or that. Nothing fun. At first, I kept busy expanding my master bath," he motions down the hall. "Then I redid the kitchen. When I ran out of house projects, I started futzing around, making models. I love the square downtown, so I made a model of the courthouse. It looked lonely, so I made the gazebo too. Then they needed some grass to tie them together." He runs his square paw across his jaw. "It took on a life of its own after that."

"How long have you been working on it?"

"A few months."

"Liar!" Weaver yells from the other room. "It had already hit obsessive proportions when I moved in. And that's almost a year ago."

"Watch your fishing show, Gramps." Turning back to me, he points at the streets surrounding the grassy square. "It's just that, once I added Whiskey Row, I had to balance the other sides of the square, so I started filling in the other streets."

"You should have someone from the *Daily Courier* come do an article. It's really amazing." The platform it's built on takes up all but the rounded ends of the dining table. "I guess you don't entertain much."

He laughs. "Nope. Weaver and me, we eat at the table in the kitchen." He lowers his voice. "Or in front of the TV if he nags me about watching one of his shows. He's addicted to those ghost-hunting shows. Says he plans to haunt me and he's picking up tips."

I laugh, then study the entryway to the room. "Is it built in sections? How are you ever going to get it out of here?"

"Why would I want to get it out of here?"

"What if you move?"

"No plans to move."

"You're going to live in this city, in this very house, the rest of your life?"

"That's the plan. I mean, I can't imagine moving. I love Prescott. It's the perfect size: not so big as to attract a lot of crime or to have that indifferent big-city feel, but not so small that everyone knows your business. There are no earthquakes or hurricanes or floods. It's got ideal weather too. Enough snow in the winter to make things interesting, but not enough to inflict cabin fever; and the summers, well, no matter how hot they get, it always cools down at night. Perfect."

How can it be perfect when there's no ocean? Still, I know Selene never plans to leave Prescott either, so that's good for the two of them. I smile and say, "I better get going."

I turn to leave and see Weaver balling up the foil I brought the scones in. He tosses the ball back onto the coffee table. "Jane, those were delicious! Milo agrees." I notice Milo scouring the carpet around Weaver's chair for stray crumbs.

Kai snorts and shakes his head while I laugh.

CHAPTER 20

YOU CAN FIX A BAD LEG, BUT YOU CAN'T FIX STUPID

A light tap at the kitchen door catches my attention. I'm standing at the sink rinsing breakfast dishes. "Hello?" a woman's voice calls through the closed door. "Sorry to bother you."

Wow, someone who actually knocks and acknowledges our private space. I'm shocked. Still, I hope this will be something quick since Selene's down in the laundry shed folding towels. "Come on in," I shout, drying my hands on my jeans.

It's Mrs. . . . I don't know. I can never remember guests' names. A quiet lady, as skinny as Maybe, who's been in black yoga pants every time I've seen her. I'm certain she's the one who sent an almost-full plate back to the kitchen. She's got more makeup on at 9:30 a.m. than I ever have on at any time of day or night.

"Can I help you?" I ask as she stands in the doorway.

"Sorry to bother you. Would it be okay if I do some yoga in the game room?" She points over her shoulder to the room beyond the dining room. Uncle Graham and Aunt Sugar call it the parlor, but most people refer to it as the game room or the library, as if the few board games and a couple of shelves filled with musty hardcover books and garage sale paperbacks are worthy of such lofty-sounding names.

"Sure, as long as there's no one else in there." There's almost never anyone in there. The room is wasted space.

"I checked, and it's empty. I hate to impose, but there's not enough space in our room upstairs. I—oh my God!" I'd heard Maybe's tags jingling as she hopped out from the back rooms, no doubt drawn by the sound of voices and a chance for some attention, but with this woman's outburst, I spin around, yelling, "What?" I fear Maybe somehow tore open her incision, and expect to see a trail of blood.

But no. She's fine. She hops over, happy as can be, tail waving, butt wiggling. She jumps up and plants her paw on my stomach. I bend down and let her kiss me, and turn back to the woman, confused. "Is there a problem?" I return Maybe's paw to the floor and hope it will stay planted there.

"Good lord, what happened to her? I'm sorry I shrieked. I didn't mean to, but I've never seen such a huge incision before." She winces as Maybe hops toward her, trying to say hi. "I'm a bit squeamish."

Personally, I think her incision looks great. I want to say, "You should have seen it last week," but settle for, "I know it's a bit of a shock. We usually have a T-shirt on her, but I thought I'd let it air out a bit." I go over to the breakfast nook table and grab Maybe's latest fashion statement—a faded Diamondbacks tank top Selene contributed to Maybe's wardrobe. "Come here, Maybe." I slip the shirt over her head.

The woman takes a silent single step into the kitchen. "What happened to her leg? Did she have an accident or something?"

I say, "Nope, she has bone cancer," straightforward, the same way I'd say, "She's a rescue." I'm proud of how well she's doing, and I'm not expecting, nor do I want, any pity. Neither does Maybe.

"Ohmigod, bone cancer! Isn't that supposed to be excruciating?"

I smile and massage Maybe's hips. "Not if you remove the bad bone." I mean, come on, lady. Does this look like a dog in pain? Maybe, enjoying the rubbing, stands at ease with her mouth hanging open in a smile that would give Julia Roberts a run for her money.

"How awful. I can't imagine putting a dog through that." Her hand grazes her heart. "There are some things you shouldn't put a dog through. You probably don't want to hear this, but sometimes it's best to put a dog down."

I stand up. Maybe circles me, wondering why I stopped the massaging. Sometimes, I think I'd like to be a dog. I'd like to have hackles so that I could show this woman that they're raised. "You're right. I don't want to hear that. What the hell do you—"

"What's going on?" Selene comes in with a gust of cold air and a basket full of fresh towels on her hip. She bumps the towels up onto the kitchen counter. "Is there something I can help with, Mrs. Newland?"

Newland. That's what this witch's name is. I glare at her. I know people can be rude and overstep their bounds, but this is about the worst thing anyone has ever said to me. Can't she see how happy Maybe is? I crouch down to Maybe's level and let her plaster my face with kisses so I can show this woman what an idiot she is, and how happy Maybe is to be alive.

Mrs. Newland waves her hand in a circle. "I was wondering if I could do some yoga in the game room." Thank God she doesn't repeat what she said to me, because if I hear it a second time, I might have to break my promise about not throwing food at the guests anymore.

"Sure," Selene says. "I'll help you move the table to one side."

Selene glances back at me, her face a question, wondering why she heard my raised voice. I know she's going to want to talk when she gets back, but I'm not in the mood.

"I need to take Maybe out." I yank Maybe's leash off its hook, and we storm out. (Well, I storm; Maybe happily bounces.) I've helped her down the steps, before realizing I didn't think to grab my jacket. No big deal. My anger will keep me warm.

We jog toward the stream, since Maybe has an easier time moving at a faster pace. Now that she has her staples out and is off her pain meds, it's time to start rebuilding her stamina. A venture down by the stream will be good for her—and will get me away from the house.

Maybe has no clue what's transpired. She's just glad to be back at her beloved stream. She sniffs the rocks at the water's edge, no doubt looking for signs of Milo or the tree squirrels that frequent the area. I unhook her leash and let her sniff and explore, while I plunk down in an Adirondack chair and wrap my arms tight across my chest.

What an imbecile. *"Sometimes it's best to put a dog down."* I can't believe she said that. I would never say anything like that to anyone. Geez Louise, do I hate people who can't mind their own business.

A scrambling noise in the bushes announces Milo's arrival. He bursts onto the path and is at Maybe's side quicker than it takes the tip of her tail to trace one of its usual figure eights. They've spent almost a month apart, since Maybe started limping so badly on New Year's Eve weekend.

I glance up and notice Kai ambling along the path toward us. He's wearing that darn forest-green shirt again, the one that makes his eyes a deeper shade of blue. He sits in the chair next to me, and we watch the furry friends kiss and tussle.

"He's missed her," Kai says, with a smile.

"I can see that." I smile back, then concentrate on watching the dogs play.

Maybe, again, amazes me. I thought she might be leery of playing with another dog, now that she's missing her right jab, but they go back to their old wrestling routine like nothing's changed. Maybe's tongue hangs out the side of her mouth, like she's grinning and giddy. I shake my head and groan, thinking back to that woman again. I wish she could see Maybe playing her heart out. Put her down. Idiot!

"Something wrong?" Kai asks.

"Not really." I nod in the direction of the Chick, without taking my eyes off Maybe. "Something a guest said. It's nothing."

"About Maybe?"

"Yeah. People can be so stupid. I mean, look at these two." I point at the dogs, up on their hind legs in a wrestling bear hug. Or, half a bear hug for Maybe. "Milo hasn't even noticed Maybe lost her leg."

"Dogs don't care about that stuff." He nods. "Truth be told, I prefer them to people."

I offer him a high five. "Me too." My hand dives back into my sweatshirt pocket for warmth.

"Aren't you freezing?" Kai asks. I look over, envious of his heavy suede jacket. He notices and adds, "Do you want my jacket?"

It's thoughtful of him to offer, but then he'd be freezing. Plus, it just seems too . . . intimate to wear his coat. "No, that's okay. We can't stay long." I thrust my chin at Maybe. "Don't want her to overdo it on her first day back in the ring."

The dogs growl and bark. Maybe pins Milo and stands over him with her tripod stance.

"Wow, Milo." Kai says. "Pinned by a girl. A three-legged girl at that."

Milo, as if embarrassed at being called out by his dad, rolls and leaps up in a single acrobatic maneuver that sends a spray of dirt our way.

"Ow," I say, blinking as something flies into my eye. I stand and shake my head, hoping that what feels like a small boulder will fall out.

Kai jumps up and comes close. "Here, let me see."

Before I can object, he puts his hand under my chin and lifts my face to his. He's only an inch or two taller than me, so we're almost eye to eye, or we would be if I could keep mine open.

"It hurts." I blink and look up. "See anything?"

"Hang on." He holds my face in his large hands, while I open my eyes wide for him to examine. His hands are rough, but warm. His breath smells like cinnamon gum.

"See anything?" I repeat, feeling awkward and wishing he'd hurry up. I keep my eyes pointed up. I'm suddenly self-conscious about what my breath might smell like. Coffee, probably.

"Yep." He licks the end of his finger and dabs at my eye. I want to object and say, "That's gross," but he removes the boulder, and it feels so good, I go limp. I blink a few times, letting my chin rest more heavily in his hand. I close my eyes and sigh a grateful, "Thank you."

When I open my eyes, he's still holding my face, his blue eyes inches from mine. I blink rapidly, and swallow. I take a quick step backward, and he lets his hand fall to his side.

"Um, thanks again," I say, looking down. "Ya know, you're right; I am freezing." I rub my hands together to demonstrate. It sounds like I'm rubbing two pieces of sandpaper, my hands are so dry from the weather and all the dish washing. It makes me think of how his hands felt on my cheek. I know I'm blushing as red as my sweatshirt. "We better get going." I call Maybe and head off, not waiting to see if she's coming, but trusting that she will. I glance back and Kai hasn't moved.

On our way back to the house, it begins to snow. Swell.

Coming in through the side door, I'm not shocked to find another guest in the kitchen—it's that kind of day. This time it's *Mr.* Newland, which I consider a strike against him. Not only is he in the kitchen, but he's standing in front of the open refrigerator, eating cottage cheese out of the container.

"Oh, hi." No sign of guilt or remorse passes over his pudgy face. He holds up the cottage cheese container. "I couldn't find a bowl."

"That's the dog's cottage cheese." I point at Maybe, who wiggles next to me, anxious to greet her new friend. "That she eats straight from the container."

"Oh." He sets the container down on the counter. "I guess I've had enough."

"And the kitchen—including the fridge—isn't open to everyone." I wait for him to notice Maybe's incision and brace myself for another rude remark.

"It's my wife. She's got me on this diet, and I'm starving all the time."

Yes, well, your wife is a piece of work. I guess I should feel sorry for him, married to that woman. "You must have been the 'egg whites and fruit' request this morning, huh?"

"Yeah. Anyway, sorry, pup," he says to Maybe, bending down. "Who's a pretty doggy?" Maybe rushes him. He makes a small *oof* sound when she pegs him in the chest with her lone front paw. "And who's so soft?" He accepts her crazed kisses while rubbing her neck. "She does great on three legs," he says to me, now crouching to rub Maybe's belly, since she's gone paws up on the kitchen floor. Her Diamondbacks tank rides up, revealing part of her incision. "Looks like it was recent, from the scar."

"Yeah, it hasn't been that long. She's pretty amazing."

"I'll say!"

Okay, this guest's not so bad after all. At least he's nice to the dog.

"If you want, I could sneak some white cheddar into your egg-white omelet tomorrow."

His face lights up, matching Maybe's.

CHAPTER 21

BED & BURRITO . . .
BRILLIANT

Back from running errands, I find a shiny silver Ford truck in the driveway. The "Sturgis Motorcycle Rally" bumper stickers can only mean one thing: Harrison, Aunt Sugar's son. Awesome. What's he doing here?

Harrison sits at the kitchen table with Selene. They're sipping beers. I happen to know we have very few Stellas left, so I'm not thrilled to see that he's drinking the last of our inventory.

"Look who dropped in," Selene says as Harrison gets up.

"Jaaane." He walks toward me with outstretched Godzilla arms, moving in for a hug, but Maybe bursts in from the den, having heard me. (Or smelled me, which is a worrying thought. Did I shower today?)

"Harrison," I say, avoiding the hug by crouching down for Maybe's enthusiastic hello kisses. "What a surprise."

I haven't seen my stepcousin since my dad died. He looks worse now, but then again, the last time, he was cleaned up for the funeral.

His pale blond hair, at least what's left on top, wafts like underwater seaweed, while the longer bits at the back are braided into a thin rat-tail. He wears a pale blue T-shirt with a black splatter-paint design on it, or it might be actual paint. The ragged threads, where sleeves used to be, drape over muscular shoulders, but the stretch of the shirt across his gut gives away the fact that his workout regimen doesn't include cardio. It's too chilly for a muscle shirt, but I know he likes to show off his "ink" since he works at a tattoo parlor. A worn leather jacket hangs on the back of his chair.

"Hey, uh, sorry I didn't make it out to Philly for Roger's funeral," he says.

"Ryan. And it's okay. It's far. I understood." I would have been shocked if he'd come.

"I thought I'd drop in and check on things," he says. "See how everything's going." He looks around the room like Papa Bear after Goldilocks trespassed. Is he checking up on us? Geez, he gets on my nerves. Actually, that's not entirely true. What gets on my nerves is how Aunt Sugar effuses about him, when he's never done anything to be effused over in his life, unless you count his unbroken attendance record at the Sturgis Motorcycle Rally for the past fifteen years. Which she does. I'd love to see him do something once that would earn Aunt Sugar some real bragging rights.

She chose his name, thinking it sounded presidential—after William Harrison, the ninth US president. She thought he'd achieve great things. I guess no one told her that Harrison died, after a mere thirty-two days in office, from the pneumonia he contracted while delivering his long-winded inaugural address. It turned out to be a pretty apt name for my hot-air-filled stepcousin.

"I was just telling him everything's fine," Selene says. "If a little quiet." She nods toward the beers and adds, "Harrison suggested an early happy hour." She looks guilty, like I've caught her goofing off in the middle of the day—which is ridiculous, but guilt is a given with her. "Anyway," she says, standing, "We've got two couples checking in tonight." She dumps what's left of her unfinished beer into the sink, then moves toward the swinging door. "So, I need to go check that their rooms are ready." I know their rooms are ready, and I know she knows it too. "I'll let you two cousins catch up."

"Stepcousins," I mutter, while Harrison goes to the fridge and grabs the last two beers. Although he's family, it annoys me to see him fetching food like he lives here.

"Come on and sit." He takes his spot at the table and waves me to an empty chair. "We do have some catching up to do. What's new?"

Besides my husband being dead and my lack of employment? There's pretty much no aspect of my life that I want to discuss with him. But, again, Maybe saves me. She hops over and flops on the floor between us. "Maybe's new. Selene told you about your mom adopting her?"

"Yeah. She told me about the whole cancer thing too. Man, that sucks."

"Yes. Yes, it does." We both nod and stare at the checkered table-cloth. "So, you still work at the tattoo place?"

"Not the same one. The place I was at before wouldn't give me time off to go to Sturgis last August." Ah, South Dakota in August. What could be better? "Said it wasn't a good time to take off because of all the new students in town getting tattoos." Flagstaff is home to Northern Arizona University, and apparently the students make up much of the shop's clientele.

"It's good you could find another job in Flag." I try to hide my surprise. From what I've seen, he's not the greatest artist. The ones on his arms, although faded, are cool; but obviously, he didn't ink them himself. No, the one he did is an island-vibe turtle on his left thigh. I've seen it in warmer weather, when he wears shorts. Surprised he's not wearing them today, since he's overly proud of the thing.

"It was no big. I can take these skills anywhere."

If only I had such marketable skills. Sadly, business analysis needs are limited to big companies in big cities. "So, are you planning to stay for the weekend?" *Please say no. Darn it, Selene. Did you have to let on that we have empty rooms?*

"No, I'm heading down to Phoenix to visit a buddy. Thought I'd stop by on the way." Prescott is not technically on the way from Flag to Phoenix, so I wonder why he's really here. He holds up a beer as if toasting. "This is the life, eh? Drinking beer in the afternoon, while the corporate drones work away in their cubes." He takes a big swig. "Man, I love this place."

"Really? I mean, your mom said you don't make it by too often." I remember her making excuses on Thanksgiving for why Harrison didn't join us. I also remember Uncle Graham going tight-lipped and getting up from the table when his name came up. Poor Uncle Graham. I know he tries hard to be a good stepdad, but Harrison never seemed to leave that pissed-off-kid-with-a-chip-on-his-shoulder phase. He's always acted like his mom owed him something for his dad leaving. I remember my uncle complained once to my mom about Sugar buying Harrison a new car, while they continued to drive their old clunker Pontiac. It stuck with me, since that was the only time I ever heard my uncle sound angry with his "bride." Picturing Harrison's shiny truck out back, I have to wonder if Sugar helped fund it.

"I'd love to make it here more often, but, you know, it's far." It's a mere two hours, partly on roads that are pretty much tailor-made for a motorcycle ride. "And I'm busy at work, but I think about this place a lot. I mean, after all, it'll be mine someday."

I almost spit my mouthful of beer across the table. *His* someday? "You're planning to buy it when they retire?"

He scoffs. "No! Where would I get the money? I mean, I'm in high demand, but my job don't pay *that* well. They're leaving me the place."

"Oh." That makes zero sense. How are they going to leave it to him? Do they have enough money to retire on, without selling this place? And Harrison? He couldn't run a sack race, let alone a business. "So, you're going to be an innkeeper?"

"Yup. I have a great rapport with people. I interact with the public every day at work. That's what this biz is about: knowing how to shoot the shit with folks."

Is there much overlap between the tattoo-purchasing public and the average B&B-goer, I wonder? What I do know is that there's way more to running an inn than shooting the shit. "Uh-huh," I say. Selene must not know about this or she'd have said something.

"You gotta be able to cook too. I make a mean breakfast burrito. Perfect for a hangover."

"Awesome."

"Hey! B&B—bed and burrito! I could even let folks roll their own." He hoots. "That's a good idea. Just put a bunch of burrito innards on the table. I bet people would prefer that, yeah?"

"Sure." Very classy. Can't believe no one ever thought of that idea before. Pure genius.

"Going to be easy money, man. Of course, I'll have to change the name. The whole chicken theme is quaint for my mom and all, but it's not me."

"When do you suppose you'll be taking over?"

"Damn, that's insensitive, ain't it?" He finishes his beer and gets up. "It's not like I'm waiting for Mom and Graham to die." He rummages through the fridge. "I mean, someday I'll inherit this place, but I'm not, like, hoping it'll be anytime real soon. You know you're out of beer?"

Wow. I don't understand. They'll live and work here until they die? How is that even possible? Aunt Sugar's already in poor health. They should sell the place and enjoy life while they're still able. I've got to have a serious talk with my uncle.

"I should go see if Selene needs help." I stand and collect the empty beer bottles.

"I should get going anyway. Want to get to Phoenix by happy hour."

Didn't we just have happy hour? With most people, I'd worry about them driving after two beers, but I'm pretty sure he's had practice handling his liquor.

"Hey, uh, do you think Selene will stay on when this place is mine?"

Doubtful. "You'd have to ask her." I busy myself rinsing bottles.

He jerks his eyebrows in the general direction of upstairs where Selene hides, lucky thing. "It'd be way more fun running this place if I had a doll like that to do the cleaning."

Lovely. "Selene does a lot more than that around here. And everybody helps clean."

"I'm not great on cleaning." He scratches his belly. "That'll have to change."

So, he thinks his days will consist of setting out some burrito ingredients each morning, yakking with the guests, ogling the help, and enjoying a beer or three every afternoon. He looks around the kitchen, and I imagine he's painting over the stenciled chickens with his eyes; he'll probably replace them with those naked-lady silhouettes you see on truck mud flaps. I'm not in love with the Chick, but I hate the thought of him running it into the ground after my aunt and uncle have put in so many years of hard work and love.

"Great seeing you," he says. I walk him out since I know Maybe's always up for some fresh air. She flies down the stairs ahead of us, having gotten the hang of them now, and he comments on her agility. She's doing incredibly well, considering it's only been three weeks.

Before he drives away, he rolls down his window. "Hey, when I own this place, maybe you could fill in for me every year when I go to Sturgis. It'd be like a vacation for you from your career. A nice break from life in a cube. Good idea, huh? How about it?"

I force a smile and nod, hoping he'll drive away before I'm tempted to scream, "Right, because running this place is such a vacation!" It's maddening when people equate running a B&B with *staying* at a B&B. As his truck crunches down the gravel drive, Maybe and I begin to circumnavigate the fence line. (I've avoided the stream since that awkward dirt-in-the-eye moment a few days ago with Kai. He likes Selene, and regardless, I'm leaving soon, so I have no business getting all red cheeked and hot-under-the-sweatshirt over him.)

While Maybe sniffs at a fence post, I take a deep breath. The air is so crisp it burns my lungs. My head spins with this new info. Although, as we near the end of our walk, it's nothing to do with Harrison taking over the Chick that reverberates most in my mind. Instead, it's that phrase he tossed out: "Life in a cube."

*

LATER, I FIND Selene folding sheets in the laundry room. I lean against the table. "Harrison said my aunt and uncle are gonna leave this place to him. Can you believe it?"

She freezes for a second, then goes back to attempting to fold a fitted sheet. "You mean, they're not going to sell the place when they retire?"

"That's just it; it sounds like they're not going to retire at all. He made it sound like they'd run the place until they drop—which is crazy enough in and of itself—but then, when they do, he'll take over. Which goes to a whole new level of nuttiness." I wait for Selene to jump in, to get frustrated with me at what a stupid idea this is, but she focuses on the sheet. She makes a mess of it, balls it up, then snaps it out and starts over. "Does that make any sense?"

Her "no" comes out as a peep, rather than the robust agreement I'm looking for. She bends over the table, reaching to the far side to fuss with the elasticized corners.

I bend too, trying to see her face. "You okay?" She avoids me. "It's a long way off. They're not going to keel over tomorrow. Knock on wood." I rap on the table in front of me. "It could be another five or ten years. Whatever this big secret dream of yours is, I'm sure you'll be ready to forge ahead by then. In the meantime, you'll still have a job here, and you can keep saving up."

"Fuck." It comes out high and squeaky, as if Minnie Mouse had taken up cussing. I'm shocked, because Selene never swears.

"What? What's wrong? What did I say?"

"My big secret dream is that I'm saving up to offer to buy the Chick." She turns toward me, and her big, brown eyes look even bigger magnified by her tears.

This explains her saving every penny, and the accounting classes, but I don't understand why it's a secret. "That's great. Really, really great."

"Not if they're giving the place to Harrison."

"But I'm sure they'd reconsider if they knew. I mean, we can convince my uncle for certain. And Aunt Sugar would love knowing the Chick would be in the hands of someone who loves it as much as they do. I bet they'll see things differently now that my aunt's had this medical problem. They've got to understand that it's not realistic to try and run this place forever. We have to let her know you want to buy it. Let's call them!"

"No! I haven't been realistic either. I thought I'd have a lot more saved up by now. I never wanted to tell them, because they're so generous; they'd offer me a huge deal. I don't want to take advantage. I wanted to wait until they were putting it on the market, so I'd know their *real* asking price. And I thought, by the time they were ready to retire, I'd be ready to buy. But no. They're saving the place for frickin' Harrison. I'm sorry, but that makes me sick. He'll ruin it." She shakes her head, and the tears spill over onto her cheeks. She's one of those pretty criers. Like in the movies. How does she keep her nose from turning red?

"I agree! And I know my uncle must see it too. We just have to convince my aunt."

"But I don't have enough money saved for a decent down payment yet, and nobody's going to give me a loan for the difference. My big dream has been just that—a total dream. It's time to wake up."

"But—"

"Jane, your uncle has let me help with the books since I started my accounting classes. I know how much this place makes. I know how much I can afford to spend on it, and I know what my loan payments would be. I've done my research. I'd have to convince the bank that I could have this place full a lot more than it's been lately. And to fill the place up, it needs upgrades. Once it's redone, I can bump up the room rates a bit. But I don't have the money for the work plus the down payment yet. And I'd never let them sell it to me at some ridiculous bargain." She wipes her eyes with her hand. Luckily, I find a clean tissue in my pocket and offer it up. She blows her nose. "I had all these ideas." She lays out her plans: redo the rooms in a more upscale style, but with the same country charm; make a deal with a local spa to offer in-room massages; spruce up the grounds; turn the unused "parlor" into a yoga and meditation room. She's talked to Kai about it, and he's given her an estimate that's more than fair—but still expensive. Her ideas are great, but beyond the elbow grease she could put in on her own, they'll take a lot of capital.

I don't know what to tell her. I guess if I were a better friend I'd say, "There'll be another place," or "Maybe it'll still work out—in a couple of years." But I'm not going to say things that I don't know are true. I'd have to look at her calculations to be sure, but she's probably right: if she doesn't have the money for the upgrades, she won't be able to bring in more guests and justify raising the rates, and the loan payments would bury her. What can you say when you're watching your friend realize her dream is dead? Instead of saying anything, I give her a hug.

CHAPTER 22

MY TWIN

Maybe and I arrive downtown thirty minutes early for her blood-work checkup. I figured we'd walk around the grass at the courthouse for a change of scenery, which I'm sure she'll like, and it will take the edge off her energy before her appointment.

Downtown Prescott is, for the most part, pretty darn idyllic. At its center is the big courthouse, with its Doric columns and sweeping staircase entrance—just like the miniature version in Kai's dining room. A thick lawn of emerald-green grass and a cobbled brick walkway surround it. In one corner, the quaint white gazebo looks as though it ought to house a barbershop quartet singing old-time melodies. Shops line the streets that form the square, their bright fabric awnings and painted windows advertising New Age books and handmade jewelry. Of course, the traffic, the tourists, the cars that get backed up and honk while some geezer waits for a handicapped parking space—all that sort of takes away from the idyllic-ness of the picture, but if the sounds could be turned down and about half the people erased, like in Kai's rendition, it'd be perfectly charming. And, today, on a quiet, sunny afternoon in early February, with the air as cool, sharp, and inviting as a lime popsicle, I can almost imagine we're back in the days of black-and-white television.

Maybe beelines toward the grass. She plunks down in a shady patch and rolls on her back, luxuriating like a Playboy Bunny on a bearskin rug. I just stand there, attached to the other end of her leash. She isn't going anywhere anytime soon.

Oh, to be oblivious like Maybe is. To think we're out here to take in some air and enjoy the fine day, instead of knowing we are on our way for another checkup. All this little girl knows is the wonderful feel of the prickly blades on her back. She wriggles, then lets her back legs flop open, while her lone front leg sticks straight up into the air. It's a bit embarrassing how much she's enjoying this. I look around at the people strolling past. Since her staples came out two weeks ago, we've been foregoing the T-shirts. I hope no one will be frightened by her scar, but it's healed well. So far, no one in the square seems to notice her. A pair of older couples walks bedroom slipper–size dogs; a sheriff talks to a man in a suit on the courthouse steps; and, my favorite, a man in skinny jeans with a skinny moustache and a cigarette box sticking out of his pocket does Tai Chi. It's an interesting group here today, that's for sure.

I'm still watching Mr. Tai Chi Smoker, when I hear a raspy voice say, "That's weird."

I turn and look. It's got to be Betty, the barfly—my twin. She wobbles up to me, one hand shoved in the back pocket of her dirty faded jeans. (I'm aware that I, too, am wearing dirty faded jeans. I try to stand more erect. I hope no one will think we're sisters.)

She points at Maybe. "Happened to its leg?" She says, pointing. "'S'weird," she says again. "Kinda creepy. Gives me the shivers."

Oh, hold the phone. She's calling my dog weird? Er, my aunt and uncle's dog. I'm so mad I can't think of a snappy retort. What blurts out of my mouth—with all the volume of my anger behind it—is, "Well, I think *you're* creepy!"

Tugging Maybe's leash, I hope she'll pop right up, and we can stomp (hop) off in righteous indignation, but she pulls against the leash and squirms to her left.

I look around to see if anyone noticed me having an "I'm rubber, you're glue" spat with Betty, and see that we've caught the sheriff's attention. Betty notices, too, and decides it's time to saunter off, muttering about me and my "weird freakin' dog."

"Everything all right, ma'am?" the sheriff asks when he gets closer.

I'm still fuming, but I'm also embarrassed about losing my cool with a pathetic old drunk. "It's fine. Everything's fine."

Maybe finally decides to hop up. I try to get her to flee the scene, but she pulls away and jumps on the sheriff. She stamps a perfect wet paw print onto his previously spotless khaki uniform pants, nailing him inches from his crotch. She jumps up again, trying to kiss him. I pull her back and grab her collar. "Oh God, I'm so sorry. I didn't realize the grass was damp."

He brushes at his pants. "It's okay. It's just water." He bends down and talks to Maybe in a high-pitched voice that's unexpected from this barrel-chested man. "Aren't you a pretty girl?" I'm relieved he's not upset about her jumping on him, and even more relieved that he sees her as the pretty girl she still is, and not a freak sideshow dog. Maybe wiggles her behind at him; her tail whips huge figure eights, like it always does when she's at her happiest.

"I thought she wouldn't be able to jump on people like that anymore after her surgery. Don't know why; after all, she's still got those big, strong back legs."

"You mean like people who have a brush with death, and then you think they'll straighten up and fly right?" He scoffs. "Believe me. I see that a lot in my line of work. Never lasts."

I laugh. "Yeah, I guess that is kind of what I thought, that she'd be on her best behavior out of worry that we'd cut something else off her."

He laughs, too, and pets Maybe's back. Although it's winter, she's shedding like a dandelion in a windstorm, and with each stroke, another handful of hair wafts away on the breeze.

A boy of about seven, walking by with his dad, stops to watch the sheriff petting Maybe.

"Do you want to pet her too?" I ask. His face lights up, and he drops his dad's hand.

As the boy comes toward us, he asks, "Is her leg gonna grow back?"

The officer and I exchange smiles. "Nope," I say. "It's gone for good."

The boy seems okay with that. He pets Maybe, and she thanks him with several kisses on his neck and chin, bringing on fits of giggles. Which in turn, brings more kisses. And more giggles. I'm beginning to think we might be here all day, but his dad comes over and collects him. The boy waves as they walk away, and the officer and I wave back.

"Cute kid," the officer says. Then, turning his attention to Maybe again, he asks, "So, how'd she lose the leg? Car accident?"

"No. She has cancer." I brace myself, expecting a lecture on not letting a dog suffer. Instead, his eyes go soft, and he cups Maybe's chin. "Aw, shoot. I lost my last dog to cancer." He looks into Maybe's eyes, but I can tell he's looking for traces of his own dog.

"Me too." He looks up, and our eyes meet. We've both been at that dark and desperate place of losing a beloved dog to the demon that is cancer.

"Did they get it all?" He seems tentative, afraid to ask.

"We won't know for a while. So far so good. Her lungs and her lymph nodes are clear."

He looks back down at Maybe. "You give that cancer a good ass-whooping, you hear?" To me he says, "What's her name?"

I tell him, and as he walks away, he says, "I'll keep Maybe in my prayers tonight."

I watch him go. I can only describe the feeling that wells up inside me as warm and fuzzy. That's not a phrase I use often. I'm not the sort of person who usually experiences such feelings—especially regarding a total stranger. But since Maybe *is* warm and fuzzy, I know how wonderful that feels, and it seems an accurate description of my insides.

*

MAYBE BREEZES THROUGH her blood-work appointment; she's a pro now at these vet visits. Dr. Leo congratulates me on her blood work and weight being perfect, and rewards Maybe with a handful of treats.

When we get back to the Chick, a couple, whom I've secretly been calling Edie and Eddie Bauer all weekend, due to their penchant for khakis and Pendleton wool shirts, are loading their bags into the back of their Explorer.

I let Maybe out of the car, and she runs to them, always the friendly greeter.

"A tri-pawed!" Edie (I have no idea what her real name is) is unfazed by Maybe jumping up on her red Gore-Tex jacket.

"Maybe! Off." I yell, and then apologize, for what—the hundredth time? I've got to work on that with her.

Edie waves me off. "It's fine. My parents used to have a three-legged dog." She pats Maybe's back. "She's gorgeous."

"She sure doesn't miss that leg," her husband adds.

"It's less than a month," I say. "But she gets around like she's always been on three legs." As if she understands, Maybe romps around us, showing off her agility. "I forget sometimes, for a second, about the surgery, and then when I see her and that missing limb, I think, aw, poor thing. Which is ridiculous because she doesn't miss it, and she's not wasting any time feeling sorry for herself." As I talk, I realize this is the most I've ever said to any of the guests. I guess it's not so bad to talk to them, as long as they want to talk about Maybe.

"Dogs sure can teach us to live in the moment," Mr. Bauer says.

Maybe comes and leans against me, her new tripod lean that I've noticed her do against walls or Selene or me—taking some weight off the remaining legs. Smart girl.

They ask what happened to the leg, and I tell them about the cancer and her, so far, clear lungs and lymph nodes. Is it weird to talk to strangers about a dog's lymph nodes? I've heard that dog owners often share the most intimate details of their dogs' lives with each other, but of course with Barnum, we were both happy to keep to ourselves.

"Well, she looks like she doesn't have a care in the world," Edie says. "We better get going. Gotta get home to our own dog. I sure miss him." She kisses Maybe on the forehead. "Maybe, I hope you stay cancer-free." She waves good-bye as her husband backs out.

Inside, Maybe heads for her water bowl while I make myself some tea. As I wait for the water to boil, I think about what the man said about living in the moment.

If I knew I was going to die, the way Ryan did, how would I want to spend my last few months? I sure wouldn't be worrying about finding another office job, that's for sure. For Ryan, it was different: he loved working with his dad, so he kept going into the office until he didn't have the strength anymore. But me? There's no way I'd want to spend my remaining days in an upholstered cubicle, under fluorescent lighting. I'd want to be outside as much as possible: going to the beach, swimming in the ocean, hiking.

I don't know. This whole "live for today" thing doesn't really make sense—at least not from a practical standpoint. If we only had *today*, no one would work. No one would pay their bills, or recycle, or floss. I wouldn't be drinking this tasteless green tea that's supposed to fight cancer and rev up my metabolism. I wouldn't care. I wouldn't need to.

When it comes right down to it, you can't completely live like there's no tomorrow.

And it's not like I didn't already learn something from this cancer crap—I do realize life's too short. Aren't I planning to lecture my aunt and uncle about that very thing when they get back? And I left Philly so I could move back to San Diego and be near the ocean again. Of course, I haven't fulfilled that quest yet, but I'm working on it.

Seriously, Cancer, I'm working on it. So cut me some fricking slack and stop trying to teach me shit.

THAT NIGHT, I try to focus on the pleasant conversation I had with the couple outside the Chick, or on that nice sheriff and his offer of a prayer for Maybe, but I can't help it. I keep replaying the scene with Betty over and over in my mind. I make a list of comebacks for the next time some idiot has something negative to say about Maybe:

1. "My vet charges an arm or a leg. We're still paying off the bill."
2. "She still has one more than you."
3. "A dog this good, you don't eat all at once." (A variation on a joke my dad used to love to tell about a farmer and his multi-talented pig. Dad would have loved Maybe.)
4. "Oh hey; you're right. She's missing a leg! I knew I saw her burying something in the yard . . ."
5. Or I could have "Nothing Up My Sleeve" printed on a T-shirt for her.

CHAPTER 23
WHEN DID I BECOME
SO CLUELESS?

It's going to be a busy weekend at the Chick. Not only is it Valentine's Day weekend, with the contrived day of romance falling on Sunday, but it's also Ryan's birthday on Saturday, so my former in-laws arrive Friday afternoon, which is a mere thirty or so hours away. We have a lot to do to get the inn ready for its first fully booked weekend in a month, and I need to wear Maybe out so I can get to work. Reluctantly, I head down with her to the stream, because it's the quickest way to tire her out.

We're not there five minutes, when Kai and Milo appear. Other than the occasional wave as he drives off in his van, I haven't seen him since the last time we were down here.

He sits next to me. I offer a "hey" by way of greeting, before retreating into a long sip from my coffee mug.

"How's things?" he asks.

"Fine."

"Good."

"Yup."

"How's Selene?"

Ah, Selene. Now here's a safe topic of conversation. I'm embarrassed about how red I could feel my cheeks turning the last time we were here together, but I doubt he noticed. He's too busy being hot for Selene.

"Selene's good," I say.

"Good."

Geez, this guy's shy. I should encourage him to let on that he likes her. "I like working with her. She's a lot of fun to be around."

"Yeah, she's nice."

Nice? That's it? I suppose, for a shy guy like him, it would be embarrassing to admit to me that he's interested. I think I'll try to get it out of him, for fun. "She *is* nice. And sweet." I wait. He says nothing, just watches the dogs. "She's gorgeous too."

He looks at me. He doesn't seem to be imagining our lovely Selene, but then, I can't tell what he's thinking. He's apparently mulling something over. "She is," he agrees in a noncommittal tone.

"Before Maybe got sick, we did some hiking together. She's in killer shape."

"Yep." He nods while turning his gaze to the dogs again. "She is that."

This guy's a hard nut to crack. "So, how long have you known each other?"

"Selene?" *Yes, that's who we're talking about. Duh.* "I don't know. I guess since shortly after I moved here." He nods up toward his house. "'Bout five years."

And he's only just now interested? Of course, she was dating Devon before.

"How long was she with Devon?"

"I'm not sure exactly, but a long time. They were already together when I moved in."

Aha. That explains it. He's been biding his time.

"Do you mind if I ask you something?" he says. He runs his right hand over his crew cut. Isn't his fuzzy head cold out here? Mine is, and I've got a full head of hair. In fact, thinking about it, I realize how cold I am and pull my hood up. "How long were you with your partner?"

What? I peek around the edge of my hood. "My . . . partner? You mean my husband?"

"Oh." He squints at me, then blinks rapidly. "Yeah. Your husband."

"Did you think I was a lesbian? I mean, it's no big deal, but . . ."

"I didn't before, but I just realized that when Selene told me you were a widow, she never said, you know, one way or the other." He shrugs. "And then I thought, uh, that maybe you were interested in Selene."

"Why would I be interested in Selene?"

"Because she's nice and sweet and gorgeous and in killer shape." He counts off the compliments I've just given Selene on his fingers. "And she's a lesbian."

"Selene's a lesbian?" Wait a minute. Devon's a girl? Why wouldn't she tell me? I wouldn't care. One of my very best friends back home, Karen, is a lesbian. "So, you thought I was interested in her?" I'm so confused. "But I thought . . . Are you sure about Selene?"

"I've met Devon, so yeah, I'm one hundred percent sure."

Whoa. Back up the turnip truck. If he knows Selene is a lesbian, then he's obviously not interested in Selene. Which means . . . the girl he talked about to Weaver is . . . I stand up. "I gotta go." I pull my hood farther down over my face. "I don't want Maybe to overdo it. She's still building up her stamina. Come on, Maybe."

He stands as well. "Oh, uh, okay. I hope I didn't say anything to offend you," he says to my back as I hurry up the hill behind the hopping Maybe.

"No, 's'fine," I yell, without turning back. I dart my hand up in a quick wave that I know he'll see; I can feel him watching us.

On our way back up to the house, we pass a couple on their way down to the stream. I nod and give a rote smile, my usual quick pass of the guests. They beam at me. *What was that about?* I think as we march toward the house. I look down at Maybe, wondering if she'll have an answer. Of course, she *is* the answer. They were smiling at this wonderful, inspiring dog. But as amazing and smart as this girl is, I bet *she* didn't realize Selene's a lesbian either. Or that Kai might like me and not Selene.

*

ON HANDS AND knees, I reach behind the pedestal sink in Iowa Blue's bathroom, scrubbing every corner and crevice. Why am I doing this? After all, Barbara won't be on her hands and knees in this bathroom. In fact, I imagine she won't even be barefooted in here. (I picture her tiptoeing around with her still-taut ballerina's calves, grimacing with each dainty step.) And yet, I cannot stop myself from cleaning every inch. After Selene has already cleaned it. Dip sponge in bucket, scrub in frantic circles, repeat.

We're putting them in Iowa because it's the best room—with the Jacuzzi tub and the fireplace and all—but still, even the nicest room may not be up to Barbara's fussy standards.

It seems that ever since Mr. Martin left a bad review of the Chick on his travel blog, I'm seeing more and more problems with the place. His review glossed over his muffin run-in with me (he made a passing reference to the "surly kitchen staff") and focused on the Chick itself. He wrote, "The place tries for an air of country shabby chic, but is instead simply shabby." I thought that was pretty harsh when I read it, but confess that since then, and since Selene talked about all the work the Chick needs, I've been seeing the place with new eyes. Now, I see how the wallpaper in the Rhode Island Red room curls at some of the seams. And how a traffic pattern in the rug highlights the path from the kitchen to the dining table, and some of the furniture bears scars from years of use and abuse. And that the flaking paint outside needs to be scraped away and redone. But other things add to the place's old-home charm—like the squeaky front porch steps, and the crack in one panel of the rose window in the stairwell, and I sort of like the way the wind howls at the front door when a storm comes calling.

Still, there's no doubt the place needs a face-lift. In my mind, I transform into a blond genie, à la *I Dream of Jeannie*. I fold my arms and, with a quick head jerk and flick of my silky ponytail, the old wallpaper vanishes. Another nod, and in a flash, new paint freshens every wall. Head jerk: old grout looks white as toothpaste. Again: new carpet. Even in my imagination, I begin to get whiplash. Selene was right; the place needs a serious infusion of capital, backed by vats of elbow grease.

Sitting on my heels for a break, I survey the bathroom. I should really be helping do other things; since we're fully booked for the weekend, there's a lot more pressing stuff to do than recleaning this room. It would have been nice if Jeffrey and Barbara had picked a different weekend to come, but then again, being busy working will mean less time I have to spend entertaining them, so I guess it's a good thing that Ryan's birthday falls the day before Valentine's.

I shrug and get to my feet. This bathroom is as clean as it's going to get, barring an acid wash.

"Sorry, did I miss something in here?" Selene pokes her head in.

"No, it's fine." I brush a stray hair off my face and follow her into the bedroom. I can't help looking around the room once more, to see if I've missed anything. "It's just . . ." My voice trails off as a spot on the windowsill attracts my attention. I attack it with my sponge.

Selene watches me, then goes over and fluffs the oversize pillows on the bed. She leaves a gap between the two pillows that looks messy;

I make a mental note to refluff them after she leaves. "Your in-laws are coming to see you, right? Not to see if our vents are dusted."

"Oh no, the vents." I look up at the white metal grill. Is that a cobweb clinging there? When the heat's on, that thing'll be swinging in the breeze, and Barbara will notice it for sure. "You're right. I better get the step stool."

She follows my gaze and shakes her head. "I doubt they're going to notice."

"You don't know my former mother-in-law. She's very . . . fastidious. We're talking plastic covers on the lampshades. Wait till you see her. Not a hair out of place."

"Okay, but still. It's not like they're coming to visit you in your own home. If it's not up to her standards, it's not like she's going to think it's a bad reflection on you."

I keep cleaning while we talk, spit shining ant-size blemishes on the white baseboards. Selene tries to sit down on the bed, but my "No, no, no!" stops her before she wrinkles the duvet. "Sorry," she says as she moves to the chair by the window instead.

"We hardly ever had them over to our place," I tell Selene. "She couldn't handle the dog hair." Ugh. The dog hair. Every inch of the den needs to be vacuumed. And I'll have to keep them out of my room. "Besides, I know she thought everything I cooked wasn't healthy enough. If we ate at their house, she could watch Jeffrey's caloric intake."

"She sounds a touch controlling."

"A teensy-weensy bit." I know my sarcasm comes through loud and clear.

"Still, this is maybe going to sound rude—and I apologize if it is—but you said it yourself: they're your 'former' in-laws. Why are you letting her get to you like this? They live on the other side of the country. You're probably not even going to see them very often anymore."

I stop spit shining. I go over and sit on the edge of the bed that I just tried to keep Selene away from. "You're right." Why am I freaking out? It's still the guilt, right? It's the fact that I didn't love their son like I ought to have, at the end; the fact that his birthday is going to be another handful of salt poured into their still-fresh wounds, while mine are scabbed over. But I can't talk to Selene about that. Instead I say, "I guess she always made me feel inferior. I don't think she thought I was a very good wife." I omit the kernel of truth that, indeed, I wasn't.

"I bet you were a great wife." She comes over and hugs me, which is awkward since I don't want to be hugged in the first place, and since I'm sitting, and she's standing. "I'm sure Ryan thought you were the best. And that's what matters." She plops on the bed next to me.

Um, no. You'd be incorrect.

"I don't want to talk about it anymore," I say. Like a forgotten towel in the dryer, my mind's been going over and over what Kai said earlier. I'm not sure how I feel about the fact that I'm the one he might like, not Selene, but I'll think about that later. Right now, I need to let her know what I found out about her. "Besides, we always talk about me."

I can't decide if she never mentioned being a lesbian because she's blasé about it, or because she's used to getting a negative reaction, so she avoids the subject. This seems like a good time to broach the subject, but how do I bring it up, without sounding like a jerk? I feel like suddenly volunteering information about Karen—"Hey, did I ever mention that one of my best friends is a lesbian?"—might come across like I, as the straight person, need to validate her. Hell. I hate thinking that she feels like she needs to hide her true self from me.

I get more comfortable on the bed. "Seriously, let's talk about you for a change."

"Don't be silly. We talk about me all the time. We talk about my accounting class, and my family. And you know my big, dumb, not-so-secret dream now."

"What about Devon? You never told me how long you guys were together. All you told me is how come she left." There. *She.* I snuck it in that I know.

My subtly dropped nugget hits with an almost audible ping, and her eyes widen, then go to her hands in her lap.

She licks her lips. "We were together for five and half years. Six if you count our 'break' time." She glances up at me. Her curiosity gets the better of her. "Did your aunt tell you?"

"No. Kai did."

"Oh."

"Look, I feel kinda . . . dumb, I guess, for not knowing this major thing about your life. I feel like I should have known, and if I were a better friend and talked about *you* more, well, then I would have known."

"You have been a good friend. A great friend. And I hardly have any friends here. I was so wrapped up in Devon I never took the time to maintain my other friendships. Stupid, huh?" Another glance at me with her big velvet-lashed dark eyes. She really is a gorgeous girl— inside and out. How is she still single? Maybe there aren't that many lesbians in Prescott. "And it's not like my work is a great place to make friends." She looks at me with an expression so serious I wonder if she's going to reveal some other deep secret. "Where do adults go to make friends? Wasn't it easier when we were kids?"

I smile. "No. Not for me it wasn't. Other kids sucked when I was a kid."

She laughs. "I'm going to miss your sense of humor." *Uh, yeah. Wasn't joking.* "I'm going to be so bummed when you finally move away."

"That feels a million years away right now. Anyway, I'm glad we talked about it. I'd hate to think you didn't tell me because you thought I wouldn't be able to handle it or whatever."

"I'm sorry I didn't tell you."

"Stop apologizing!"

"Sor—I mean, okay. I should have told you. I should've known you'd be cool about it. It's just . . . a lot of people love to hate. You know?"

"Yeah, well, a lot of people are jerks. I've had enough of this cleaning nonsense. Let's go get a beer."

THAT NIGHT IN bed, while trying to avoid obsessing about my in-laws' arrival tomorrow, I make a list of reasons why it's not possible that I'm the one Kai mentioned to Weaver:

1. Weaver used the word "girl," and I'm certain I stopped being a girl at least ten, if not twelve or so, years ago. (But then, when you're practically ninety, does every woman under fifty seem like a girl? Or, wait, did he say "gal"? Am I a gal? Probably. Damn.)

2. Kai thinks I look like the town drunk. I know some men are desperate enough not to mind drunken disorderliness in a woman—maybe even prefer it—but Kai's handsome and not the least bit desperate; he's definitely not one of those types.

3. Even if I don't look like the town drunk (okay, maybe sometimes I do, but not, like, all the time), I'm not the kind of woman men fall for. Okay, there was Ryan, but that's the exception that proves the rule. I'm not girly, and I don't like to waste time on makeup and hair and clothes. I almost never look my best, and even my best (brushed hair, moisturizer, clean clothes) falls short of what looks plain acceptable on most women.

4. Kai knows I'm going back to San Diego, and he said he's never moving again, so there's zero future there. He knows that.

Clearly, I'm being stupid. Although I've only gotten to number four on my list, I can see that the signs point to Weaver having misinterpreted things. I remember Weaver saying that Kai claimed that he and the "gal" were "just friends"—and that's all we are. Even if I blush like crazy whenever he touches me, we're just friends. And that's all we're going to be. So, yeah, that must be it: Weaver misunderstood.

"Right, Maybe?" I whisper into her fur. She wakes enough to make an *mwwrrmph* sound, which I take as agreement.

CHAPTER 24
THE REALLY LONG WEEKEND

A batch of my special cookies is in the oven, and the kitchen smells of cinnamon. Jeffrey and Barbara should be here any minute, and the baking has helped pass the time while we wait.

"Come and sit," Mom says from the kitchen table, where she sips tea and flips through Aunt Sugar's latest *Reader's Digest*. Mom arrived in time for lunch today, and has already changed clothes twice—once because Maybe jumped on her in greeting when she arrived and got a tiny bit of dirt on her slacks (it was only one paw's worth), and then a second time because she decided the turquoise pants she changed into weren't formal enough for Barbara. I told her not to worry, waving my hand to indicate my own not-Barbara-ready favorite jeans. At least I'm wearing my best green wool sweater—which Mom suggested I swap out for the beagle cardigan she gave me for Christmas. I lied and said it was at the dry cleaner's.

The oven timer dings at the same time I hear a car crunching up the gravel path.

I pull out the cookies and pluck a few off the tray, dropping them onto a rose-rimmed china plate.

I look out the kitchen window. "It's them." My tone sounds like I'm announcing the arrival of a plague of locusts. Mom squeals. We go out onto the porch. Mom waves while Jeffrey parks their rental.

Maybe scratches at the closed kitchen door, trapped until we can say calm hellos without an overeager three-legged dog stamping her mark on the festivities. She whines, but I ignore her; she'll have to wait.

Jeffrey toots the horn, then hops out of the car. Not waiting for Barbara, he bounds up the steps two at a time. "Jane!" He grabs me in a bear hug, pulling me up onto my toes. Enveloped in his beige Burberry trench coat, I remember the hugs Ryan used to give me—he'd stretch back and pull my feet up off the ground. When you are five foot eleven, it's rare that someone else lifts you up. It always struck me as a unique and wonderful experience. Ryan was the one person whose hugs I truly enjoyed. I should have told him that.

Barbara picks her way across the gravel in her pointy-toed—*Who travels in shoes like that?*—pumps. After a cross-country flight and a two-hour drive up from Phoenix, she still looks freshly cleaned, pressed, and laundered, with her black coat, deep burgundy talon nails, and shiny black purse. Ah, but there it is, the slight sign of wear and tear when her porcelain foundation makeup cracks as she smiles and leans in for the old shoulder-clutching hug that I haven't missed.

"Come in." Mom waves them in, as if it's her house.

"Maybe, no jumping," I say as we file into the kitchen. Maybe careens around the room, rubbing against human and table legs, swishing her tail behind her like an Olympic gymnast's ribbon. Jeffrey notices the plate of cookies and snatches one. He breaks off a pecan and offers it to Maybe before popping the rest in his mouth. With that and a bit of smooth talking and some butt scratching, Maybe is all his. Barbara says, "What a lovely dog," but I notice she doesn't pet her.

"These are delicious." Jeffrey takes another cookie while Barbara frowns at him.

"They're good for you," I fib. I'd wanted to make Jeffrey his favorite, decadent peanut butter cookies with chocolate chunks, but knew that wouldn't go over well with Barbara. Instead I made healthy-*sounding* cookies. "Whole grain antioxidant cookies—they've got oatmeal, and some pecans and dark chocolate." I don't mention the two sticks of butter or the cup of sugar.

"If they're good for me, I'll have another."

The four of us do the whole how-was-your-flight and how-was-the-drive routine. We go through the now-expected exchange about Maybe: "What happened to her leg?" "She has cancer." Which I hate to bring up with them. They've been here all of two minutes. Barbara looks around the room when I say the C-word; "Awww," Jeffrey says, getting down on one knee so Maybe can kiss his proffered chin. "She sure looks healthy."

To change the subject, I offer to help bring in luggage. We get their bags from the car, and I show them to Iowa Blue. We run into Selene on the stair landing and do introductions. Once in their room, Barbara's face remains impassive as she scans her eyes over the place. They rest a beat too long on the crocheted doily atop the dresser, causing me to notice the coffee stain. *How did I miss that?* Barbara seems reluctant to take off her coat, as if it's a sign that they're giving in and actually staying here. Jeffrey booms that the room is perfect as he shucks Barbara out of her coat, and we go back downstairs to the private den.

We make it through the first night with a trip to Hassayampa Inn for dinner. It's classy, and even Barbara seems impressed. Luckily, they are tired from the time difference, so they head up to their room early. Selene helps me prep some things for Saturday morning, and then I crash on the sofa with Maybe.

At breakfast the next morning, which the Chick serves from 7:30 to 9:30 a.m., Barbara and Jeffrey are the first guests down. Jeffrey ducks his head into the kitchen and says good morning. I tell him they can help themselves to coffee and the food will be right out. I'm glad when he goes back out to the dining room, because I can't cook and talk at the same time.

It occurs to me, as I tuck the warm low-fat apple bran muffins into their serving basket, that I haven't spent a night under the same roof with my in-laws since we moved Ryan into their house after the hospital had given up on him. Was that only five months ago? It seems like forever.

Geez Louise! It's Ryan's birthday. Of course I know that—after all, it's the reason they're here. But it didn't pop into my head first thing when I woke up. I should have said something to Jeffrey. I grab the basket of muffins and the butter—and the fake butter for Barbara. In the dining room, two of the other couples have come down, and Selene chats with everyone. I'm not going to say anything in front of strangers, so I whisper to Barbara that the muffins are low fat, and dash back into the kitchen to check on the frittata.

Mom shuffles into the kitchen and heads for me, arms extended. *She* remembered that it's Ryan's birthday right away. But then, she's a much better person than I ever was or ever will be.

"How are you this morning?" She hugs me, her chemical Aqua Net smell overpowering the savory scent of the frittata. She backs away and looks into my face. "I know today's going to be hard. You should take it easy. What can I do to help?"

"I don't need to take it easy." I go back to slicing the frittata.

"I know how you are. Work, work, work. Keep your mind off things. You never want to talk about things."

"I'm not avoiding my feelings, if that's what you're implying." It feels like she's waiting, watching, hoping for me to break down so she can gather up the pieces. "Anyway, I can't talk now. If you want to help, you can make more coffee."

We get through the meal, and as we clean the kitchen, we hear Jeffrey, Barbara, and the other guests chatting while they linger over coffee. This happens all the time, but I find it weird. Why do people want to sit around and yammer with strangers? It's their vacation. Don't they want to go outside and do something?

Mom sits to read the paper. I free Maybe from the den, and we go to my room to check e-mail. It's been almost five weeks since I sent my resume to that biotech company, Golden Triangle Technologies, and I still haven't heard anything. The position's probably been filled already, or they're in the process of filling it—with someone who has biotech experience—but still, I keep hoping I'll hear back. Of course, I know, logically, that I won't get an e-mail from them or an alert about new job postings on a Saturday, but I can't help checking every morning after breakfast. Nothing in my inbox except a message from Karen. That's one great thing about her new baby—she e-mails more often, and it seems like motherhood has taken the edge off her workaholic tendencies. As usual, though, it's just a quick note ("Took up running again to get ready for volleyball season. Egad. When are you going to get here?? Need you to help get my rear in gear. Plus, you are missing all this cuteness!") and includes a link on Picasa to the latest batch of baby pictures. Indy is pretty darn cute, I must admit, and this week's photos are a series of food-smeared close-ups. Mom comes in and can't get enough of the pics; she watches over my shoulder as I click through them.

"Slow down. Wait, go back." While we wait for the photo to reload, she asks, "Indy? What kind of name is that for a baby?"

I shrug. "Elaine's from Indiana." I kind of like it for a girl's name, being a fan of *Raiders of the Lost Ark* and all. Hopefully, she'll grow up to be a kick-butt woman.

"It sounds like a dog's name. Oh, that one's precious. I could eat her up."

"They'd frown on it if you did. They're vegetarian."

Mom shoves my shoulder in response. When I get to the last one, she says, "Jeffrey and Barbara are talking with Selene in the kitchen. Have you said anything to them, yet, about today?"

I slump in my chair. "I don't know what to say."

"Let them know that you're here for them. And it would probably help them if you talked about Ryan." I know she's thinking that it's not normal that I never want to talk about him. Now that his parents are here, I guess she figures I'll have to. "Let's go; they're waiting. They came here to be with you, after all."

Jeffrey and Barbara are sitting at the kitchen table. Mom joins them. Selene excuses herself to go switch over a load of laundry. Maybe circles the room looking for attention and, after getting pats from Jeffrey, collapses onto the floor with a "we never do anything fun around here anymore" look on her face.

I lean against the kitchen counter and rub Maybe's behind with the toe of my sneaker. I ask my former in-laws how they enjoyed breakfast. Jeffrey raves and pats his stomach. Barbara manages a smile. Everyone falls silent and seems to wait.

"I know today's going to be hard," I venture.

Jeffrey nods, looks down. "Of course, a day doesn't go by that we don't think of our son and miss him terribly." He looks over at Barbara, and places his hand on top of hers. "But some days are tougher to take."

Selene pokes her head through the doorway and quietly comes into the kitchen. Maybe hops up to greet her as if she's been gone a week. "It's beautiful out there. What are you guys going to do today?"

"We haven't talked about that yet." Our discussion of Ryan interrupted, I glance at Barbara, who's studying Jeffrey's hand, so large it all but hides hers from view.

"It's a nice day for a drive over to Jerome," Selene suggests.

"That'd be fun," Mom says. "We could have lunch there and look around the shops."

"What's Jerome?" Jeffrey asks.

"It's a charming spot, perched on a hillside," Mom explains, like she's from the tourist bureau. "It used to be a big mining town. It's less than an hour from here."

It's decided. Selene offers to take Maybe to Watson Lake while we're gone. As we discuss whose car to take, Mom whispers, "Is that what you're wearing?"

It's hard to say which of us will be more embarrassed by the other's outfit. I think I look fine. I wear jeans (my good pair) and a button-down shirt. Okay, it's a plaid flannel shirt, nothing fancy, with my zip-up gray sweatshirt over it. It wouldn't make the fashion pages, but no holes, stains, or worn spots stick out. At the other end of the spectrum, we have Mom decked out in the turquoise ensemble that she deemed not somber enough for last night. The sequined silhouette of a howling coyote covers the back of the blouse. To me it screams "Arizona tourist," even though the woman has been a local for years now. We roll our eyes at each other.

We decide to take Mom's Lincoln, and I chauffeur them to Jerome. It's a gorgeous day. I don't think I've ever seen the sky this particular shade of blue anywhere but in Arizona. It's so blue it looks fake—a Hollywood or Disney creation. The temperature hovered at freezing when I first woke, but now, the sun warms the car. In the backseat, Jeffrey makes huffing sounds. The rest of us fall silent so he can sleep. We hit a winding downhill section of Highway 89, and we rock in unison, left, then right, then left again. I can't believe Jeffrey can sleep through this, but Barbara whispers that he's been up since three thirty due to the time difference.

The day passes pleasantly enough. We wander through antique shops and galleries; visit the mining museum; sit on benches and look at the view over the valley below; and, finally at lunch, we reminisce about Ryan. Jeffrey orders a bottle of wine, and we toast Ryan and the fortieth birthday he did not see. Barbara weeps, Mom sniffles, and

Jeffrey clears his throat. I tear up when Jeffrey says, "Ryan, you are greatly missed."

The stories about Ryan flow from the first toast until the waiter tries to ply us with dessert. Instead of ordering something, my mom tells the Waynesfields a dessert-related memory, although they've heard the story many times. It was the first time my parents met Ryan; they came to dinner at my old San Diego apartment. He wanted to impress them, so insisted on helping. I knew he was clueless in the kitchen, so asked him to make a simple dessert. I gave him my easiest recipes to pick from, but of course, being a typical boy, he wanted to make something he could set fire to. He decided on bananas Foster. I figured he couldn't do too much damage, since I had a glass tabletop. But I wasn't counting on the napkin draped over his arm, like he was a waiter in a fancy restaurant, which he proceeded to flambé, along with the bananas. And then, in a panic, he dropped it on the rug. No security deposit returned at that place. But it always made for a good story.

Of course, for me, the annoying memory that follows is how he used that as an excuse to never help in the kitchen again.

When we get back to the Chick, Barbara says she'd like to lie down for a bit. Mom says it's a good idea since "being a tourist is exhausting." I'm hoping Jeffrey will follow Barbara upstairs so I can have some alone time.

"Jane, is there somewhere we could go and talk? Someplace more private?"

So much for alone time. "There's a spot out back that I like. You might want to put your jacket on. It can be chilly in the shade."

As we settle into the Adirondack chairs, Jeffrey leans forward and rests his elbows on his khaki-covered knees. He clasps his hands and watches the stream, as if it has some hidden wisdom (which I think it does). I wait, since he's the one that called this meeting. I was right—it is cold out here. I wish I'd brought some gloves. I shove my hands under my thighs.

"I've practiced a few different ways of approaching this," he says, which makes me wonder what the hell he's going to say. He looks down at his leather loafers. "Oh, Jane. God sure makes you feel foolish sometimes, with all your dreaming and hoping." He tilts his head back and looks up at the branches overhead. He takes a deep breath. "As soon as I got the idea to start my own business, it was my dream to have Ryan come work with me. We'd build the place up together and sell it. Make enough money that both our families would be comfortable. Boy, the way it all worked out." He turns to me. "I found a buyer. I'm selling."

I can't believe it. Finally. What I had hoped for all those years in Philly. *Now* it happens. Now that Ryan's gone. Now that it doesn't matter to me anymore. I realize Jeffrey's waiting for me to say something. "That's great. Congratulations."

"Thanks. But, it's doesn't feel right without Ryan here. The ridiculous thing is, they're paying me a fortune—twenty-five million—and I can't even get excited about it." He shakes his head as if still unable to believe his news.

"Wow." I'd fall out of my chair—if it weren't an Adirondack. That's an amazing amount of money, but he seems unmoved by it. "I know Ryan always said the company had huge potential." Their specialized software for pharmacies had struggled to find a foothold at first, but sales had been good—*really* good—the last year or so. "It's a testament to what you built. Maybe in time, you'll be able to enjoy . . ." My words trail off. There is no enjoyment for him without Ryan there to share in it.

"There is one thing that would make me happy. It involves you."

"Me? What do I have to do with anything?"

He reaches into his jacket and pulls out a white envelope. "Open it."

Lifting the unsealed flap reveals a check, typed in no-nonsense font on a pale blue background. I haven't even pulled it all the way out when I notice the amount—five *hundred thousand* dollars—and then see my name on it. Stunned, I'm no longer aware of the chill air. My neck feels hot; my sweatshirt becomes a sauna. My mind races ahead. I could move to San Diego. Tomorrow. It would be so much better to search for a job while living there.

But, it's not right.

I can't take Jeffrey's money. I slip the check back in the envelope. I feel Jeffrey studying my face. "I can't." I try to hand it back, but he holds up his hands.

"I knew you'd refuse," he says. "In fact, I wanted to make the check out for more than that, but I figured this was the most I'd be able to talk you into. It's only two percent, Jane."

"No. Thank you, sincerely, for thinking of me, but there's no way I can take this money." I try again to hand it back to him, but he ignores the gesture. I lay the envelope on my knees and stare at it.

"Ryan would want you to accept it. I know he didn't have life insurance. He might have had it as an employee benefit if he still worked for a big company like he did in San Diego."

"Well, this is a helluva lot more than life insurance would have paid out." I shake my head. "I can't take it. I don't . . ." I want to say "deserve it," but instead go with, "need it. I have a good career. I'm sure I'm going to find a job in San Diego soon. I'll be back on my feet in no time. It's very thoughtful of you, but it's not necessary."

"This isn't about whether you need it or not."

"I just can't accept this. I'm sorry. But that's all there is to it." If things had worked out differently, if Ryan hadn't gotten sick, I'd have walked out on him a year ago. I'd have been back in San Diego long before the business was sold. The money would have been split between Jeffrey and Ryan and had nothing to do with me. Jeffrey's offer to me is a gift based on something he thought was there, but which didn't exist.

"I expected you to react this way, and I think I know why you feel you can't take the money." He pauses, looking down at his immaculate fingernails. "Ryan told me about the problems you two were having. I . . . I know you didn't love him anymore."

He looks back up at me, but I can't meet his eyes.

I can't believe he knows—has known all along. I look down at my grubby nails, broken and brittle from the months of parched air and daily chores. I look at them in contrast to the smooth white envelope resting under my fingertips. I've fooled a lot of people, playing the sad widow, but not Jeffrey. He's seen through me all this time. I feel like such an idiot. Worse than an idiot—a liar. A total bitch. Why doesn't he hate me? Why is he giving me this money? I don't understand, although one thing is clear to me: he must not have told Barbara. I'm sure she would have cut me out of their lives if she knew the truth.

I wish I knew exactly what Ryan told Jeffrey, but I don't deserve to ask. I think back to that horrible night when Ryan died, and tears begin to slip down my cheeks.

Jeffrey puts his hand on mine. His skin is soft, and I know mine feels like sandpaper. I don't deserve his comfort.

"I didn't want him to know I didn't love him anymore. I thought I was doing such a good job of hiding it. I really did *try* to hide it. But I found out that he knew, the night he died."

With my elbows on my knees, I drop my face into my hands. Jeffrey puts his arm around my shoulder.

"What happened that night?" Jeffrey asks. "I always had the feeling you never told us exactly what went on."

He's right. I didn't. I couldn't.

CHAPTER 25

REGRETS. YEAH, YOU COULD SAY I'VE HAD A FEW

That night, which I think of so often, comes to me again. I'm back in that guest room with its gold carpet, the dim light from the bedside lamp with its fussy pink Victorian shade, and the Air Wick soothing-jasmine air-smotherer competing with the musty, almost-metallic smell that hovers over Ryan's bed. Barnum snores at my feet; Ryan drifts in and out of sleep.

Barbara and Jeffrey had gone to bed. I was the only one awake, sitting in the recliner that Jeffrey'd brought in from the living room.

We'd carved out a routine by then. While Jeffrey worked, Barbara and I took turns being with Ryan. Mornings were hers, while I did whatever needed doing—walking Barnum or making drugstore runs. For lunch, the four of us, counting Barnum, gathered in Ryan's room. As if we didn't already know, *that* was a sure sign that Ryan was dying; otherwise, no way in hell would Barbara let meals be taken outside the dining room. Ryan wasn't eating much by then, maybe some broth or a few sips of a shake. (How bad has life become when everything—even a chocolate shake—tastes like chalk?) We felt guilty eating in front of the skin and bones he'd become, even if it was just one of Barbara's thin soups or a sandwich as flat as a deck of cards. But he liked us joining him, said it made him feel more normal.

Afternoons were my turn. I'd read aloud. Neither of us had ever been poetry lovers, but we took to it in those last weeks. We didn't have the staying power for a novel (besides, Ryan lamely joked that he might never hear the ending), and even short stories took more focus than we could muster. So I started reading from a book of *Best Loved Poems* I found on Barbara's bookshelf. They were perfect vignettes about nature, love, and sometimes—if I screwed up and didn't scan them first—death.

By the time I'd read two or three, Ryan would nap. I'd pull out my laptop and go through work e-mails. I was on leave then, but it made me feel useful to check in. I'd answer any questions, forward requests that had come in, add my one cent to discussions. I wasn't up to two cents, what with the worrying and waiting and dreading: Will today be his last? I wasn't ready for that last day. I didn't know how to say good-bye.

In the evenings, when Jeffrey got home, we'd give father and son some time alone. I'd often overhear Jeffrey telling Ryan about work issues, asking his advice about accounting and finance issues. Ryan perked up during those conversations, sitting up a little higher on his changed-daily pillows. He'd unpack his arms from under the layers of blanket that Barbara smothered him with, and lace his fingers on his chest.

After dinner, I'd read the paper to Ryan. This would not have been my activity of choice if I were in his shoes. (Of course, by then it had been ages since he'd worn shoes—he was always either barefoot or wearing those dingy blue-gray hospital socks with the rubber nubs on the bottom. But maybe that was it. Maybe when you're reduced to wearing nothing but socks with rubber nubs, you feel the world passing you by like it's the express train and you're on the "Local" platform.) Anyway, I'd try to skip the really bad news and stick to the . . . well, almost none of it was good news, but some of it was less depressing. I'd savor the rare funny items, the ones where Ryan's chapped lips would part and a half cough, half laugh would come out. I remember the story I read that night, remember the last time I heard that dry laugh.

"A man was arrested for trying to revive a dead opossum by the side of the highway in Punxsutawney."

"Mouth-to-mouth?" Ryan's voice was almost a whisper. "Or just chest compressions?" I couldn't believe he was still making jokes. I had to laugh.

"It doesn't say. Maybe he thought it was that groundhog, Punxsutawney Phil; maybe he thought it was his civic duty. What do you suppose they arrested him for? Is it illegal to revive a rodent?"

Barbara came in and asked what was so funny; she didn't see the humor when I read it to her. "Disgusting." She remummified Ryan in his blankets. "Good night, love." She kissed him high on his forehead, on his hair, once so full and thick. "Not too much more, Jane," she said on the way out, as if we were kids hiding with *Mad* magazine and a flashlight under the blankets.

"What about . . . Business?" he asked, fading.

To humor him, I pretended to scan the Business section. "There's nothing much." I dropped the paper on the floor, with the rest of the pile. "Time for bed." I didn't want to read him the grim news about the economy. I knew he worried about what my financial situation would be. I'd told him many times there was nothing to be concerned about. "I'll be fine," I'd say. "I have a good job." Of course, I never mentioned that I planned to quit my job or that I'd need extra money to escape back to San Diego. I couldn't bring myself to tell him my plans, which was silly, because we both knew that I would move. He would have had to be crazy to think I'd stay. But still, I couldn't voice it. Saying, "I'm moving back home" would have been like saying, "I'm *finally* getting my way!" It felt too much like, "Hurry up and die already."

I sat there that night, thinking of the things unsaid between us, piling up like the Great Wall of Denial, while I watched him struggle to keep his eyes open. I wanted his last days to be peaceful. I didn't want to revisit any of the stressful topics we'd fought over. I wanted to pretend, for his sake, that everything was fine, like I'd been doing since he got sick.

But what did I think? That he was a child? That he was oblivious?

Yeah. I guess I kind of did, because I wasn't ready for it when he said, with his eyes shut, "I know you're going to move back." He paused to try to swallow. He opened his eyes; I grabbed his water and held the straw to his lips. He took a small sip, had a coughing fit, and let his head sink back into the pillow, exhausted. "I'm glad," he continued. "I want you . . . to be happy. I'm sorry I didn't . . . make you happy."

"Oh, Ryan." I leaned in toward the bed. I wanted to hold his hand, but Barbara had him tucked in tight. I brushed the back of my hand along his cheek, felt the coolness of his skin. My stomach knotted. He opened his eyes and looked at me, his eyes that were once such a bright green, now dulled from the medications. His jaw hung slack, as if he lacked the strength to close his mouth after speaking. His eyes widened. He drew a sharp but shallow breath.

"What is it? Are you okay? Should I go get your mom?"

"No." His voice was low, a whisper. He struggled under the blankets.

"Are you uncomfortable?" I folded the blankets down, laid his arms on top of them, and held his hand. Blue quarter moons rose on his fingernails.

He moaned, moved his mouth to say something.

"Do you want some more morphine? Hang on; I'm going to give you some." I'd placed a few drops under his tongue a while ago. Was it okay to give him more? Jesus, it couldn't hurt. I didn't know what the hell I was doing. I wanted to call Barbara, call the hospice people. I couldn't handle this. I wondered why it couldn't be like with pets. Why couldn't I crawl in bed with Ryan and wrap my arms around him while some nice doctor with a soothing voice administered a shot; Ryan would quietly, comfortably go limp. That was my one consolation, three weeks later, with Barnum's death—seeing the pain fade from his eyes, the peace he felt at the end. The only thing I could do for Ryan was try to help numb him to it all. I reached for the bottle on the side table.

"No." He gripped my hand with surprising strength. His brittle nails dug into me.

His lips moved; his mouth worked. I leaned closer, afraid I'd miss his words. "And . . . I know . . ." His eyelids slid slowly down, but he still held my hand.

What he was talking about? What else did he know? I was scared. I knew this was the end and didn't know if I could handle it alone. I thought again of running to get Barbara and Jeffrey. Big, strong Jeffrey would know what to do. But Ryan wouldn't let go of my hand.

"Don't talk, Ry. Rest." I started to cry. What the hell did he need to rest for when he was heading for eternal rest? I was just afraid of what he'd say.

"Let . . . finish." He opened his eyes. His head tilted back at an odd angle. He looked uncomfortable. I yearned to give him another drop of his morphine. I wanted to numb him, to numb myself. I blinked back tears.

"I'm listening." I pressed my lips together.

"You don't . . . love me." He paused, gathered himself. "It's okay." I didn't know what to say. My throat closed. I couldn't speak. I squeezed his hand. Tears rolled down my cheeks. I started to shake.

He knew. Of course he did. The man wasn't an idiot. He had to have known, had to have realized things weren't the same between us in those months before he got sick.

I was the idiot. I should have known I couldn't pull off that good of an acting job. I'd always been a terrible liar. How did I think I could fool him?

Ryan opened his mouth to say more. I braced myself, waiting. He had every right to let me have it, but *now*?

"Tha—" Nothing else came out. It was frustrating and painful to watch him struggle. "Tha—" Desperation filled his eyes; they locked on mine. I prayed for it to be over. "It's okay," I managed to say. I stroked his forehead. "I'm here; it's okay."

*

I TELL JEFFREY everything except the last part, about how Ryan tried to say more. I feel like it's my fault that he couldn't get out his last words, probably because I'd given him too much morphine earlier. And I'd wanted to give him more! I don't tell Jeffrey how I ruined his son's chance to say whatever else it was he wanted to get off his chest before he died.

I also don't tell him how Ryan's passing wasn't the peaceful drifting off I'd been sold by Hollywood. It's the one final lie I'll stick to. The same lie I told them that night when I gathered myself to go wake them. I lied to spare them. I don't want them to know how he looked so desperate, so scared. I said he went so quickly and quietly there wasn't time to fetch them. It was the least I could do then. It's still the least I can do.

Jeffrey's had his arm around my shoulders through my story. We're silent, except for my snuffling. I pull away so I can blow my nose on the handkerchief Jeffrey has produced. They don't make men like him anymore. Dapper men, like Cary Grant, ready with a handkerchief when a woman needs to dab her eyes. Or to blow her runny nose, with a blast like a foghorn.

"I wish he hadn't known." One more sob fights its way out. "I was a fool to think he wouldn't realize things were different." Back when I'd first found out Ryan was sick, I thought I'd done a good job of burying my feelings. He was fighting for his life, for Pete's sake; he didn't need to think he was fighting for his wife's affection as well. But no. He knew all along. And then, at the very end, I should have said I loved him; I wasn't *in* love with him, but still . . . I tell Jeffrey how I said it afterward. "Ryan? I love you, Ryan." He had to know that. I shook him. He had to hear me. I wanted to scream, but it was too late. He was gone. "Jeffrey, I totally screwed up saying good-bye to him."

Jeffrey rubs my back. I'm shivering, and my teeth chatter. "It's okay. He knew. I know you probably think you're a terrible person. I'm assuming you feel pretty guilty about how everything . . . ended. But, you did the right thing. You stayed with Ryan when he needed you most. If you fell out of love with him, I can't judge you for that. Oh, I did at first. When Ryan told me, I was upset. But people change; they want different things out of life. And I know, through it all, that Ryan still loved you. If you'd left him, he'd have been devastated. He was grateful to you for staying. He said, 'A lesser woman wouldn't stick around for the ugly stuff.'" He claps his hand on my shoulder one last time. "He thought you were a very strong woman, and he was thankful to have you in his life."

"He was?"

"He was. I want you to think about that." He stands and removes his jacket, draping it over me. It's warm and smells like his musky aftershave. "You stay out here and collect yourself. I'll say you went for a walk. And, Jane"—he points a finger at me—"you are going to keep that check. Ryan made me promise that if I sold the business I'd make sure you were taken care of. You wouldn't want me to go back on a promise to my dying son, now would you?"

He turns and walks back up to the house. I'm left to process the fact that my husband—the man I thought wanted to give me a piece of his mind on his deathbed—was grateful to me. Could that be it? The last thing Ryan struggled to say: "Thank you"?

*

WHILE I SIT, I hear Selene's old truck sputter into the yard, back from Watson Lake. I don't turn around, just stay hunched over, my chin in my hands, elbows on my knees. I hear Maybe's paws tromp down the path. Selene must have let her loose, knowing she'd go to me. Her nose is the first thing I see. She pushes my hand away so she can get at me. Her tongue, warm and thorough, mops up my tears. When she's done, she nestles between my knees and watches the stream with me. She pants, happy from her walk with Selene.

Her presence calms me. When I'm breathing normally again, and I think my face looks more like its old self—which takes a long time, even with Maybe's helpful kisses—I head up to the house. It's a good thing I rarely wear makeup, because if I'd had some on today, my raccoon eyes would give me away. As it is, if my face burns a shade too red, I'll blame it on the crisp air.

Inside, everyone's hanging around the kitchen. Mom asks if I want to help get things ready for dinner, and everyone goes back to chatting.

Barbara, refreshed from her nap, apparently insisted on making one of her "famous" soups. She stands at the stove, wearing one of Aunt Sugar's frilly aprons over her no-nonsense navy A-line dress. Mom carves leftover ham. I warm up some cheddar scones from this morning that will help round out the meal. Selene joins us for dinner, and the five of us sit, knee to knee, at the kitchen table. I'm beat. Lost inside my own head, I register the hum of talk around me. I want to go to bed, which is not an option since I'm sleeping in the den. But I can't manage the sitting around and chatting thing. I want to be alone. So as soon as dinner is over, I announce that I think I'm catching a cold and am going to take a long bath.

The bathtub provides refuge. Sinking down, I stop only when my nose almost touches the water line. Memories of Ryan's last night compete with replays of my talk with Jeffrey. I thought I'd crushed Ryan, but Jeffrey made it sound like he'd long ago accepted the fact that I didn't love him anymore and had even forgiven me for it.

Maybe now, I can forgive myself too?

IT'S HARD to sleep knowing there is a check with so many zeros, made out to me, tucked in my jeans' pocket mere feet away. Am I going to take the money? Tonight's list of the pros and cons of cashing the check can't be avoided:

1. Con: I don't deserve it.
2. Con: I don't really need the money. I will eventually have a good job again.
3. Con: If I take it, I'll feel beholden to Jeffrey, which is not so bad, but that also means, by extension, being beholden to Barbara. If I take the money, I'll always wonder, in the future, if I am only staying in touch with them out of a sense of obligation. (But isn't that already what I'm doing?)
4. Pro: I sure could use the money right now though. I could use it to move, and it would be so much easier to find a job while living in San Diego. Plus I could buy a house. I wouldn't have to rent something and move again later.
5. Pro: It would mean I could stop working here as soon as my aunt and uncle get back.
6. Pro: It's what Ryan wanted, according to Jeffrey. We can't ignore that, can we? Ryan's probably already annoyed about how they ignored his wishes for the funeral, so we shouldn't ignore this wish too. (Did he really want this for me? Did he think it through?)
7. Pro: The money would help me fulfill another of Ryan's dying wishes, because I'd be able to afford to fly to Maui.
8. Con: I really, really, really don't deserve it.

CHAPTER 26

SETTING SAIL UP SHIT CREEK

The next morning, I suggest to Mom that she should join the Waynesfields and the other guests in the dining room for breakfast, but she stays and bumbles around my kitchen.

Huh. *My* kitchen. That's funny.

But I guess I do think of it as mine now. After all, I do every bit of the cooking and most of the cleaning in here. I'd rather clean the kitchen any day than the guests' bathrooms. Selene is cool with that, so she leaves the kitchen as my domain. And even if it does have floral wallpaper and a rooster clock and a set of ceramic hens on the window-sill, it does feel like it's mine. I love baking in here. I love the view out the kitchen window. I love how Maybe leans against the backs of my legs, looking for attention while I cook.

I'll miss this place when I move. If I decide to accept the check, then that might be soon. But I don't know if it's right for me to accept it. I spent all night thinking about it.

"Honey?"

"Huh?" I realize I've been staring out the window. I'd come over to wash the scone batter off my hands, and now I'm still standing here, wet hands resting on the edge of the sink.

"Where were you just now? I asked if you want me to sprinkle the sugar on top of the scones."

"I'll do it. You go sit and read the paper."

"But I like to help."

"I know, but I can't concentrate when there's someone else in the kitchen." I almost said *my* kitchen.

She harrumphs, but sits.

With breakfast done, and the dishes cleaned, the Waynesfields and my mom gather around the kitchen table over one last cup of coffee before my former in-laws head back to Phoenix to catch their flight.

"So, Jane, what did you decide about the check?" Jeffrey says. I'm surprised he's asking me in front of everyone, although it's not like I've given him a chance to get me alone. "You're going to deposit it, right?"

"What check?" Mom asks.

I explain to her about the pending sale of Jeffrey's company. "He wants to give me a very generous check."

My mother's eyebrows disappear into her perfect barrel-rolled bangs. She looks from me to Jeffrey. Everyone waits for me to speak. I lick my bottom lip. I'd love to take the money, but I still don't feel like it's right.

Jeffrey must see my hesitation. "Remember what I told you. I made a promise to my son, and I'm not going back on it."

"I'm still thinking." I stare into my coffee cup, as if answers might swirl there.

When I look up, Jeffrey frowns at me. He opens his mouth, but Barbara puts her hand on his arm. "You must take it," she says. "We must honor Ryan's wishes." She waves her hand in a magnanimous—and very ballerinaesque—gesture.

I force my brow to remain smooth and impassive as I try to figure this woman out. I don't understand her. Since when is she on board with what Ryan wanted? I'm so damn confused.

"Honey, if it's what Ryan wanted . . ." my mother says. No one has mentioned the size of the check. My mother has no inkling about what Jeffrey's business is, and therefore no clue how much money it could be worth. She probably thinks we're talking about a small amount. "You could certainly use the money, since you're out of work and all."

I don't want to talk about my needing the money, so I simply say, "True."

"I have a great idea!" Mom says. "You could use some of the money to take Ryan's ashes to Maui. Your anniversary's coming up soon; you could go then."

As soon as she says "Ryan's ashes," I know I'm screwed.

Through clenched teeth, I get the word "Mom" out. She looks at me with a questioning, what-did-I-do look. I high beam the whites of my eyes at her. I've been leaning against the kitchen island, while everyone else is bunched in around the table. If I were sitting with them, I'd kick her. I'd like to go over and kick her now. I don't know what to do with my hands. I run them through my hair, trying to think.

"What do you mean, Cordelia?" Barbara leans across the table, tilting her head in confusion. "What about Ryan's ashes?"

I try to think of something to say, something to cover for Mom's slip, but my brain slows to obese-hamster-on-a-rusty-wheel speed. "She, she . . ."

Mom waves a hand at me in dismissal. "Jane's worried that I'm going to push her to turn taking Ryan's ashes to Maui into a big production."

This is a complete and total disaster. A nine on the Richter scale earthquake. I should be ducking and covering, crawling under something solid, but I freeze.

Jeffrey's head takes on the same tilt as Barbara's. "Jane's taking Ryan's ashes to Maui? Excuse me?"

"It's just a symbolic thing," I say. I can save this. This can work. I'll tell them I had his . . . his . . . his . . . clothes burned? No, they know I didn't keep many of Ryan's clothes. Photos? No, that sounds bad, like I want to get rid of the memories. I can come up with something that will make this work, but I need a second to think.

"Yes," my oh-so-helpful mother chimes in. "Of course it's symbolic, since it's where you two got married." I'm still trying to think of what ashes I can say I'm throwing into the ocean, when Mom adds, as if confused about why everyone doesn't understand, "She's taking the part of Ryan's ashes that weren't buried."

I've been up shit creek before. Even without a paddle, I always made it out. However, this is no creek—this is a tsunami. And not only do I *not* have a paddle, I don't have a boat or raft or life preserver either. Drowning looks certain.

"Part. Of Ryan. Wasn't buried?" Barbara half rises in her seat, but she's trapped between Jeffrey and my mother. "Jane, please explain to me what your mother's talking about."

I walk out of the room. I have no choice but to tell them now, but I'm hoping when they see how little of him I took, they'll come around; they'll be okay with it. *It's only a couple of scoops!* I mean, I won't say it in those words, but I'm hoping the visual will ease their minds. It's an insignificant amount. He's in a sandwich bag, but he'd fit in the snack size, easy.

Barbara asks where I'm going. My mother answers, but I don't hear what she says, only the "we'll sort this right out" tone that she uses.

In my room, I pull the Williams-Sonoma peppermint bark tin out of my dresser. There's no way I can show them that he's been in a candy box, so I yank off the duct tape and open the lid. The bag confronts me with "Ryan: Maui or Bust" inked across it. Geez Louise. Forgot about that. Not going to go over well, but there's no time to transfer him to something else.

Back in the kitchen, they're talking over each other, but stop mid-word when I walk in. Standing at the edge of the table, looking at them seated before me, I hold the bag in my hand with the writing turned toward me in hopes they won't notice.

I go with the straight-up truth. "I took some of Ryan's ashes."

Barbara puts her hand on her chest, which rises as she gasps. "You didn't." Her other hand flails toward the bag, but I take a half step back.

"I did. The day of the burial."

"Oh my God," Barbara says. Jeffrey sits open mouthed, silent.

"I don't understand," Mom says. "Honey, you told me you divided Ryan's ashes with the Waynesfields."

"She did no such thing. She stole him! He's . . . he's . . ." Barbara looks like the room might be spinning. I'm expecting her head to fall back, her body to go slack, but she surprises me. She braces her slender ballerina arms, in her perfect cashmere twinset, against the heavy wooden table, and shoves it out of the way so she can get up. She darts around the table, swiping at the bag. She's fast, but not fast enough. Besides, she's eight inches shorter than I am. I make a move to swing the bag up over my head and out of reach, but she jumps at it and catches a corner with her maroon claws. The bag stretches between the two of us. One of her nails pierces the plastic.

My eyes are fixed on the bag. *Please don't rip.* If I have to, I'm prepared to slap my former mother-in-law to get her to drop her end. I hear my mom muttering, "No, no, no." And breathing like she's having palpitations.

I draw my hand back.

"Enough!" Jeffrey lunges at us, reaching across the table with his long arms. His hand envelops the bag, and I let go of my end. I've never seen Jeffrey this angry before. "Let go, Barbara. So help me God, if you spill—" He can't finish, he's shaking so hard.

Barbara reaches up with her other hand and sheepishly holds the bag while retracting her caught nail. She smooths her pencil skirt. It's a good thing I did have Ryan in the bigger bag, or else ash would have poured out the instant her nail punctured the plastic. As it is, the hole is about halfway up. Jeffrey holds it at an angle, and the gray dust slips to the bottom corner. He hands it to me.

I'm surprised, but I don't say a word.

"Jeffrey, what are you—" Barbara hangs on his arm. He holds her as if she might fly at me again, but the fight drains out of her.

"Those ashes are for Jane." He waits a moment. "I helped her take them."

"You what?" Barbara looks into her husband's face, wide-eyed. I'm sure my face looks like a mirror image, but luckily she doesn't look my way. "But, the burial . . . Father Llewellyn said—" In the commotion, Barbara's bun has come loose. It's the only time I've seen her hair down, other than the night I went to their room to tell them Ryan was gone. That dark, disheveled hair falling around her shoulders makes her seem so vulnerable. She looks tinier than usual.

"Jane promised Ryan she'd take his ashes to Maui. It wasn't right of us to get in the way of that." He turns to me. "I'm sorry; we should have understood all along." He puts his arm around his wife and kisses the top of her head. "I need to apologize to you, too, Barbara. I'm sorry I didn't tell you about it, but we need to keep *all* our promises to Ryan. Not just the ones we agreed with." She leans into his chest, but keeps looking at the floor.

"Thanks, Jeffrey," I say. I hug the bag to me. "I appreciate it."

"You realize it's the same with the check. You have to cash it."

CHAPTER 27

UNIVERSE, ARE YOU TRYING TO GET BACK ON MY GOOD SIDE?

Sometimes the universe doesn't suck after all. It's Monday afternoon, and the weekend guests are gone. Mom's already called to let me know she got home safely. (She added that she's still "suffering from fits" every time she relives Barbara and me fighting over Ryan's ashes.) I'm in my room, checking e-mail, when an interview request arrives from Golden Triangle Technologies, the biotech firm I applied to weeks ago.

I pound the table, and Maybe jumps up to see what's so exciting. I now not only have the money I need to move back to San Diego, but I also might have an actual reason to return as well. Things are finally going my way.

I rub Maybe's neck while rereading the e-mail. They want me to do a phone interview with HR first. Perfect. I'm better on the phone than in person anyway, so hopefully, I'll ace that. If all goes well, they'll schedule an in-person interview with the hiring manager as soon as it's convenient.

Tomorrow is convenient! Okay, well, maybe not tomorrow, but I could do Wednesday. The Chick doesn't have anyone checking in until late Friday, and it's just one couple, so I'm sure Selene could hold down the fort if I needed to disappear for a couple of days.

I fire off a reply.

Rather than stare at the screen, waiting for a reply, I call my aunt. Her rehab wrapped up last week, and they're creeping back home in the RV.

She answers on the second ring. "Is everything okay with Maybe?"

"Yes, she's doing great. Didn't you get the pictures I sent?"

"We got them. She looks wonderful, but we worry so about her. There's nothing you're keeping from us, is there?"

"No, I promise." *Well, except for some bills.* "She's a very happy girl. She's sitting right here next to me." Maybe sits up on her back legs and bats at me. I grab her paw and shake it. I didn't think she'd still be able to sit up and shake after her surgery. What a rock star. "The vet says we're not out of the woods, the cancer could still metastasize some-where, but she said, at this point, Maybe's body doesn't really know it has cancer. She's as happy and energetic as any other eighteen-month-old puppy."

"We're praying she stays that way. I know you're doing your best to help keep her healthy. You're such an angel, Jane."

I consider arguing the point, but we've had this conversation before. "Where are you guys?"

"Pascagoula, Mississippi. We took a detour off the highway so we could see the world's biggest shrimp that they got on display here." Her voice is full of wonder. "Such a country—so many fascinating things to see and do."

Leave it to Aunt Sugar to describe a jumbo shrimp as fascinating. But I need to remind her of this conversation when they get back.

This can be one of my arguments in favor of them selling the B&B to Selene. I'm sure I can convince them how much fun it would be to get back on the road, exploring, in a couple of years. Note to self: print out a list of quirky tourist stops to entice them. I should buy a big map and mark out a theoretical route. If Aunt Sugar thinks a big crustacean is exciting, wait until she hears about the world's biggest ball of paint. I saw something on TV about it awhile back. She'd be all over it.

I know Selene said she doesn't want me to say anything, but it's not like they need to retire tomorrow. They can wait a year or two, or until she has the down payment saved. It's still better than working until they drop. In fact, it's best for everyone—for them, for Selene, for the inn itself. Heck, it's definitely best for any future guests. It's even good for Harrison, because he doesn't know the amount of work he'd be in for.

"I might have an interview in San Diego soon." I tell my aunt as I cross my fingers, hoping that will remove any jinx I've just put on myself by getting ahead of things.

"That's great!" I hear her share the news with my uncle, which she misconstrues as if I've already got an offer.

"Whoa, I don't have the job yet," I say when she's back. "I haven't even had the phone interview. I don't want to stress you out and make you come back faster than planned, but I just wanted to let you know that I'll be ready to move when you guys get home." Even if I don't get this job, I can move any time after they get back. I've started mentally packing.

"Nonsense, we've imposed on you enough. If you need to get going, we will too. We'll look at the maps tonight and let you know. There'll be time someday to visit the world's largest—" The reception is garbled for a moment, but it sounds like she says, "World's largest kitty litter box." Can't be. I don't ask.

"Don't speed on my account." She promises they won't and that they'll be careful as "a fly in the ointment," which makes zero sense. We say good-bye, but not before she instructs me to give Maybe a hug and a kiss from her. Which I do, as soon as I hang up.

*

THE SCHEDULING OF the phone interview falls into place so fast that I've already aced it, and been informed that I'm moving on to the "in-person" round, before I get a chance to tell Selene the news. The interview is so short and so easy that I assume its sole purpose was to establish that I'm not a blithering idiot before wasting the hiring manager's time. I was even able to bond a little with the HR manager, since she also used to live in Philly. She tells me she still has half a closet full of winter outerwear that she never uses, and I tell her I gave mine away to charity. She tells me that was smart, and, hey, I have to agree. It was smart. *I'm* smart. They need me.

I burst out of my room, Maybe at my heels, and find Selene in the kitchen, staring into the fridge. "I have an interview in San Diego! Soon!"

"That's fantastic. We should do something to celebrate."

"We'll celebrate if I get the job."

"*When* you get the job."

Maybe leaps up, excited by our raised voices, and she and I do a quick tango, spinning circles across the kitchen. We stop, and she races off to find a toy while I fill Selene in on the details and how I might be gone for a few days. "But even if the interview is Friday, I can be back here late Friday night, in time for the weekend guests."

"I can totally manage here. You do what you've got to do."

What I've got to do is get this job. I've got to nail this interview and get back to my life in San Diego.

*

FIRST THING TUESDAY, the universe continues to shine upon me, with an e-mail from Golden Triangle scheduling the interview for Thursday morning. I'll meet with the hiring manager, and as long as he likes me, then the other members of the team. I send back a "Hell yes, I can make it" reply, only in business speak, which I'm out of touch with after so many months away from an office. (I should go online and check out the latest corporate buzzwords. Do people still use the word *synergies* in every other sentence? I hope not.)

Then comes the scary part of Tuesday—taking Maybe for her follow-up chest X-ray. It's been just over a month since her amp. Dr. Leo said we should do an X-ray to see how her lungs look—hopefully, all clear—and then, going forward, do them every three months.

As I pull in to park, I wonder if this is where the universe will let me have it. I've already got the check from Jeffrey, plus the interview lined up, so how much more good luck can I expect? Things are said to happen in threes, but is that only bad things? Hopefully, good things come in threes as well, and Maybe's X-ray will be fine. But still, worry sits heavy in my stomach, like one of the painted stone gnomes in Aunt Sugar's flower beds. I shut my eyes for a moment as Maybe bats at the car door, anxious to see the adoring fans that she knows await her entrance. *Please let the X-rays be clear.*

As we walk across the parking lot, an old red Honda backing out of one of the other spaces stops, the window lowers, and the woman behind the wheel hollers, "Love your dog!" as she drives away. It's nice to have random people express their love for Maybe, and it puts a smile on my face as we head into the vet's office.

"Maybe!" the receptionist hollers, getting up from behind the desk to hug Maybe. "Dr. Leo's running a few minutes behind; she'll be right with you."

I take a seat in the waiting room, across from a woman sitting on her hands, staring at her boots. She looks up, because there is no ignoring Maybe's exuberance. It would be like trying to ignore a swarm of bees. Maybe hops about the small area, her tags jangling with each bounce. She works her way along the chairs next to me, sniffing the floor. When she gets to the end of the slack on the leash, I'm forced to stand and follow. She's headed, as usual, for the display cabinets along the back wall that house the various prescription dog foods and treats. Sure enough, she stands on her strong back legs to facilitate shelf surfing her way down the row. She stops to inspect a particularly interesting bag.

I hear the woman laugh, and look over to smile at her.

"She gets around great. What an awesome dog."

"Thanks," I say. Maybe decides the woman is more interesting than the treats and goes to say hello.

"You're so soft," the woman coos, and Maybe eats it up, wiggling and waggling and trying to press more of her furry flesh against the woman.

"Maybe, you're being a pest." I tug at her leash.

"No, she's fine. I had to leave my dog here overnight, so I could use some doggy love right about now. I'm waiting for them to bring him out."

"I hope everything's okay."

"I hope so too. He had a lump removed. We won't know if it's cancer for a few days."

I wince. I know how waiting for the news sucks. And I know how much worse it sucks when it's not the answer you want. "I'll keep a good thought for you."

She points at Maybe. "Is that why . . . ?"

"Yep." I look at Maybe, who has now flopped into her favorite rub-my-belly position. The woman obliges.

"Well, she sure seems happy. If my Atticus does have it, God forbid, I hope he'll be as obviously pain-free as she is. She's an inspiration."

The door to the waiting area opens, and one of the techs leads out Atticus, a big, beautiful German shepherd, looking very forlorn in his cone. His tail wags as soon as he sees the woman, and he hobbles over to her, favoring his bandaged back leg. Maybe horns in on their reunion and hands out kisses to both Atticus and the woman, but mostly Atticus. His tail wags faster.

"She's a terrible flirt," I say.

The woman laughs again, then rises to leave.

As they head toward the door, I call out good luck, and she turns. "I'm sure those kisses from Maybe will bring us luck." She rubs the shepherd's neck. "That was a very special girl, Atticus," I hear her say as they exit.

I take the seat vacated by the woman, and Maybe leans against me. "You *are* a very special girl," I whisper. I think about how scared the woman looked when we came in, compared with the smile she had on the way out.

"Maybe!" Another of the techs comes out offering pats and salmon treats. "You can come on back." Maybe hops up, excited to follow him.

He shows us to one of the exam rooms, then takes Maybe's leash. "I'll take her on back for her X-ray, and Dr. Leo will come in and speak to you after."

And then I'm alone. Waiting. Just me in a hard chair in the exam room, with my thoughts.

What if the news is bad? What if the cancer fills her lungs already? That can't be though. Every possible outward sign points to a happy, healthy dog.

But maybe she's just happy. And not healthy.

Why didn't I bring something to do? I hate the waiting. My stomach churns. The clock on the wall seems to be on strike, because it says I've been in here only five minutes. I check my phone. Five minutes. How long is this going to take?

I'm going to drive myself insane. The waiting and the fretting and the imagining and the worrying. It's a bad reminder of waiting for results with Ryan and Barnum.

And look how that turned out.

No, not Maybe. It's got to be different this time. I can't handle it otherwise.

Please, please, please let her be okay.

It'll all be fine. It'll all be fine. It'll all be fine.

When I start to think it's been way too long and therefore must be bad news and Dr. Leo is trying to find the words to come break it to me, she swings the door wide open, with a big smile on her face. Maybe races to me, and I know, without a word, that the X-rays are clear.

So far, so good. So very, very good.

CHAPTER 28
I CAN GO HOME AGAIN!

I drive west, truly alone for the first time in months. Heaven. I tap my fingers on the steering wheel to the beat of the music, thinking about how the next time I make this drive, the car will be filled with my belongings—I'll be moving home for good. For now, it will just be a quick in and out: get to San Diego later today and check into my hotel room, ace my interview tomorrow (I've left the whole day clear in case the interviews run long), have an early lunch with my friends on Friday, and then head back to Prescott in time to help Selene with Saturday-morning breakfast.

As the drive wears on, parts of it through the desert—the long, straight, hot stretches—bore me to the brink of a heavy-lidded coma, so I blast my music and chomp stick after stick of gum. But other parts are beautiful. I love the rolling hills outside Prescott, dotted with saguaro cacti, like giant Gumbys of the desert. But the best part is the mountain I climb past El Centro, studded with huge cream- and pink-hued boulders. As soon as I crest that mountain, I roll down my window. The air is refreshing, and the smell hints of the ocean beyond.

I feel freer, happier, moister, than I've felt in a while. My chapped lips no longer threaten to fall off. My hair stops clinging to the collar of my sweatshirt. I'm almost home.

*

SAN DIEGO, OF course, is as beautiful as I remembered it. It's around noon, right after my interview, and I'm overlooking the ocean at Torrey Pines State Reserve, my favorite hike within city limits. The ochre-colored hills stand out in sharp contrast to the brilliant blue Pacific below. My number-one favorite thing about San Diego is being able to swim at La Jolla Cove, but the handy hiking options run a close second. The canyons that crisscross the county, with their hiking, biking, and walking trails, are easily reachable by a ten- to fifteen-minute drive. And they add to the area's beauty—no endless miles of housing and strip malls here.

Since my old wet suit is out of commission, and the water's too cold for a swim without one, I'm happy to spend the afternoon hiking.

I think about the interview while I charge down the trail. I nailed it. Like, with a high-speed, pneumatic power hammer. Questions. Answers. Witty comments. Bam, bam, bam. The job is mine.

Not technically. Not yet, anyway. They didn't offer it to me there on the spot, as I'd fantasized, but I'm pretty sure they will. The manager has a market research background, but wants to expand the department's fledgling market intelligence duties. That's where I come in. They've been making do, but I've got the education, the experience, and the ideas. I rattled off three quick ways we can get the MI side of the department up to speed, plus several longer-term undertakings. On top of that, I scored points by commenting on the pictures of her chocolate Lab. We talked about dogs for a good ten minutes. The job is mine. I know it is.

I fill my lungs with the salty air and search the shoreline for dolphins, remembering how often I used to spot them here. Soon, very soon, I'll be back for good. Finally. I'll be able to swim and hike and take advantage of all this (I'm tempted to throw my arms wide—all *this*!—and twirl à la Julie Andrews in *Sound of Music*, but I'm not the twirling type). Settling for mentally twirling, I think about how I'll be able to come down here all the time.

Or, not all the time. *Most* of the time, I'll be back in a cube. But, on the weekends.

Of course, I remember how crowded it can get here on Saturdays and Sundays. It's not the same as it is now, on a quiet winter weekday afternoon.

Maybe would love it here. Dogs aren't allowed at Torrey Pines, though, so she'll never know, but . . . I wonder how she's doing. I wonder if she misses me.

I bet I'm out of sight, out of mind. I'm sure she's having a great time with Selene. I hope Selene has time to take her down to the stream to see Milo. And over to Watson Lake. She loves it there. I should call them. No, that's silly. I'm sure they're fine. And soon, Maybe's mom and dad will be home. It's time for her to forget about me anyway.

*

LUNCH THE NEXT day doesn't start well. It takes less time than I thought to get there, so I arrive early. As I pull up, I see Elaine already inside at the counter. Damn. I'd been hoping she wouldn't make it. I was thinking I might tell Mir and Karen the whole story about Ryan and me, but I don't want to go into it with Elaine here. Since she and Karen met after I moved away, I don't feel like I know her that well. She never even met Ryan, since I usually flew home to visit by myself.

I watch her through my windshield. She's sipping something green through a straw and studying the overhead chalkboard menu. Why did she have to come along? You don't see Mir's hubby, Max, here, trying to horn in on our Three Musketeers fun.

And why is it we're at *Elaine's* favorite health food spot, Ki's? Mirabella groaned when I said this was the place Karen suggested. Mir wanted to go for Italian, but since Elaine's a vegan (and, who knows, maybe Karen is, too, these days), I had to convince Mir that Ki's was the best option. Luckily, everyone was okay with meeting early, since afterward, I need to get on the road for the six-hour drive back to the Chick.

At least I won't be sleepy while driving after a big Italian meal.

Looking down at my cell, I pretend to be engrossed in texting so I don't have to go in and make small talk with Elaine. A few minutes later, Karen pounds on my driver's side window. Feigning absorption in my faux text, I drop the phone in my purse and hop out of the car.

The thing I find the most awkward about hugging is that initial "are we or aren't we going to?" dance. One person kind of moves in, the other one doesn't; plus, there's the added question of whether to air-kiss, do the big *mwah* thing, maybe press a bit of cheek—so many permutations. The good thing about Karen and Mirabella, though, (and also my mom and aunt and uncle) is that I *know* they're going to hug me. And I know *how* they're going to hug. So it's fine and not awkward. Karen gives me a long bear hug (no cheek action, no *mwah*!), and I squeeze her right back. We both lie about how great the other one looks (she looks tired and drawn, and I am not the athlete she used to know).

"Why are you waiting out here? Didn't you see Elaine?" She's wearing her no-nonsense lawyer suit and her no-nonsense heels. It's nice to be around a tall girlfriend again. I stand up straighter while pretending to just now catch sight of Elaine inside.

"Oh, I didn't see her there."

I'm not sure whether Elaine will hug me, but she bounces over and gives me a longer hug than the one I got from Karen. I end it by saying how hungry I am and turning to study the menu. We wait a few more minutes for Mirabella, then decide to order and wait for her on the second-floor patio.

"Did you hear from her?" Karen asks me.

"No, I assumed she'd be here."

"I thought maybe that was who you were texting."

"Oh no. I was texting . . ." I can't say my mother because I told them what a technophobe Mom is, after Karen had offered to start sending the Indy pictorial updates straight to Mom. "Um, Selene. My friend at the B&B. Seeing how things are going."

"And?"

"Good. Everything's good."

"So, how is it? Working there, I mean. It must be hell for you. I can't see you in the service industry." She laughs and takes a sip of the green sludge she ordered for herself. What the hell is that?

"I know. Weird, right? But it's okay. Mostly okay. I did kinda lose it one time."

"That sounds like a story."

"Only if you want to hear about me zinging minimuffins at a guest's head."

Karen laughs and says, "Of course!" While Elaine adds an "Oh my."

"Jane!" I turn, and there's Mirabella. I jump up. (Mir does her usual side-to-side hug, accompanied by hearty *mwahs*.) She both smells and looks fabulous, in her turquoise form-fitting jacket and slim black pants. Although on closer inspection—and even with her heavy high-def-camera-ready layers of professional makeup—I see signs of sleep deprivation. Both my friends look thin and sleepy. I guess that comes with the territory of having babies on top of demanding full-time jobs. Not to mention that Mirabella has to get up at 3:00 a.m. every day. Yes, she has a somewhat glamorous job and a handsome husband and a gorgeous house and a big loving family, but I wouldn't want her life for anything. It all sounds too exhausting. And loud. Her relatives are very, very loud.

She pulls back and assesses my face. "You look really good. The small-town innkeeper's life agrees with you." She doesn't even glance at my jeans and sweatshirt ensemble. Unlike my mother, Mir gave up on trying to get me to dress "cuter" about twenty years ago.

"I don't know about that. I've been getting more exercise, though, compared to when I saw you at the funeral."

At the mention of the funeral, Karen and Elaine both apologize again for not making it.

I wish I hadn't brought it up.

"How are you doing?" The words come from Karen's mouth, but all three ladies lean in with knitted-brow concern.

Okay, here it comes. The poor-widow thing. "I'm fine. Really. Didn't you guys just tell me I look fine?"

"Better than fine. You look great." Mir squeezes my arm.

I deflect the conversation from me and my widowhood by asking about Indy and the twins. Phones are passed with pictures that I ooh and aah over while hearing the kids' latest exploits. The twins sound like a handful, but they're a hoot.

"Oh my gosh, what are we doing?" Mirabella says after we finish laughing about how she can't get any alone time in her bathroom. She grabs her bottle of SmartWater and holds it up. "We need to toast your new job. Here's to moving back to San Diego!"

"I don't have the job yet."

"But you will. And then you'll be back here for good." Karen and Elaine thud their green smoothies with Mir's water bottle, and wait for me to hold up my iced coffee. (Trying to get a serious flow of caffeine going for my drive home.)

"Ready to start swimming at the cove again when I get back?" I say to Karen as we set our drinks down.

"Um." She wipes her mouth. "The early morning workout thing is kind of hard now, with Indiana and all."

"Oh, of course. But what about our Fridays at Five swim?" We were like clockwork with that. We were very smug about going for our mile swim, while others headed to happy hour in the bars lining La Jolla's Prospect Avenue, a block up from where we plunged into the chilly ocean water. "We've got to start that up again."

"Yeah, we'll see." Not a super-enthusiastic commitment. She exchanges a glance with Elaine, gives an almost imperceptible shake of her head. Almost. She has no intention of starting up swimming three times a week with me again like the old days. Maybe not even once a week. I bet I'll be lucky to get out with her once a month. "But you're still going to join my volleyball team, right?" she adds.

"Definitely. I need to get in some practice time though. It's been awhile."

"It's okay; you'll be back in the swing in no time. We need you and your killer serve. It's going to be great."

Before I can say how excited I am, a guy who looks like he just stumbled up from the beach after a surf session arrives with a tray brimming with our lunches on biodegradable plates.

Mirabella takes hers and lifts the bread off the top of her sandwich. "Hold on," she says. "I ordered this without sprouts." She points a manicured finger, and something about her tone and her nails and her perfect hair reminds me of the snooty woman who, months ago, came into the Chick's kitchen to bitch about the pumpkin bread. *Oh, Mir, I don't like seeing you as that woman.*

"Pick them off," Karen says, shrugging.

The waiter teeters, unsure what to do. It's not the kind of establishment where people send their paper plates back to the chef.

"Want to switch?" I offer her my organic chicken wrap.

"All right." She dismisses the confused boy and takes a dainty bite of the wrap, but her face gives no sign of enjoyment. "So, tell us what you've been up to. How's your mom? How's the inn?"

While some of us eat and some of us pick at our food, I tell them about the inn and Selene and my mom. I tell them about Maybe, glossing over the cancer details, but leave nothing out about how amazing she is on three legs. I tell them about my former in-laws' visit.

"The main reason they came out to see me was because Jeffrey sold his business."

"Wow, really?" Mir says, wiping her mouth. How does she manage to eat and still keep her lipstick looking perfect? "How ironic. After you waited for that all those years." Although they don't know about the fights, my friends at least know that Ryan had promised we'd move back to San Diego as soon as his dad sold the business. "But why'd he want to tell you about that in person?"

"He said he made a promise to Ryan that if the business sold, I'd be 'taken care of.'" I make air quotes, then shake my head. I still can't believe it. "He gave me a very generous check. Totally unexpected."

"How much?" Mir asks.

I'm surprised at Mir asking such a question. She's always so Emily Post about what's polite or not. Before I can answer, Karen mutters, "Of course."

"What?" Mir's voice takes on an exasperated edge.

"It's rude. You don't ask people that."

"Jane is our closest friend. If her life isn't my business, then—"

"Not everything in this world is about the almighty dollar. You're so . . ."

"Karen, it's okay—" I try to jump in.

"Let her finish." Mirabella fluffs her paper napkin on her lap, as if it's the finest linen. "Clearly she has things to get off her chest."

"I don't mind if Mir asks about the check. I was going to tell you guys anyway. It's fine."

"No, it isn't," Karen pushes her plate away. "You haven't been here. She's like this *all* the time now."

"What's that supposed to mean?" A gust of wind snatches away Mirabella's napkin, but she ignores it. Elaine dashes to catch it.

"You're so materialistic. You boil everything down to how much it costs, and every*one* down to how much they make."

These two have always been prone to little jabs at one another, but never like this. I look back and forth between them. It's been so long; I've lost my knack for defusing these things.

"Ladies, come on," Elaine says. I guess she's the one who defuses things these days.

"Could you let me finish a conversation with Karen for *once,*" Mirabella says, her voice raised. People at the surrounding tables look in our direction.

Apparently, one defusing too many.

Karen loses it with Mir for "attacking" Elaine. From there, it degenerates further. They each try to talk over the other. When they tire of trying to make their points with each other, they turn and talk/yell at me. ("When I told her we were adopting Indiana, the first words out of her mouth were, 'Do you have any idea how much raising a kid costs?'" "She tries to lay a guilt trip on me every time I wear something new—like I'm a soulless narcissist or something. I have to look nice for my job!") The other patrons point, and it looks as though one man recognizes Mir from the morning broadcast.

My two best friends seem to be dredging up every hurt feeling and stepped-on toe from all the years I've been gone. I feel responsible; I was always in the position of pressure release valve in our threefold friendship. They've always gotten on each other's nerves in certain ways, but I always knew how much steam to let them blow off before it got to volcanic proportions. They've needed me as much as I've needed them.

I close my eyes for a second and hope it will stop. It doesn't. I open my eyes, glance around, and announce, "The man in the corner is filming you with his iPhone." I'm sure he's waiting for them to start pulling hair and throwing drinks, but luckily we haven't quite sunk to the level of a reality TV show.

Elaine, no longer shrinking back in her chair from being snapped at by Mirabella, tries to smooth things over. "I'm sure we've all said some things we didn't really mean." That's kind of her. She could have taken Karen's side and made things worse. I give her a half smile of encouragement, while Karen becomes interested in rearranging the contents of her pita pocket, and Mir busies herself checking e-mail on her phone.

What a great idea this lunch was. Maybe I should have gotten together with each of them separately.

*

IN THE CAR on the way home, I think of that phrase people always say: "You can't go home again." I never understood that. The roads still go there. Of course you can go home again. I guess it means that you *can*, but don't expect it to be like it was when you left.

But we'll get back into a routine, even if it's an altered one. If today showed me anything, it's that my friends need me as much as I need them. Once I'm back, it'll all be fine.

I WENT TO bed at nine, exhausted from the six-hour drive; but it's eleven now, and I'm still tossing and turning. I decide to list the obvious and tackle this sleeplessness thing head on with the reasons I can't sleep:

1. Way too much Diet Coke. Stopping at 7-Eleven before hitting the road was bad enough, but I never should have let them supersize everything when I stopped for an early drive-through dinner. (That sprout-filled sandwich proved not to be super satisfying. What a surprise.)

2. Too many M&M's. I thought there was no such thing as too many M&M's, but there is. Should not have bought the "sharing-size" bag. (Do they really expect people to share? I think it's printed there so the M&M-buying public can lie to themselves: "I'm not going to eat these by myself; I'm going to share them with all my friends!")

3. A weird churning in my stomach. The cause of this could be the surfeit of M&M's and Diet Coke and drive-through chicken tenders, but I bet it's actually excitement. I'm moving! Soon. I'm getting what I've been waiting for all this time. I'm lying in this ridiculous canopied bed, but mentally, I'm packing my junk in my car. Then again . . . could it be dread? What the hell was with that fight today? No. No, it's excitement. I'm sure.

4. Maybe. She keeps nudging and bumping and kissing me. She was ridiculously excited to see me when I got home. I mean here. (This is not home.) It was nice. And now, she sneaks kisses on my hand and my wrist and, oh so ticklishly, on the inside of my elbow. She keeps curling into a tighter and tighter ball beside me. I stroke her soft fur and tell her I missed her too.

CHAPTER 29

SHOULD HAVE BEEN MORE CAREFUL ABOUT WHAT I WISHED FOR

I wake in a sweat. What a weird dream. I was swimming at the cove with Karen, but then she fell way behind me, and I kept going, which is weird because we always stick together, no matter how crappy one of us might feel. I kept going, and I felt okay about it. But then a gigantic bear started swimming after me. This was like the Michael Phelps of bears, gaining on me with every stroke. I woke up, gasping, as he wrapped a huge paw around my ankle.

The weird thing was, his paw felt like a human hand.

What the hell was that supposed to mean?

Is this about my real-life dream—the dream that I've been chasing for so long of getting back to San Diego, getting back to the ocean? If so, then why do I feel like the one who's being chased?

I'm giving it too much thought. It was a bizarre dream, brought on by chocolate and cola and compressed chicken parts. Why did I eat all that junk?

Maybe breathes steadily next to me. We sleep like sardines in a can, her head by my feet, her back pressed up against my side. I reach out and stroke her soft fur.

I'll miss this girl. I'll miss a lot of things here, if I'm being honest with myself. Not the guests, of course, but having no set schedule is nice, and the lack of a cubicle is wonderful. Wearing whatever the hell I want while I work is a definite bonus. And Selene earns the Nicest Coworker Ever award. But I'll miss Maybe most of all.

Damn my aunt and uncle. I knew they got her in the hopes that I'd fall in love and keep her for myself. But I can't take her away from the fantastic life she has here. As much as I'd love to, I can't subject her to an empty house, waiting for me to come home from work every day. That's not a good life for her.

Edie and Eddie Bauer, the guests who were so impressed with Maybe, pop into my head. I remember Eddie saying something about dogs teaching us to live in the moment.

Geez. When's the last time I lived in the moment? I've been dreaming of my future in San Diego for so long, I think I forgot how to be *present*. Now I'm almost back there, and yet . . . I've got doubts.

My mind drifts to Ryan. There's no present, no future for him. If there's one thing I need to take from everything that's happened this year—Ryan's death, Barnum's, Maybe's cancer—it's that nothing is guaranteed. We are promised nothing more than right here, right now. The rest is a crapshoot.

Maybe lives in the moment. All dogs do. But her moments need to be the best they can be. She may not get the quantity she deserves from life, but she damn well is going to have the quality. She needs to be here, at the Chick.

What if I'm meant to be here with her? Huh.

Another scene replays in my mind: Kai, so handsome in that green shirt, telling me about his name, how it means "the ocean."

I've spent the last six-plus years dreaming about moving back to San Diego, wishing I were back living by the ocean again. Huh.

*

THE NEXT MORNING, I don't say anything to Selene. It's been my experience that ideas that seem brilliant at three a.m. seldom hold up to scrutiny in the harsh light of day.

We go about our usual routine. I make breakfast; she chats with the guests. Afterward, I take Maybe down to the stream. It's Saturday, so I know we'll run into Kai and Milo and, sure enough, there they are.

"How was San Diego?" Selene must have told him about my quick trip for the interview.

"Okay."

"You're smiling. You must have been offered the job." He doesn't smile back at me.

"Am I?" Self-conscious, I stop. "No. They didn't. I mean, not yet. I'm pretty sure they will though."

"I guess congratulations are in order."

"We'll see." I smile again. I stand. I don't feel like sitting. "I think I'll take Maybe over to Watson Lake this afternoon. She loves it there. You guys want to come along?"

That gets a grin out of him. "Yeah," he says, running his hands over his hair. It seems less stubby today. Is he growing it out? I never really noticed the color before. It looks grizzly bear brown. "Milo'd love that."

"I'd better let Maybe rest up until then." I call Maybe over and wave good-bye as we walk back up to the house. "See you later. Like two-ish?"

"Perfect."

Up at the house, I find Selene shoving the vacuum back in the hall closet. "Do you want to come along to Watson Lake with Maybe and me this afternoon?"

"Sure. I'm going to miss hiking with you. I need to get my fix before you go."

"Kai and Milo are coming too."

"Oh shoot. I just remembered. I can't go . . . I have to finish packing. Sorry, count me out." My aunt and uncle are due back today, and Selene is moving back to her sister's.

I shake my head because I know what she's thinking. "It's not a date."

"He's a nice guy, and cute."

"Yes, I know. But it doesn't matter how nice or how cute he is. I'm not ready to date anybody right now. He could be George Clooney, and I still wouldn't want this to be a date. It's a walk with the dogs. And my friends. Come with us."

"I really have to pack. In fact, come talk to me for a minute while I start." I follow her into my aunt and uncle's room, and Maybe hops along behind. I flop on the bed while Selene pulls her few belongings out of the dresser. Maybe picks up a dropped sock, circles in the corner, and settles in to mouth it.

I look around the neat room. "It's going to take you all of ten minutes to pack."

She picks up a laundry basket full of tees and sweatshirts from the floor and drops it in the middle of the bed. "I have to fold all that stuff too."

"Okay, fifteen minutes."

"All right, I'll go." Her smile slips into an exaggerated frown. "But only because I just realized this might be my last chance. I know you're anxious to get out of here. She's leaving us, Maybe." She snatches the sock away and ruffles the fur on the back of Maybe's neck.

"I wouldn't say 'anxious.'" I grab a sweatshirt and help fold.

"*Excited* at least. You've been grinning like the cat that ate the canary all morning. That trip home must have been pretty great. I think you're holding out on me."

I'd told her when I got back last night that the interview went well. When she pressed me about how the trip went, I told her it was fine. "Forget about me; let's talk about you." I clutch the folded sweatshirt in my lap and tell her to sit.

"What about me?" she asks, sitting cross-legged on the other side of the bed.

"Once my aunt and uncle get resettled"—I pause and take a breath—"I'm going to do my best to convince them to retire early and sell the Chick. I'm thinking my uncle will agree, and then all we have to do is convince my aunt to sell this place to you—" Selene opens her mouth, but I rush ahead. "Not until you're ready with the down payment, of course. I'll bet you anything they'll both be on board with the idea. They love you." I grab another T-shirt to fold because I'm afraid to watch her face. "So, I was also thinking . . . remember when you showed me your business plan?" She'd shown it to me after Harrison's visit, and we'd gone over some of the numbers together. "And you'd factored in a salary for an employee?"

"Yeah. I *could* run the place by myself. Obviously, I'd make more money that way, but I'd have no time for any sort of life, except maybe in January and February, when it's slower."

"Did you ever think about getting a partner instead of an employee?" I start refolding the same T-shirt again.

"That'd be great. I mean, if I was lucky enough to meet someone who wanted to run the place with me. Maybe someday."

"I'm sure you'll meet someone, like a *real* partner, someday. In the meantime . . . what about me?" I give up on the T-shirt and look up.

"You? You're going back to San Diego." She's smiling, but disbelief shows in her eyes. "Like, you'd be my silent partner? I'd still have to hire someone to help with the work."

"No, I'd be your loud partner. Well, not *super* loud, because I'd keep hiding out in the kitchen and behind the scenes, like I've been doing. Does that sound nutty? You and me, running this place?" Am I making another of my rash decisions? I know it hit me quickly, but I'm so excited about being with Maybe and being my own boss that it feels right, even if it is rash. I have to admit, I've grown to the love the Chick, and this town. And now, I've got friends here too. This really does feel right.

Her smile broadens. "Oh my God, yes. That sounds completely nutty. Fun and awesome, but nutty. Are you smoking something? I thought you hated the guests. Haven't you been counting the minutes until you could get back to San Diego?"

"Yeah, but I think I've been dreaming all this time of going back to something that's not there anymore. I know it sounds crazy, but right now, the most important thing to me is Maybe."

"That part doesn't sound crazy at all. Maybe's the best." We both look over at her; she lifts her gaze to us while keeping her chin on the rug.

"Come here, you silly," I say, and she hops onto the bed. Selene pushes the laundry basket out of the way to make room. Maybe rolls over and stretches, and we rub her tummy. "I want her to be happy and have a great life. And I know she already has that here. I need to be part of that."

"I get that. But are you sure that making Maybe happy is going to make *you* happy?"

"I'm sure I'll be happy here. And being part of making Maybe happy is the icing on the cupcake. Plus, the thought of going back to the corporate ladder–climbing routine, sitting in a cube, commuting in traffic—it all sounds like hell." I never gave it much thought before, while I was living that life, but now that I've had a break, I'm not interested in going back. I've stopped rubbing Maybe's tummy while I talk, and she kicks at me with a powerful back leg. "Geez, okay. Pushy!" I laugh and go back to scratching her. "I've realized the guests—even the otherwise-annoying asshat ones—aren't so bad if I get them talking about Maybe or their own pets." I shrug.

"You've come a long way, willing to converse with annoying asshats about their pets." Selene laughs.

"That's thanks to Maybe." I lower my face toward Maybe's. "Thank you, sweet pea," I say as she squirms around to be able to reach me for a thorough chin kissing.

I have a sudden memory of Barnum's kisses. Not as frantic as Maybe's, but as numerous. I can't help but think how different things would be if Barnum—and Ryan—were still alive. I don't know what it is about humans that we search for the good in everything—especially tragedies—but I guess, if there can possibly be a "bright" side to Ryan's death, it's that it taught me to go after what I want. At first, I thought that was being in San Diego, but now, I realize it's about being where I'm happiest. And, shockingly, that's here.

Then I think of Barnum, again. I would have loved to have more years with him, but he was old. It was his time. Plus, if he'd been with me that day in the car when I found Maybe, I'd have had to leave her behind. All I could have done was call Animal Control and hope they'd catch her. There's no way Barnum would have let me put a strange dog in the car. It feels wrong now to think I wish I'd had more time with him, because if I'd had that gift of extra time, then I wouldn't have Maybe in my life. Who knows what would have happened to her? I shudder, thinking about her being alone, scared, and hungry, dumped at that rest area.

"Earth to Jane." Selene laughs as I blink and return to our conversation. "You're not having partner's remorse already, are you? Because I'm ready to shake on it."

I hold out my hand. "No remorse here. Partners?"

She grabs my hand and gives it a strong squeeze. We shake over Maybe, and she bats at our clasped hands with her lone front paw. "Partners!"

We're still grinning when we hear the creaks and crunching that signal the arrival of my uncle's RV on the gravel drive.

CHAPTER 30
MAYBE THIS TIME

Almost five weeks later, my aunt and uncle, who've booked a room and insisted on paying full price, drive up from Phoenix with my mom for the grand reopening of the Farm Hound B&B. Selene and I think the new name gives just the right vibe, now that we're dog friendly, but still maintains our country roots.

We removed every chicken tchotchke, painted over every stenciled chicken conga line, and renamed the rooms—which are simply numbered now. The Chick is no more!

Luckily, Selene turned out to have quite an eye for decorating. Outside, we had the building repainted, ditched the plastics tulips in favor of English lavender and butterfly bushes, and put bright purple cushions on the rockers on the porch. Inside, we've redone all the rooms in warm, welcoming colors: pale cornflower-blue walls, cream-color bedding, and accents in cranberry red. There are color-coordinated dog beds in various sizes if the guests need one. The old parlor is the same serene blue shade, but the old furniture is gone, replaced by yoga mats and an assortment of weights, if someone wants to work out. The games and books, now neatly displayed in white-washed bookcases, have been moved into the hallway so guests can still borrow them and take them up to their rooms. Best of all, we painted my kitchen a buttery yellow, and I'm planning to hire Kai to put in the same butcher-block countertops that he has in his kitchen. But that will probably have to wait until things are quiet again next winter.

Tonight, we've got all eight rooms booked, five with pets. Maybe and I will be celebrating our sold-out grand reopening night sleeping on the sofa since Mom's got my room. It doesn't matter, though, because I'll be too excited to sleep anyway.

We're having a special champagne and hors d'oeuvres happy hour indoors and yappy hour out back. I made Selene's mother's empanada recipe, and a guest comes up to me, waving a half-eaten empanada, and says, "If you serve these at every happy hour, we'll be coming here for life." I agree with him that they're like little pockets of heaven and offer him another from the tray.

It's such a nice evening that most of the guests opt to mingle outside, watching the dogs in the newly fenced play area. I hear several of the guests commenting on Maybe and how impressive she is. Everyone wants to know how she lost her leg, and I never get tired of reporting how well she's doing. "It's only been a few months?" is the general astounded reaction. "She gets around like it's been years." If they seem sad about the cancer, I boast about her latest clear lung X-ray. I tell them Maybe plans to beat the odds. And that, no matter what happens, she'll have the best life possible.

The nightly happy/yappy hour was Selene's idea. She says it will give the owners and the dogs something to do, and tired dogs are good dogs. I ask her if tired guests are also good guests, and she says they are, as long as we limit them to one small glass of free wine each.

I get my uncle alone and ask how Harrison's adjusted to the fact that he's not going to be the owner of the Hound, as Selene and I call it now.

"He put his poor mother through a rough few days at first." He raises his hands, fingers curled. "I'd like to take that man and shake the stuffing out of him. Once he found out he was still in the will to receive the house in Phoenix, he was playing the model son again."

"That must have shown her that he was only after the money behind the Chick. The whole thing about wanting to run it was a bunch of bs."

He sighs. "Your aunt has a mighty big blind spot where that son of hers is concerned—Oh! Here comes my lovely bride now."

"The place looks so nice, Jane," Aunt Sugar says as she walks up with Selene. "Selene gave me the tour of all that you've done."

"We didn't change that much. Minor things, here and there."

"You're downplaying it. The place looks wonderful. You two are putting your own stamp on it."

"It's Selene's stamp. I just help." I wonder again, as I did the day we loaded the plastic deer in the moving van, if my aunt isn't maybe a bit hurt at all the changes we've made. But when I see her and my uncle beaming at Selene, I know they couldn't be happier for her if she was their own daughter.

"I think we're going to go lie down for a while before dinner," Aunt Sugar says. The five of us are going out later to Hassayampa Inn to celebrate. They excuse themselves, and I hear Uncle Graham say as he takes her arm, "Won't it be fun, sleeping in one of the guest rooms?"

After they're gone, Selene bumps me with her shoulder. "Whaddya think, partner? Pretty great so far, huh?"

"It's day one."

"I know, but come on. Don't you feel like it's going to be great?"

I chew my lower lip and survey the play yard. Dogs race around, their owners standing and watching, resting their plastic champagne glasses on the top of the fence. "Yeah. I think it might be pretty great." We clink our glasses together and take long drinks; the bubbles burn my nose. "But swear to me that you're going to stick to our plan. If you meet someone someday who wants to run the place with you, you two can buy out my share. I'm happy to move on to something else. Open a bakery or something. This is *your* dream, and I don't want to get in the way if you find a more perfect partner."

"We'll cross that bridge when we come to it. Right now it feels like I'm going to be single forever. There are zero prospects around here for me."

"You're gorgeous, and you're going to meet someone someday. So promise."

"Okay, I promise." She raises her eyebrows and hides her mouth behind her champagne glass. "Speaking of prospects . . ."

I turn in the direction she's looking and see Kai walking up the hill with Milo. "Shush, you," I say, jabbing her with my elbow. Kai lets Milo into the play yard, where he's greeted with an enthusiastic bop on the shoulder from Maybe. Selene and I have been busy from dawn until dusk, scrapping wallpaper, painting, redecorating, and working in the yard, so I've barely seen Kai, except for quick play sessions with the dogs down at the stream. His hair has grown out a bit now. It's thick and wavy. I like it.

Kai says hello and hands Selene a bottle of champagne tied with a red bow. "This is from Weaver. He wishes you ladies the best of luck. And he said the next time the four of us go out, drinks are on him."

"I'm in," I say.

Selene says, "He's so sweet. Tell him thanks. I'm going to go put this in the fridge."

Kai rests his elbows on the fence, like I'm now doing, watching Maybe and Milo play.

"I've got a present for you too. I mean, it's sort of for both you and Selene, but mostly you." A small cardboard tube appears from out of the depths of his big suede jacket.

"Should I wait for Selene?" I hold it up to my ear and shake it, gleaning only that it's some sort of paper. A drawing or art for the house? I hope not, because I hate when other people try to buy me art. "What is it?"

"Open it and see."

I pop the white plastic top off and turn the single sheet of rolled paper out into my hand. The blue pencil lines on thin white paper give away the fact that it's some sort of architectural design. "What is this?"

"It's plans for turning the storage shed into a one-room studio." He takes the paper from my hand and unrolls it along the top of the fence. "I thought you might like to have your own space."

I study the plans. The original entrance is still there, and the washer and dryer are in the same place, but he's added a partitioning wall, and a separate entrance around the other side of the building, which has been enlarged to allow space for a queen-size bed and a sitting area. A bathroom with a tub sits on the other side of the shared laundry room wall.

"I didn't put in a kitchenette. I figured you'd still eat in the main house, but if you want me to add one, I can." He reaches out as if to take the drawing back, but I snatch it away.

"No. It's perfect as is." I look at it again. It's just the right size for Maybe and me. As much as I love Selene, and enjoy hanging out with her, it would be great to have my own space. "How did you know?"

"Know what?"

"That I was worried about living with Selene under the same roof 24-7."

"It doesn't take a clairvoyant to figure out you like some alone time. I thought this might help set your partnership up for success."

"I can't believe this. This is the most amazing gift I've ever gotten." I look back again at the gorgeous space that will someday be mine. *All* mine. And Maybe's. "Of course, I'm not sure how soon we'll be able to afford to build it. I mean, we have to finish getting this place up and rolling first."

"The present's not only the drawing. I thought I could help you build it. You told me how handy you are. Now you can put your . . . well, not your money, because the labor will be free, but your . . . your hammer where your mouth is." He cocks his head and runs his hand over his head, only now there's hair to run his fingers through. "That doesn't sound right, does it?"

I laugh. "No, it doesn't. But that's way too generous. I can't let you do that."

"It's not that big of a deal. It's a pretty simple plan—a box with a bathroom. Between the two of us, we can handle it. I don't take jobs on weekends, unless someone's got an emergency, and you've generally got some time in the afternoons, right? And we can work in the early evenings, now that it's staying light later."

"You've got this all figured out. I don't know what to say."

"How about 'thank you'?"

"That won't do. I mean, God, yes, thank you! But that's not enough. I'll think of something. Something that will be a *real* thank-you." He's still holding the plans along the top of the fence, and I put my hand on top of his and squeeze it. I look into his eyes, and he smiles. I can't believe I never noticed the fullness of his lower lip before. I imagine giving him a thank-you kiss, and my cheeks burn. I let go of his hand and reach for the plans. I bury my face in them for a moment, then roll the paper back up and wave it back and forth. "I've got to go show Selene."

I turn and start off toward the house, then stop and come back. I hope he doesn't think this means we'll get together. I'm not ready for that. Hell, I thought I wanted to stay single. I think I'm better at being single. And after rushing into things with Ryan, if anything is ever going to happen between Kai and me, well, it's going to have to happen slowly. If I jump into something and it doesn't work out, how awkward would that be with him living right next door? Right now, I just want us to be friends. And not friends with benefits. I hope he's not imagining that if he builds me a bedroom, there'll be bedroom privileges. Maybe I should make that clear before we get into this whole project. "Why are you doing this?"

"I want things to work out for you and Selene. I . . . I like you . . . you ladies." His hand goes to his hair again.

"So, you just want to help out your friends?"

"Yeah, I want to see you both succeed."

"Ah, I get it. You're worried we'll go under, and you'll end up with God-knows-what for neighbors." I smile, and he grins back at me.

"Yeah. That's right. This is simply in my own self-interest."

"Mm-hmm. That's what I figured."

"But wait, there's more," he says in his best late-night TV sales pitch voice.

"No, no, no," I shake my head and waggle the plans at him. "This is too much already."

He reaches into his jacket pocket. "This part's something small, and it's not for you to keep." He unfurls the fingers of his big paw-like hand and reveals two small carvings: a three-legged dog, and a tall, skinny blonde.

"Awww!" I reach for the tiny version of Maybe and hold it up, turning it over and noticing what a great paint job he's done depicting her multicolored coat. "Oh, I love it. She's perfect."

"I thought since you guys are staying, I'd add you to the courthouse square."

I pick up the mini-me and study it. "You're sure this isn't Betty? Is that a tiny Budweiser I see in her hand?"

He smirks. I'm not sure if it's an "I deserved that one" or a "What do *you* think?" smirk, but it makes me laugh. "I'm teasing. These are amazing. I'm honored that you thought to include us. Maybe loves to go down to the square."

"We should go down there sometime. Walk the dogs and grab a bite."

"We'll see. We're going to be awfully busy building my new room. Anyway, I've got to go show Selene the plans." I waver, on the verge of giving him a thank-you hug. I decide against it, but it's too late. He must have seen my arms rise ever so slightly before I aborted the idea. He leans in, and his big bear arms envelop me. I wasn't ready, so my delay means I end up with my arms wrapped around him inside his jacket. Holy cow. I feel the hard muscles of his back and the heat of him through his shirt. He smells wonderfully of cinnamon gum. My cheek presses against his neck and my face flashes from cold to hot in an instant. I could stay like this for hours.

"We're crushing the plans," I say, my voice thick, when I realize we've been hugging for an embarrassingly long time. He releases me. Smoothing and rerolling the plans, I hope he won't notice my flushed face. I glance up, smile, mutter thanks once more, then turn and run to show Selene.

*

THAT NIGHT ON the sofa, as predicted, I can't sleep. It's been a helluva grand-opening party. Everyone seemed to have a fun time, especially the dogs. Maybe sleeps stretched along my legs, exhausted from all the playing. I've got so many things running through my brain: plans for the Hound, worries about Maybe, thoughts about Kai and how it'll be fun to work with him on my little apartment under the cottonwoods. It'll be a good way to get to know him, and hopefully, we'll become even better friends.

Maybe we should also start offering a doggy day-care service to some of the locals. Their dogs could come and play during the day with Maybe and whatever guest dogs are visiting, and we'd make some extra money.

Maybe everything will be okay with the next set of follow-up chest X-rays. Maybe I'm worrying for nothing. Maybe she'll be in the 10 percent of dogs that beat this horrible disease. Maybe she's really going to kick bone cancer's ass, and be the miracle dog everyone already thinks she is.

Maybe one day, when Selene meets someone and they want to run the place together, they'll buy out my share, and I'll start a bakery in town. Maybe that would be fun.

Maybe, when there's time for me to take a vacation, I could give Kai tickets to Maui. That would be a spectacular thank-you present. Maybe we'd go together—for moral support, while I scatter Ryan's ashes and he looks for his mom. I'd get to enjoy him seeing the ocean for the first time. That would be pretty cool. And maybe, just maybe, in the future there will be bedroom privileges.

Maybe everything's going to work out great this time.

No, definitely.

AUTHOR'S NOTE

This book is a work of fiction, but as I stated in the dedication, my hubs and I had our own "Barnum" and our own "Maybe."

We lost Bailey, our beagle, to cancer at age twelve. We'd had her since she was eight weeks old; she was our first pet as a couple, and the hubby's first dog ever. Oh, how we loved that crazy kid. We were both devastated when she passed from hemangiosarcoma (a tumor on her heart). I started writing this book at that time. I found the best way for me to deal with my grief was to write about another person—and, thus, the character of Jane was born—dealing with the death of *her* dog.

To add a twist, I decided her husband would also have just died, but she was sadder about the dog. Now, why would that be, I wondered? And, thus, the entire book was born. (This was a disturbing concept to my hubs, and I apologize to him for that!)

Six weeks after Bailey passed away, we adopted four-month-old Abby from the shelter where I volunteer. I fell in love with her gorgeous face and sweet manner, and convinced the hubs that we needed her. He wasn't completely ready for another dog, but I talked him into it.

Her sweet demeanor lasted, oh, twenty-four hours or so. She was all sharp puppy teeth and hyper energy, and I lost six pounds trying to keep her worn out. (If you've ever had one, you'll know that it really is true, as Selene says, that a tired puppy is a good puppy!)

Sadly, when Abby was only fifteen months old, and almost exactly a year after we lost Bailey, she started limping. If you've read the book, you know that led to finding out she had osteosarcoma. (If you haven't read the book already, shoo! Go read it. *Now.* Unless you want to find out part of how it ends. Although, the book doesn't end the same way our story did.)

We received the news on a Monday, and by that Friday, Abby was in surgery having her right front leg amputated. After a tough two weeks of recovery, she quickly learned to adapt, and once she had her stamina back, she did amazingly well on three legs. (And I've got the videos on YouTube to prove it.)

We took her to the bay at least three or four times a week. She could easily run and play (with lots of rest breaks, of course) for an hour or more. She was so fast, people often commented that they didn't notice she was missing a leg until she stood still.

Many of the things that happen with Maybe in the book happened to Abby and me: a little boy asked if her leg would grow back; a "friend" suggested we put her down and not put her through the cancer fight; people would stop their cars in the middle of the street and yell, "I love your dog!"

But, some things in the book are not the same. We actually did chemo with Abby. She handled it very well, but still, I'm not sure I would do it again. It's really impossible to know what "works," so even though we had an amazing fifteen months with Abby post-amp, following a mixed chemo/holistic approach (which I called "*half*istic"), if I had to go through it again, I might go totally holistic.

We lost Abby when she was only two and a half years old. I still had much work left to do on the book. I'd planned all along for the book to have a happy and hopeful ending. It made it very hard to keep working, since I'd hoped for the same for Abby. I put the book aside and focused on marketing my other novel, *What the Dog Ate*.

If you've read *What the Dog Ate*, or simply seen the book, you know there's a gorgeous chocolate Lab on the cover. I "met" Charley and his mom on Yahoo's "Bone Cancer Dogs" support group.

Charley's amputation was the day before Abby's (so they became "amp buddies"). As I write this, Charley is coming up on four and a half years postdiagnosis. He has been cancer-free all this time. It seems he is one of the lucky dogs in the 10 percent that beat the disease. I like to think that Charley's angel, Abby, is looking out for him.

Although Abby was cheated on the quantity front, she had an amazing quality of life. Abby lived large and would smile broadly when we were out and about. Hers is a short story, but it is still a happy, hopeful one. And Charley is proof that some dogs do well even after such a devastating diagnosis.

Really, none of us is guaranteed a tomorrow. Even later today might be sketchy, so make the most of the here and now. That is what we learned from our Abby, and I hope that's the message you will take away after reading *Rescue Me, Maybe*.

PS—To learn more about Abby or her bone cancer journey, please visit my blog at www.poochsmooches.com and go back to the archived entries from 2010 through 2011.

PPS—I know Jane lets Maybe off leash while they're hiking. Jane only does it because no one else is around. It doesn't mean that I advocate letting your dog off leash, especially while you're out in the wilderness. Please don't do it! (No dogs were harmed in the writing of this book.)

PPPS—I'm sorry, City of Brotherly Love, that Jane did not have sisterly love for you. It's not you; it's her. I lived in Philly for eighteen months, and I loved your history and parks and those chocolate-covered strawberry cordials at Lore's.

ACKNOWLEDGMENTS

There are so many people (and pooches) I want to thank for their help, input, and support. I'll start with the cutest.

Tummy rubs and kisses to my dogs—past and present—who have inspired me to write about the funny, touching things they do. And also for making me get out and walk every day, whether I want to or not.

I truly appreciate the time and feedback from my early readers, Louisa and Micki, and from Leslie who read the *this*-close-to-being-done version.

I don't know what I would have done without my author friends: Peggy Frezon, Tracie Banister, and Samantha Stroh Bailey. Thank you, Peggy, for turning my "brain drizzle" of title ideas into an actual storm, and coming up with *Rescue Me, Maybe*. Wish I could say I thought of it myself, but I didn't! Tracie and Sam, your input on the manuscript and the title were a huge help; but mostly, I want to thank you for your never-ending support! I'm so glad to have met all of you along the way on this publishing journey.

I also owe a huge thank-you to my sister Terry for all the time she put in proofreading the early drafts; to my editor, Amara Holstein, for her eagle eye and for helping me make the words on the page align with the ideas in my head; to my agents, Kevan Lyon and Taryn Fagerness, for all the work they've done to get me to this point in my writing career; and to Jodi Warshaw and everyone at Lake Union/Amazon Publishing for their help.

As with my previous book, I want to give a shout-out of appreciation to my mom and the rest of my siblings—but this time I'll add in thanks to their furry family members as well. I've used the names of at least one of each of their pets for character names—both human and four legged. So special thanks to Sugar, Llewellyn (aka Lou), Topi, Roxie, Danielle, Leo, and Indy. I had a lot of fun working their names into the book, and I hope you all appreciated the little surprise of seeing their names in print (or pixel, as the case may be).

Most of all, thank you to the hubs for his support and encouragement. He is the best thing that ever happened to me and ever will.

READERS' GUIDE

1. Jane is definitely an introvert. Introverts aren't necessarily shy; they just find being with others a drain on their energy, and they re-energize by spending time alone. Extroverts, on the other hand, thrive on the energy of being around others. Which better describes you—introvert or extrovert? Are there times when you are one or the other?

2. Jeffrey tells Jane that his mother would say that finding a penny from heaven is a little sign that a loved one who's passed is doing okay. Later, when Jane finds Barnum's squirrel toy and it squeaks for the first time in ages, she takes it as a sign that Barnum wants to let her know he's okay. Have you ever had an experience that you felt was a sign from a loved one who'd passed?

3. Pet lovers know that when you bring home a pet, you are signing up for future heartbreak, since our pets don't live as long as we wish they would. When Jane's beloved Barnum dies, she swears she won't get another dog, but then Maybe comes along and helps Jane's heart heal. Many people share Jane's opinion, and once they lose a beloved pet, they can't go through that

again. Others believe a new pet helps piece your heart back together. What do you think?

4. Not every story has a classic villain. Do you think *Rescue Me, Maybe* has a villain? If so, is it Barbara? Or is cancer the real villain here?

5. Jane admits to being more demonstrative with the dog than with her husband—even when she was still in love with Ryan. Why do you think some people find it easier to be completely vulnerable with pets rather than other people? How did this make you feel about Jane?

6. Since B&Bs are known for their hospitality, and usually include a family-style breakfast, this starts out as the worst possible workplace for an introvert like Jane. Some people love B&Bs, while others definitely prefer an impersonal hotel stay. Those who love B&Bs often fantasize that running one would be like staying at one. Do you like B&Bs? Does running one seem like a dream job? Or a nightmare?

7. In honor of Aunt Sugar, if you were a baked good, what would you be?

8. How do you feel about Jane? Are there things you have in common with her? When Jane makes a list of ways she used being a widow, she theorizes that trying to work some widow pity into her job hunt would make her a worse person than she already is. Do you think Jane is a bad person? Do you think everyone has both some good and bad in them?

9. Jane and Jeffrey both made promises to Ryan that they intended to keep. What do the living owe the dead? If a dying loved one wanted you to promise something you didn't agree with, what would you do? Humor them, like Barbara did, then ignore their wishes? Who, in this situation, should have the power to make this decision—the spouse or the deceased's family members?

10. Have you had a pet that taught you life lessons? What did you learn?

AN EXCERPT FROM
JACKIE BOUCHARD'S
HOUSE TRAINED

CHAPTER 1

This morning I overheard my husband talking to his penis. He was getting in the shower and thought I'd already left; that's how I unintentionally snuck up on him. Or rather, *them*.

His words stopped me in my kitten-heeled tracks there in our bedroom. A cartoon traffic pileup of emotions plowed into me one after the other: guilt (I'm not in the habit of eavesdropping on Barry, or anyone else for that matter); confusion (I was unaware he had discussions with this particular member of our family unit); embarrassment—for him (it was an awkward moment); and a little anger (does this often happen when I'm not around?).

I raised my arm to push open the bathroom door and say, "Hey, what are you two talking about?" but caught sight of my watch. I only had twenty minutes to get to Montecito, and I try my damnedest to never be late for a meeting, especially with a new client.

Zooming south on the 101, I still felt confused, as if I hadn't had enough coffee or something. Had Barry done anything else out of the ordinary? I replayed the morning in my head. The day had started with our typical Saturday routine: the dog and I slept in while Barry went for his usual long run. I ate, took Marie for a walk, and showered. I'd finished my makeup and was stepping into my linen skirt, still warm from the iron, when I heard Barry come home. Marie's tags jangled as she ran to greet her daddy, and I heard him ask how his "pretty girl" was doing.

I walked out to the kitchen to say hi, and we had our standard "How was the run?" "Fine, how'd you sleep?" exchange.

"Does this skirt look okay?" I turned and gave him the back view, wiggling my hips.

"'S'cute." He pulled up his Coolmax T-shirt to wipe the sweat from his face. I rolled my eyes at his favorite running shorts, the ones I'd tried to throw away because of the bleach stain. At least he'd left his dirty Nikes in the garage. He padded in his running sock–covered feet to the fridge, leaving ghost feet markings behind on the hardwood. "Glad I didn't bring Marie. Hot."

Marie perked up at her name and joined her daddy gazing into the fridge. She nose-poked the cheese drawer, then slumped on the mat, dejected when he merely grabbed the orange juice. Barry leaned on the granite counter and guzzled juice from the carton, though we both knew that I would give him grief about it.

"I wish you wouldn't do that. It's gross."

"Not if I finish it."

He stripped off his running hat and pushed a handful of dark, wet hair off his forehead. Having spent fifteen minutes straightening my own flyaway wavy hair, I envied Barry and his run-your-fingers-through-and-you're-good-to-go hairdo. Barry has thick, shiny shampoo-ad hair. He got it from his mom, a gorgeous, petite woman whose parents came to California from South Korea when she was a baby. Next to her, I always felt like an Amazon. One of those B-movie-poster buxom blondes: *Attack of the Fifty-Foot Interior Designer*. Happily, Barry got his height from his Nordic warrior–looking dad.

"I bought that carton yesterday. You're not going to finish it," I said, reaching for my clutch. "I'm not giving up on you, Bear. I know I haven't had total success training you these past fifteen years"—I paused to check my lipstick in the mirror on the inside flap of my purse—"but one of these days, I'll have you fully dialed in to my specs." I made kissy lips at him.

"Yeah, we'll see how that works out for you." Barry air-kissed my cheek, because he knows not to mess up my makeup when I'm dressed for work.

I jingled my keys, and Marie pranced over, hearing the signal for a good-bye treat. Marie's a big dog—long legged and close to sixty pounds—but she's as graceful as a dancer. She dropped her ivory-colored, curly-haired behind onto the floor. Her dark eyes followed my every move, and her shiny black nose twitched as I got a biscuit out of the cupboard.

I said good-bye, gave Marie her treat, and then headed out with my portfolio. Within seconds of pulling out of the garage, I realized I'd forgotten my sunglasses. (I'm so damn forgetful lately. Barry teases me that it comes with being the Big Four-O—and I tease him right back that he should know, since he's been in his forties longer than I have—but I prefer to chalk it up to stress.) Wearing sunglasses is key if you live in sunny central California and are trying to avoid the Clint Eastwood squinty-eyed look, so I had no choice but to go back into the house for them.

Marie greeted me with her long, silky ears perked up and a "You're back!" expression on her fuzzy face. Marie is an intelligent dog, like most labradoodles—her sweet nature is from her Labrador side, and her brainpower is from her poodle side—but judging time lapses isn't her strong suit. She was poised on her long legs, ready to grab her ball if I gave the word, but I simply said, "Sorry, missy," and ruffled her floppy bangs on my way to the cubby in the kitchen where we stash our mail and keys. No sunglasses. But then I remembered I'd left them on our dresser.

I dashed down the hall. As I neared our master suite, I heard the patter of our rain-style showerhead on the glass tiles and figured Barry was in the shower. I reached the half-open bathroom door and heard his voice. At first I thought he was on the phone, but in the shower? It seemed odd, so I peeked in. There he stood, in all his wiry, nude, marathon-runner glory, his little white butt turned my direction. He had one leg up on the step of the shower, waiting for the water to get warm. His head hung low as he spoke to his crotch.

"This is basically all because of you, Skippy." He reached in to test the temperature. "Or, wait . . . Do you think she planned it that way?" He shook his head and stepped into the shower.

What did I plan *what* way? I stood there balancing on the balls of my feet. Momentum urged me forward, but I had to get going to my appointment. Talking about this would have to wait. Sunglasses in hand, I ran back out to my BMW, leaving Marie looking miffed at the absence of a second good-bye treat.

Which brings me to here and now. While I drive, dodging the Santa Barbara city traffic and the weekend beachgoers, I turn down the radio so I can think. Other than the overheard shower conversation, the morning all seemed normal enough. Barry was maybe a little more taciturn than usual, but he's always like that after a run. Especially a twelve-mile run in the summer heat.

Of course, he didn't seem quite as uncommunicative with his penis. What was it he'd said? "This is all because of you . . . Or do you think she planned it that way?" What did that mean? And what the hell was up with "Skippy"? I didn't know it had a name. My two college boyfriends and the man I dated before I got together with Barry all had names for their penises ("The King," "Patton," and "Benjamin"— after the Dustin Hoffman character in *The Graduate*), but they were all so young. Barry was a very mature thirty-one-year-old when we started dating, and he had never mentioned a name in the years since, so it stunned me. I assumed naming one's penis was something only a younger, less mature guy would do. Not my Bear.

And the name itself. *Skippy?* I mean, it's okay for a Jack Russell terrier or a ferret, but for a penis? It's so . . . preppy. And Barry is the antithesis of preppy. I would have thought he'd go for something more, I don't know, classic, maybe. Wesley or Heathcliff. Or one of his favorite scientists' names, like he did with Marie. Maybe Sir Isaac or Copernicus. Yeah, Copernicus would be an excellent name for a penis. But Skippy?

With a bit of speeding, I manage to make it to my appointment at the Van Dierdons' house, where two bleach-bottle-white smiles welcome me inside. Their home is probably over seven thousand square feet and backs up to an immaculate golf course. My heart beats with covetous lust. The place looks like the grand-prize dream house for an HGTV contest: Spanish-style architecture, beamed ceiling, great room with massive stone fireplace, distressed hardwood floors, and huge oak-trimmed windows overlooking verdant landscaping.

"You have a beautiful home," I say, hoping I'm not drooling, and wondering why they've asked me here. The place oozes perfection.

"Thank you, Alexandra. And thanks for coming on a Saturday," says Mrs. Van Dierdon with her burgundy designer loungewear and perfect tan.

"It's not a problem, and, please, call me Alex."

"Well, Alex, we moved in recently; we're newlyweds." She blinds me with a flash of her anvil-size diamond, and I wish I still had my sunglasses on. "We desperately need your help in the bedroom."

Silver-haired Mr. Van Dierdon lets out a TV-anchorman chuckle. "It doesn't sound very good when you put it that way, little lioness." Her nickname suits her; her gaunt cheeks and slinky saunter give her an on-the-prowl look.

She bats him on the arm. "Tiger, of course that's not what I meant."

I give them my best aren't-you-two-adorable smile. "Why don't you show me the room and we can get started?"

We hike back to the master suite, and Mrs. Van Dierdon says, "First of all, these doors have to go." She stops in front of partially open French doors leading to their room. They're lovely—dark mahogany frames with frosted-glass panels down the center. "The previous owners installed these, and they're quite annoying when we have guests." She points out other rooms down the hall with the same type of door. "If guests stay up reading, their light shines through these ridiculous doors and keeps us up."

"My bride doesn't need beauty sleep, but *I* do," Mr. Van Dierdon says with a wink.

"I'm sure we can find something more to your liking. I'd never select something for a design simply because it was beautiful. Everything has to work together and work for your lifestyle," I reassure them. "I'm not a form-over-function designer; you can count on that." Designing simply for aesthetics is a huge pet peeve of mine. Sure, it will look great in a glossy portfolio photo, but how are people supposed to live in those sterile, ultrasleek living rooms? Yes, the faucet mounted on the counter-to-ceiling mirror behind the vessel sink gives modern flair to the guest bath, but how's a person supposed to wash their hands without splashing water everywhere?

"I'm pleased to hear that," Mrs. Van Dierdon says. "Now, on to the room." She pushes the doors open, holding her skeletal arms out as I take in the expansive room, large enough to hold all three of the bedrooms in my house. It's pretty, but impersonal. We could be in any top hotel chain. "We're picturing something serene, spa-like."

"Perfect. I can draw up something simple but elegant. We should start with the color. There are a lot of options for a serene feeling: sea greens, pewter, pale bl—"

"No, no, no." Hubby shakes his head. "Red. We definitely want red walls."

Wifey picks up a page torn from a magazine. "Something like this."

The picture shows what looks like a luxurious resort in the tropics. It's austere, with a color palette in wheat, eggshell, and a lovely shade of celadon. I nod. "I can give you something very similar to this."

They nod back. "Great. But in red."

I spend the next thirty minutes covering their coffee table with photos from my portfolio and design magazines. I show them a formal dining room my employee, Rachel, and I did with garnet-colored walls. "See how this room is so vibrant? You're not going to get the relaxing effect you're after if we go with red." I remind them they got my name from Mrs. Van Dierdon's hairdresser, and isn't Salon Bellissima oh so serene in those luscious creamy tones? (Rachel and I redid the day spa for free early last year before the market dropped; it's been great publicity, which, as a fairly new business in a crappy economy, we need.) Then I pull out the big guns: some research Barry looked up for me on the science of color and how it affects our moods.

"But red's our favorite color." She offers to show me photos of their red-themed wedding.

I draw the last arrow from my quiver. "Have you ever noticed how fast-food restaurants always use red in their logos and their decor?"

"Oh, Alex, we don't do fast food."

"But you've seen the logos, right?" They nod their perfectly coiffed heads in unison, and I continue. "They're red because it's stimulating; they want to stimulate the appetite."

"Stimulating the appetite sounds good, doesn't it, my lioness?"

Lioness growls at Tiger. Time for me to exit, so I stand. "What I'll do is draw up a design for a red room as well as one using beach tones, and you can select the one you prefer."

They show me out, and on the drive home, with the glare of the ocean on my left and the air conditioner and my music cranked high, I think about my job, which I generally love. I thrive on taking an empty space—or better yet, an ugly space—and converting it into a thing of beauty. Someplace my clients can relax. A place where they can walk in the door after a hard day and exhale, feel their shoulders drop away from their ears, and say "I'm home."

But trying to please demanding (and/or confused) clients goes hand in hand with the fun, creative side of the job. If money and the opinions of society (and my mother) were no object, I'd probably turn into one of those reclusive artistic hermit types. I'd get a cabin in the middle of nowhere, hole up there with my dog and husband, and just *create*. Not sure what, since you can only redo your cabin so many times, but I'd make something. Maybe I'd learn to sculpt or throw pots.

However, the reality is that money and the opinions of society (and my mother) matter. Mostly the money. Especially now, since I've, uh, "borrowed" a major chunk of the money Barry was saving for a new car to try to keep my business afloat. And Barry doesn't exactly know. God, I feel sick every time I think about it.

I grip the steering wheel, wanting to beat my head against it. I've got to make these people happy. Sometimes it's hard, though, balancing what you know is right with what the client thinks they want. I wonder aloud, "How can I give them a room that's serene *and* red?" We've got to nail this job so they'll tell their fabulously wealthy friends. My money problems will be over, and Barry will never even know they'd existed in the first place.

I've got to get this contract. I wonder if the Van Dierdons will go for bisque with red accents.

I try to de-stress by mentally drifting back to our serene dream cabin. I need something for Barry to do so he's not underfoot while I'm sculpting. Gardening! He loves that. I picture him tending our veggie patch. Then I hear him say to a summer squash, "Do you think she planned it that way?"

I shake my head to get the image out of my mind. But what did he mean by that?

Could he think I purposely set up my meeting with the Van Dierdons on a Saturday to get out of our usual nap? We've been having some issues in terms of our . . . marital relations lately. We've always kind of been ships that pass in the bed. I'm a night owl, staying up late to work or devour a murder mystery. Barry's a morning person, and I'm still comatose when he springs up to go out on a run. We've always solved this problem with weekend "naps." But since striking out on my own, I've had to do everything I can to get new customers, and sometimes that means weekend meetings. And Rachel can't take the meetings, since I'm the one with the design degree, and it's my company. (I don't want to say Rache is "just" an upholsterer, because she's not—she's more like a fabric whisperer. She does things with a sewing machine and a staple gun that would make a person consider upholstering the fireplace. Or Grandpa. Her work is *that* gorgeous.) Anyway, whenever I've got a weekend meeting, it's adios to the siesta.

I bet that's what he meant. But it's only one o'clock. Plenty of time for a nap. I can get going on some sketches later. A lazy afternoon would be nice, and it'll make Barry happy.

My cozy image of us tucked in our sleigh bed vanishes when I turn into our cul-de-sac, and the latest monstrosity on our neighbor's lawn looms large. My molars rub together. The Jansens roll out hideous inflato-decor for Every. Single. Holiday. On Arbor Day, they put out a huge plastic palm tree—hiding the real tree in their yard. And, I swear to God, on Mother's Day she puts out a blow-up uterus. Now an immense, angry bald eagle, visible from space, signals the impending Fourth of July holiday.

I shout, unheard from within the sealed sanctuary of my car. "You're bringing down the whole neighborhood aesthetic! Can't you just hang out a flag, like normal people?" Good grief, their trash bin is still out too. Friday morning is pickup day. "And trash cans are supposed to be removed within twelve hours of pickup!"

Leaving their lawn in my rearview mirror, I think, *This is why I love Santa Barbara so much. The city's as crazy about these types of regulations as I'd be if I ran things.*

I whip into our driveway and hit the garage door opener. As the door rises, it reveals Barry's truck isn't there. And then it hits me: maybe *I'm* not the "she" Barry was talking about.

ABOUT THE AUTHOR

Photo © 2012 Theresa Hanten

Jackie Bouchard, a *USA Today* bestselling author, writes what she calls Fido-friendly fiction: humorous and heartwarming stories about women and the dogs that profoundly impact their lives.

Bouchard has lived in Southern California, Canada, and Bermuda and now lives in San Diego with her husband and dog. Her novels include *What the Dog Ate, House Trained*, and *Rescue Me, Maybe*.

For more information, visit www.jackiebouchard.com.

Her blog: www.poochsmooches.com

Facebook: www.facebook.com/JackieBouchardWriter

Twitter: http://twitter.com/@JackieBouchard